We the People

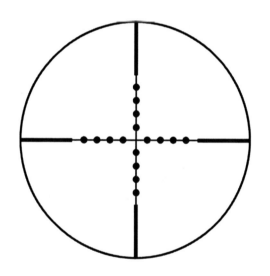

MIKE CLOWES

Wasteland Press
Shelbyville, KY USA
www.wastelandpress.net

We the People
by Mike Clowes

First Printing – July 2010
ISBN: 978-1-60047-467-5
Library of Congress Control Number: 2010931745

We the People is a work of fiction; the names of characters were selected arbitrarily. Any similarity to real people or events is coincidental.

Printed in the U.S.A.

To all those who serve in the armed forces (past, present, and future), who courageously defend our great nation, the principles of our Founding Fathers, and the Constitution of the United States

To Earl & Annie

I hope you enjoy reading the novel as much as I did writing it.

Mike Flowes

Class of 58

Acknowledgements

To my wife Trudy who never questioned my ability to write this novel—serving as a sounding board for ideas—and to the rest of the family who supported me as only a family can...

To my friend Steve for his enthusiastic support and for assuming the mantle of critic *extraordinaire*...

To Susan, my editor and mentor, who magically transformed a series of words into an intelligible story...

There are others from whom ideas, statistics, and technical information were gleaned. To all involved, I extend my heartfelt thanks.

PROLOGUE

THE CRIMINAL JUSTICE SYSTEM IS BROKEN, and Mike O'Reilly, the dynamic governor of Oklahoma and soon to be dark horse candidate for the highest office in the land, knows how to fix it. As governor, he had already received national acclaim by spearheading a no-nonsense approach to prison reform. By ridding the state of lenient and inept judges and eliminating bail and parole for hardened repeat offenders, he all but eliminated the revolving door syndrome that is the crux of our dysfunctional, overburdened criminal justice system. Statistics were showing that his tough approach to crime, along with swift, harsh punishment for those convicted, had already greatly reduced the incidents of crime in Oklahoma…*Why not in the United States?*

WHAT MIKE DID NOT KNOW…he was getting unsolicited help from a sophisticated, covert organization, operating under the radar of federal and state law enforcement, unencumbered by policies and procedures that always seemed to favor the criminal. *Enough is enough!* No longer would tens of thousands of vicious, remorseless predators—released daily by a dysfunctional criminal justice system—be allowed to go unchecked to *again* commit heinous crimes against American citizens.

Sean O'Reilly, Mike's father, a decorated war hero, chairman of one of the largest privately owned corporations in America, and patriarch of the O'Reilly family, also knew how to fix the problem of escalating, unchecked crime in America. His solution could not be found on any bar exam: *An eye for an eye, saith the Lord!*

AMERICANS have an innate propensity for rugged individualism, self-reliance and an aptitude for handling their own problems. It stems from their short but colorful history where survival depended on tough self-sufficiency and immediate justice, usually through their inalienable right to bear arms. Aside from the insidious conditioning associated with the erosion of rights and freedoms, which has led most Americans to believe they have little if any power to bring about change, nothing has changed!

We the people must go forward with a single voice to reclaim our right to self-government. We must demand that elected officials and members of the judiciary meet the highest standard of honesty and integrity; that their actions are taken with the best interests of the people in mind, ensuring their safety and welfare through strict enforcement of the laws of the land.

To the O'Reillys, *anything less is unacceptable!*

The good of the people is the highest law.

Cicero

1

Vicious lightning illuminated the plush executive offices as dark clouds rolled low over the Oklahoma sky, giving one a sense of foreboding, as if the subject being discussed were not scary enough.

"Jeff, the only reason you're on the payroll is I know you're handicapped, and not from combat wounds as you would have everyone believe. God manifested one of his cruelest jokes when he carefully inserted an egg-sized blob into your cranium.

"Now in as few words as possible, and hopefully during my lifetime, what are you trying to tell me?"

Mike O'Reilly, the dark horse candidate for the highest office in the land and ex-CIA operative Jeff Stone had known each other since 1960 when they had served together—Mike as sniper team leader, 75th Rangers, and Jeff as a CIA asset on loan to the task force commander as a special advisor—on a *humanitarian* mission to the Congo.

In actuality, it was a scantily publicized military operation involving U.S. Army Rangers, Special Forces and army aviation assets, resulting in the rescue of hundreds of refugees and the annihilation of approximately 500 soldiers loyal to Mobutu, the ruthless dictator of the Republic of Congo.

Mobutu, who had given free reign to his soldiers, thought that butchering white farmers and merchants living in and around Leopoldville was a team sport.

Jeff had resigned in disgust from the CIA shortly after his seventh year in Southeast Asia and was now reunited with his longtime friend, serving as a special advisor and head of Mike's security detail.

"What I'm trying to tell you, my hard-headed friend, is I believe law enforcement is getting unsolicited help from persons unknown in their ongoing effort to take hardened criminals, big-time drug dealers, and other bad guys off the streets."

Jeff eased back in his chair, giving Mike a chance to think about what he had said for a minute, and then continued. "Remember, buddy, I'm *super spook* and I have gut feelings about these things."

Mike's mind raced back to the Congo and the times Jeff's instincts had saved his young butt. As he measured the man sitting in the chair across from him, he smiled. "Bullshit, Jeff, you probably had burritos for lunch and your gut feel is little more than your body's desire to pass gas."

Jeff ran his hand over the back of his neck to massage the scar that served as a lasting memory of close combat in the jungles of Laos. And in a feigned Irish brogue said, "Mikey, me boy, you're a bright Irish lad, you are, but sometimes, and I'm sure it's just to piss me off, you can be dumb as a bloody stump."

Mike laughed, bounced out of his chair, coffee cup in hand, and walked around the desk. "Let's get a fresh cup of this stuff and then you can tell me all about your gas attack."

Jeff followed him to the specialty coffee station that had recently been installed in Mike's outer offices. With the push of a button, freshly ground exotic beans from around the world started the aromatic brewing process. Moments later, they both took sips of the delicious brew.

"Remember the first cup of mud we had together? I believe we were in the Tac Ops Center in the Congo. That was some bad stuff, man. I would say this is a giant step up. In fact, just so you know, this is the only reason I put up with your crap. If you ever remove this machine, I'm outta here!"

Mike was a fair-sized man at 6'3" and 220 pounds. He still possessed the military bearing that had been drilled into him at West Point. The confidence gained as an army ranger was ever-present. His gregarious way and good looks were clearly political attributes that had served him well as governor of Oklahoma. He was now beginning his bid for president of the United States—

clearly a long shot in his mind. He was far from being a Washington insider and his piercing blue eyes and candid, no-nonsense approach made most politicians uncomfortable. He did, however, have a few things going for him.

His demonstrated record as governor of Oklahoma in crime reduction, education and innovative back-to-work welfare initiatives had gained him national acclaim. He was also one of the wealthiest men in the country. Thanks, in great part, to his father, who had amassed a fortune through his interests in oil, cattle, real estate and myriad business enterprises.

Perhaps his greatest asset in his bid for the presidency was his ability to relate to the people. He possessed an innate respect for his fellowman and had an affinity for blue collar workers. He never lied and kept every promise he ever made to the people, even if he had to use his own resources to do it.

His greatest concern at the moment was how to navigate through the treacherous, uncharted waters of political compromise.

As the two men returned to the office and settled back in their chairs, Mike said, "OK, Jeff, tell me what you know."

Jeff took a sip of coffee and then set the cup on the corner of the ornate desktop. "There are a disturbing number of seemingly coincidental deaths of bad guys showing up on the scope. I've got my contacts checking other parts of the country to see what *they* have. They're also checking to see how far back these mysterious incidents may go. It won't be a perfect trail, but if there are operational similarities or patterns, I think I'll recognize them. Remember the old adage 'birds of a feather'? I have a feeling I may have trained some of *these* birds."

"Who else is in the loop on this one?" asked Mike.

"Just you and me at the moment. I'm low-profiling all of my requests under the guise of background data for future campaign speeches."

"Good, let's keep it that way for now."

Jeff nodded. "In my former life, I was one of the in-country operatives responsible for monitoring and in some cases controlling government reconnaissance units—an innocuous name for U.S.-led assassination teams—composed of Special Forces and either Mong or Montagnard tribesmen that were on my payroll.

Aside from special assignments, they operated in a sphere of influence."

Mike leaned forward with his elbows on the desk and his hands clasped together. "Just what does *sphere of influence* mean?"

"Picture a map of any given area and then overlay interconnecting circles placed in such a way as to cover the entire area of operation. These circles are spheres of influence. Each sphere had a GRU group responsible for liquidating—actually the word is neutralizing—special targets."

"And what constituted a special target?" Mike asked.

"Primarily, political officers in the villages that had them, hamlet chieftains known to aid the Viet Cong or North Vietnamese Army, senior officers, communications specialists, foreign army advisors, and the like. I can recall on several occasions being directed to go after certain high level political figures that were expected to be in the area. I have to be somewhat ambiguous about these targets because some of that shit is still classified Top Secret NOFORN."

Leaning back, Mike asked, "Jeff, are you suggesting there is a covert network of operatives taking out bad guys on U.S. soil?"

"Not yet, boss. What I *am* saying is there are certain skill sets that have unmistakable characteristics. I've used most of them myself at one time or another. Hell, you used some of them yourself in your former life. I've experienced a phenomenon very similar to what I believe I'm seeing here. If it checks out, and I should know something in the next few weeks or so, I'll give you a clearer picture and may be in a better position to share my opinion."

Mike stretched his arms in front of him. "You're a hard case, Jeff."

"Me!" responded Jeff, with feigned indignity. "If memory serves me, it was *you, sir,* and that group of knuckle-dragging apes you called army rangers that lit up the jungle and sent 150 or so of Mobutu's warriors floating tits up merrily down the river. What the hell was that all about? *That's* a hard case! I guess that explains why we've been friends all these years. If you haven't lived it, no way could anyone ever understand it."

Mike then asked the obvious question. "How could a group large enough to cover the entire country operate covertly without someone spilling his guts? I'm not sure anonymity could be maintained, given the number of boots on the ground."

"Think back to your ranger days, buddy. We were all patriots and had a common goal. Great effort was taken to train out the weakest link before you went into combat. Can you think of a single trooper you would not have entrusted the safety of your family with?"

Mike thought for a moment and then said, "No, not really. We were a brotherhood like no other, baptized by fire and dedicated to mission success, regardless of where or the dangers involved."

Jeff looked across the desk and winked. "There you have it, boss. At some point, dedicated, well-trained patriots are either discharged or retired. Why couldn't they band together, under excellent leadership, on a courageous mission to rid the country of predators that are poisoning society with drugs and associated crime?

"We both know our criminal justice system is in the toilet. It is overburdened to the point of being dysfunctional and incapable of coping effectively with crimes against society.

"And by the way, inept judges and lawyers, particularly the ACLU, are part of the problem, not part of the solution.

"Let me give you an example. Not too long ago, Maryland State Troopers stopped a car for an illegal lane change and were subsequently given consent to search the vehicle. They called in a canine unit and found forty pounds of cocaine in a secret compartment." Jeff emphasized the point by reiterating, "*Forty pounds*, my friend!

"A judge ruled to suppress the drugs as evidence because it violated the Fourth Amendment rights [to be free from unlawful seizure] of the two scum suckers. They walked with a minor lane change violation."

"Are you making this up to magnify your point or did this really happen?"

"Mike, it happened! This judge has a track record or I should say *had* a track record of suppressing drugs as evidence in a number of cases over the last few years. He was unreasonably lenient in almost all drug-related cases. Thank God the bastard's dead."

Mike leaned back in his chair, "What happened to him?"

Jeff took a swig of cold coffee and shifted in his seat before answering. "That's the interesting part, and it magnifies my earlier comments concerning coincidental deaths. My source says he was on vacation somewhere in Georgia, a little German town called Helen or Helena, something like that, and was having lunch when he died of an apparent heart attack."

"And why is that interesting? People die of heart attacks everyday, Jeff."

"Yeah, that's true. But most don't wind up face down in a plate of sauerkraut, and most autopsies reveal a damaged heart. Evidently that was not the case here."

"I can name several poisons in our covert arsenal, on the other hand, that work very quickly and mimic heart failure. It's something to think about, boss, particularly if bad guys and their enablers keep croaking under mysterious circumstances.

"I can't think of a more efficient way to clean up the criminal justice system than to whack bad guys and inept members of the judiciary that seem hell-bent on getting them released back into society so they can continue to ply their illicit trade, can you?"

He thought about Jeff's comments for a moment. "That's unsettling, bud. I hope like hell you're wrong."

The ex-CIA operative added, "To be perfectly honest, boss, I might join such an operation myself *if* it existed. Highly trained specialists—*killing machines*—don't lose their skills or desire to use them just because they're no longer in government service.

After Jeff left the office, Mike sat back closing his eyes to think, as he often did when he was troubled about something but couldn't quite put his finger on it. He was accustomed to instant recall, so not being able to pull up the troubling data really bothered him. He knew it had something to do with what his father had said years ago. He and his dad were having lunch with Ronald Snyder, long-time family friend, in the executive dining room of Ron's Chicago-based law firm, Greene Laverish Santine & Snyder. But what was said and why was it lingering in his mind?

They had been discussing campaign strategies for his entry into the Oklahoma gubernatorial race when, out of the blue, his dad had openly confessed to killing the man who had, many years before, been instrumental in the death of Donovan, Mike's older brother.

Think! What the hell did Pops say? He remembered thinking how protective he could be and that a person would have far more success trying to stick a straw up a wildcat's ass than messing with a member of the O'Reilly family, because the patriarch would hunt them down and snap their spine like a toothpick.

That's it! Pops said he "believed in justice, but it was obvious to him justice was not going to be served in Alabama, at least not for the O'Reilly family." So he *fixed* the problem. He also said something to the effect, "We don't have to wallow in our own fat any longer. We can set a course as a people united to correct the blight that the country is presently and will forever experience if we don't fix the problem."

Mike knew his father was not into big words—or words at all, for that matter—and was far more apt to act than to pontificate. He grabbed a yellow legal pad from the corner of his desk and doodled for a moment, a technique he used to stimulate thought. He then started building a block diagram, similar to those he had created to envision the strategies needed to successfully win oil and mineral rights claims for clients when he was a junior partner at the law firm of his mentor, Ron Snyder. It was his way of pictorially displaying specific thoughts and ordering them until they created a crystal clear presentation of the issue(s) at hand.

At the top of the page he wrote his dad's name and circled it. To the right he drew lines to smaller circles surrounding the words *patriotic/loves his country, wealthy, capable of murder*, and *deeds, not words*. Mike scratched through *deeds, not words* and moved them to the top of the page under a circle containing the phrase *family motto*. He then started inserting his own interpretation of what his dad had said. Mike drew a vertical line down to *does not trust criminal justice system—broken* and circled it. Below that he wrote *Donny's death* and quickly circled it as all of his senses kicked in and focused on the issue. From this circle, he drew a horizontal line to *fix the problem* and circled it. He kept circling this phrase, as he felt the full weight of the significance of those three words.

Somewhere in Alabama, a body lay in a grave covered with dirt. A family no doubt had mourned their loss, never suspecting that Mike's father had snapped the neck of the stupid bastard. A wry grin crossed Mike's face as he thought, not good to cross the big guy!

Mike interpreted the phrase, *wallow in our own fat* to mean that law enforcement and the criminal justice system was so encumbered by rules and antiquated laws, as to be rendered ineffective—even impotent—and unable to protect the people. He wrote *cops & judges can't protect the people* and circled it in the center of the paper. *Set about as a people united to correct the blight.* Now, there was an interesting phrase. Blight probably referred to criminals or perhaps the whole set of societal problems stemming from drug-related crimes.

His father often had said we could greatly reduce the country's lawlessness simply by ridding ourselves of drug dealers. He circled *drug-related crime & lawlessness*. He drew another horizontal line and circled *fix the problem.* If Dad used this phrase in the same connotation as he had when referring to justice for Donny…Mike let that thought hang, not wanting to recognize or even think about the implications.

He then looked at a *people united* and determined it had to mean an organization or perhaps bi-partisan cooperation of Congress—not likely, but possible—in an effort to pass laws in the best interests of the people. He circled the words *organization & planning* and underlined it several times thinking these are the key elements to mission success and knew first hand his father had amassed a fortune by mastering both.

Mike ripped the page from the pad, wadded it up and threw it in the polished rosewood trash can, disgusted for even thinking his own father might be capable of such things.

As he leaned back in his chair, it was as if one of the violent lightning strikes ravaging the Oklahoma plains outside his window had suddenly struck him. *Who the hell am I kidding*? Given his father's background and self-proclaimed track record, he was *more* than capable of whacking anyone who posed a threat to his family or his country.

Mike reached down, retrieved the crumpled paper, smoothed it out and stuck it in his desk drawer. He then pushed the intercom button to page his secretary.

"Mary Elaine, would you come in for a moment, please."

She entered his office with pad and pencil in hand. "Mr. O'Reilly, why can't you just call me Mary, like everyone else?"

Mike smiled. "It's a southern thing, I guess. Besides, given the salary I'm paying you, my dear, I'm entitled to call you about anything that lights my fire as long as it's respectful. You can take the boy out of the South, but you can never take the South out of the boy, or something like that. If I give you a raise, may I continue calling you Mary Elaine?"

"For a raise, sir, I'll answer to anything."

"Well, it was a hypothetical question. It's only been five or six years [it had actually been three months] since I bumped your salary and I like Mary Elaine. It has a nice ring to it. Times are tough, sweetheart."

His secretary rolled her eyes, "Yeah, boss, I can see things are pretty tight right now, given the shiny airplanes and this twenty-four story glass shanty. So with your permission, I'll start supplying my own pencils."

Mike smiled. "Permission granted, my dear. You don't by chance recall why I called you in, do you? Oh, yes, I desperately need a cup of coffee, a donut and Jeffrey, if he is still around."

"Do you want them in that order?"

"Yes, my dear. That would be lovely."

As she turned to leave, she looked over her shoulder with a smile. "Save all of the gushy, sweet stuff for the campaign, boss. You're going to need it. Besides, I'm past the point where it would have any effect on me. Your slave-driving tactics have turned me into a hardened hussy. The only difference between me and a streetwalker is they make a lot more money."

Mike smiled saying, "Poor baby! Just a little cranky today, are we?"

2

Weeks later – FOX News interview

Prior to airtime, Robert Bozeman, the veteran news anchor chosen to host Fox News Tonight, a new talk show, approached Mike as he entered the posh main lobby of Fox headquarters in New York. "Mr. O'Reilly, a pleasure to finally meet you. I have been monitoring your campaign with great interest and if I may say so, sir, your ads are a breath of fresh air."

As the two men shook hands, Mike said, "Thanks, I appreciate that. Mr. Bozman, do you by chance have a pot of coffee handy?"

"Absolutely, let's go to my office and go over the main topics we will be discussing. I'll have refreshments brought in."

"That's fine, but if we talk about what we are going to discuss on the show, that means I'll have to do it twice and that is tantamount to a rehearsal. I don't do rehearsals, sir. You can ask whatever you choose to ask."

"I just don't want to surprise you with questions you may not be prepared for or want to answer. I know of no one that goes on national television cold turkey."

"You do now, sir!"

Once the two men settled into chairs at a small table, Robert, for the first time, stared into the purest, most unsettling blue eyes he had ever seen and knew immediately that Mike O'Reilly was a force to be reckoned with. He now understood why other candidates during recent debates always seemed to be behind the proverbial power curve.

Mike's eyes reminded Robert of a cat of prey, seeming to laser through him as they stared at some distant object. He found some comfort in the disarming smile and gregarious nature of the man sitting across from him.

"Sir, your campaign ads are positive and upbeat with little, if any, negativism toward your opponents. Given the *strike first* nature of politics, don't you find that a bit risky?"

Mike drank some coffee and set the cup down. "A couple of things we need to clear up before show time. One, I assume this is just comfort talk and won't be one of the questions when they turn the lights on. I've already said I don't do rehearsals. Secondly, I don't view the other candidates running for my party's nomination as opponents and have no animosity toward them whatsoever. So why would I want to body slam them? I will consider them, until proven otherwise, as patriotic Americans interested in giving something back to the country by way of holding high public office. How do you see them?"

Robert crossed his legs and leaned forward to pick up his talking points paper to inconspicuously scratch through the campaign ad question that he did indeed plan on asking again on the air. "Well, sir, I've been in this business a long time and quite frankly I have been conditioned to see politics as a no-holds-barred free-for-all. The nastiest candidate with the most money wins. As sad as that sounds, most Americans feel that way."

"Well, then," Mike said with a wry smile. "Let's give them renewed hope in the system."

After the make-up gang finished touching up both men—a ritual Mike hated but had learned to tolerate—they proceeded down the hall to the program set and took their assigned places moments before the lights, fans and cameras came on.

"Good evening, ladies and gentlemen, and welcome to Fox News Tonight for our first airing before a live audience. I will be your host this evening. With us tonight is Mike O'Reilly, one of the Republican Party's leading presidential candidates. His innovative approach to welfare reform and education and his tough stance on crime as the former governor of Oklahoma has received national acclaim and, on occasion, been cloaked in controversy. It is a pleasure having you here, sir."

"Thank you, Robert, I'm happy to be here. In fact, after a very rough plane ride through some downright nasty weather, I'm happy to be anywhere." There was polite laughter from the audience as they got their first close look at the dynamic candidate.

"Mr. O'Reilly, race always seems to play a role in the pursuit of high political office, each party doing and saying whatever they believe will win the minority vote. What is your position and why do you feel your platform will be appealing to all voters, black and white?"

Mike looked straight into the camera, knowing his opening remarks would make or break the rest of the evening. "True, race *is* always an issue that most politicians tread lightly around, but it shouldn't be. I take exception to the phrase *voters, black and white*. I have always felt and have said on numerous occasions that we may subliminally stimulate racial issues facing this country by referring to citizens as black or white. Why not use the phrase *American voters* instead?

"All of us—rather our ancestors emigrated from other countries for a variety of reasons. We do not routinely refer to citizens whose ancestors may have come from England or, in my case Ireland, as English Americans or Irish Americans, so why should citizens with African ancestry be singled out as African Americans? That in itself is racial. Certainly we all should take pride in our respective genealogies; I know I do. As a kid, if I slipped up and said anything derogatory or off color about the Irish, no matter what it was, I got my ears boxed. I suspect a lot of you did, too.

"Remember, folks, those of you that can trace your ancestry through the ugly practice of slavery are not alone. Many, many immigrants from the British Isles and Europe arrived in this country as indentured servants—slaves by any measure—and stayed that way until the day they died."

Mike took a drink of water as he surveyed the audience. "The short answer to your question of whether or not the platform I have chosen will be appealing to both black and white voters: I did not tailor what I stand for to a specific ethnicity. We are all Americans and, in my view, the three most important issues facing us today is overhauling of a dysfunctional welfare program, providing a good education for our children and establishing a no-nonsense judiciary to combat what I believe is unchecked crime. These issues pertain to and impact every American citizen.

"We could learn a lot from crayons." Mike paused for affect and smiled at the perplexed look on the faces of his host and many in the audience. He then looked directly at the camera and continued, "Think about it. In fact, the first opportunity you have to open a box of crayons, look inside. Some of them will be sharp and some dull. Some have weird names and come in many different colors, but they *all* have to live and co-exist in the same box. Americans are those crayons, ladies and gentlemen, and we need to care for one another and do all we can to live in harmony." The audience nodded approval of this simple analogy and applauded.

When everyone had settled down, Robert looked at Mike. "On a different note, other candidates are seasoned politicians who know their way around Congress and are familiar with the inner workings of Washington politics. Do you view this as a campaign disadvantage and, if so, how do you propose to overcome it?"

Mike thought about the question for a moment. "That's an interesting question and one that I have thought about a great deal. Is it a disadvantage? I'm sure all of us would feel more comfortable walking a trail knowing where all the land mines were."

The audience was clearly enjoying the candidate's unique and easy-going mannerisms.

"There is a flip side, however. It is difficult to think outside the box if you know nothing beyond business as usual.

"I hate to be the harbinger of bad news, but the very people we have elected to govern us do not necessarily have the best interests of the people in mind. Their decisions are self-serving and only a few of them vote on legislation from a position of knowledge. Rather, they read summary sheets prepared by junior staff members. That's a bit scary to me. Left unchecked, it could bankrupt or cause irreparable damage to the country.

"The federal government operates on the theory that there is an endless supply of money. *There is not*! Superimpose that over irresponsible fiscal management, and you have a formula for disaster.

"Ladies and gentlemen, other than edification to identify things that need to be changed, I don't want to know how the seasoned 'good ole boys' do it. Let me be clear. Some good comes out of Congress and some elected officials are making a concerted effort to get things done. However, they are fighting an uphill battle against a system that is inherently inefficient.

"Unfortunately, Americans have adjusted their expectations to align with marginal performance and assume that is the way it has to be. That's a *bad* assumption.

"Let's take, for example, a bill that is sponsored by whomever and offered up for vote with the intent of passing. I need to take a drink of water before we get into this mess, because the whole process gets me hot as a three-dollar pistol." He paused to take a few sips of water.

"That hypothetical bill I just mentioned is very much like an onion. The core of the proposed bill may be good, even needed. It may even be honorable. But by the time you peel off layer after layer of superfluous pork barrel add-ons, it's enough to make your eyes water. That's one of the ways the proposed bill's sponsor gets the support he needs. Tab after tab—amendments, if you will—of costly line items that are no more in the best interest of the people than the man in the moon.

"Just to give you a taste of this nonsense, I'll tell you what was attached to a bill that subsequently has been passed into law. I'll use no names. Not far from Boston there exists a new two-way bridge leading to...*nowhere*! That would be okay if a new bridge were actually needed and it served a high number of our citizens. One, the bridge that was replaced was serviceable, albeit an eyesore. The inhabitants of this small island enclave coincidently are very wealthy supporters of the bill's sponsor, as well as a few family members and the sponsor himself. One does not have to be super clever to see that there's a rat in the sandbox.

"This is only one example of the shenanigans taking place across the country, using hundreds of millions of your tax dollars. I don't like it at all and will do my dead level best to nip it in the bud as your president.

"Can I do it alone? Absolutely not, but we *can* do it with a united voice of folks just like you, telling Congress it has to stop or they're out. You will see far fewer needless bridges and arrogant waste of our tax dollars if you are willing to take a stand.

"Robert, I know we need to move on, but you opened this can of worms, and the good citizens listening tonight need to be aware of what is taking place."

The host nodded. "Please continue, sir."

"Here is another interesting point. If our representatives in Congress are truly looking out for the best interests of the people, why don't they have the same Social Security plan we have? Their plan is different and one hell of a lot better, just as their pension plan far exceeds the wildest dreams of the people they represent. Folks, that's nonsense, pure and simple.

"I believe every American should be enrolled in the same Social Security program. There is only one America. Different programs for our congressional representatives simply will not stand the test of logic. I can guarantee you that the country's failing, soon to be bankrupt Social Security system would be on the front burner if these *mullets* we elected to Congress were part of it. Think about it.

"We put them there, and we can collectively make them go away if they don't get their act together and put in place the changes necessary to get this country back on the straight and narrow where it belongs.

"In my view, it takes a lot of guts to vote in a congressional pay raise when your overall performance is marginal at best. Pay raises in the companies under the umbrella of the O'Reilly Corporation are given for superior performance. We fire underachievers! However, that is what Congress does, and as a citizen and businessman, I find that unconscionable. Again, your hard-earned tax dollars at work.

"Let me share with you one of my favorite analogies concerning politicians in general. Politicians are like bananas. They start out green; have a short period where they're good, and then they turn rotten and have to be thrown out.

"You asked earlier, Robert, if I thought I was at a disadvantage. Oh yeah! My path will not only have land mines, but also booby traps and snipers. I wouldn't have it any other way. I'm up to the challenge. The question is are the American voters willing to work with me to bring about drastic and long-needed changes in the way our government conducts its business? We will soon see."

"Sir, you have been called the law and order candidate. Would you care to expound on that?"

"I have heard that. It's not because I believe all of the laws that govern us are good. Rather, I believe all laws—to remain on the books—should be in the best interest of law-abiding citizens and not designed by left wing, bleeding heart liberals who go overboard to ensure the civil rights of hardened criminals.

"As far as I'm concerned, they forfeited most of their rights when they committed heinous crimes against society. All one..." Applause interrupted and he waited a moment before continuing.

"All one needs to do to understand my position on crime is to look at what the legislature, the judiciary and I accomplished in a reasonably short time in Oklahoma. Be assured, ladies and gentlemen, high on my list of things to do will be prison reform. The approach, in spite of the collective efforts of the ACLU, will be an expansion of those policies and laws that are working so well in my home state.

"Are you aware that for every prisoner incarcerated across this great nation of ours, it costs the taxpayer about $40,000 annually? The exception is Oklahoma and Maricopa County, Arizona where it costs a fraction of that.

"There are roughly two million men and women locked up today. Do the math. Hell, we have criminals on death row that have been there for as long as twenty-seven years, with the average time being about fifteen. That's *nuts*!

"Once a jury finds a person guilty of a capital crime and receives a death sentence, that person should be entitled to a single appeal and no more. Given the inefficiency of the courts, it may still take three or four years. Why does an appeal take that long? Beats the hell out of me, but you can be assured I will have a committee looking into it before the end of my first week in office. It is absurd.

"While we're on the subject, I might also add that I will work hard to have laws pertaining to statute of limitations repealed. What is that all about? The crime was committed against someone. Who gives a damn how long it takes to find the perpetrator? A statute of limitations on crimes as traumatic as rape and robbery? Not on *my* watch.

"There will be no bail and likely as not, felons—particularly repeat offenders—will be incarcerated in the middle of nowhere living in a large tent. All the reasons for the revolving door syndrome that brings these hardheads back time and time again will be removed. No air-conditioned cells; no weight rooms to make them stronger and more dangerous when they are released, should that day ever come; and no full access to the courts, flooding the system with nonsensical, frivolous appeals and the like.

"This approach, though harsh, works! The national average of repeat offenders is well over 50 percent. The state average in Oklahoma is now about 18 percent. The byproduct, in addition to lowering crime rates, is the large sum of money saved.

"This money can then be dedicated to educating our children and funding vocational programs to get large numbers of able-bodied welfare recipients off of the rolls and into jobs that help the economic growth of the nation.

"This is not hypothetical mumbo jumbo to get your support. Everything I have said is presently in place, working and a matter of public record. All we have to do is expand these policies.

"Now I'm not naïve. There will be lots of national 'not invented here' posturing. We have to work our way through it and accept every *no* answer as one step closer to *yes*.

"I can tell you unequivocally I have never met a problem or challenge I could not work my way through. Well, that is not exactly right. In my former life as an infantry soldier I had my wrist shattered by an enemy bullet which forced me to alter career paths from an infantry officer to a civilian lawyer and businessman." As Mike said that, he held his stiffened wrist in front of him and rubbed it.

"It was a change that did not come easily for me. O'Reilly men have been serving in the infantry dating back to the late sixteenth century. I was fortunate enough, however, to serve in our armed forces as an army ranger up to the time of my injury. In all of America's history, there are only two defining forces that have ever offered to die for you…Jesus Christ and members of our armed forces. I am proud to have been part of that legacy."

After taking a quick break for commercials, which gave Mike and his host an opportunity to relax for a moment and get a fresh glass of water, the talk show host continued.

"Mr. O'Reilly, we have time for perhaps one or two more questions. I would like to hear your views concerning foreign aid and our role in the United Nations."

"Wow! Are you part of a conspiracy to sink my ship before it leaves port?"

The audience by now was behind the candidate and clearly enjoyed his glib humor. They hung onto every word, agreeing—for the most part—with about everything he had said up to this time.

Robert chuckled. "You know as well as I do, sir, your ship can't be sunk, regardless of the outcome of the nomination."

"Let me address the foreign aid part of the question to include world affairs in general. Primarily I am not an isolationist. I believe the world population, each and everyone, should help one another, however possible. The O'Reilly Corporation has been doing just that for many years and we will continue to do it.

"Aiding those in need is a good start as long as we take care of our own desperate souls first. We look foolish in the eyes of the world when we send planeloads of aid to foreign countries while our own citizens in places like Appalachia, the Deep South and slums across the country are in need of help. Let's take care of our own so we are in a better position to help others. Remember every society is judged by how it treats its least fortunate amongst them."

"Foreign trade is where I have a problem. We need to have it, certainly, but it needs to be more equitable. Presently the playing field is not level. For every trade dollar gained we lose ten in trade deficit. The rules, trade tariffs and agreements with our trading partners need to be restructured with fair trade clauses. Not necessarily dollar for dollar, but something more equitable, taking into account offsets, military bases that are strategically located around the world, and things like military-assistance packages.

"When the smoke clears and all of these things are brought into play, we should just about have a wash as opposed to the huge foreign trade deficits we are presently experiencing, don't you think?" The audience again applauded.

"I also believe the United States Government should be very cautious about approving the sale of U.S. real estate and corporations to foreign countries. I think that's not a good policy. We need to change our views on it before it's too late, even if it irritates the world at large.

"We have only a few real allies anyway, so why lose sleep over the rest of the world getting their colon twisted? It is our country; it is up to us to safeguard it from foreign interests.

"With regard to the United Nations, *it's a mess*! It is wallowing in its own fat and all too often rife with corruption. I don't know how it was in the beginning; perhaps it worked well. But today, it is little more than a paper tiger that has to be fed through a straw. It has no teeth.

"We need to force change, because it cannot police itself. Short of that, we should consider getting out. We, the United States, pick up about 28 percent of the tab. That gets us *one* vote!

"Notwithstanding those few allies I mentioned earlier, the rest see us as a *cash cow*, someone to carry the brunt of the dangerous international policing actions. It is clear they don't like Americans, either because of jealousy or cultural differences. I see no advantage to being a member under the present set of circumstances.

"The organization is corrupt, inefficient and almost totally ineffective. It is a laughing stock to countries that choose to violate established international law. The violators know nothing will happen beyond an unenforceable embargo of some type that has little impact on the country and, in all probability, will be lifted before it starts. In my view, it is a losing proposition.

"One thing for sure that needs to be done: hold all foreign diplomats responsible for their actions on U.S. soil, regardless of where they are assigned. If they violate our laws, prosecute them. There are over 19,000 outstanding traffic tickets associated with members of the United Nations. Impound those shiny new Benzes, Beamers and limousines and sell them to offset the cost of the tickets.

"From a business standpoint, the United Nations building, though dated, could be refurbished and would make pretty comfortable digs for federal and state government agencies that are now housed in an array of high-dollar real estate throughout New York City. Lease the unneeded space for commercial use. That, ladies and gentlemen, is known as a *win–win* scenario.

"We must start thinking outside the proverbial box if we are to bring about positive change in this country. I'm more than prepared to do that, but it cannot be done by one man. It will take the voice of a united citizenry demanding that elected representatives lead, follow or get the hell out of the way. I say enough of this partisan nonsense. We need to give the country back to the people and start acting like we have some sense."

When it was obvious he was finished speaking, the audience gave him a standing ovation. Mike was taken aback by this warm and somewhat unexpected reception and self-consciously took a long drink while waiting for the audience to settle down.

Robert Bozeman took the necessary steps to regain control. "Mr. O'Reilly, obviously the viewing audience approves of your position on the subjects you've discussed. Sir, given your position on sensitive issues, do you have any concerns for your well-being?"

"No, not really,"

"Why is that, sir? It has been reported you have received several threatening letters, and there have been unsuccessful attempts on your life."

"As you may be aware, I have my own security detail, trained by America's finest, and they are *very* good at what they do. One would think an open forum like we have here this evening would be somewhat risky. It really isn't. Let me demonstrate for the sake of the audience, since you asked the question.

"Gentlemen, if you please." The full extent of Mike's security detail became obvious as each member of the team turned on eye-safe lasers, similar to the one attached to their individual weapons.

The audience gasped in awe as laser beams crisscrossed one another and seemed to fill every void of the Fox News Tonight set.

Mike smiled broadly as he raised his hand and all the lasers were turned off in unison.

"Now, given that every one of these guys can place fourteen rounds in a circle about the size of a coffee cup at fifty feet and do it in less than eight seconds with either hand, you have to feel pretty comfortable with that. Unless, of course, you made one of them mad. Then that would *not* be good. So I always carry a good supply of raw meat to keep them pacified and under control."

After the audience settled down, Robert said, "Any last thoughts you would like to share with the viewing audience this evening, sir?"

Mike smiled saying, "My advice to everyone would be to not be fooled by articulate talking heads. Examine their records. What have they actually accomplished?

"I clean up pretty good, but at the core, I'm still a simple rancher. The family's motto is 'Deeds, not words.' I live by that motto, and my goal is simple: to be as good a person as my daughter and my dog already thinks I am. Thank you, Robert, for the invitation and the opportunity to speak to the good folks across this great nation of ours. God bless you and America."

3

Mike O'Reilly was born to Irish farmers whose forefathers long ago had opted to go west instead of settling, as so many immigrant Irish families did, in Boston and New York.

Sean, Mike's father, was a large man with a thick chest and ruddy complexion. He was an honest, no-nonsense disciplinarian. When it came to raising his two sons, Mike and Donovan, he would accept nothing but their best effort, no matter what the task.

He taught them to be honest in their dealings, to say what they meant and to mean what they said, to be self reliant, tough, and to tolerate no nonsense from another man. These were more than just character traits. They were principles to live by.

Honor, courage and loyalty were longstanding O'Reilly family traits, stemming from over 300 years of military service. Mike would one day join the long line of infantry soldiers, dating back to the sixteenth century and ancestral duty with the Queen's Own 18th Royal Grenadiers. He would learn first hand the principles of honor, courage and loyalty…the hard way.

Locals in Pushmataha County, Oklahoma where the O'Reilly family eventually settled had heard rumors the family had prudently moved from rural Coffee County, Alabama after the patriarch confronted a high school principal for viciously paddling his son Donovan.

Truth be known, Donovan was jumped by two older boys, intent on taking a medallion of the family crest, which he wore around his neck on a braided horsehair necklace.

It didn't turn out quite like they expected. Donovan severely pounded both antagonists, as well as a third unwise bystander who thought his two buddies could use a little help. The two boys that started the fight were not seriously hurt, just bloodied up a bit, although they needed stitches to close their wounds.

Unfortunately the bystander's intrusion somehow didn't set well with Donovan's sense of fair play. It really pissed him off. He had to be pulled off the guy by two coaches who had heard there was a fight outside the gym.

The O'Reilly boy had busted the kid's nose, broken two ribs and ripped part of his left ear off before they could be separated.

To make matters worse, the wayward intruder was the bullying son of the high school principal.

By the time Sean and Donovan entered the principal's office later the same day, large, discolored welts covered all of the boy's buttocks and much of the lower torso. There were two inch-wide bruises approximately twelve inches long across the back where the principal had maliciously struck Donovan with the side of the paddle.

The discussion was short. Sean asked the principal if he had done this to his son, to which the principal replied, "Damn right I did, and I'd do it..." Before he had a chance to complete his statement about what he would do again, the big man knocked him senseless.

Sean, guided by his sense of fair play and family honor, immediately called the Coffee County sheriff's office. About fifteen minutes later, two deputies and a pair of ambulance drivers with limited first aid training burst through the school's double doors.

Typical of southern deputies in the 1950s, they were fat, tobacco-chewing meatheads, with limited formal police training. Both spoke with a deep southern drawl that most people have a tendency to mistakenly associate with ignorance. In this case, however, the association would be correct. Both men were dumb as doorknobs, exacerbating the situation.

The smaller of the two inquired as to whether or not the principal was still alive. It was obvious he was. His chest was rising and falling with each breath taken, and his legs were involuntarily twitching as a neurological reaction to a solid blow to the left temple. One of the medics looked up in disgust, asking the deputy somewhat sarcastically if he had ever seen a dead man twitch like that, and then went back to reviving the fallen principal with smelling salts.

In the interim, Sean had picked up the overturned chair, placed it neatly behind the desk and was picking up books and papers that had been scattered when the principal fell against a bookcase on his way to the floor.

The smarter of the two brain-dead deputies asked if there were any witnesses to the fight.

"It was not really a fight," Sean replied. "My son Donovan and I were the only ones in the office."

"You ain't no witnesses. Ya'll caused this!"

Sean raised the torn shirt of his son and stated that the man on the floor had admitted to the beating.

Both lawmen and the ambulance driver stared in disbelief that a principal could inflict such a beating on a student. The medic asked the boy if he felt sick or lightheaded.

"I still feel kind of tingly here," Donovan said, pointing to his left hamstring.

The medic gave him two aspirins, which was about the limit of his medical prowess, and told Sean to keep an eye on his son for the next couple of days and to get him to the hospital if he became nauseous or passed out.

The principal finally responded to efforts made to revive him and was placed on a stretcher for transport to the hospital for observation. The deputies placed Sean under arrest but were unable to figure out a way to handcuff him. He stood 6 foot 8 and weighed 285 pounds. Years of hard physical labor had contributed to the development of massive forearms and wrists.

They did the next best thing. Bubba number one—the fatter and slightly smarter of the two deputies—told him to get in his truck and follow them to the courthouse in downtown Enterprise to the police station and jail. On the way, the deputies stopped at a café to get coffee.

Sean waited patiently in his truck with Donovan wondering how these buffoons could ever be entrusted with a weapon, a loaded one, at that.

They arrived at the station, went through the booking process, and appeared before a justice of the peace. In the early 1950s and 60s in most of the South, a justice of the peace could be just about anyone. Of course if you knew a little about the law, it was a real plus. Sean stated the events of the day accurately, but as one might expect, it had little impact on the forthcoming decision.

Justice of the Peace Roy Babcock set the fine at $25.00 or 30 days in jail and slammed his homemade gavel down on an old wooden military surplus desk.

Sean told the man, whose only means of support was raising fighting cocks and running illegal chicken fights over in New Brockton, that he only had $12.65 on him.

Mr. Babcock was either in a very good mood, didn't know what to do with young Donovan if he put his dad in jail, or he had a payment due on something. He picked up the booking form, which had been mimeographed so many times that most of the words were barely legible, drew a line through $25.00 and entered $12.65. With the second pounding of the gavel, this case was closed or so everyone thought.

No one actually remembers, but sometime during the next seven to ten days, Donovan, the 200-pound Allstate linebacker from Coffee County High School, collapsed during football practice and died as he was being transported to the hospital.

The subsequent autopsy revealed the cause of death to be a massive clot blocking blood flow to the heart. The most probable cause of death, according to the coroner, was blunt force trauma to the lower torso.

4

After the burial of his eldest son and following a period of mourning, Sean and his youngest son Mike went to the judge advocate general's office—the military law office that helps military personnel and veterans with legal assistance, including procedures for pressing criminal charges—located at nearby Fort Rucker.

After getting authorization to enter the post from military police at the Daleville gate, Sean and Mike made their way to the two-story wooden building just off Rucker Blvd. They were met by a young corporal from the 509th Airborne Infantry (Pathfinders) who had broken a leg on a night jump and had been assigned temporary duty to the understaffed JAG office.

"Corporal Best, can I help you, sir?"

"Yes, you can, corporal. My name is Sean O'Reilly and I have an appointment at 1400 hours with Captain Snyder."

"Wait one minute, sir, and I'll see if the captain is available."

The young soldier lifted himself onto his crutches and hobbled down a long hallway. Moments later, he returned with a flushed face and sheepishly said, "The captain will be with you shortly, sir. He told me to tell the big ugly son-of-a-bitch to be patient."

Little Mike's eyes almost bulged out of his head. He knew his dad allowed no man to speak to him in that manner, and that the continued well-being of the captain and possibly even the corporal could now be measured in seconds.

Sean, sensing his son's uneasiness, placed a hand on his knee. "Things are not always as they seem. Understand all of the facts before you go off half cocked. Always remember that, son; it's an *important* lesson."

Corporal Best, showing some uneasiness, knowing this mammoth of a man could dispatch him to paratrooper heaven with one blow from his tree trunk arms, said, "Sir, I want you to know I'm not part of this outfit. I'm just helping out while this frigging leg heals. Don't shoot the messenger!"

The big man burst out laughing, to the dismay of both the corporal and his son.

About that time, a loud voice boomed from down the hall, "Hold down the noise out there. This is a law office, not a bloody whorehouse!" From the hallway emerged a balding man of small stature who walked with a pronounced limp.

"Captain Snyder, I presume?"

Ron Snyder responded to Sean's fugal attempt at a Sherlock Holmes impersonation by saying, "Aye, matey, that be me" as he gave the corporal and the young man standing beside him his best Long John Silver wink. The two men then embraced, hugging each other in a display of emotion only combat veterans, past or present, could relate to or even understand.

"Corporal Best, would you please round up some coffee and a bottle of pop for the young Mr. O'Reilly. And if you would, bring a notepad. I may need you to take a few notes." Sean and Mike followed Captain Snyder down the hallway to his office.

"Have a seat anywhere, gentlemen."

Sean then introduced Mike to his old friend, Ronald Detmeir Snyder III, Esq.

"Your dad and I served together in the 101st Airborne Division, Mikey. We were known as the Screaming Eagles and later picked up the label everyone associates with the 101st Airborne—the Battered Bastards of Bastogne!"

Sean interjected, "Those were the days. That was the scariest, hungriest and coldest I've ever been in my life, buddy. You remember that?"

"Oh, yeah, I remember! What I really remember is this giant of a man running through an enemy artillery barrage and picking me and another poor soul up like sacks of flour, one under each arm, and carrying us back to the aid station before I bled to death. Your dad saved fourteen men that day, Mikey, and sustained severe wounds to his back, legs and, as I recall, a piece of shrapnel reamed him a new asshole."

Sean laughed, "OK, partner, enough of this crap!"

"Pops, you never told Donny and me any of this stuff. How come?"

"I guess I never got around to it, son. I don't much care to talk about things that serve no purpose." As hard as the big man tried to hold back the tears, it was not to be. "I guess it's a little late for Donny Boy to hear it anyway," Sean said.

Ron intervened saying, "Son, would you mind giving Corporal Best a hand with the drinks?"

Mike had barely left the room when all of the emotions stored up between men who have shared the horrors of war overflowed.

Sean said tearfully, "Ronny, I'm sorry about this. I thought if I had Mikey with me I could get through this. Guess I was wrong."

"For God's sake, Tiny, you just lost one of your sons. Don't be so hard on yourself."

As Ron raised his pant leg to show the prosthesis, he said, "You can get through this, just as I got through the shock of losing a leg. You can do it! You *must* do it for Mikey's sake. You're all he has and this is a real tough time for him, too. The latrine's down the hall on the right. Why don't you take a moment to freshen up before they get back, buddy. Make you feel better, and I'm sure it'll improve your looks a hell of a lot, or at least as good as one can hope for with a mug like yours."

Ron walked around the desk and hugged the man to whom he owed his life.

As Sean was making his way back to the office, he met his son and the young soldier. "Let me get the door for you, boys," he said as he opened the door and stepped inside.

"Corporal Best, this is *your* lucky day."

"Why is that, sir?"

"You're in the presence of a real American hero. One of the most decorated soldiers of World War II and Korea. Mr. O'Reilly here, because of his soldierly skills and demonstrated leadership, received a battlefield commission as part of Task Force Smith at the outbreak of the Korean conflict.

"He is also one of the few living recipients of the highest decoration for valor this country has to offer—the Congressional

Medal of Honor. And I'm here today because of his selfless, heroic actions that I might enlighten you young gentlemen of this fact."

"Jesus Christ, Dad, when were you…"

Before his son could get the next word out, Sean stood and glared at his son with stone-cold eyes. "If you use the Lord's name in vain again, I'll throw your little ass through the damn window, understood? Now apologize to Captain Snyder and Corporal Best."

Mike, embarrassed and a little shaken, said, "Yes, sir! I'm sorry. I know better, but I'm just now hearing stuff I should already know. You should have told us, Dad."

Ron reached over and squeezed Mike's small arm and said, "No apology necessary, son. If this bonehead had a hair on his ass, he would've told you himself a long time ago."

In an effort to change the subject, Sean interrupted. "Can we get down to business now?"

"Yes, sir, as you wish. I've done a preliminary review of the salient points. It is my learned opinion that the principal's actions are, in all probability, the cause of Donovan's death. However, tying the beating and later demise together will be difficult to prove because of the time lapse between incident and death.

"There is circumstantial evidence, for sure, but I believe it will not carry the day. As important as any evidence or lack thereof, the principal's ancestry has roots here in Alabama dating back over 150 years. It is a well-respected name, consisting of educators, lawyers and two prominent judges."

"Sir, he killed my only brother," Mike said tearfully, "and he should pay for it. Why does all that other stuff matter?"

"I know how you must feel, son" Ron said, "but the law and the way things work is not always right, and certainly not always fair."

"One day," Mike blurted out, "the law will change and what's right for the people *will* matter." Tears came to his eyes and his throat tightened as he spoke. "We just studied the Constitution and Bill of Rights in school, and there's none of this shit in it."

Sean looked over at his son. "I know your upset, Mikey, and therefore I'm going to cut you a little slack on your choice of words."

"Tiny, I'll do whatever you ask of me, but I thought it wise to lay it on the table, so to speak, so we have no false illusions about the daunting task that lies before us.

"It will be expensive in terms of emotional strain and could carry on for months. My tour of duty here at Mother Rucker–as Ft. Rucker was affectionately known–ends in about seven months. Your case, in all probability, will be assigned to my replacement, and that's a grab bag. He may have just graduated law school and have less experience then Corporal Best here. I'm afraid that's the real world we face."

As the big man and his son stood to leave, Sean said, "Ronny, thanks for being here at a time when I really needed you."

Ron smiled, winked at Mike and said, "If you weren't so big and ugly, you'd have more friends. I can't do this every day, you know. It's not like I *owe* you my life."

As the corporal and Mike left the office, Ron grabbed his friend by the arm to stop him. "Buddy, I can't help you very much in a legal sense, but if I were you, I'd do what you do best and take care of business. I say this one trooper to another. You understand?" Sean nodded and squeezed his friend's shoulder as he left the office.

When they were in the truck on the way back to the farm, Mike looked over at his dad and asked, "What did Captain Snyder mean, Pops, when he told you to do what you do best?"

Sean shrugged as he gripped the steering wheel a little tighter and said, "It's just a saying, son. It don't mean nothing."

5

Six months later

In July of the following year, Sean attended Major Ron Snyder's promotion party at the Ft. Rucker Officer's Club Annex located at Lake Tholocco. The Lake Lodge, as it was known, was a spacious, open building of rustic design overlooking one of the best fishing lakes in Alabama.

It was a popular place for fishing, swimming and water sports. The neat thing about the lake, it was a private reserve located on a military reservation and only military personnel, their families and invited guests were allowed to use it.

Since Sean was no longer military, he had to stop at the guard gate to gain authorization to enter the post. This was handled in one of two ways. Each gate was issued an access list of expected guests, which was about as effective as trying to piss up a rope, or the military police would call the guest's sponsor for authorization. As chance would have it, Sean's name was on the list.

As he drove through the remote and heavily forested back roads leading to the lodge, he thought perhaps subconsciously that if a guy were to run off the road back here, he might never be found.

Prior to Sean's arrival at the lodge, Major Snyder ensured that the commanding general, along with his senior staff, was made aware that one of his invited guests was a highly decorated veteran of two wars and had been awarded the Congressional Medal of Honor by President Truman.

Major General Wymore inquired as to the particulars surrounding the award of such a prestigious combat decoration, instructing his aide-de-camp, Captain Roger Smythe, to take copious notes. He then thanked the newly promoted major for the heads-up, adding that he would ensure proper military protocol would be followed.

Moments later the general tapped on a whiskey glass to gain the attention of the guests. When a general officer clangs on anything at a military function, the room magically falls silent.

"Ladies and gentlemen, we are about to be honored with the presence of Sean O'Reilly. In his former military life he served with Major Snyder as a ranger in the 101st Airborne Division. What rank did he hold then, Major Snyder?"

"He was a sergeant, sir."

General Wymore continued, "Sergeant O'Reilly is the recipient of the Congressional Medal of Honor. For the edification of Major Snyder's civilian guests, that is the highest combat decoration awarded for valor this beloved country of ours has to give. It is an award few soldiers, even our most gallant warriors, have the privilege of wearing.

"As such, there are special considerations and recognitions that are bestowed upon a Medal of Honor recipient out of respect and to honor his achievement and sacrifice. I say sacrifice, because more often than not, the Medal of Honor is awarded posthumously. Mr. O'Reilly is entitled to, and shall receive this evening, a salute by every soldier present, regardless of rank. It will be a privilege to lead all of my officers in attendance in honoring this highly decorated soldier.

"Once he arrives, I will first propose a toast and respectfully request all guests to participate. All officers and any enlisted personnel that are part of the club's staff will then be asked to take my lead, rather my adjutant's lead, as we render the hand salute called for by military protocol.

"Captain Smythe, would you please so inform the club manager and see that any enlisted men working here tonight are available to participate?"

"Right away, sir."

Shortly thereafter, Sean walked through the heavy wooden doors and into the foyer. Though he had received a battlefield commission in Korea as part of Task Force Smith, he had surrendered—rather resigned—that distinction when he returned to the states and was subsequently honorably discharged from the army.

His battlefield commission to lieutenant was a matter of convenience for the army, based on his demonstrated leadership skills and the army's desperate need for platoon leaders in Korea. As a matter of record, the life expectancy of young infantry lieutenants was very short indeed.

In no way did Sean, as he was standing in the lodge foyer, see himself as anything but a "dogface" infantryman, also fondly known as a grunt. He did not possess the upbringing, background, education or sophistication he associated with the Officer Corps. Therefore he was more than just a little uncomfortable as he stepped into the main hall searching for the one face he knew. Sean was almost a foot taller than anyone in the room, which made his search easy.

As he made his way to the bar where Ron was standing with a small cluster of fellow officers, he could not help notice the stares, smiles and gentle nodding of heads as he crossed the room. He was accustomed to occasional stares, because of his immense size, but this was beyond anything he had previously experienced. It made him self-conscious and he wondered if he was dressed inappropriately. Or perhaps his fly was open. Wouldn't that be cute!

Ron spotted his friend and picked up two glasses of bourbon, freshly poured by the bartender, and headed through the crowd to meet him. "Glad you could make it, Tiny. This shindig wouldn't be complete without you being here."

"Thanks for the invite. What's with all the stares? People are looking at me like I'm a bloody ape or, even worse, my fly is open."

"Well, *you* are a bloody ape, but that notwithstanding, let me be the first to tell you how dapper you look. I'm amazed Dothan Tent & Awning could make such a nice jacket."

"Piss off, you little shit. I should have left your raggedy ass in the mud." Sean downed the glass of bourbon and almost immediately felt better. "Is there a limit to how many of these a guest can have?"

"In your case there is, because everyone knows the bloody Irish can't hold their liquor."

Sean laid a huge arm over his friend's shoulders. "Walk with me to the bar, kind sir, and we'll see who can hold what."

Ron put an arm around his friend's waist, the only place he could comfortably reach, and said, "Come on then, I'll see if I can get special dispensation for you to have one more."

"I really like this place, Ronny, me boy, do you think I fit in?"

"Oh, yeah, perfectly," Ron said, waving his arm in the general direction of the masses. "They are the little cowboys and you're the 2,000-pound bull. Yippee, kayee!" Both men laughed as they headed for the bar.

As the bartender poured each of them fresh bourbon, Ron said in a rather serious tone, "Sean, I have something for you and little Mikey, but before I give it to you, I want you to promise you'll accept it. If for no other reason, do it because we are friends and I want you to have it."

Wary of a practical joke in the making, Sean looked into his friend's eyes and what he saw made him uncomfortable and anxious. His friend was serious. "Hell, Ron, as long as it's not your hand-me-down size thirty-two suits or a spare wooden leg, I guess I'll accept it. You're not dying on me, are you?"

Ron smiled. "That would be a real kick in the ass, given you dragged my skinny butt through the mud for miles. No, I'm not dying, but my father did some time back. He is the genesis of this gift."

"I'm truly sorry about your father, buddy, but what the hell's a *genesis*?"

"You've got to be the dumbest son-of-a-bitch alive. No wonder you're a hero. You probably thought the fire you felt when that shrapnel was ripping you a new asshole was a hot flash!"

As they both roared with bourbon-induced laughter, General Wymore again clanged on his glass.

A hush fell over the banquet room, as the general began to speak. "Ladies and gentlemen, I would like to propose a toast." He raised his glass. "To honor, courage and loyalty, may God forever bless and protect those who live by this creed." In concert, the men and women, including Sean, responded by saying, "here, here," as they raised their glasses.

General Wymore then asked Sean to come forward. As he set his drink on the bar, he looked at Ron and thought he saw a sly grin or a twinkle in his eye. Sean said, as he walked toward the general, "You sneaky little bastard, I'll get you for this."

"Mr. O'Reilly, we are only following long-established military tradition and protocol here and, because of a severe shortage of JAG officers, we sincerely hope you will forego the urge to kill our newly appointed major." The room filled with anxious laughter.

"With your permission, sir, it is with great honor and respect that I and all of the officers and soldiers present salute you."

The post adjutant, who was standing to the left of General Wymore, said in an exaggerated command, "Present arms." In perfect unison, officers and enlisted alike rendered a salute. A few seconds later, the adjutant commanded, "Order arms," upon which, everyone saluting dropped their right hand quickly to their side.

A moment later, the general said, "I would like to propose another toast...to the lovely ladies and the gallant men in their flying machines." All of the men, at least the officers, responded by saying, "To the ladies."

The general turned to Sean. "Let me escort you back to the bar. I would consider it a privilege if you would have a drink with me."

"General, it would be my pleasure to have a drink with you and your officers."

The general said rather loudly, "All officers to the bar."

The Officer Corps is a very tightly knit group, quick to rally around one of their own and even quicker to rally if directed to do so by their commanding general. And if libation is the crux of the command, it is not safe to stand in their way.

As the other invited guests went about socializing, trying not to look offended for not having been invited to drink with the general, his officers and honored guest, General Wymore started to highlight Sean's heroic actions for the benefit of his officers. That accomplished, he asked Sean what he did for a living.

"I'm a farmer, sir. I have a couple hundred acres just north of here and my son Mike and I raise a few head of cattle and grow peanuts, cotton, soy beans and the like."

"What prompted you to settle in Alabama, if I might ask?"

"My great grandfather settled here, sir, more than a hundred years ago. God only knows what he was thinking at the time. My best guess is he was drunk, broke a wagon wheel or just liked the misery associated with trying to grow things in rock hard red clay. Irishmen are funny that way.

"He fought in the Civil War with the Kentucky Long Rifles and later died from complications of an old war wound. He's buried out there on the old homestead, along with the rest of my family. My wife, however, is buried in the cemetery over in Enterprise, due to something about the law not allowing home burial plots anymore.

"It's just as well, sir. I'm going to sell our place as soon as possible. Last year's flood just about did us in. The previous year's poor crops, on top of the damage done by the flood, has put us so far behind with the bank that I'll just about break even by selling the place."

"I'm really sorry to hear that, Mr. O'Reilly. I know things have been hard for most folks in the area, but I really hate to hear about veterans having a tough time."

"Call me Sean, sir, and thanks for your concern but we'll do just fine."

"What happened to your wife, if I may ask? I know you said she passed away."

"Sir, she died in an aircraft accident on her way back from Atlanta a couple years ago. The airline is supposed to be giving everybody a settlement of some kind, but I have no idea what that will be or when. Hopefully it will be enough to give Mike and me a new start somewhere."

Captain Smythe, the general's aide-de-camp, hung up the telephone sitting on the bar and whispered something to the general. "Gentlemen, I'm needed back at post headquarters. Major Snyder, congratulations on your well-deserved promotion and thanks for the invitation. Sean, it is an honor to have met you, sir, and I hope to see you again soon. Good luck on whatever the future has in store for you."

"Gentlemen, let's have another toast before I leave and while you are still able to stand." The general raised his almost empty glass, "To the United States Army Aviation Center." The officers raised their glasses and responded, "Above the best, sir."

After the general departed, with his aide at his heels, things became noticeably more relaxed. The senior officers had another drink or two and then, one by one, they left the party. By then, the disc jockey that Ron had hired was playing louder music and everyone was dancing and feeling no pain.

The Lake Lodge closed at midnight on Fridays and by about fifteen till, all but a few diehards at the bar including Ron and Sean had left.

Ron indicated there were still some things he wanted to talk about and asked Sean if he would be interested in going over to Ozark for a cup of coffee.

"Yeah, I'll go as long as we can get something to eat. Because of the bullshit you put me through I never got even a wee morsel of food."

As they stood to leave, Ron handed the bartender a twenty, thanking him for his service.

In the parking lot they decided Sean should drive for a couple of reasons. He had managed to hold his liquor better than the smaller major and, more importantly, they had to navigate off and then back on post. The military police manning the Ozark gate might stop them on the way out because of the late hour and would most assuredly stop them on the way back on post to pick up Sean's truck at the lodge. For an officer, particularly a field grade officer, to be detained for DWI was the kiss of death insofar as a military career was concerned.

They took Ron's car because it had blue post decals, signifying it was registered to an officer and would therefore be less likely to be stopped at the gate. Also Sean's means of transportation was a dirty farm truck. It just seemed nicer to cruise after hours in a brand new Cadillac convertible.

Sean left the top up until they were through the Ozark gate, simply because it would be harder for the gate guards to get a good look at the condition of the men inside. As they left the post, he pulled off of the road and, with the help of his friend, managed to lower the top.

Located on Highway 231 just north of Ozark was an all-night truck stop, used not only by truckers, but also by local bar hoppers in need of early morning sustenance. Sean pulled up in front of the café and stopped.

Major Snyder reached into the back seat and retrieved a briefcase made of fine leather and engraved with his initials, a gift from his father on passing the bar in New York and Illinois, the locations of his father's well-established and highly respected law firm.

The two men settled into a rear booth for privacy, as a waitress approached. In a slow, almost silky voice, she asked, "Can I help ya'll this morning?"

The newly promoted major spoke first, "You may, my young lassie."

"What's he sayin' anyway?" the waitress inquired with a cute smile.

"Ignore him, Miss. He's an idiot! Could you bring us a pot of coffee?"

"I can't bring a pot, but I'll make sure ya'lls' cups are never empty. Would that be okay?"

"You bet! Major Snyder, are you ready to order, sir?"

"Aye, matey, that I am. I'll have coffee and a piece of apple pie, if that be okay with ya'll?"

The waitress smiled—really more of a smirk, since she knew this strange little man was making fun of her southern drawl—as she took his order and turned to Sean, rolled her eyes as if to say, 'you're right; he is an idiot.'

"And what will you have, sir?"

Sean stretched, repositioning his large frame. "Miss, I'll have six eggs scrambled, eight or ten pieces of crisp bacon, hash browns, some grits, toast and jelly, a large glass of orange juice, and keep the coffee coming."

"Did you say six eggs?" the waitress asked with an incredulous look.

"Yep, six eggs scrambled and if you would, bring me a bottle of hot sauce."

"OK! I don't even know what all that will cost, but I'll find out, OK?"

"It makes no difference sweetheart. My Yankee friend here is picking up the tab."

Ron looked over in disbelief. "Thank God it's payday! No damn wonder you can't make a living on just 200 acres. Your grocery bill runs as high as the national debt."

As the waitress left to place their order, Ron, who was facing the order window, saw her and the short order cook exchange looks and laugh, as though the order was *slightly* out of the ordinary.

After the two men had finished their breakfast, the table was cleared and the waitress poured fresh coffee, Ron looked over at his friend and asked if he had had enough to eat.

"You bet. Thanks."

"May I assume then that I can proceed with the business end of this little foray?"

"Please do, sir!"

Ron placed the briefcase on the table and extracted a smaller leather sheath about eight by twelve inches in size. "Before I open this, you need to know a little about my family, particularly my father."

"Hell, Ronny, its damn near two in the morning already. Another hour or so won't make a flippin' bit of difference. I'll just go straight home, jump on my tractor and hope like hell I can stay awake and not kill somebody."

6

Ron knew that Sean would never accept the gift he would soon offer if he did not carefully lay the framework. The only way he could think of diminishing the magnitude of the gift was to somehow convince him that it was not as significant as it might initially sound. He had thought about the subject a great deal over the last few days and struck on the idea of a short family background story.

The only problem was the quickest thing that ever happened to him in his life was his bar mitzvah on his thirteenth birthday, and that had taken all day. His New York Jewish heritage and his decision to become a lawyer essentially removed 'quick' from his consciousness. But he had to try.

"My grandfather was a very affluent diamond broker from Austria and Switzerland. Just saying he was wealthy doesn't quite do justice to his ranking on the hierarchal pyramid. When they immigrated to the United States in 1922, he ensured my father's acceptance into Harvard School of Law by building a new science center. You get the general idea here?"

Sean merely shrugged his massive shoulders and drank his coffee. At that moment, he had about ninety-five cents to his name, so any tale of great wealth was about as intriguing as "Little Red Riding Hood," "The Three Pigs," or anything else that started with "Once upon a time."

"I can see I've got you right on the edge of your seat, so let me fast forward this tale before you fall asleep. The long and the short of it, Dad became a successful partner in a prestigious law firm owned by friends of my grandfather.

"My father, just as my grandfather had done, paid cash for everything and kept the bulk of his resources in precious metals and gems, so when the market crashed in 1929, he lost very little.

"The 1930s brought more misery to the country via the most severe drought ever recorded. The Midwest was affected most severely. Texas, Oklahoma and Kansas—the bread basket states—took the brunt of the blow. It was so severe and it persisted for such a long time that it became known as the Dust Bowl. Crops withered and died year after year. Cattle died for lack of water and hay. Eventually ranchers and farmers just gave up, left their homesteads and many of them moved west. The movie "Grapes of Wrath" portrayed just how miserable times were for this group of people in the thirties.

"Desperate to get their families to safety, ranches and farms were sold for as little as ten cents on the dollar and, in some cases, they were given away to anyone willing to pay off outstanding debts or bankroll the landowners' trip west.

"It was in this unhappy set of circumstances that my father acquired large tracts of land in Oklahoma. Land at the time of purchase, for all practical purposes, was useless and there was no relief in sight.

"My father suffered from stiff and swollen joints, probably brought on by the long periods of sitting associated with his work at the law firm. Because of this affliction, he made frequent pilgrimages to Hot Springs, Arkansas for mineral bath treatments. Normally he flew from New York to Little Rock and then rented a car from one of the locals for a week and drove to Hot Springs.

"On one of these trips he chanced upon a middle-aged Indian and his beautiful sixteen-year-old daughter standing in the rain along a deserted stretch of Arkansas highway. My father had always been a compassionate and generous man who cared for the well-being of others, so he stopped to see if he could help them. The decision to stop would prove to be fortuitous."

Sean sensed this story was about to get interesting, so he sat up and started paying more attention.

"The two rain-soaked souls walking slowly along the side of the road had no money and really no way of surviving, given the racial overtones of the day. Unknown to my father, a city boy from New York, Indians were not the chosen race. In fact, the same cruel prejudice that Americans of African descent endure here in the South was indiscriminately applied to all Indians in Arkansas, Texas, Oklahoma, and other western states with Native American populations.

"It's a disgusting thought, Sean, but the prejudices of the thirties still exist to this day. I know!"

Sean responded with a nod, "Yep, it wasn't long ago the Irish had their hands full with that crap. Once we took over the police role and started knocking the shit out of the dumb bastards, they backed off. I'm not sure that is exactly how the transition happened, but it has a nice ring to it and makes me feel good, so I'm sure it's right."

Major Snyder waved the waitress over for more coffee and continued. "According to what the Indian man later told my father, a couple of transients, which he and his daughter had been somewhat coerced into giving a ride to when they had stopped for gas just outside of Memphis, had forced the father to drive west while they both got in the back seat with his daughter.

"For the next couple of hours or so, nothing happened. The men were drinking moonshine, and it wasn't long before they made the girl drink some of it and took turns kissing her. From a very early age most Indians had been taught—perhaps conditioned is a better word—not to resist white men, because it made them mad and they would hurt them somehow.

"We're talking about the twenties and thirties now; a lot has changed since then, but that's how it was then, according to my father.

"Kissing soon turned to fondling of the girl's breasts. When she didn't resist, the drunkards interpreted that to mean she liked it, and they pulled her dress over her thighs and started roughly groping her breasts and putting their hands between her legs. Though she had been given quite a bit to drink, the roughness caused her to whimper. That served to excite the two thugs even more.

"Somewhere along the way, the larger of the two jerked his head toward the front, which was his way of telling his drunken buddy to get his scrawny ass into the front seat and to keep an eye on the old man. The smelly, drunk transient then forced the girl down, pulled her panties off and threw them at the guy in the front seat, laughing.

"Her father tried to stop the car but the transient pulled a knife, held it to his throat and told him to keep driving or they would kill them both.

"The guy in the back, winded from struggling with his hapless victim, told his friend to look for a place to pull off the road and into the woods. He then busied himself with the task at hand—brutally stealing the innocence of the young Indian girl.

"At some point, they found a secluded place and once the car stopped, they tied the old man up, put him in the trunk of the car and pulled the girl from the back seat. A short distance from the car, they found a stand of pine trees, where they took turns raping the girl until they were too exhausted to continue.

"Evidently the old man could hear his daughter's cries, intermingled with occasional slaps and the drunken laughter of the two transients, as they clumsily went about violating her and, indirectly, her father.

"A short time later, the two men pulled the Indian from the trunk and dragged him over to his daughter, who lay on her side with her legs pulled tightly to her bare breasts in a fetal position. She was trembling, and the old man feared she may die from shock.

"The two men took the Indian's money and before stealing his car, threw the girl's panties and the old man's jacket out into the darkness. They drove off leaving the father and daughter alone in what would have to be described as hostile territory.

"My father was naive and had no idea what difficulty he would have in trying to be a Good Samaritan. To set the stage for this piece of the story, Sean, picture yourself in a situation where you were dirty, cold, soaked to the bone, hungry and scared to death. On top of that, it's dark and you are, for all practical purposes, surrounded by hostile human beings that want you dead."

Sean sat up straight. "My friend, you have just described Bastogne. You and I both know how they must have felt, though their fear may have been a bit different; it had to have been scary. I'm sure they had a sense of utter hopelessness. Damn, how can people do that to one another?"

"I don't know, Tiny. It happened decades ago, but my heart still goes out to them.

"The first thing my father did was to get them into the car so they could start warming themselves. It took some coaxing, as you might imagine but they finally acquiesced.

"My father was not a big drinker, but he often carried a silver flask of Jaegermeister when it was cold out, just to take the chill out of his bones. It came in handy that night.

"He also had a couple of ham and cheese sandwiches and a bottle of pop he picked up in Little Rock just in case he couldn't find a café open on his way to Hot Springs. Hanging off the front bumper was a canvas water bag for the radiator in the event the car overheated. However, it was good water and aside from the strange taste that water has when stored in a waterproof canvas pouch, it was good for drinking. All of those items were used.

"The Indian man, after thanking my father for picking them up and explaining the terrible events of the day, broke down and cried as he held his daughter. My father tried to console the man as best he could and assured him that what happened to his daughter was not his fault and his inaction probably had saved their lives.

"The man, whose name was Samuel Eagle, and his daughter Winona were Osage Indians trying to get home. They had no money and no way of contacting anyone in Oklahoma to come get them. My father immediately changed his plans. He turned the car around and headed north toward Ft. Smith, Arkansas."

Sean again interrupted, "Your dad changed all of his plans and took it upon himself to help these poor folks whom, just a few hours before, he didn't know?"

"Speaks volumes about the character of the man, doesn't it?"

"I'm not sure I could do that, buddy," Sean said as he took another drink of cold coffee.

Ron looked incredulous at his large friend. "Look, numb nuts, that's exactly what *you* did in your former life. That's why I'm here today. Because of you, I lived! I'm sure you weren't hiding behind a big oak tree praying for an artillery strike just so you could dash out in the mud and muck to save a dumb shit from Able Company."

Sean shrugged. "There may be a little similarity, but combat is different."

"You and combat have a lot in common. You are definitely *different!*" Ron added sarcastically.

He smiled at Sean and continued his story, anxious to wrap it up and call it a night. "Over time, Samuel Eagle became talkative and spoke of the difficulties facing Oklahomans. He said that much land had to be sold to pay debts because of crop failures. With no grass and the prohibitive cost of bringing in hay from the north, cattle either starved to death or were killed.

"This was news to my father. He admittedly was not in tune with happenings outside of the eastern seaboard and furthermore he led an affluent and insulated lifestyle.

"Samuel Eagle told my father that the draught was upon the land because the white man violated Mother Earth and did not take care of her properly.

"He went on to say the Osage had money, collected from the white man for the rights to drill for oil on tribal lands, which for the most part had not been affected by the draught. The Osage, unlike poorer tribes, were wealthy Indians.

"Always the consummate businessman, my father heard key words while Samuel Eagle described the plight of Oklahomans ...indebtedness, cheap land, mineral rights and oil.

"When they reached the little town of Sallisaw, Oklahoma, about fifteen miles or so west of Ft. Smith, my father called his Chicago office and instructed them to research mineral and property rights law, particularly as it pertained to oil in the State of Oklahoma and to make an initial determination whether or not this might be a new field of interest for the firm.

"The story gets a little hazy at this point, but from what I have pieced together, it appears Samuel and my father became good friends over a short period of time. After much talk and a long drive on less than desirable roads, they reached Samuel's home just outside of Muskogee, Oklahoma.

"My father spent a number of days there and during that time Samuel was instrumental in helping him locate and purchase large tracts of land and negotiate mineral rights with the Osage tribal leaders.

"During this process, my father became acquainted with the legal movers and shakers in Tulsa, where most of the legal work took place. He soon discovered through a lawyer he had met that his new friend was, in fact, chief of the Osage nation, wealthy and very influential.

"The legal haranguing associated with his newly acquired properties and mineral rights that normally would have taken several months took less than a week."

Sean stood, stretching his large frame and looking down at Ron, smiling. "You're gonna give me and Mikey a little piece of land, aren't you?"

"I'm not giving you jack shit if you don't let me finish. Mikey, God love him, has no chance at normalcy being raised by the likes of you."

"Yep, probably right, but right now I have to take a leak. Order up some more coffee and a couple pieces of that coconut pie we saw on the way in. I'll be right back." Sean disappeared through the swinging door.

About that same time, several loud and very drunk locals sat down at the counter. They, like many rednecks, carried an old Coke bottle to use as a spittoon for the nasty juice produced from their constant use of chewing tobacco.

The loud banter suggested they had just come in from fishing on the Choctawahatchee River. By the looks of things, there had been a whole lot more drinking going on than fishing.

Obviously looking for trouble, they scanned the cafe for a likely candidate. With the exception of a couple of truckers on their way out, the only paying customer left was Ron. His small stature, neat appearance and implied success associated with a major in the U.S. Army, made him an easy target.

Why is the smallest drunk always the loudest? The runt of this litter made uncomplimentary comments about the officer and was in the process of working himself into a really stupid mistake when the waitress sauntered over.

"Coffee for you boys?"

The little guy's response was predictable. "Boys! I got a pound of salami and a sack full of balls. Who ya callin' boy?"

She smiled as she poured three cups of coffee and cocked her head in the direction of Ron. "Ya'll might wanta sip a little coffee before ya stagger over there and start showin' your ass. Or ya might be carryin' that mammoth salami and little sack of bb's home in a slop jar. The kind gentleman in the corner ain't alone."

The three men flexed a little as only drunks know how to do, and as Sean came through the swinging door, one of them turned his back to the big man saying to no one in particular, "Damn! Look at the size of *that* son-of-a-bitch!"

After Sean settled back in his seat and took a bite or two of his pie, Ron said, "Now, sir, are we agreed that such a gift, even if it is a 'little piece of land,' would be graciously accepted by the rather large Irish eating machine?"

Sean finished the last bite of pie, washed it down with coffee and gently placed a hand on his friend's forearm. "I can't think of anything that would help Mikey and me more at this time. A piece of good land and the money from the airlines when it comes would be the answer to my prayers."

Ron opened the small leather document wrap, laid the prepared papers on the table and pointed to six places requiring Sean's signature. He then smiled, "Sign by the X, preferably not with an X!"

Sean could feel his emotions starting to well up inside and hurried to sign the papers.

Ron looked across the table and said, "You, sir, are now the proud owner of a little piece of Oklahoma. The deeds are free, clear and unencumbered to include all mineral rights."

"Hang on just a minute, Ronny," Sean, now teary-eyed, said in a choked-up voice, "What exactly does unencumbered mean?"

"In this case, it means that under no set of circumstances, now or in the future, can persons, parties, organizations or corporations legally claim as their own your property and the associated mineral rights, whether or not the land is occupied, as long as all taxes are paid.

"You will never have to worry about paying property taxes. My law firm has already been instructed to take care of that and to serve as your legal counsel without fee in all matters concerning these properties. These same arrangements automatically transfer to Mike in the event you are no longer with us."

Sean wiped tears away with his hand. "These mineral rights you're talking about, are they worth anything?"

"It all depends what's there. Some of the largest oil deposits in the country are in Oklahoma. If oil is found on the property, it could be worth millions. On the other hand, it may be good for raising crops, cattle or chasing rattlesnakes. Who knows, I've never seen it."

Sean stared at Ron. "You what?"

"I've never seen the property. I have an idea of about where it is. I know there are parts of it leased to ranchers and farmers. That will provide you with some annual income until you get established. Just how much, I'm not sure. Additionally, there are some mineral rights leased to Phillips Petroleum, Texaco and several independents. They also generate annual income.

"Don't worry about the small stuff. All of that information will be prepared and sent directly to you once I call the office and tell them you have accepted the property. I need to know your checking account number so I can have the proceeds from leases sent to you."

"Hell, Ronny, I don't even have a checking account. What little cash I have, I keep hid out in the barn. I pay cash for everything. I borrow from the bank for seed and stuff and hope like hell we make enough to pay it off each year. That's not been the case the last couple of years. The grocery store runs a tab on what little groceries I have to buy, and I pay them when I can. Right now I'm in the hole, but I'll get it taken care of sooner or later, and they know that. I'm not joshing you, buddy. I'm poor as Job's turkey."

Ron smiled. "If I may ask, who is Job?"

"Don't you read the Bible? Of course you don't. Job was the hero of the Book of Job who endured many afflictions with fortitude and faith. His turkey, if he had one, surely suffered even worse."

Ron shook his head. "I see, very enlightening. With your permission, sir, I would like to make a futile attempt to bring you out of the Stone Age and into the twentieth century. Let's start by opening a checking account. What bank do you *borrow* from now?"

Sean took a quick sip of coffee and said, "Bank of Ozark."

"Okay. Later today we will go over there and open checking and savings accounts and fill out the necessary paperwork to have funds transferred from my firm directly into your accounts. That will keep you from having to mess with it. The bank will send you a monthly statement telling you how much is in savings and checking. Later I'll explain how to keep track of what is left in checking. You strike me as the kind of guy that might think he has money as long as he has blank checks."

"You're a funny man. You'd look real funny hopping out of here on one leg, wouldn't you?" They both chuckled. "On a more serious note, Ronny, where exactly is this property you have never seen?"

"I thought you might ask, so I brought a map. Of course the deeds provide an exact location, but this map will give you a rough idea." He took the atlas from his briefcase and opened it to the State of Oklahoma. "I had the office give me a general idea of where it is. One piece is located in the vicinity of Kiefer and Glenpool, Oklahoma. It is my understanding that is south and a little west of Tulsa."

"Which is it, Kiefer or Glenpool? They look to be about ten miles apart on the map."

"Both. This piece of land covers approximately twenty-three square miles."

Sean's body went limp, and the color rapidly drained from his face as he started to perspire profusely.

Ron raised his arm and waved the waitress over to the table. "Miss, my friend is not feeling well. Could we have a cold rag or a glass of ice or something?"

She quickly returned with both ice and a cold rag. As she applied the cold rag to the back of Sean's neck, she said, "As much as he ate, I'm surprised he's even living." Sean recovered almost immediately.

"Damn, Tiny, if you react that way, I'd better not tell you about the big piece! Hell, you might keel over and die."

"I'm fine now, buddy, and thanks for the cold rag," Sean said as he regained his composure. "Are you pulling my crank or is this for real?"

"One of the largest oil deposits in the country is located in the vicinity of Glenpool. I believe that is where some of the mineral rights leases are. I've not had time to look into it in detail, but I believe that's right. Now just south of the little town of Bristow, there are several parcels of land that total approximately twelve square miles."

Sean just looked at his long-time friend with a blank stare. There was nothing to be said in a situation like this, which had never before occurred in the history of mankind. No one gives away this much land!

"The third and final parcel, approximately thirty-seven square miles and the one my father said was most likely to be the one a person might want to homestead—given one is into that sort of thing, is located along the Kiamichi River, north of a place called Antlers, Oklahoma in what is now Pushmataha County.

"They do have a way with words out there, don't they? You should blend right in. I'm going to speculate what your Indian name might be once they get to know you…Large Walking Eagle. The English translation…bird so full of shit he can't fly!"

Both men burst into laughter. When people have been up for twenty-four hours or so, they tend to get a little giddy. So was the case with these two friends that had endured the horrors of war together.

As they returned to Ft. Rucker, Sean said, "Did I hear you say *your* law firm, Ronny?"

"You did, indeed. That's another thing I wanted to tell you. As soon as it can be arranged, I will leave the military to take over the law firm of Greene Laverish Santine & Snyder. Mssrs. Greene and Santine have passed away and Joseph Laverish has been in full retirement for a number of years.

It is a matter of respect that their names remain on the partnership documents. I am the senior and controlling member of the firm, even though Howard Laverish, the eldest son of Joseph, manages the day-to-day operations.

"He has done a sterling job of taking care of the firm's business interests and has orchestrated, with occasional suggestions from me, the firm's tremendous growth over the last fifteen years or so. Our main offices are in New York and Chicago, and we now have on board something like 300 lawyers, paralegals and support staff. Not bad for a one-legged Jewish boy."

Sean was quiet as they drove back to base. Out of the blue he said, "There is nothing I can say to you, my friend. Mikey and I will be forever indebted to you."

"You saved my life, Sean. It makes the deeding of a few acres of land pale in comparison. I'm a diehard city slicker, you know that. If I lived to be a hundred, I would never use this land. On the other hand, you will cherish and take care of it and some day pass it on to Mikey.

"I saw something in his demeanor when you were in my office. I can't put my finger on it, but I intuitively know he is destined to do great things. By accepting this land you will make me a part of that legacy; and the gift will ultimately provide the resources he needs to achieve whatever goals he sets for himself. Just say *thank you* and we'll call it a day. I'm beat."

Sean reached over and put his hand on Ron's shoulder as they pulled into the parking lot of the Lake Lodge. "Thanks for all you've done for us, buddy. We won't ever forget it. By the way, when you come to Oklahoma, just refer to me as 'Your majesty, Large Walking Eagle.' I like that."

7

It took several days for Sean to reconcile the events of the previous week. Unimaginable new land holdings in Oklahoma; the guarantee from his trusted friend that Mike, his only son, would be provided for should something happen to him; and a transfer of funds into his own account, though he really didn't know how much. He was overwhelmed and had to go out in the drought-damaged fields so his son wouldn't see him cry.

Later in the afternoon, on a hot summer day in Alabama, he and Mike drove to Ozark in their old battered pickup. Sean parked on the town square and gave his son fifty cents for a hamburger and milkshake at the drugstore while he went to the bank to check his accounts.

Sean gave the account numbers to the elderly teller and waited at the counter. A few moments later the manager, a stooped gentleman with gray hair and bad breath, came around the counter holding a sheet of paper.

"Mr. O'Reilly."

"Yes, sir. Is something wrong?"

"No, not at all, I just make it a point to get to know our large account holders."

Sean smiled. "It can't be very large; it was opened only last week."

"I know, and since then we have received four wire transfers from your legal representatives totaling, let's see, $82,000 to checking and $321,000 to savings. Does that sound about right?"

Sean stood there staring at the sheet of paper as blood drained from his head, turning his weathered brown face sheet white.

"Mr. O'Reilly, are you OK?"

After a moment he nodded. "What was your name again, sir?"

"McDonald, sir. Edwin McDonald."

"Mr. McDonald, what does all that money represent? I mean, what's it for?"

"It says here, sir, it is a partial transfer for leases on property and mineral rights in Oklahoma. It also states that the specific breakout of parcels and associated mineral rights involved will follow within the next few days."

Sean smiled, saying more to himself than anyone else, 'that son-of-a-bitch! That's why he was so evasive about the money side of it. He knew I wouldn't accept the gift if I knew the amounts involved. That dirty, little, one-legged son-of-a-bitch!'

Taken aback, Mr. McDonald, a true southern gentleman, replied, "I beg your pardon, sir. Am I to assume someone gave you these Oklahoma leases?"

"That is correct, sir. The sneaky little bastard deeded free and clear about seventy-two square miles of Oklahoma to include all mineral rights."

"Is this gentleman a relative, sir?"

"I'm 100 percent Irish, given the Roman legions didn't have their way with a distant ancestor. My friend, Major Ronald Snyder, is Jewish. No way are we blood relatives, but I love the little bastard like a brother."

The banker, now appearing even more confused than before, said, "I know Major Snyder. He is one of our largest account holders and seems to be a very likable fellow."

"He is that, sir, if nothing else."

Mr. McDonald, because of the bizarre circumstances surrounding the day's events, then asked, "As you might expect, Mr. O'Reilly, I *am* curious as to why a friend would be so generous."

"Many years ago, I pulled his skinny little butt out of a mud hole in a place called Bastogne." For a moment, Sean seemed lost in thought as his mind drifted back to another time. Then he said, "The Battered Bastards of Bastogne! We were young men then, Army Rangers with the 101st Airborne Division. I happened upon him during one of the worst German artillery barrages I can remember. He was in bad shape, and I carried him and a few others to an aid station that had been set up in an old church. That's all there was to it. We've been best friends ever since.

"I'm kind of new at this check-writing thing, Mr. McDonald. Can I write a check on this account now?"

"Yes, sir, you can. Do you already have checks?"

"I have a few the bank gave me last week," Sean said, pulling a small packet from his shirt pocket.

"These are counter checks, sir, and will do nicely. We do offer something new in the checking industry: personalized checks."

"What exactly are they?"

The old gentleman smiled. "They are checks printed with your name, address and telephone number. It saves a little time when you cash a check."

"How much do they cost?"

"A box of 200 costs $1.75."

Sean winced. "That's a lot of money to spend on a check I can get for free. No, thanks, I'll just use these."

Mr. McDonald smiled politely, asking if he needed help writing whatever checks he needed.

"I need to write one to you for my seed loan."

"Let me get the payoff amount for you, sir."

"I know the amount. I owe you $712." Sean wrote the check smiling like a little kid in a candy store and handed it to the banker.

"This is kinda like magic. Scribble your name and *poof,* it's paid for. What will they think of next? Mr. McDonald, if I were to go buy a new truck today, would they accept one of these checks or do I need cash?"

"You should have no problem, Mr. O'Reilly, but if for any reason they won't accept your check, have the dealer call me and I'll take care of it. On the other hand, don't you think it would be fun to pay hard cash money for a new truck?"

"Yes, sir, I believe Mikey would get a big kick out of that. Give me, uh, say two thousand dollars cash and I'll pay off the grocery store, too."

Sean left the bank feeling whole for the first time in many years. He had not felt this good or nervous since President Truman had personally hung the Congressional Medal of Honor around his neck.

He went to the drugstore to get his son and to celebrate with a chocolate shake. On the way home they stopped at the Chevrolet dealership in Enterprise and picked out a shiny new red pick-up truck, complete with radio, armrests and outside mirrors. What a day!

8

Down a rutted dirt road not far from where Sean turned off to go to his farm lived a black sharecropper he saw now and again when he went into town for supplies. He often stopped and gave the man a ride.

On impulse, he turned down the road and pulled up in front of a sharecropper's rundown shack with no front door or windows, just openings where they should be. The shack had a rusted tin roof and an outside privy that stood about fifty yards or so from the shack.

There was a heavy-set black woman in front of the house sweeping the dirt yard with what looked like twigs, or perhaps straw, tied to the end of a small branch. That struck Sean as odd, but he dismissed it as a cultural thing and got out of the truck.

Running from the back of the shack were four dirty little kids he figured to be from two to six years of age. The two older boys wore tattered overalls. The little girl appeared to be about four or so and wore a soiled dress made of a printed feed sack. The youngest wore nothing. All the kids were barefoot.

They appeared startled. Sean reasoned they did not often see a white man in their yard, particularly a very large white man. However, kids are kids and they quickly recovered and ran up to the shiny red truck to have a look.

At about the same time the O'Reillys got out of the truck, the black man appeared out of a chicken coop carrying two chickens by their feet. When he saw who it was, he gave a quick cranking motion to the neck of each chicken, twisting the heads off and tossing them in the hog pen. The chickens began spurting blood from the neck and flopping all over the place. Mike was fascinated and just stood there watching at what looked like some exotic mating dance.

As the black man approached, Sean realized he didn't even know his name. How could that be? He had given him a ride half a dozen times. Embarrassed, he extended his hand to the man, "I'm Sean O'Reilly, and this is my son Mike."

The black man, dressed in dirty, well-worn overalls and a long-sleeved denim shirt, firmly clasped Sean's hand and with a deep Southern drawl said, "Pleased to know ya. Name's Ezekiel, and this is my missus, Lawonda. Don't have nothin' to offer ya, but we can sit for a spell, iffin ya like. Gonna fry up those birds when they stop carryin' on. Ya'll welcome to stay."

"Thanks, Ezekiel, but we have to get back to the farm. Been gone most of the day and I have some livestock that need tending."

"Mr. Sean, that sure is a pretty truck," Ezekiel said, as he moved in for a closer look.

"In a way, that's why I'm here. I have just come into some good fortune, and I thought I might share some of it with a man that I know works hard, takes care of his family as best he can and most importantly, deserves a break."

"Mr. Sean, ya lost me there. What ya proposin'?"

"Let's go sit on the porch for a minute and try to work out a way that I might be able to help you."

"Mr. Sean, I don't have much, but doin' okay, thanks to the Lord. We have enough to eat most of the time and most folks pretty much leaves us be."

"Ezekiel, it's summer now but it won't be long before winter will whip through that front door like a freight train."

"That's tha truth; it surely will. Old man Briley, he owns this place, and he said he'd put in windows and doors and I could just add it to the money I owe him from last year's sharecroppin' shortages. I swear I can't get nothin' put away. I told him we could get along without um."

The two men and Mike moved to the dilapidated porch and sat down on the dusty steps.

"Does this place have electricity?" Sean asked.

"No, sir. No, sir, it surely don't."

"Ezekiel, if I gave you my truck, would that help in any way?"

Ezekiel raised his face toward the roof and let out a belly laugh that could be heard a mile away. "Mr. Sean, I like ya. I surely do, but all that would help is to get me killed by the town folk. I can see ole Ezekiel drivin' into town, pretty as ya please, in that shiny red truck, I surely can. Everybody knows I got nothin'. I can't read or write so I got no drivin' papers. I got no money, so when the gas runs out, I'd have to leave it where it be. I'm sure some kind-hearted southern gentleman, maybe the law, would come along and claim I stole it.

"Mr. Sean, they *hang* negra men in these parts for lookin' at a white woman; for not steppin' aside for a white man, or for goin' to a privy marked 'whites only.' What ya reckin' they do to a negra in a shiny red truck?"

Sean pondered the man's response for a little bit. "Ezekiel, I've got a good friend that claims I'm the dumbest man that ever walked the Earth. You just proved him right. It was a stupid offer."

"Mr. Sean, it was a good thing to do. Times just ain't right for it."

Mike had been listening to his father and Ezekiel talk for some time when he said, "Why are folks so mean? Why can't you go where you want and look at who you want? It's not right, Dad. Negroes fought in all our wars. Why does everyone think they're so different?"

"Fortunately, son, everyone doesn't. What you want to learn from this is to treat everyone with respect until they give you a reason not to, regardless of color. Be fair and just in all your dealings. Be honest."

Ezekiel sat next to Sean nodding his head in approval and then said, "Amen, Mr. Sean, amen. You listen to your pa, little man, and you be doin' fine."

"Ezekiel, while the missus fries up those chickens, would you mind taking a short ride with me? It'll take a little while for her to boil the water to pluck those birds. The kids might get a kick out of riding in the back. Mike here can keep a close eye on them."

Ezekiel's face lit up with a smile, "I surely would like a ride, Mr. Sean."

"Then let's go. Kids, jump in the back. Mike, you help the little ones in and hold onto them so they don't bail out."

The men walked over to the truck while the kids screamed with joy and climbed in. Sean turned around in the freshly swept dirt that constituted the front yard. They were on the main road only a moment or two before he turned down the road leading to his farm. A few minutes later, he pulled into the dirt drive, crossed over the cattle grate and drove up the long driveway.

There was nothing fancy about the O'Reilly homestead. The old double-door barn was unpainted, but in good shape, as was the other shed that he used as a workshop. The farmhouse set some distance from the barn, next to the dirt driveway that made a big loop around a huge oak tree. Under the tree were four metal lawn chairs, where Sean and Mike often sat in the evening to capture what little breeze there was.

A two-person wooden swing that Sean had built for his wife hung from one of the tree's huge branches. The house sported a five-year-old coat of white paint with red shutters, something he had promised his wife he would do if there was money left over from the sale of crops. It had been a banner crop that year and he kept his promise.

Most southern farmhouses in the 1950s had tin roofs. This one was no different. The inside was kept clean and neat or at least as presentable as could be expected, given there was no longer a woman around. The house consisted of a kitchen, living room, bath and two small bedrooms. Modest is the word that comes to mind, but everything is relative.

As he stopped the truck, the kids piled out, screaming with delight, as they raced for the swing. Sean looked at Mike and asked him to keep an eye on the kids while he and Ezekiel talked.

"Ezekiel, let's go in and fix these kids some ice cold lemonade, and then I'll show you around the place."

"That sounds mighty fine, Mr. Sean. It surely does."

The kids got their lemonade, and the two men sat on the back porch to talk. Setting on a small stool was a rotating fan that made the summer heat almost bearable. Sean pointed to the field that stretched before them. "Isn't that about the most pitiful cotton field you ever saw? The last couple of years have been hard on everyone, except maybe politicians and moon shiners."

Ezekiel smiled. "That is surely true, surely true, Mr. Sean."

After they had finished their lemonade, the two men walked outside stopping at the three-acre, spring-fed pond to wash off some of the dust and sweat.

"Has it ever been hotter than this?" Sean asked.

"Oh, yeah, a couple of wars ago, maybe even before that, it was bad. Cows dried up, mules fell over dead. Little children and old folks dropped like flies. It was bad, real bad!"

As they sat in the shade of willow trees along the edge of the pond, Sean said, "Ezekiel, I'm not going to beat around the bush. I want to give this place to you and the missus. Now before you turn me down, hear me out."

The black man shifted his position on the hard clay dirt and listened. "There are approximately 200 acres here and a lake, so you'll always have water. The house has electricity and water so you can live better than you do now. Your family deserves that. This piece of land has been in my family for over a hundred years. I own it free and clear."

"Mr. Sean, I has had nothin' but trouble from white folks my whole life. I know you be a good man, but you see the problem I'm havin'?"

Sean nodded. "Ezekiel, the good Lord wants us to treat each other with love and understanding and to help one another. The Good Book says it. Do you believe that?"

"I surely do, Mr. Sean. I surely do."

"During World War II, I saved a man's life. He is now my best friend on Earth. A few days ago he gave me some land out in Oklahoma. I won't get into it, but it's a lot of land. My son and I are moving out there once I wrap up some details here in Alabama. He provided me with the answer to my prayers...a fresh start somewhere else. I have been prompted somehow to come to you that I might be the answer to your prayers."

"I ain't never had no prayers as big as 200 acres! I pray for health, to keep food on the table. I pray my li'l ones can get some schoolin', maybe learn to read and add numbers, things I don't know. But mostly, I just give thanks for what I have, Mr. Sean."

"I believe every word you say, and by my giving you this place—as scary as it may seem at the moment—it will be good for your family. That's what it's all about, family."

"Yes, sir, Mr. Sean, it surely is."

"Take this place and start farming for yourself. Old man Briley don't care about anything but himself, isn't that true?"

"Yep, it surely is."

"I noticed while I was over at your place the fields had already been tilled and looked about ready for planting. Go ahead and seed, then tell old man Briley he has to get himself another sharecropper because you just got your own land and won't have time to help him out."

Ezekiel smiled and then chuckled as he thought about the look on old man Briley's face when he told him all this. Then, he started laughing and couldn't stop. The magnitude of this life-altering development all of a sudden hit this deeply spiritual man, and soft sobs quickly turned to an uncontrollable outpouring of emotions to the extent his whole upper body was shaking.

Sean reached over and laid a hand on the man's forearm. "I know exactly how you feel, sir. I reacted the same way just a few days ago. Best thing to do is to go out into the field alone and thank God for your life and good fortune."

In an effort to lift the weight of the moment from the man's shoulders, Sean asked, "How much money do you owe old man Briley and the store?"

Between sobs Ezekiel said, "I don't rightly know, Mr. Sean. Mr. Briley shows me numbers and all, but I can't make sense of them. I know they changes from time to time, 'cause the shapes ain't the same."

"Here's what we can do," Sean replied. "I'll come get you tomorrow, and we'll go into town and have the deed to my place turned over to you. You can make your mark. It's as good as a signature. Then, we'll stop by the general store and settle your bill. We then go over to old man Briley's place and pay him off."

"I thought I had to seed before I told Mr. Briley about me havin' my own land?"

"You're right, Ezekiel. We'll save old man Briley for later."

"I'll do it, Mr. Sean. I'll make my mark tomorrow."

"Good man! Now, I'm not taking much with me to Oklahoma, so you can have the whole place, lock, stock and barrel, including my old International Harvester tractor you saw out in the barn. It's pretty fast, and you don't need a license to drive it. That should take care of your having to walk everywhere you go. OK?"

"God bless ya, Mr. Sean. That's all I can say."

"That says it all, Ezekiel." The big man put his arm around his new friend, gave him a reassuring hug and said, "We better get you and the kids back home now, before the missus gets worried and comes after me with that broom she was using."

After Sean and Mike returned home, they made a pitcher of iced tea and sat on the swing. Sean explained everything that had transpired over the last week or so: Ron's gift of over seventy square miles of land in Oklahoma; the incomprehensible bank deposits generated by leases and mineral rights which he showed Mike; the decision to give the farm to Ezekiel and his family; and the biggest shocker of all, the idea of moving to Oklahoma in the near future.

The following day Sean picked up Ezekiel, as promised, and drove into Enterprise to transfer the property and pay off the general store, where they both had charged goods for many years.

Both of these events attracted far more attention than either man felt comfortable with. The 1950s was a great time to be alive for most people, unless you were black and living in the Deep South, or a white man who had befriended a black. Beneath the thin veneer of civility lay deep-rooted prejudices and outright meanness.

Some time later, Ezekiel completed planting, and they paid Mr. Briley a visit to settle accounts and to inform him he would have to find another person willing to sharecrop.

When old man Briley stated what was owed by Ezekiel, Sean was stunned at the outrageous sum mentioned. "May I have a look at that ledger, Mr. Briley?"

"You may *not*, sir! This is between me and the n.....r."

"Sean stood up saying, "You mean Ezekiel, don't you, sir?"

"Ah, yes. The matter is between me and *that* man," he said, waving his hand in the general direction of Ezekiel.

"You mean Ezekiel?"

By this time it was obvious to the man that Sean O'Reilly, because of his persistence, size and cold hard stare, was a force to be reckoned with.

"Ah, yes, I do mean Ezekiel."

Sean looked menacingly at the man and in his most pleasant southern drawl said, "There now, that wasn't so hard, was it? What the hell's wrong with you stupid assholes? What makes you so much better than this man out there doing honest work? Turn that ledger around or I'll turn it around for you."

Mr. Briley, visibly shaken by the threat of this huge man and now sweating profusely, reluctantly turned the ledger.

As Sean was reviewing the entries, Mr. Briley regained some of his composure. "You're heading for a heap of trouble, mister."

Sean looked at the man through piercing, dark eyes, as if to say 'you're now on my permanent shit list.' "No, Mr. Briley, trouble is being surrounded by a German Panzer Division, knowing you have only one ammo clip left. That's trouble! Everything else pales in comparison.

"Now I want you to delete every double entry that's on this ledger." Sean pointed to specific entries on the book. "These seven items are for hay and horse feed, which has nothing to do with Ezekiel. This entry is for two tires for a pickup truck. Ezekiel, you have a truck?"

"No, Mr. Sean, I surely don't."

"Ezekiel, would you leave us alone for a few minutes? I need to talk to Mr. Briley in private."

As Ezekiel closed the door behind him, Sean fixed this weasel of a man with the meanest stare he could muster. "I won't ask you why you would take advantage of this gentleman. I already know. You're a miserable little shit-head of a man. Here's your choices, sir. Accept $200 cash money right now instead of the nearly $1,200 in bogus entries reflected on the ledger, or I'll take the ledger somewhere out of Coffee County and have it audited. I'm going to guess, using your term, a *heap* of improper entries might be found."

Mr. Briley bristled slightly. "So what! There ain't a county in the whole state that gives a damn what a law-abiding citizen charges his Nigra help."

"I believe the word you're having so much trouble with is *Negro,* you stupid sheet-wearing son-of-a-bitch. I've had a taste of Alabama justice, sir, and based on that experience, I'm inclined to agree with you. So I have another choice for you. Accept the $200, which is probably more than is owed anyway, or I'll take you out in the middle of that cotton field and deep plow your raggedy ass under, never to be seen again. I'm prepared to do that right now!"

Mr. Briley paled noticeably and, after a brief moment, nodded and accepted the money.

As a parting shot Sean said, "Mr. Briley, I suspect your brain is about the size of a peanut, but I'm about to tell you something important that has a direct impact on how long your sorry ass will be allowed to dwell on Earth. Our conversation about the imperfections of Alabama's justice system has reminded me of some unfinished business that needs tending to. When finished, I'm leaving Alabama.

"I leave behind over a hundred years of homesteading and a number of relatives in and around this area. This is the important part I was telling you about. If I get word that anything, and I mean anything, happens to Ezekiel or his family that even remotely looks suspicious to me, I'm coming back. I want you to be clear on this. It makes no difference if the problem is caused by the law, your other sheet-wearing, chicken-shit buddies or you. I hold you personally responsible.

"If I have to come back, I'll cut off your ugly head and impale your skinny white torso on a sharpened fence post at the entrance to your property. Do you understand?"

Mr. Briley, by this time, was lightheaded and faint. All he could do was to nod that he understood. Sean got a paid-in-full receipt for Ezekiel and left determined to clear up all unfinished business before leaving on a new adventure...Oklahoma.

9

Ron, upon hearing Sean had deeded his farm to a man named Ezekiel and had to vacate the premises immediately, called a friend, the officer in charge of post billeting. Arrangements were made for Sean and Mike to stay in one of the cottages at Lake Tholocco. These accommodations were normally reserved for senior officers on temporary duty or officers awaiting on-post housing. It was not likely, however, that anyone would deny temporary housing to the recipient of the Congressional Medal of Honor, regardless of rank.

Along with the key to the cottage, Ron provided his friend with a seven-day temporary gate pass that allowed him to move freely around Ft. Rucker without being stopped by military police.

Early the next morning, after unloading suitcases and the few other belongings Sean planned to take to Oklahoma, he and Mike walked about a block to the boat dock. The lake surface was like glass with a light fog suspended over the water.

"Son, maybe the place in Oklahoma will have a lake. If it does, we'll get us a boat."

Mike looked at his father with concern. "Pops, I'm a little scared about moving to Oklahoma. I don't know anybody there, and I'll be leaving all my friends here. We have no family there to visit or nothing."

"All that's true, Mikey, and it will take some getting used to for both of us. Try to look at it as a new adventure because that's what it is. Hell, son, two weeks ago I wasn't sure where I was going to get the money for your clothes and school supplies for the upcoming school year." Sean's eyes were moist and he could feel the emotion swelling in his chest. "I was really worried about it, bud."

"You didn't look worried."

"I know, son. Remember when we were in Major Snyder's office and I told you things were not always as they seem? You have to learn to control your emotions."

Sean wrapped a massive arm around the little boy. "There are a couple of *lessons* you can learn from this that will help you later on in life. No matter how you feel or what you're thinking, never let it show. Secondly, never be afraid of the unknown. I want you to have a warrior's spirit. Take the bull by the horns and don't shy away from difficult challenges. These are important lessons, son; don't forget them."

"How could I, Pops? Every time I turn around I'm getting another important lesson."

In one quick motion, Sean grabbed his son by the belt, raised him over his head and walked to the edge of the dock. "Do you or do you not like your dad's important lessons? Speak quickly, I'm getting tired and may have to drop you."

Mike was laughing, but he knew his dad would not hesitate to throw him in the lake. "I really, *really* like your important lessons, Pops; just don't throw me in." Sean swung him wildly over the water again, before setting him back down on the bench.

Once safely on the dock, Mike walked over to the edge to check out something he had seen on his whirlwind ride over the water. Looking down at one of the pilings that supported the dock, he said, "Dad, come look at this."

Sean kneeled down to take a look. "It's a good thing I didn't throw you in, bud. That's a nest of water moccasins stirring up the water like that. During mating season, they entwine themselves into a ball, sometimes fifty or more snakes. A cottonmouth is a nasty, aggressive snake to begin with, but when they're like this, they can be downright mean and will come after you. Their venom can kill a man. You get a bunch of bites and there's no chance of living through it."

Mike stood up saying, "Let's get out of here. These things give me the creeps!"

Later that evening, Sean left Mike sleeping as he slipped out the back door. There was still one last piece of unfinished business to be taken care of before leaving for Oklahoma. As he pulled out of the gravel driveway, thunder was rumbling in the distance and a light rain had already started.

Earlier in the week, he had reconnoitered various access routes—other than main gates—onto Ft. Rucker and had found a dirt road leading off Highway 27 into the gunnery ranges. This road was primarily used by range personnel to inspect the old tank hulls which served as targets for National Guard armor and artillery units during summer training exercises. Inspect is probably not a good choice of words. This was an impact area with a gazillion unexploded tank and artillery rounds. Seldom, if ever, did anyone actually venture off of the dirt road to inspect anything.

The road itself, however, worked its way across the impact area in a serpentine trail, coming out on a seldom-used road just to the north of the Girl Scout camp located on the other side of the lake. It was perfect.

10

Gene Tidwell, principal of Coffee County High School, lived in a nice, unpretentious house a couple of blocks off Highway 84, just outside Enterprise, Alabama. Sean knew the area well and had been preparing for this night for the better part of six months.

In the 1950s few people ever locked their doors and during the summer months, everyone slept with their bedroom windows open, out of necessity, to capture any rogue breeze that might pass their way.

In a pecan grove next to the principal's house, Sean parked his truck which he had covered with mud in the impact area. The drizzle that continued to fall worked in his favor by dampening the leaves. He approached the house without any noise.

Because of his size, he opted to enter by the rear door of the house. He had brought along a treat of raw meat in case he encountered a neighborhood dog. He knew, through hours of observation, that the Tidwells didn't have a dog, but it was wise to have a contingency plan. As an army ranger, Sean had learned that lesson well. He was now drawing on that experience to close one of the worst chapters of his life.

Given the circumstances, he was unusually calm as he stood just inside the back door to allow his eyes to adjust to the darkness. Once he could see, he noticed the rear entrance to the house was through the kitchen. To his left was a utility rack with a couple of mops and a broom. He removed one of the mops, dampened it and set it by the door as a physical reminder to clean his way out of the house.

He then removed his rubber work boots and placed them just outside the door. As he was making his way toward the center of the house, he heard a man cough and a few moments later saw the silhouette of Gene Tidwell as he passed down the hall in front of him.

The bathroom light flicked on. Fortunately the bathroom was further down the hall, and Sean's night vision was not affected by the dim light. He closed one eye anyway to preserve his night vision as he walked toward the bathroom.

He knew that once Tidwell left the brightly lit bathroom, he wouldn't be able to see anything. He would die in total darkness without a conscious thought of how his life ended so quickly.

Sean positioned himself against the wall and waited. Moments later, the man exited the bathroom. He never made it back to bed.

Sean quietly slipped behind the man who had viciously beaten his son and ultimately caused his death and expertly placed one massive arm around Tidwell's face, covering his mouth, just as he had done years ago in combat, and with one quick twist, broke Gene Tidwell's neck.

He carried the lifeless body back to the bathroom and placed it on the floor. As quietly as possible, he slammed the principal's neck against the rim of the commode. Sean then threw a cup of water on the floor and over the feet of the lifeless body to make it appear that he had slipped on the wet floor, hit his head on the commode and expired. If the coroner, given one was notified, didn't look too closely, he would determine that the bruising on the neck matched the rim of the commode and that would be the end of it.

In any event, the O'Reilly family honor had been upheld; it was time to move on. Sean mopped his way out the back door, put his boots on and returned to the pecan grove as rain pummeled the tin shed where the *late* Gene Tidwell parked his car.

By the time Sean reached the Girl Scout camp on the west side of Lake Tholocco, an hour and a half had past, partly because he had made two wrong turns in the impact area and had to backtrack.

Sean thought himself lucky for not being blown to hell and back by a dud. Things looked a lot different in the dark with no moon or discernible landmarks to help guide him; it was easy to get disoriented.

The weather continued to deteriorate and by the time Sean pulled his truck onto the hard surface road leading back to the cottage, he was in the middle of a torrential downpour that washed most of the mud off his new truck. As lightning streaked and thunder rattled around him, he thought how ironic the circumstances surrounding the demise of Gene Tidwell had been.

Sean had planned to kidnap the principal, beat him with a board so he could experience the pain his son had endured, and then drop him off the boat dock so he could feel his life ebbing as the cottonmouths repeatedly drove their fangs deep into his pale flesh, pumping deadly venom directly into his bloodstream. Nonetheless, O'Reilly justice had been meted out; it was the end game that really mattered.

It took Sean several days to wrap up loose ends. He took Mike out of school; visited with Ezekiel to ensure everything was working out; and left him a few thousand dollars for emergencies, food, seed and the like. He stopped by the bank, one last time, to get a little traveling money, and spent some time visiting relatives.

Early the next morning, he and Mike were up, packed and ready to hit the road by 0800 hours. Sean drove over to the billeting office to settle accounts and to return the cottage key. He then stopped by the JAG office to say good-bye to his old friend.

As they walked into the office, Corporal Best followed with coffee. The two warriors hugged each other and as he settled his massive frame into a chair, Ron threw a folded newspaper at him, "Check out page two and the obits. Looks like our favorite principal had an accident."

Mike stood behind his dad as they read the short article about the accidental death of Gene Tidwell.

"Man, you were right, Pops, when you said God works in strange ways."

As Mike sat back down, Sean turned to the obituaries, read for a moment, and then placed the newspaper on the desk. He took a couple swigs of coffee and looked up to see Ron's eyes locked on him. Sean smiled. "Too bad!" he said in an emotionless tone. "Shit happens to assholes. What can I say?"

After saying their good-byes, the O'Reillys got up to leave. As they reached the door, Ron said, "My Chicago office is now involved in mineral rights, oil claims and land leases. Our major clients, as luck would have it, are several Native American tribes in Oklahoma and other parts of the Southwest. I now have a reason to come visit, and I will. I'll remember to ask for God or Large Walking Eagle."

Sean hugged Ron again, put his arm around Mike's shoulder and headed toward their truck. As they drove off, embarking on a new life, Mike looked over at his dad, "What's with the God or Large Eagle stuff, Pops?"

"It means nothing, son. I already told you the little shit's crazy as a coot!"

11

Several years later

Life in Oklahoma was great; the years seemed to fly by for Mike. Now eighteen and a senior in high school, he was a gifted athlete, an excellent student, and had been nominated class president.

He had grown into a commanding presence physically, standing 6'2" and already topping the scale at 200 pounds. His deep southern drawl and handsome features endeared him to most classmates, especially girls.

Of all the activities Mike participated in, being president of the debate team was what he enjoyed most. Since most debate topics had to do with politics and international affairs, it was a fitting beginning for a future United States presidential candidate.

Over time, Sean became one of the most powerful voices in the cattleman's association, a prominent civic leader and philanthropist. He contributed large sums of money to education, museums, various political candidates and, most importantly, to organizations that helped the poor and homeless.

Though he was a prominent figure and stayed very busy increasing land, cattle, oil and other holdings, he never let it interfere with his primary responsibility of raising his son properly. Sean believed in a day's work for a day's pay and instilled this work ethic in his son.

It never entered Mike's mind to ask his dad for a car when he turned sixteen. Instead, he worked all summer following the combines, bailing hay through Oklahoma, Kansas and as far north as Nebraska. When he returned, he bought his first car...a 1942 Ford Coupe.

His friends drove newer, fancier cars, paid for by their parents, but Mike never gave it a second thought. Insofar as girls were concerned, he could have been driving a two-wheeled push scooter. They thought he was the cat's meow, and most of them did everything in their power to make sure he knew they were available, willing and able.

Prior to graduation, Mike received word that he had been accepted to attend the U. S. Military Academy at West Point. Though he had received academic and athletic scholarships to a number of universities, he took his father's sage advice and accepted the appointment.

He felt a sense of honor and patriotism, a continuation of the O'Reilly family's longstanding tradition of military service and most recently, his father's. In addition to the Congressional Medal of Honor for valor in the last world war, he had received two silver stars, three purple hearts and a chest full of ancillary awards and decorations for his exploits while serving in Task Force Smith against hostile forces in Korea.

It wasn't until Mike's pre-appointment interview with Oklahoma Senator Wesley Henderson—a prerequisite to acceptance into West Point—that the full realization of his father's military accomplishments hit him. His dad was one of the most decorated soldiers of WWII and Korea. Perhaps he *was* qualified, after all, to teach important lessons.

As one might expect from having a father like Sean, Mike was accustomed to hard physical work. His life had been quite structured from day one, so he had no problem adjusting to life as a cadet. The first year was filled with all of the traditional nonsense that goes along with being a plebe.

Over the next three years he excelled in academics, language arts, marksmanship and military tactics. Always an avid hunter and excellent shot, he particularly liked marksmanship. Mike had successfully completed airborne school at Ft. Benning, Georgia as an upperclassman and graduated third in his class as second lieutenant, infantry. There were other perhaps safer alternatives afforded him, but O'Reilly men had all been infantryman and he would not be the exception.

During his four-year stay at West Point, he had listened to literally hundreds of guest speakers covering every conceivable subject that had the slightest military implication or relevance. Most cadets slid into a semi-comatose state during these sessions and did so while appearing to be alert and attentive, an art form honed to perfection. However, during his senior year, one session in particular kept coming to the fore of his consciousness.

A Fort Bragg, North Carolina demonstration team of the recently formed U.S. Army Special Forces really put on a show. He had studied the heroic exploits of the Office of Strategic Services, better known as the OSS, and it was his understanding that Special Forces were something tantamount to OSS reincarnate. That was all Mike knew about the Green Berets.

By the time these guys had finished demonstrating hand-to-hand combat and knife-fighting techniques, all at normal speed, he was convinced they were the meanest, best trained fighting force that ever walked through the proverbial valley of death. As the team concluded their on-stage carnage, they identified themselves, their A-Team duties and capabilities, each speaking first in a foreign language and then in English.

These were not the actions of a knuckle-dragger, a term loosely used by the professional military cadre to describe army rangers, and now Special Forces. The inference being, they were all big, mindless, indiscriminate killers of whatever moved. That was not what Mike saw.

All of these guys were articulate, bi-lingual and as professional as any soldiers with whom he had studied in the last four years. Some of them spoke multiple languages and in a couple of cases several dialects of the same language. Mike knew he wanted to be a part of this elite fighting force, just as his dad had wanted to be an army ranger. What the hell is wrong with O'Reilly men?

Unfortunately at the time, Special Forces were not accepting officer applicants straight out of the academy, since they were all inexperienced butter-bar lieutenants, and pussies at that.

Mike had no problem understanding their position. In fact, he was relieved to hear it. He wanted no part of these guys until he had totally prepared himself. Second Lieutenant Mike O'Reilly needed military seasoning before taking on the Special Forces challenge, so he requested and was accepted into ranger school.

Jump school instructors at Ft. Benning threw him out of an aircraft a few more times to ensure he was current. Fortunately he was!

Ranger school was so damn bad that Mike, who was always up for a challenge, didn't want to even talk about it. There was no way to describe how brain-numbing tired the training was all the time. He was a big guy and always starving. If one had happened by, he mused, he would have eaten the ass-end out of a Teddy bear.

Seasoned combat-tested rangers still conjure up ugly memories every time they hear of Ft. Benning, Dahlonega, Georgia and Eglin Air Force Base, Florida. Dahlonega and Eglin are where the mountain and jungle phases of ranger training are conducted.

It was during the final two weeks of mountain training that he broke one of his fingers while rappelling. Rather than going to the aid station for treatment and almost certainly being sent back to the next class, he opted to tape the broken finger tightly to his index finger and load up on aspirin. No way in hell was he going to be sent back and go through this shit again! He learned to live with the pain and successfully completed the course. The training was extremely difficult and the weak-willed and faint-of-heart were quickly weeded out.

The trade-off for all the misery, sleep deprivation and associated pain was an abundance of confidence. Mike knew when he was awarded his ranger tab, he had entered a fraternal order of elite fighting men who knew they could successfully complete any combat mission assigned.

After ranger school, while other graduates were heading off to assignments in airborne and conventional infantry units around the world, Mike curiously received orders to attend sniper school at Ft. Benning. Sniper training is reserved for the 'best of the best' insofar as marksmanship and infantry-related skills are concerned, and very few officers are selected.

However, from an early age, Mike had shown unique shooting skills with his dad's coaching. He learned how to blend in with natural surroundings but most importantly, he learned patience. He had better than 20/20 eyesight to include peripheral vision that seemed to exceed 90 degrees. He was a natural.

Throughout military history, including the early years of World War II, U.S. Army Snipers didn't receive special training; their rifles were conventional weapons modified to accommodate whatever optics happened to be available. Snipers were simply good shots with a rifle and made up the needed skill sets as they went along. Commanders had no clue about how to optimize or employ this *unique* resource.

The psyche of soldiers who chose to become snipers—primarily loners and unconventional thinkers—was so different from their peers, they were ignored and in some cases, shunned like lepers.

Other soldiers were afraid of them because they knew the snipers were cold, calculating killers, yet that was not how they perceived themselves. How ironic. A soldier trained to kill would see himself differently than a soldier trained to kill more efficiently.

After the fall of Dien Bien Phu in May 1954 and analysis of the lessons learned about Viet Minh unconventional tactics, the U. S. Army determined that well-trained marksmen possessing unconventional tactical skills would be needed in the future.

Officers would also be needed to perform leadership roles in the army's elite special operations units. Officers trained in unconventional warfare tactics understood the psychological impact the presence of snipers have on enemy morale.

There really is nothing that will screw up lunch faster than having your buddy's head explode all over your C-ration pound cake. The only good thing about it is you don't have to eat the pound cake, a piece of crap so hard and heavy that it could just as easily serve as a boat anchor.

In addition to the fear factor, it makes you want to leave the field of battle and go home to mommy. That's the intent! To psychologically overwhelm the enemy by demonstrating in horrific ways that there is no safe place, even in secured areas.

12

Infantrymen and hostile environments are attracted to one another like steel to a magnet. After sniper school, Mike was assigned as a sniper team leader with the 75th Ranger Regiment. Early one morning, he was told by the Regimental S-3 (operations officer) to have his twenty-man team ready for overseas deployment at 0600 hours the following day.

His team was to be part of a strike force consisting of a ranger sniper team, Special Forces B-Team, elements of the 503rd Aviation Company, located in Hanau, Germany, and logistical airlift support units from the USAF. Destination: Africa.

Typical of this type of operation, strike force personnel were kept in the dark until the last moment. The scuttlebutt, however, was that Mobutu, the Congo dictator, had loosed his soldiers for reasons unknown on the civilian population. Specifically white farmers living in the rural areas around Brazzaville and Leopoldville, turning the mutilation of these poor souls with machetes into a team sport.

It was determined at the highest level of government that a humanitarian initiative would be mounted to protect the defenseless civilians and assist them, however possible, in escaping across the Congo River to a safe refuge.

Three days later, the strike force was in a forward deployment area in Cameroon, a small country bordering the Congo. Given that units were coming from a number of U.S. locations and Germany, the transition into a cohesive operational unit went relatively smoothly, except for communications.

In the early sixties, field radios, tactical switchboards and even avionics left a lot to be desired. In this case, the hot, humid weather and other atmospheric conditions created many problems. Army and air force switchboards could not be stacked to function as a single, seamless communications network.

The enlisted men and noncoms found ways to work around the problems and in short order everything worked. The devious mind—wizardry, if you will—of the enlisted soldier and his ability to get the job done in *spite* of standing operating procedures has always amazed the Officer Corps and is part of the armed forces mystique. God willing, it will always be that way.

Helicopters airlifted tactical units into various locations and Special Forces deployed A-Teams to conduct recon forays across the river to reconnoiter and make recommendations to the task force commander on how best to complete the extraction mission.

Initially Mike and his rangers were tasked to set up a perimeter defense to protect the command post and mission essential equipment on the east side of the river and to provide armed escort for uninvited civilian officials that seemed to crawl out of the woodwork on missions like this.

He knew his unit was not organized or equipped to perform such duties. His two-man sniper teams were armed with high-powered rifles and an assortment of scopes. They also had binoculars and carried 1911A1, .45 caliber semi-automatic side arms. These would not normally be the weapons of choice for perimeter defense. Nonetheless he knew this was a temporary deal and his guys would hopefully be properly deployed soon.

Later that evening, after checking his defensive positions, Mike returned to the command post (CP) for final instructions before settling in with his team. There, drinking stale coffee from a steel canteen cup was a face he hadn't seen before. The man stood apart from the others. His foot was hiked up on the chair of an army field desk as he observed a small gaggle of officers engrossed in studying a plastic-covered map.

The man was dark and weathered, a look associated with men who spend their lives outdoors. Mike's father, Sean, had that same look. This man was about 5'10"—perhaps a little less—and was dressed in camouflage fatigues, something Mike had never seen up to this point.

What drew him to this stranger was his face. He had a sinister-looking scar running diagonally from just above the right eye downward to about mid-cheek. The stranger had dangerous eyes. They spoke volumes about the character of the man, what he had endured and experienced. It was the cold, calculating stare of a serious battle-hardened man, quite capable of killing.

Mike pushed the lever on the coffee urn, took a quick sip of the wretched brew, winced and walked over with outstretched hand. "Mike O'Reilly, 75th Rangers." He could see the man carefully measuring him as he approached. The man's sinister, dark eyes were locked onto Mike's and never looked away. One of his father's important lessons had been to always look a man in the eye. To look away was a sign of weakness or submission and questioned the strength of one's character.

The man switched his canteen cup to his left hand and without showing the slightest sign of friendliness, shook the young lieutenant's extended hand. "Jeff Stone."

"What brings you to the wilds of the Congo, Jeff?"

"According to the masterminds behind this rat screw operation, *experience* seems to be the reason I'm here. How about you?"

"Well," Mike said, "it's not experience. I wouldn't know a Simba warrior from a hat rack. I'm the sniper team leader, presently providing perimeter defense for this fine facility."

Jeff smirked, his best effort at a smile. "Based on the current situation, if a black head shows up in your scopes, tap it! Chances are real good it's *not* a hat rack."

During the ensuing conversation, it became apparent, aside from experience, that Mike and Jeff had quite a bit in common and would soon become friends. Jeff, it turned out, was a CIA operative with extensive field experience in Africa, South America and Southeast Asia. A graduate of USC, Jeff had been recruited right out of college and within three or four years was up to his clavicle in covert operations.

He told Mike he had arrived about a week before the task force and had been getting a first-hand feel for the makings of a first class political cluster screw. He also provided the unsolicited fact that most of these low-intensity skirmishes that they seemed to find themselves in, the United States, in one way or another, created in the first place.

In this case, the United States—specifically the CIA—some time back had been instrumental in overthrowing the corrupt Republic of Congo Government. Since Mobutu had helped the CIA on a number of occasions and was a prominent figure in the Congolese military and political arenas, the agency did what was necessary to ensure his bid for power was successful.

Unfortunately the United States found out too late that Mobutu was ten times worse than the previous government and assumed the role of absolute dictator.

The U.S. Government thought he would be a willing partner in its efforts to exploit the vast natural resources of the area and help establish a stable democratic form of government. Wrong again! Instead, Mobutu was uncontrollable; he had manipulated the CIA into fulfilling his personal agenda. He was a ruthless, blood-thirsty racist!

"So, Mike, here we go again. From a selfish standpoint, we ought to be tickled to death. These dumb-ass decisions and lack of forethought ensures long-term job security for guys like us."

"Why don't you come along while I troop the line? You might see ways of making the area more secure. I'd welcome any comments you might make."

Jeff ground out his cigarette, threw what little coffee was left in his canteen cup on the ground and said, "Be happy to, sport. Watching these guys peruse a useless forty-five-year-old map has lost its appeal."

As the two men exited the GP medium tent that was serving as the Tactical Operations Center, Mike stepped out smartly in the direction of his defensive positions.

Jeff grabbed him by the arm and said, "Easy, buddy. Kneel down here for a few minutes while our eyes adjust to the darkness. This is not a training exercise. These black bastards are cunning and mean as hell, so don't underestimate them. I assure you they are out there *watching*, and I don't mean from across the river."

"You are, of course, pulling my crank, right, Jeff?"

"For the moment, let's assume I'm not. You asked for my comments. That's appreciated, buddy, but rest assured I was going to give them to you whether you asked or not. You're as deep in the friggin' bush as you're ever going to get. The first rule out here is to watch out for one another and don't do anything stupid. A dumb mistake can get a lot of folks killed, and new guys have a tendency to make dumb mistakes. I've taken a liking to you and want you to come out of this thing alive, so don't take what I say too damn personal."

"We could have used some of this advice in ranger school."

"Don't sell the school short, buddy. You learned the important shit. Now I'm going to teach you the *super*-important shit. I define super-important shit as those nice-to-know things that keep your sorry ass alive. Then you pass it on to your troopers, and hopefully we all get to go home."

As the two moved away from the TOC into total darkness, Jeff leaned in close to Mike's ear and said, "If you must speak, do so in something less than a whisper. When possible use hand and arm signals. Your troopers need to know this tonight, so take the time necessary to tell each one personally just as I'm telling you now, OK?" Mike nodded.

"Can you smell that?" Jeff whispered.

"Smell what?"

"Someone's smoking."

"It won't be my guys. We did a shake, rattle, and roll before we went into our defensive positions and part of the standing orders was no smoking, no chocolate, no chewing gum, lights or movement. I can tell you, bud; these guys would rather milk a female grizzly than get sideways with me." Though it was too dark to see Jeff's smile, Mike felt a pat on his shoulder and for some reason it was reassuring.

It took a little less than an hour to inspect all of the defensive positions and to relay the sage advice Jeff had shared earlier in the evening. At about 0200 hours, Jeff nudged Mike. They low-crawled about 50 yards south of the southernmost position, and then stopped.

Jeff pointed two fingers at his eyes and then slowly pointed in the direction he wanted Mike to look. He then held up five fingers to indicate the number of hostiles and made a cocking motion with his wrist to indicate they were moving toward the river.

Twenty minutes later, Jeff, Mike and Sniper Team NCOIC, SFC Miguel Alvarez entered the TOC to report what they had seen. Major Bob Doherty, commanding officer of the aviation company, was holding down the fort. He looked up as they unzipped the tent flap and walked in.

Major Doherty was an affable, aging, out-of-shape artillery officer with absolutely no command presence. Mike was the first to speak. "Major, sir, we observed five hostiles just outside our defensive perimeter moving back toward the river."

"How sure are you they were hostile, Lieutenant?"

Jeff contemptuously interjected before Mike could reply, "Pretty damn sure. Hard to build a case for a midnight stroll given the locals know only really bad things move through the jungle at night. You know things like tigers, black mambas, Simba warriors with machetes, those sorts of things!"

The two men could see that the major was searching deep in the recesses of his aging memory, hoping to catch a glimpse of what might be an appropriate action given this situation. There was nothing there.

Jeff stated undiplomatically that in his view the five hostiles were mapping out the location of the defensive positions, the helicopters and probably the TOC, assuming they were adept enough to know one should exist.

When Jeff had finished verbally drawing a scary scenario, Mike said, "Sir, I recommend we pull our perimeter in and tighten security around mission essential equipment. That will negate or at least diminish the accuracy of the intelligence Mobutu's guys will have. I also suggest, sir, we put the task force on full alert and establish listening posts (LPs) at river's edge to give us early warning of an impending attack. We need to do this now, Major!"

Jeff proved to be a man of few words and didn't waste any here. "Major, I've spent a good deal of my adult life in situations just like this. I think Lieutenant O'Reilly's assessment and recommended actions are right on the money. I figure we have two, maybe three, hours to get ready for these bastards. I suggest you get off your dead ass and start moving."

Surprisingly Major Doherty kept his cool and did not challenge Jeff or his advice. Truth be known, he was probably relieved to have two competent warriors to sort through what had to be done. All he had to do was pick up the field phone and initiate the actions required. That's what he did. The major then turned to Lt. O'Reilly. "How many LPs do we need?"

"I believe four will do it, sir. That will make it very difficult for anyone to slip by unseen. We will give each post a radio and direct them to turn the squelch and volume as low as possible. That way each post can push the transmit button and the task force commander will know when they are crossing the river without conversation."

"Better yet, Mike, the LPs can key their radio and actually use it as a counter to let the TOC know about how many of the slimy bastards are coming."

"Gentlemen, I appreciate your insight and help. Lieutenant, set your LPs out immediately."

Mike turned to SFC Alvarez, "Sarge, get the troops cracking. Be sure the men manning the LPs know withdrawal routes and passwords for tonight. Challenge is 'Little' and the counter is 'Big Horn.' Got it?"

"Yes, sir."

"Also knock out a quick sketch of the new perimeter and be sure the B-Team commander who will tie into your right or southernmost defensive position knows where our guys are. Tell him we need a couple of machine guns down by the river. See if he's in a position to help us.

"Stand fast, Sarge. I just thought of something. Sir, if all four LPs see the same thing and start simultaneously keying their mikes, some clicks may be overridden or, worse, the TOC may think the attacking force is four times larger than it really is. That would not be helpful. We can avoid that bit of confusion by setting all four radios on different frequencies. That will also tell us exactly which LP is reporting."

Major Doherty replied, "Good, let's set it up. We have three fox mikes (FM radios) in the TOC, and two are mounted on the old man's Jeep. We can pull one of them in here." Jeff moved toward the exit without saying a word.

By the time Jeff had returned five minutes later, labels were prepared for all four radios, signifying the LP to be assigned that particular frequency and Mike, in the absence of a communications officer, had designated frequencies for the four radios, ensuring they were spares and not already assigned.

He gave the frequencies to SFC Alvarez. "Good, sergeant. Your idea to bring along extra radios for the team was prophetic.

Good thinking. I'll meet you back here at 0330 to review the new positions. We can then troop the line and make any adjustments that need to be made."

"Yes, sir," SFC Alvarez said, as he left the TOC.

A few minutes later, after finalizing a few details, Mike and Jeff left the TOC to prepare for what was shaping up to be an interesting evening.

13

As they settled in at one of the LPs, Mike tapped Jeff on the arm to get his attention and handed him a C-ration can of pork and beans. Since pork and beans was as good as C-rations got, he figured Jeff had earned it by providing a short course, "How to stay alive."

As he opened a can of mystery meat, Mike theorized: One day some asshole's going to figure out that light infantry can't hump a hundred pounds of C-ration cans on their friggin' backs! Next time I see a quartermaster officer, assuming I ever get that far back in the rear echelon, I'm going to kick him in the nuts! I'd bet a paycheck the route step bastards would quickly find a better concept if they had to hump this shit. Now that I think about it, *shit* is the perfect description for most C-rations. *Assholes*!

The jungle, regardless of which continent it happens to be on, is beautiful, foreboding, and scary at night. Except for one of his sergeants who had been a Hungarian Freedom Fighter, Mike's troopers had never fired at another human being. Therefore he and Jeff frequently checked the positions, reassuring the men.

Jeff's jungle experiences proved invaluable. He suggested spotters focus on identifying areas that were unusually shiny on the far bank and on the river as well. Sweaty black skin is extremely reflective. He also told the men that Mobutu's soldiers, though more at home in the jungle, could not see any better than they could and may use flashlights to lead the attacking force to the river.

"They have been known to wear miners' lamps when moving at night. So if you see a light that keeps changing position, put the light at the top of the scope's vertical crosshair and go for a chest or gut shot.

"With the flash and noise suppressors on your sniper rifles, they won't know for a few moments if the guy was bitten by a big ass snake or the monkey gods put a hole in his chest for giggles. They're all superstitious as hell and most are dumb as a stump. Nonetheless they are good fighters and, given the opportunity, they *will* kill you!"

The lunar cycle was at about half-moon and the river in front of the defenders was only about 400 or 500 yards wide, so it was possible to see movement on the opposite bank with the aid of binoculars.

Mike and Jeff agreed that the optimum engagement range would be mid-river, where the targets would be silhouetted to some degree by the water's reflective surface. Further, the river was swift enough to carry any would-be attacker that found himself in the water away from the fight, where they would pose no immediate danger. Many natives were poor swimmers; there was always the possibility that some of the slimy bastards might drown. In any event, the swim to shore would take a lot of fight out of them and that was a plus.

At 0400 hours, a sniper at LP-1, the westernmost position, engaged a target at the outer limits of visible range...one shot, one kill!

At about the same time, emerging from the darkness of the upstream river bank, twelve to fifteen canoes carrying eight to ten warriors each made their way toward the ranger positions. The TOC FM radios came to life with a constant clicking, each click representing an enemy warrior.

Colonel J.B. Hawkins, the battle-tested task force commander took another sip of coffee, and then asked, "Major, which LP is making this spot report?"

"LP-1, sir."

"Okay, let the games begin! Major, hot foot it back to your guys and bring your sector to full combat alert. I know your men are aviation and not necessarily trained for this sort of thing, but they're now infantry and I expect them to hunker down and fight like infantry.

"Your pilots and helicopters are considered mission essential, that's why Major Wilkinson, B-Team commander has some of his Special Forces troopers in close proximity to the aircraft. I don't want any of your pilots manning defensive positions. Keep them close to their assigned aircraft and instruct them to fight only if their aircraft are threatened. You got it?"

"Yes, sir."

"Move out, Major, and give me a commo check when you're in position."

"Are you sure you won't need me here, sir?"

"I said move out, Major."

"Yes, sir." Major Doherty reluctantly left the TOC to participate in what was very likely to be his first taste of combat.

"Dave, alert Major Wilkinson of the situation and instruct him not, *I say again,* not to put out any probes in front of the aviwhackers. These folks are straphangers at best and will shoot anything that moves. I feel sorry for any spider monkeys that might be out foraging in front of these guys!"

Captain Dave Best was pulled into the operation at the last moment by Col. Hawkins because of his demonstrated tactical operations and planning skills at the Special Operations Center— later known as the JFK Special Warfare Center— in Fort Bragg, North Carolina. He had worked with Hawkins for the better part of eighteen months as the Assistant S-3, Plans & Operations.

Dave had earlier distinguished himself for his concepts in the development of a tailored rapid deployment force to meet low-intensity conflict situations around the world. Years later some of these concepts would be used in the formulation of the army's Force Package One.

Dave laughed as he reached for the FM radio handset to alert the B-Team commander. "Snake 36, this is Tomahawk."

"This is 36, five by."

"36, be advised enemy force approximately 150 strong, I say again, 1-5-0 strong, now crossing river in front of LP-1. Killer 6 advises full combat alert now! Killer 6 adamantly states no, I say again, *no* Alfa Team probes in front of positions manned by aviation personnel."

"Roger. Understand enemy strength 150; full combat alert and no probes in vicinity of aviwhacker positions. There is a God! Be advised, I have two machine gun crews in support of LPs. Belt ammo for guns is four to one." [Meaning every fifth round was a phosphorous tracer projectile used to adjust fire on target.]

Dave smiled. "Roger, 36, out."

"Did you hear that, boss?"

Col. Hawkins nodded as he lit a cigarette. "Yes, sir, I did. Bruce sounded relieved about the probe bit." Both men chuckled and immediately refocused on the business at hand.

"Dave, what's the name of that young officer in charge of the knuckle draggers from the 75th?"

"Lieutenant Mike O'Reilly. According to Jeff, he's a super sharp trooper."

"Yeah, well, we'll soon find out, won't we? Send a runner down to the river to inform the lieutenant that as soon as the machine guns engage the enemy, all future transmissions can be made in the clear. Hard to maintain the element of surprise with tracer rounds going off all over the damn place.

"The placement of LPs by the river was a damn good idea. We might be able to wrap this thing up right there."

"Yes, sir, Lieutenant O'Reilly's idea to do that."

Captain Best grabbed one of the TOC clerks by the arm, gave him the message to be delivered and left the tent with him to ensure he got on the right trail leading to the river and the four LPs. "If you get lost, Private, head back in the direction of gunfire." The soldier left without saying a word.

Mike finished alerting his four LPs about transmitting in the clear and took up a position at LP-2. Between him and LP-1, he had one of the machine gun crews; the other placed further to the east between LP-3 and LP-4. All of the positions had excellent fields of fire on the approaching force.

Mike thought the straight-on tactic being used by Mobutu's warriors was a bit squirrelly. With all the natural cover available, including darkness and the ability to cross the river at any point they might choose, why here?

One of his dad's many important lessons while Mike was still at West Point was, "Regardless of the situation, if you wouldn't do it, then chances are neither would the enemy, unless they had a damn good reason." It took him only a moment or two to work his way through the limited good reasons in this case. The river crossing was a ploy, and all of these warriors were human sacrifices.

He grabbed the FM radio handset, turned the volume up and began transmitting in the clear, "Tomahawk, this is Panther 26 in the clear, urgent."

"26, go ahead."

"Tomahawk, inform Killer 6 that I believe this river crossing is a diversion and the real attack will come from the south in the vicinity of the aircraft, over."

Before Dave could respond, Col. Hawkins grabbed the handset, "26, this is Killer 6, what makes you think the river crossing is a ploy?"

"Killer, in about five minutes, when the canoes are mid-river, this is going to turn into a turkey shoot. It's dumb as dirt. It *can't* be the main attack."

J.B. Hawkins was well aware—from his combat experiences during the Korean conflict—of the importance of intuitions and competent situational analysis. "Stand by, 26. Dave, get Jeff up here ASAP."

Col. Hawkins then got on the horn to the B-Team commander. "Snake 36, this is Killer."

"36, go."

"36, have your recon guys picked up anything?"

"Negative, Killer, but we're going out only about 500 yards or so. About 0400 one of our guys on recon thought he heard something further south that sounded a little like the tailgate of a truck, a metal sound, but there's a small village a couple kilometers out in that general direction, and I suspect it came from there. Over."

Col. Hawkins thought about that for a moment and then keyed his handset again. "36, Panther 26 believes the attack from the river is a diversion and that the main attack will come from the south in the vicinity of the aircraft. Your thoughts?"

"Makes sense to me. I'll send a recon team toward the village. Check your map for a road down that way."

Col. Hawkins motioned for Dave to check the map for any reference to a road south of their position. "36, at your discretion, position several of your 60mm pack mortars so they can provide close fire support in front of the aviation positions."

"Wilco, 36, out."

Dave quickly checked the map and informed the task force commander that there was a road about three kilometers south of the TOC. "36, this is Killer. Be advised there is a road three klicks [kilometers] south of your position."

"Roger, Killer, my guy's heading in that direction now. Spot report to follow."

Engaging a hostile force is an unparalleled adrenaline rush, no question about it. The period leading up to that engagement, however, can be the most stressful period of all. Especially for soldiers who are not battle tested and really don't know what to expect.

The known threat in this case was moving slowly but steadily across the Congo River toward the LPs along the river's edge. The unknown but suspected main threat was closing quickly on the southernmost positions, the aviation sector.

Army rangers manning the LPs had engaged perhaps a dozen targets of opportunity on the far shore, since the canoes were spotted, but Mike wanted to delay engaging the enemy with his machine guns until they were deep in his kill zone, about mid-stream. Then he thought of a way to end this situation quickly.

He keyed his handset and spoke in an even, calm voice, "Killer 6, this is Panther 26."

"26, this is Killer."

"Killer, reporting twelve enemy KIA's (killed in action) on the far shore at this time. If I had illumination when the canoes reach mid-stream about five or ten minutes from now, my guys could end this thing in short order. Request a helicopter to light up the river with landing lights, over."

About that time Jeff entered the TOC.

"Stand by, 26. Jeff, what's your take on O'Reilly?"

"J.B., he tagged three bad guys. Two of those shots had to be 600 yards. Unbelievable!"

"That counts, but my question was broader than that, Jeff. I'm interested in his judgment and leadership skills."

"Let me put it to you this way, if you were not in command here and I was king for a day, I'd choose Mike over the more senior, highly qualified leaders that are available. That should give you some idea of the confidence I have in him."

J.B. took a sip of cold, rancid coffee as he eyed the CIA operative, whose judgment and advice he valued. "Dave, call Major Doherty. Tell him to kick the tires and light the fire on two H-34s. No pre-flights! I want them on station at the river in five minutes. Be sure they have Panther 26's frequency. Do it now!"

Dave was already keying his handset before the task force commander finished issuing the order. That's what J.B. liked about his operations officer. He was bright and damned decisive.

"Eagle 6, this is Tomahawk. Killer 6 wants two H-34s airborne and on station at Panther 26's location to provide landing light illumination of enemy canoes expected to be mid-river in five minutes."

"This is Eagle 6, cranking now, out."

Major Doherty, operating in his world–aviation–was an effective officer. He took off at a dead run toward the aircraft some seventy-five yards away. He approached the aircraft, totally winded, and in a raspy voice, he directed the pilots to get airborne immediately. By the time he reached the aircraft, the blades were turning.

He climbed in the main door and stuck his head up in the cockpit between the two pilots and said, "Hop over to the river," as he pointed toward Lt. O'Reilly's position. "The LPs have observed canoes heading toward their position and have requested we use our landing lights to illuminate them as they reach mid-stream. Panther 26's frequency is 67.5. Call him for specific instructions when you get airborne.

"I'll have the crew chiefs set out some bean bags [a canvas-covered base about eight inches square, filled with beans or sand, with an upward facing light to mark hastily prepared landing sites] to mark the helipads before you get back. If you have to ditch, do it on this side of the river. Any questions? Take off!"

Major Doherty exited the aircraft and moved to the left front of the closest helicopter and gave the command pilot a thumb's up. As the choppers lifted to a hover, the major turned his back to the aircraft and held on to his cap to keep it from blowing away.

Once the aircraft were airborne, he instructed the maintenance sergeant to have his guys mark the landing site. He then returned to his Jeep that was parked fifty yards or so inside the southernmost defensive perimeter. From there, he could be in a position to observe his area of responsibility and maintain radio contact with the TOC, his first sergeant and any airborne aircraft.

The flight to the river took less than two minutes. "Panther 26, this is Killer 6. You should have two choppers closing on your position now. They will be up on your frequency so talk directly to them as you coordinate the attack."

"Roger that, Killer. Thanks."

Mike quickly briefed his men, including the two machine-gun crews, about his intent to illuminate the enemy canoes with instructions to commence firing once the target was lit up. "I want a total kill, no prisoners. On my command, I want LPs 1, 3 and 4 to pull back to the TOC to serve as a Ready Reaction Force (RRF). LP-2 will stay in place to ensure we are not surprised by reinforcements. The two machine-gun crews report back to your unit. Are there any questions? Stand by, show time in about one minute."

"Panther 26, this is Eagle Flight."

"Eagle Flight, in one minute, I want you to direct your landing lights mid-stream abreast my position. Do you have the canoes in sight?"

"Roger, Panther. I think we can get a little better illumination at 200 feet."

"Eagle, try not to light up my position, which is about 200 yards north of you at this time."

"Roger, Panther, lighting up in thirty seconds, out."

The two A-Teams, dispatched some forty-five minutes earlier to recon the southern approach to friendly positions, started reporting movement. The teams were about a quarter of a mile apart on either side of the southernmost defensive positions and moving south roughly a kilometer in front of the aviation sector when contact was made.

The terrain in this area was primarily flat crop fields and patches of mahogany trees on approach to the river, and friendly defensive positions.

"Killer 6, this is Snake 36, spot report. At 0520 hours, observed uniformed force of about 200 soldiers one klick south of your position, moving north through what appears to be cornfields. Force is armed with AK47s and a mixture of older, unidentifiable weapons. They appear to be in a loose but organized formation.

My guys think they're a trained military force. No crew-served weapons observed."

"Roger, 36. Be advised Panther 26 just engaged enemy force in the river, stand by."

As the two H-34 helicopters turned on their landing lights and shifted slightly upstream to fully illuminate the enemy force, all four LPs and the two machine gun positions commenced firing. The barrels on the machine guns were smoking as round after round found their marks in the tightly packed canoes.

Snipers concentrated on those that had jumped into the river to avoid the withering fire of the two machine guns. The night air was filled with the screams of the dying; the smell of phosphorous from hundreds of expended rounds of ammunition; and the fear that accompanies mortal combat.

Mobutu's force was taken by surprise and able to return only sporadic fire from a few antiquated bolt-action rifles. The carnage associated with that moment was instantly and indelibly etched into the memory of every trooper.

Lt. O'Reilly called for a ceasefire once he was satisfied there were no survivors and immediately ordered his force to report to the TOC as an RRF contingent. The two machine-gun crews headed back to their unit and LP-2 remained in position along the river as a rear guard. Truth be known, a sniper team made a piss-poor rear guard element, but in this case, it would be adequate.

Once Mike had ensured that the two troopers manning LP-2 had ammo and water and their heads were screwed on straight, he radioed the B-Team commander to thank him for his help and to let him know his guys had performed magnificently.

Furthermore he recommended the barrels on the two machine guns be checked for warping and replaced if necessary before the guns were put into service again. He then called Eagle Flight to release them back to their unit and to express his thanks for a job well done.

Mike headed up the trail toward the TOC, his first combat action now behind him. Only then did he realize he was shaking and actually felt a little weak. He found a downed tree along the trail and sat down to collect his thoughts and take a drink of water. He couldn't believe how dry his throat was; he gulped water until his canteen was empty.

After a few minutes, he realized he had not contacted the TOC with his after-action report. Mike also became aware for the first time that he had sent his radio operator back as part of the RRF. He pounded his fist down on the log...*Mike, your one brain-dead butter bar. Don't ever make this mistake again.*

As he approached the TOC, he saw his men standing beside the task force commander's Jeep and walked over to them. "Is everyone OK? Anyone hit? Be sure to recheck your weapons and fill your canteens before you go out on the line. Where's my radio operator?"

"Butch, get your ass over here. The next time I even look like I want to send you further than a couple of feet from me, you have my permission to kick me dead in the nuts. Understood?"

Butch Gulledge was a good ole boy from Arkansas and, in addition to being the assigned radio operator he also had served as Mike's spotter when they were employed as a sniper team. It was not intended that would happen very often, but if an additional team was needed, they were very capable of completing the mission.

Butch grinned. "Yes, sir, understood. Is that order retroactive?"

Mike lightly punched his shoulder, as he turned to enter the TOC and said with a smile, "Nice try, you little shit."

The rest of the group looked on approvingly and chuckled as the lieutenant disappeared into the TOC. They knew how fortunate they were to have a leader like Mike O'Reilly.

By the time he entered the TOC, he had regained his composure. Col. Hawkins looked over at him and with a cold stare asked, "Well, Lieutenant, your radio crap out? Where the hell you been?"

"No, sir, radio's fine. This dumb-ass lieutenant sent his radio operator back to the TOC as part of an RRF in the event we had a breach early in the fight. Good lesson learned, sir. It won't happen again."

The task force commander stared at him for a moment and then smiled. "That's a damn good answer, son. You'd make one hell of a good politician if you weren't so damned honest. How'd it go down there?"

Relieved he had escaped the colonel's wrath, Mike said, "Sir, we engaged an enemy force estimated at 150 men and as best I could tell, we had 150 KIA. Other than minor burns to the right hand of one of the machine gunners, who accidentally touched the barrel of his gun, we sustained no casualties."

"Outstanding, Lieutenant, well done! Grab yourself a cup of coffee and stand by."

"Sir, I have seven troopers outside that could sure use a cup right about now and a place to smoke a cigarette without lighting up the world."

"Bring those knuckle-dragging bastards in, lieutenant, and get 'em fixed up. They damn sure earned it!"

Mike walked to the flap of the tent, stuck his head out and said, "The colonel has invited you knuckle-dragging bastards in for coffee and a smoke. Do us all a favor and clear your weapons first."

As the rangers entered the TOC, one of them reminded Mike they had left their cigarettes behind, on his orders, when they moved into defensive positions.

"Oh, shit, that's right. Let me see if I can find a pack for you. Jeff, you don't by chance have a pack of smokes I can bum, do you?"

Before Jeff could respond, Dave tossed a fresh pack of Camels to him, and smiled. "Army rangers are like trained monkeys. They do what they do best, *kill* things, which *we* trained them to do, and then they want a banana! Jesus, sir, what's this army coming to."

J.B. laughed. "Lieutenant, better give them that pack of bananas before they get rowdy and tear the place apart."

"Yes, sir. Grab some coffee, men, and relax for a few minutes while we decide which end's up."

J.B. asked Jeff how many men he thought Mobutu's force would leave behind to protect the trucks that Snake 36's troopers had spotted on the road.

"I would think no more than two or three, J.B."

The task force commander studied Jeff for a minute and then said, "What would you need to knock them out quickly?"

"Give me one of Mike's sniper teams to provide over-watch and to take care of any runners, a couple Special Forces guys, thermite grenades, a helicopter ride, and I can take care of that little trick in less than thirty minutes if all goes well."

Col. Hawkins keyed his handset, "Snake 36, this is Killer. I'm sending Jeff down to take out the trucks. I need two of your best to report to the helipad in about five."

There was no need to mention equipment needs. It was common knowledge that this kind of assignment was always done quietly, if possible. Therefore all Special Forces and army rangers carried the best fighting knives in the world and were expert in their use.

"36, are your recon teams carrying automatic weapons?"

"Affirmative, Killer, each team has a machine gun and 300 rounds."

"Can you defend your piece of the pie without them?"

"Roger, that. Panther 26 just released my gunners and we have them in place to help shore up the aviation sector. Excellent fields of fire."

"Good. I'm sending all available troopers over to help you out. They will report directly to you. Have your two recon teams move into blocking positions to prevent withdrawal of enemy force."

Once the helicopter carrying Jeff and the others had lifted off, Col. Hawkins chambered a round in his .45 caliber side arm, grabbed his M-1 Garand rifle—rather his clerk typist, M-1—and said, "Dave, I'm going over to the aviation sector. My driver will be up on the TOC frequency if you need me. Hold the fort down."

He then turned to Mike, "Lieutenant, grab your guys and let's go earn our paycheck."

The fighting over the next hour and fifteen minutes was characteristic of special operations forces, highly intense and violent! When the firefight was over, the majority of Mobutu's soldiers lay dead or dying. A few of the warriors lay within the defensive positions. Those that chose to flee ran into Major Wilkinson's blocking force and were cut down as they ran across open terrain in a failed attempt to reach their trucks which were now smoldering hulks.

The enemy force was destroyed. Friendly losses were comparatively light. Three KIA in the aviation sector, two KIA in Special Forces and nineteen wounded, including Lieutenant Mike O'Reilly, who had taken bullets in the thigh and left wrist.

The humanitarian rescue mission had evolved into a vicious fight for survival and would be known to only a few outside the

Republic of Congo and lost forever in the annals of military history.

The mission was nonetheless successfully completed with over 700 refugees airlifted to safety. The operation complete, the task force flew back to Cameroon for airlift out of Africa. First stop: Frankfurt, Germany.

14

Lieutenant Mike O'Reilly had taken up temporary residency at 97th General Hospital, Frankfurt, Germany and over the next several days had a parade of visitors.

His sniper team had come through the ordeal unscathed and stopped by to say good-bye before catching a military airlift command flight back to the States. Jeff visited several times in an effort to nurture their new friendship and to see if Mike might be interested in pursuing a career in the agency.

Special Forces troopers, Col. J.B. Hawkins and Captain Dave Best, were there when Mike's dad filled the door frame of the hospital room.

Another patient in the semi-private room saw this giant of a man first, since Mike's curtain had been pulled around his bed for privacy. "It's the Grim Reaper!"

"Where's Lieutenant O'Reilly?"

The young soldier pointed toward the closed curtain and said, "Good choice, sir, take him!"

Sean, by nature, was not a gentle man so when he yanked the curtain open, he tore it free of two of its retaining rings as he stepped toward the bed. As he entered, he bellowed in a resounding and intimidating voice, "I fought in two wars; humped the hills of Korea with a sucking chest wound for the better part of a day; and you take two little hits and lie around here smitten by a bevy of cute little nurses. Have you no pride, Lieutenant?"

The three SF visitors were taken aback, but said nothing. Mike grinned as he waved his good arm toward the intruder.

"This, gentlemen, is my father, Sean O'Reilly...a kind and gentle warrior giant." Sean momentarily ignored the introduction as he gave his son a hug and ran his hand through his hair.

As he turned to shake hands with all present, his eyes were tearing and he wiped the corner of each eye with his forefinger. He then said, "My pleasure, gentlemen. I'm happy you made it out in one piece or at least had pieces that could be fixed."

"Mike told me you lost a few. I'm sorry as hell to hear that. I know how hard it is to lose men under your command. It's hard to understand sometimes why men choose the path of a soldier. O'Reilly men have been doing it for centuries, but then we're *Irish* and not too damn smart. How about the rest of you?"

J.B. smiled as he shook the big man's hand. "I guess we all have a little Irish in us, sir. I wouldn't trade this life for any other. Civilians think we're nuts and perhaps we are. But my worst day in the bush is preferable to being stuck in some claustrophobic office shuffling stacks of paper."

"Well stated, my friend. I'm no longer in uniform, but I share your sentiments. You could never in hell make a dumb-ass civilian understand the bond between soldiers or why we do the things we do."

A pretty, petite army nurse with short brunette hair who had just entered the room to dress Mike's wounds overheard the conversation. "Why *do* you guys do what you do? And where in the world would you have to go to get shot this day and age?"

J.B. replied, "To the first question, my dear, the answer is simple: we're nuts! To the second, where we were is highly classified and insofar as you or anyone else in this facility are concerned, Lieutenant O'Reilly and other members of our party residing here are being treated for injuries sustained during a bus accident on the Autobahn. Is that clear?"

"Yes, sir, it is."

The nurse, now blushing, busied herself taking care of the young officer's wounds as his visitors left at Sean's invitation to have lunch in the hospital cafeteria for the time being.

Once seated and while staring at the poorest excuse for a hamburger he had ever seen, J.B. opened the conversation. "Sean, I feel like our paths may have crossed somewhere along the way, but

I can't quite put my finger on it. Any idea where it might have been?"

Sean thought for a moment. "You look a little young, sir, to have been OSS or an army ranger in World War II, so it must have been Ft. Benning or perhaps Korea. I was part of Task Force Smith when that fiasco started. Could that be it?"

"Could be. I had a recon unit with the 7th Infantry Division in 1951. Were you still there then?"

"I was, but I don't recall having any dealings with the 7th Division. Of course when the Chinese entered the fray, we had guys from every unit scrambling all over the damn place trying to move south. I did spend a few days in a MASH facility north of Seoul. I think it was part of the 8th Army, but I'm not sure.

"Just prior to rotating back to CONUS in '52, I took part in an 'Atta boy' ceremony in Seoul. That's about it."

Dave Best smiled. "I don't believe I'm familiar with that ceremony, sir."

Sean grinned at the young captain. "That's when you get your ass shot off and some rear echelon shit head in spit-shined boots says, 'Atta boy' and pins another medal on you."

"That's it!" J.B. said. "You were the guy sporting a leg cast seated in a wheelchair in front of the formation. If memory serves me, you received the Silver Star, your third or fourth award of the Purple Heart and Combat Infantry Badge (CIB) with star. The reason I remember, Sean, is that it struck me as odd that the CIB would be awarded at a ceremony since every infantryman baptized by fire gets one.

"In fact, this whole ceremony was different than any I had attended before. A medal of honor winner was there and the presiding officer led all present in the customary hand salute rendered all recipients of America's highest award for valor.

"I will never forget that day. In spite of my frozen feet and temporary loss of hearing from a ruptured eardrum, it was an honor to be in the presence of a real American hero."

"Well, gentleman, I can't argue that the medal is prestigious, but for my money, it belongs to the battle-tested grunts lying face down in the mud, having made the ultimate sacrifice for their fellow soldiers and country. They are the real heroes and the ones soonest forgotten.

"Because I was awarded the medal in WWII, I'm invited to speak at a number of events involving veterans each year and…"

"Jesus, Sean, were *you* the one they were recognizing? I had no idea it was you. I couldn't hear much of what was said, but I heard medal of honor in there somewhere and saluted with everyone else."

As J.B. reached across the table to shake Sean's hand, several young soldiers at the next table who had overheard their conversation came over to meet this celebrated warrior.

One of them hesitantly said, "Sir, we hate to bother you but we want to shake your hand, if that's okay with the colonel."

J.B. withdrew his hand and said with a smile, "By all means, gentlemen. This is something you can one day tell your grandchildren."

The young soldiers looked at him a little funny since at age eighteen or so they couldn't comprehend life beyond twenty.

Sean stood to shake their hands and to share an encouraging word. When he did, Dave burst into laughter.

The colonel, Sean and the young soldiers glanced over to see what the hell was so funny. "I apologize, gents, but the look on their faces when Mr. O'Reilly stood was priceless. It reminded me of a scene from 'Jack and the Beanstalk' when Jack first encountered the giant. That made my day!"

Everyone chuckled and Sean took the time to shake hands with the young soldiers and told them to keep up the good work and take care of one another.

"Well, as I was saying, I consider speaking to various organizations around the country as a way of honoring and keeping the memory of our fallen comrades alive. That's also why I've taken such an active role in veterans' affairs in the State of Oklahoma.

"Some of these guys are pretty messed up when they finally come home and often need support not readily available from the government. Many need a place to work and regroup away from all the boneheads asking stupid questions about how it feels to kill someone or telling them war is such a waste, as if they didn't already know that.

"I've got about 200 returned combat vets working in various places within my organization and have plans to bring another couple of hundred on board sometime next year. Some are able-bodied; some aren't. I treat them all the same, no preferential treatment. Depression and alcoholism seem to be the biggest problems.

"Knowing first hand the horrific things they have seen, including the terrible stench of combat, burning or, worse, rotting flesh, sulfur and the horrendous noise and chaos of battle, seems to help in the communication with these guys.

"Working with animals and breathing fresh air is good therapy, and I have lots of both back home. Though there's nothing dumber than a cow, unless perhaps it's 10,000 of them. It keeps them busy and a chance to sort things out as best they can, and most are really good workers."

What Sean neglected to say was that not all of the veterans he was recruiting needed physical and mental healing. Many were highly qualified Spec Ops operatives with unique skill sets brought into his employ for a very specific purpose.

Between bites of a dry ham and cheese sandwich, Dave asked, "Mr. O'Reilly, if you don't mind me asking, sir, how much land do you have?"

"Please, call me Sean, Dave. I have about 85,000 acres in ranch land and another 15,000 or so in various places. Most of it tied up, one way or another, in the production of oil.

"I've acquired mineral rights on another 232,000 acres on Alaska's North Slope. I'm involved in partnerships with several large oil companies to do exploration in Alaska. Guys, I'm here to tell you Alaska is one wild and beautiful place. I've never seen anything prettier or more deadly. It can and will kill you if you use poor judgment or drop your guard.

Last year we discovered vast amounts of natural gas, and we believe the North Slope area to be one of the largest oil deposits in the world."

Years later these deposits would become known as Endicott and Kuparak fields.

Sean let the scope of his holdings sink in for a minute and then proceeded, "Fellows, I'm sharing this stuff with you for a reason. Not long ago, I was the poorest dirt farmer in the State of Alabama. I didn't have enough money to buy seed for the upcoming planting season. Destitute would be an understatement!"

J.B. asked the obvious question, "How did you do it? How do you transition from destitution to where you are now so quickly?"

Sean took the last bite of the most pathetic hamburger ever made by mortal man; washed it down with a swallow of equally bad coffee; and said, "It was a miracle of sorts and I won't bore you with all of the details. Let me just say that if you place the welfare of others before your own, somewhere down the road you will be rewarded.

"Now I need your help. Mike has told me on more than one occasion he wants to be a Green Beret. If possible, I want to nip that in the bud. Let there be no question; he would make one hell of a trooper. However, he also possesses all of the character traits—integrity, loyalty and innate respect for his fellowman—that are needed to be an effective statesman. It is my belief, gentlemen, that the time is right to bring him home to start the grooming process.

"He needs to be well established as a savvy, successful businessman before age thirty, and I can make that happen. He'll need well-educated, smart people around him that he respects, trusts and can relate to.

"That's where you gentlemen come in. J.B, Mike has had nothing but praise for the way you orchestrated your most recent operation. He specifically mentioned the maturity and confident manner displayed by Dave here and how well you worked together under the most demanding of circumstances. These are the kinds of qualities I'm looking for to build a winning team.

"I know you're career soldiers and that is most honorable, but I, rather Mike needs your services and will pay you most handsomely."

Both men shifted in their seats and became noticeably uncomfortable. Sean intuitively knew it was now or never if he were to be successful in recruiting these well-educated, dedicated warriors. Though he was a very persuasive person used to getting his way, he knew he was dealing with officers with strong convictions and even stronger inner strength who had pledged allegiance to defend and protect the United States. Sean also knew there was nothing in that pledge that said one had to be in uniform to protect and defend this great nation.

"Here's my proposition which is contingent on Mike agreeing to pursue a political career. Resign your commissions or in your case, J.B., retire as quickly as possible and become the cornerstone of our team-building initiative.

"As I already said, I will pay you handsomely and give each of you a signing bonus commensurate with six months of your present pay grade including your housing allowance. I will double your present salary. If the military won't pay your relocation expenses, I'll take care of those, too.

"I'll buy each of you a house of your own choosing; the only caveat, it must be within your financial means to qualify for it and to maintain it once purchased. The deed will remain in my name for the first five years of employment. At the end of the fifth year, I will give you a bill of sale and clear deed to the property.

"You will of course be enrolled in the O'Reilly Corporation's health insurance program. The basic life insurance issued is about ten times more than that provided by the army, so I don't think that will be a point of contention.

"Now, between soldiers, our word is our bond. That's not necessarily so with wives. They have a propensity to want to see something a bit more tangible than the spoken word. Since they are the lynchpin in most of our major decisions, this one being no exception, I will provide you written contracts outlining the provisions discussed here today. How does that sound?"

After taking a moment to check reactions and to see if they had soiled their britches, it became clear that dedicated soldiers or not, they were far too smart not to give the proposition serious thought. One does not pass on a once in a lifetime opportunity like this, and that was precisely the effect Sean was shooting for.

Dave was first to speak. "Sean, I have a beautiful wife and two little girls who are not crazy about what I do for a living. Each time I walk out the door they wonder when they will see me again or, more pointedly, if I will be coming back at all. That is the nature of Special Forces.

"I'm at a decision point in my career, and you have said the right things, sir. There's only so much luck issued each trooper, and I've already used up most of mine. Count me in."

J.B. looked at his young protégé with a smile. "Damn, Dave, what happened to giving only your name, rank and serial number when questioned?"

"This is one hell of deal, sir. I want to be part of it, and I want you to be on board as well. We both have talked about Mike's command presence and judgment. Hell, you even told him he ought to be in politics. He's a no-nonsense kind of guy and you have to admire that. We could use a hefty dose of that in government, don't you think?"

J.B leaned back in his chair and mulled over Dave's words for a moment. "You're right again, Dave, for the second time in your life!"

"Dave, you going to let him get away with that?"

"Hell, sir, I have to at this point. But I'll keep it on file and the moment he retires, I'm going to take him down!"

J.B. stood, coffee cup in hand, and squeezed Dave's neck lightly as he winked at Sean saying in a holier than thou tone, "I would expect nothing less from a trooper that I have imparted so much knowledge and wisdom to."

He set his cup back on the table, "Why would I even think of going back for a second cup of this stuff?"

As the men stood to leave, the young soldiers at the next table stood and showed their respect for the officers and Sean.

One of them said, "Sir, it was an honor to have met you."

Sean shook each of their outstretched hands again. "The honor is mine, gentlemen. You represent what America is all about. I expect you to serve and to live your lives with honor, courage and integrity. Don't let me down."

"No, sir, we won't." You could tell by the look on their young faces that at that moment they felt pride never before experienced in their young lives; a moment they would remember.

As the three men left the cafeteria, Dave said, "Sean, I'd like to thank you for lunch but I thought I'd hold off a few minutes to see if food poisoning was in my immediate future."

Sean laughed and patted Dave on the shoulder. "I thought K- and C-rations were about as bad as it got. I stand corrected!"

The big man looked over at the senior officer, "Well, J.B., what're your thoughts?"

J.B. mulled over the question for a moment. "Sean, your offer leaves very little to be desired, other than perhaps timing. Relocation is not a problem. My son is in his last year of high school and will graduate in a few months. My wife is a real trooper. Relocating would be just another move to her.

"However, I'm being seriously considered for promotion. I think this last operation will all but assure my nomination. I'm a professional soldier, sir. I know nothing about politics and quite frankly, my take on most politicians is not good. They are inept, inefficient, shameless self-promoters who could give a crap less about representing their constituents."

"That's precisely why I need you, J.B. Your assessment is a mirror image of mine. I believe we can change that perception and really do some good for the country. Believe me, I know you are a professional soldier, and it is the 'can do' attitude that troopers possess that I want in my organization.

"Please take my business card and talk it over with your family before you give me an answer."

J.B. took the card. "Alright, I'll do that and get back to you in a few days."

They shook hands and the two Green Berets turned to leave the hospital lobby when Sean called after them, "Hey, before you leave, give me your telephone numbers and addresses where I can reach you. Dave, I'll have a contract and benefits package sent to you before the end of the week. Take care of yourselves and have a safe flight back home."

Sean made his way back to his son's room and arrived about the same time as Dr. Calhoun, the chief of orthopedic surgery. He had a worried look on his face as he entered the room with the latest x-rays. As with most military doctors, he had the bedside manner of a longshoreman.

"I'm afraid I have some bad news, Lieutenant. I can fix most of your shattered wrist with progressive surgeries, and you should have reasonable motion and use of it. Unfortunately, the range of motion will not meet the minimum requirements for continued active duty in the army or at least not in the army you know. If you could be content with rear echelon administrative duties, I would be willing to sign the necessary papers, but you don't strike me as the kind of officer that would be happy doing ash and trash kinds of things."

Mike was unable to speak for a few moments as he wrestled for control of his emotions. "Doc, O'Reilly men have been infantry soldiers since forever. I'm an infantry soldier and you can bet your sweet ass that under no condition would I consent to administrative duties."

Mike looked over at his dad with a forlorn look, shaking his head in disbelief. Sean could sense the helplessness and anger his son was feeling and squeezed his shoulder.

"Dr. Calhoun, is it?" Sean asked, looking down at his name tag.

"Yes, sir."

"In your opinion, do you think more could be done in a place like, let's say, the Mayo Clinic?"

The doctor thought for a moment as he reviewed the x-rays. "Mayo Clinic has some of the finest physicians in the world. Their skills and labs are second to none and they perform extraordinary things, sometimes."

He then handed the x-rays of Mike's wrist to Sean. "Having said that, sir, take a look at what we are dealing with. Notice in the frontal and oblique views of the wrist, the path of the bullet shattered most of the bones and did severe damage to the nerves and tendons. Bone fragments are presently still lodged in some of the tendons.

"That's the *next* task. I can't proceed for a day or two because of the swelling resulting from the initial surgery. The nerve damage has been repaired as evidenced by the lieutenant's reaction to stimuli to his fingertips. Most of the smaller bone fragments have been cleaned up and the larger ones we hope to save for rebuilding.

"I've intentionally avoided the medical mumbo jumbo in an effort to keep it simple and straightforward. In a nutshell, the wrist is shot, no pun intended, and when the smoke clears, bones will be fused and pins and screws used to hold it all together, hopefully. I anticipate the loss of bone to reduce the overall arm length by about half an inch shoulder to fingertip and the lateral motion of the wrist to be about 40 percent. Vertical range, however, will be nonexistent or minimal at best.

"Could Mayo Clinic do it better? In my view, given the circumstances, they could not. I have already provided copies of the x-rays and consulted with chief of surgery at Walter Reed. He concurs with my actions and diagnosis. I know this is bad news, Lieutenant, but there it is."

Sean nodded. "We appreciate your candor, Doctor. Unlike fine wine, bad news doesn't get better with time. It is best to hear it upfront. If possible, Doc, my son and I would like to have a little time alone."

"I understand, sir. If there is anything I can do to help, see the nurse and she will find me."

As the doctor closed the door behind him, Mike looked at his dad and ran his tongue over his dry lips before speaking. "I can't believe my whole life has been shit-canned in the last ten minutes. He found it hard to talk as his chest tightened and tears welled up in his eyes. "I could have made a real contribution as a career officer. I'm sure of it, Dad."

"You *have* made a great contribution already, Son. J.B. and Dave said you performed magnificently in Africa. They said they have never seen such command presence and demonstrated leadership in such a young officer and that the success of the operation was in large part due to you. That's something you can hang your hat on and take great pride in now and forever."

Sean knew his son had heard his words but his attempt to console him seemed to have failed completely as Mike turned his head to one side and wept uncontrollably. After a few minutes, he used a corner of the sheet to wipe his face and then surprised this giant of a man by saying, "Well, Pops, I guess that's it. Time to move on."

15

Oklahoma – 10 years later

Subsequent to resigning his commission, Mike attended Harvard Law School where he received a law degree while simultaneously completing the necessary course work for a master's degree in international affairs. He was blessed with not only a keen intellect, but he was also a speed reader with a photographic memory. In other words, he seldom, if ever, forgot or overlooked anything; the perfect combination for a career in business, law or politics.

He studied hard and passed the bar exams in Illinois and Oklahoma and, not surprisingly, was hired as an associate with the law firm of Greene Laverish Santine & Snyder. Ron Snyder was not only an old family friend; he was now Mike's mentor.

After an acceptable time as an associate, Mike was made a junior partner and given oversight of the legal department that managed oil leases, mineral rights, and the many facets of the O'Reilly Corporation, including family trust funds.

He had been involved in portions of his father's enterprises after returning home from the military, primarily during the summer months on short breaks from school. Only after familiarizing himself with all the documents constituting the bulk of the corporation's assets and associated funds did Mike truly understand the magnitude of the family's holdings. It was overwhelming!

Very few people own cattle ranches covering most of 100,000 acres or own land and oil leases spread over 167 square miles in

Oklahoma and Alaska, including properties acquired within the last month or so. The trust funds alone were worth millions of dollars.

Mike mused… 'It just goes to show you, even a hard-headed Irish dirt farmer from Alabama can do good if he sets his mind to it…and somebody deeds him half the State of Oklahoma.'

Late one evening, as Mike sat in his office overlooking the Chicago skyline reviewing documents for upcoming oil lease litigation, his mentor limped into his office unannounced.

"How's it going, Mike?"

Mike jerked upright, startled by the voice. "Mr. Snyder, you caught me in deep thought. What can I do for you this evening?"

"First of all, call me Ron or Ronny like your dad does when he wants to irritate me. Please save Mr. Snyder for board meetings or in the presence of clients, OK?"

"Yes, sir."

"What are you doing here at eight-thirty on a Friday night? A successful, good-looking guy like you should be in the company of a lady friend."

"Actually, I do have a date a little later this evening. First time I've been out in weeks. You guys work me like a sugar mill mule."

Ron smiled as he thought of some of the nonsensical but quaint redneck colloquialisms Mike's father had used so comfortably in daily conversation. Times like these made him realize how much he missed his old friend, and how much Mike reminded him of Sean. "Spoken like a true Haaaavad man!"

"Yeah, right! Most of my Bostonian pals, all one of them, were surprised that a guy from Oklahoma could write with something other than a crayon and could paste together a complete sentence."

Ron chuckled as he stood up to leave. "Clear your calendar tomorrow for lunch. Say twelve o'clock. OK?"

"Yes, sir." As Ron reached the door of his protégé's office, Mike said, "Just once before I leave this firm I'd like to say, 'Like to, Boss, but I just can't make it today. How about next Tuesday, around four?'"

"Try it! I'll have your sorry ass moved to a broom closet. See you at twelve." He closed the door and limped down the hall.

The following day Mike walked into the executive dining room straight up at twelve o'clock. "That's what I like about you O'Reillys, always on time. What happened to your hand?"

Mike looked down at the skinned and bruised knuckles of his right hand. "Not much, really. My date's ex-fiancé refused to step aside as we were leaving her apartment. I *moved* him!"

"Uh huh, I see, the *infantry* solution, right?"

"You might say that. I feel obligated to ask nicely only once. That's what I did."

"You're definitely your father's son! Most men go out of their way to avoid confrontation. The O'Reillys seem to thrive on it."

"I wouldn't go so far as to say *thrive* on it," said Mike. "We just don't like taking too many detours. I guess one could say it's an Irish trait."

"Speaking of big, ugly Irishmen, your dad should be here shortly."

"Pops is coming today?"

"Yes, he is, and hopefully he won't embarrass us in front of the executive staff and valued clients."

"What's the occasion?" asked Mike.

Ron shifted in his seat to find a more comfortable position. "We have an important decision to make that requires the three of us to make it. I'm sure he'll get a kick out of the bruised knuckle story, given the nature of our upcoming discussion."

Sean arrived and, as usual, his huge mass attracted a great deal of attention among the well-groomed pin-stripers having lunch in the executive dining room.

He was immaculately dressed in a dark gray Armani suit that must have cost several thousand dollars. The big man gave his son a bear hug and then walked around the table. As he bent down to kiss his best friend on the forehead, knowing everyone was watching, he winked at Mike and said in a loud voice, "I love you, my *little* Ronny!"

Ron blushed ever so slightly and then clanged on his glass to attract the attention of all in the room, as if that were necessary. In a serious apologetic tone, he offered, "I apologize for my big ugly friend's behavior, ladies and gentlemen, but he is truly harmless.

"You see, during the last war he received a severe head wound and doctors felt it best to perform a lobotomy to keep him from bullying larger men. It failed! So after lunch, I'll take him outside and whip upon his posterior gluteus major until he whines like the girly-man he is."

Quickly realizing this whole episode was a spoof among friends, the guests in the dining room smiled and nodded approval.

"Gentlemen and guests of the firm, it is my greatest privilege to introduce Sean O'Reilly, Mike's father and my dearest friend on Earth."

Sean stood and, in a final effort to embarrass his friend, curtsied to those seated in the dining room.

Ron shook his head in surrender. "You win, Tiny. Let's have some lunch."

Once lunch and a fair amount of small talk was over, Ron suggested the men retire to the smoking room for coffee and dessert. As they walked into the expensively appointed room filled with walls of books and plush leather chairs and sofas, Sean said, "Tell me again how you hosed up your good hand, Mikey."

Mike gave his dad a cold hard look. "Dad, I'm in my mid-thirties, a junior partner in one of the most prestigious law firms in the country. Don't you think it's high time to dispense with Mikey?"

"Yeah, I guess so, in public anyway. But you will always be Mikey in my heart."

"That's a good place to keep it, Pops."

As they settled into comfy chairs and were served coffee, Sean said, "Son, we want you to run for governor of Oklahoma."

Ron rolled his eyes and placed the palm of his hand to his forehead, "I thought we agreed to work our way into the conversation about a career in politics for Mike?"

"I did work my way into it. You know how I feel about words, Ronny. Talk is overrated!"

Mike started laughing. "If ever there was a classic case of a bull in a china shop, this is it. You're a real piece of work, Pops. But I do endorse your view on the overuse of words. General Eisenhower, when he became president, told his senior staff that regardless of the complexity of the issue, if they couldn't reduce it to a three-page summary, they hadn't given it enough thought."

Ron looked at Mike. "Now that we have *worked* our way into the discussion, what are your views?"

"Actually I've been giving it serious thought for the past couple of years." The two men looked at one another inquisitively as Mike continued. "Truth is, I've known for some time I wanted to be involved in bringing positive change to what I believe to be a dysfunctional criminal justice system. I'm sick and tired of watching hardened, dangerous felons being released back into society. Holding public office is the fastest way to influence it."

As Sean listened to his son, he thought…if he only knew!

"In fact," Mike said, "it has been in the back of my mind ever since we visited Ron's JAG office at Ft. Rucker. Do you remember that?"

Since neither of the older men could remember what they had for lunch the day before, Mike continued. "The two of you were discussing whether or not the high school principal responsible for Donny's death could be brought to justice with the evidence available and concluded, because of the time between the beating and his death, the case couldn't be won.

"The point that always stuck in my craw was the discussion you had about how connected the principal's family was and how it would impact the case. Something was said to the effect that the law was not always fair.

"I said, perhaps naively, because I was just a kid, 'He killed my brother and should pay for it.' I still believe that.

"Cicero once said, 'The good of the people is the highest law.' It's *true,* and somehow, I'm going to get things back on track so the laws of the land are in the best interest of the people. Folks today feel almost powerless to bring about change. Our criminal justice system is in the toilet and can't handle the criminal element, leaving law enforcement officers in the breach.

"Hell, as often as not, the criminal is back on the street before the cop has finished his report. That, gentlemen, bites the big one and is pure nonsense. We *must* bring about change so Americans are safe from egg-sucking dirt bags and to send a message to the dedicated men and women of law enforcement that someone, other than themselves, gives a shit."

"That sounds like one hell of a good platform to run on," said Ron. "I'm sure every police officer will vote for you, plus me and your dad. You have a substantial number of votes already and have yet to announce your intent to enter the gubernatorial race. Not bad! Your dad knows the people of Oklahoma probably better than anyone else. We need to take advantage of the O'Reilly name recognition and what it brings to the parade. Tiny, would you like to say a word or two about how we get started on this thing?"

As Sean set his cup back on the silver tray, he started laying out a basic strategy. "To start, most campaigns fail due to a lack of name recognition and demonstrated performance by the candidate. That's not the case here. Organization and funding shortfalls is the long pole in the tent, and we have that covered in spades.

"In an effort to please everyone, most candidates try to force-feed a platform so damn complex, folks don't have the foggiest idea what the guy stands for. Even the candidates can't keep their stories straight. The real albatross, in my view, is that most candidates are lifelong politicians playing another word game just to get elected. They lack conviction and integrity. In other words, they're douche bags and can't be trusted. We don't have that problem. Since we will be self-funded, we don't owe a passel of favors to bottom feeders waiting to gorge themselves at the political hog trough."

"You have to admit, Mike, he's a smooth talker. Every time I listen to him, which isn't often, I conjure up this mental image of Neanderthals sitting in a cave grunting at one another."

Mike grinned and shook his head, knowing his father had just provided the meat of the issue and a perfect description of most politicians.

Sean gave both men a serious look. "There is something I've been meaning to tell both of you for quite some time…years actually. It's time you both knew."

"The newspaper article about Gene Tidwell accidentally dying of a broken neck was not entirely accurate. Tidwell, son, in the event you don't remember, was the school principal that caused your brother's death so many years ago. He died of a broken neck alright, but it was no accident."

"How can you be so sure of that, Pops?"

Sean shifted in his chair and fixed his son with a cold stare. "Because I *broke* it! I believe in justice, son, and it was obvious justice was not going to be served in Alabama, at least not for the O'Reilly family. So I fixed the problem."

Mike was taken aback by this revelation. Not because he felt his father was incapable of such an act; all one needed to do was to look into Sean's chillingly cold eyes to realize he had experienced horrific things in two wars and was capable of exacting whatever justice he felt matched the crime.

Superimpose the O'Reilly ancestral belief—an eye for an eye—and you had the makings of a perfect killing machine. Mike's first thought, once he regained his composure, was what a great man his father was. Honest, courageous, patriotic to a fault, and protective of his family and those he cared about.

He hugged his father. "Pops, had I been old enough at the time, I would have done the same thing. All these years I thought the bastard had gotten away with murder."

As tears started to well up in Mike's eyes—a release of pent-up emotions he had carried around for years—his dad placed a reassuring hand on his shoulder. "O'Reilly men always have, and hopefully always will take care of their own and be firm in their convictions. We'll never speak of this again, understood?"

"Yes, sir."

"Ronny, do you have a problem with this?"

Ron looked at his friend indicating he had no problems. "This sure as hell tops the bruised-knuckle story Mike shared with us earlier. Tiny, just so you know, as soon as I saw the article in the paper years ago, I knew what had probably happened. I felt pretty confident you wouldn't leave town without taking care of business. Remember, my dear friend, I'm much smarter than you, and I'm going to guess superior in every way!"

Sean smiled at his friend. "Yeah, yeah, I've heard it all before, you little shit."

To lighten the moment and set the stage for an easy transition to the purpose of their meeting, Ron said, "Mike, did you know your dad used to keep the family money in a sock out in the barn? Pretty clever move, huh? Like I've been telling you all along, son, he's loveable and cuddly but dumb as a stump!"

"You lie like a dog, Ron," Mike said as he brushed a tear from the corner of his eye. "When you mention him at all, it's tantamount to some kind of religious experience."

Ron shrugged his shoulders, "Well, maybe I didn't say it but I'm sure I was thinking it. Can we get back to the business at hand? I have a law firm to run and life is short."

Sean laid out the four points he had made earlier. "We clearly have name recognition, not just in Oklahoma but nationally. Over the years, thanks to Ron and his influence, along with a lot of hard work, we are known around the beltway and in influential power bases throughout the nation. This will help us not only in the short term, but also will be essential should Mike decide to take the next step toward the presidency at some future date.

"The O'Reilly men have never gone back on their word. Not once. We have demonstrated our willingness to give back to the community and, in fact, have funded a number of state projects that would have been impossible otherwise.

"Son, you have personally been up to your clavicle in expanding the family business and creating a slew of new jobs for Oklahomans. That has not gone unnoticed. The people know you are a man of honor and one that can be trusted. That may be the strongest link we have.

"Funding will obviously not be a problem. In fact, part of our strategy will be to let the people know you are self-funded and owe no allegiance to special interest groups. We will maintain that theme, regardless of political office you choose to run for. It's a strong message and one that people desperately need to hear.

"As you know, for years I have been recruiting the brightest, most patriotic and competent men and women the country has to offer. Many of them are graduates of our military academies and are decorated veterans.

"J.B. and Dave form the nucleus of one of the strongest, most talented teams anyone could pull together. They will run interference for you, provide all security needs and in general see that everything runs smoothly.

"I propose we have a straightforward, easy-to-understand message that strikes directly at the heart of the most pressing issues…crime, education and welfare programs that make sense. These same messages, once we have a demonstrated track record of success, can be used as part of a broader message to the nation.

"We don't have to wallow in our own fat any longer. We can set about the task, as a people united, to correct the blights the country presently and will forever experience if we don't *fix* the problem. What are your thoughts?"

"Damn, Pops, I think *you* ought to be the one running for governor, don't you, Ron?"

"Believe me, Mike, we've talked about that very thing at great length. We decided, and wisely so, that once the people found out your dad keeps his money hidden in a sock, he might lose fiscal credibility with the people who elected him governor."

"You little shit, can you get serious for a moment or do I have to drown you in that coffee cup?" It was obvious these men had a special bond and enjoyed camaraderie shared by few.

"The big guy wants me to get serious for a moment, so I shall. Your dad and I believe he is too old and too intimidating to have the kind of connection with the people and other political figures that would be necessary to make a serious run for the governor's office and he would have no chance at the presidency.

"You probably haven't noticed, since he's your father, but he is, how shall we say, quite large! His way with words, though damned effective, also leave a bit to be desired. Simply stated, Mike, a toad in comparison would be viewed as a sophisticate.

"Furthermore, most mommies don't want their defenseless little babies picked up and hugged by a mass of humanity that blocks out the sun. In other words, we both agree you are the more likely candidate.

"You are well educated; at the right age to capture the hearts and minds of the young voters; you possess the maturity and polish that middle-aged and older folks like to see in their candidates. Don't let this go to your head, but you are good-looking, articulate, have command presence and handle yourself with an air of confidence. We believe you're the real deal and can go all the way if you elect to do so, and we hope you do."

Sean stood to stretch. "I couldn't have said it better myself, Ronny."

"Tiny, you couldn't have said it at all, way too many big words."

"You're a feisty little critter, aren't you? Do you have enough influence around here to get us some more coffee and pastries or do I have to send out for some?"

As Mike took in the bantering, a server arrived with freshly baked pastries and a pot of steaming hot coffee.

"How the hell did you do that?" asked Sean.

"Like I've always said, my friend, I know you well and I'm light years ahead of you."

"Yes, you are, sir. I willingly concede that."

Mike excused himself to go to the restroom and when he returned, he grabbed a croissant and poured a fresh cup of coffee for himself and topped off the cups of his mentor and father. "OK, guys, how do you envision this thing kicking off? When do we start and what mode of transport do we use to flit around the country?"

Ron spoke first. "It will take you a couple of weeks to bring closure on the projects you've been working on and another week to transfer responsibilities to one of the other, more senior partners. So, let's say the end of the month."

Sean pulled out several sheets of paper from his briefcase and passed them to Mike and Ron. "This is the proposed itinerary worked up by J.B. and crew."

"You must have been pretty confident about your sales pitch, Pops. What if I had said no?"

"I've never seen an O'Reilly back down from a good fight or worthwhile cause. That's what this is; so it was a pretty safe bet.

"We can take one of the corporate jets, the new G-4, out of executive service and dedicate it to your campaign. It has the latest communications gear so you can stay laced up with staff, researchers, Ron and me at all times. That way, we can keep you from being blind-sided or caught short in the event your opponents play dirty, and they will."

Mike smiled, winking at Sean as he rubbed his bruised knuckles. "In politics, can you punch someone's lights out if they use disparaging language toward you?"

"Jeez, Mike, that's one of the reasons why your father's not running. Do I have to worry about you, too?"

Sean looked over at Ron and in his best Irish brogue said, "That's *me* boy speaking."

Mike grinned mischievously. "I'm just pulling your crank, *Ronny*, me boy."

"Your dad can get away with that Ronny crap, but I'll fire your little butt on the spot."

Father and son had a good laugh at their friend's expense and as they prepared to leave the dining room, Sean said, "Let's get cracking, gentlemen. Lots of work to do before month's end."

Unknown to Mike, Sean would be leaving this meeting to hold another, a clandestine initiative authorizing covert operators to strike a target in Alabama; thus fulfilling a promise—a prophecy—the elder O'Reilly had made many, many years earlier to an ignorant man that didn't listen.

16

The race begins

One of Mike's first acts upon returning to Oklahoma was to have his staff call journalists of various newspapers, reporters and television network producers together to announce his intent to run for governor.

His real goal was to establish clear rules of conduct concerning their reporting—specifically the accuracy of their reporting—during the campaign.

The press conference was held on the grounds of the lavish 24,000-acre O'Reilly estate. J.B., campaign director, chose this place for a couple of reasons: One, he wanted to send a clear and intimidating message to anyone who might choose to vie for the governorship that they would be dealing with deep pockets and a well-organized campaign. This message was not really necessary, however, since anyone from Oklahoma who did not know the O'Reillys was either comatose or totally brain dead and therefore posed no threat.

Secondly, he knew Mike loved this place. The veranda overlooking a large spring-fed lake; the Kiamichi River in the background; miles of white, four-rail fencing around pastures containing spirited, sleek-coated quarter horses and award-winning livestock was a perfect backdrop to put everyone at ease.

On the morning of the interview, campaign staffers scurried about like field mice ensuring everything was ready. Mike, on the other hand, had just returned from a three-mile run around the lake and stopped at one of the out-buildings to admire his dad's antique tractor collection when he received his first of several frantic calls to get ready. Thirty minutes before show time, Mike showered, shaved and made his way onto the veranda.

Much to the displeasure of his staff, he was dressed in nice, but casual slacks and a polo shirt. He immediately noticed a very attractive lady whose media badge indicated she was from KVOO television in Tulsa.

"Hi, Veronica. Mike O'Reilly. Glad you could make it, and if I might add, you look absolutely stunning in that outfit. Just so there is no misunderstanding, if I were looking for a dinner date I'd pick you over that scruffy guy with a beard every time."

Veronica Witherspoon blushingly held her petite arm out as Mike shook her hand ever so gently. "Thank you...I think! Are you always so direct, Mr. O'Reilly?"

He gave her a disarming smile. "Not always. I do believe, however, words have a tendency to be overrated. May I get you a drink of some kind?"

"Iced tea would be nice," she replied.

"Iced tea, it is."

As they walked across the massive veranda, Mike asked one of the dozen or so servers for two glasses of iced tea. "Have you ever tried squeezing a lime wedge into your tea, Veronica?"

"No! Has anyone else?" she said, smiling at the handsome candidate.

"Bob, bring a couple slices of lime for the lady and if you would, sir, fix mine so I don't have to mess with it."

"Can do, boss." The ex-Green Beret headed for the bar.

"Are all of these waiters in your employ?"

Mike smiled broadly at her naivety. "Miss Veronica, I like you more by the minute. Bob, along with the other well-dressed gentlemen looking like penguins, is not a waiter. They are highly trained security personnel.

"Bob, for example, is an ex-Special Forces trooper who speaks several foreign languages and is expert in martial arts. Look down by the lake. The two gentlemen on horseback are retired marine corpsmen, designated marksmen...snipers. You will be safe here, if nothing else."

Veronica was clearly surprised and perhaps even a little uneasy. Most people she met didn't surround themselves with killing machines. After a moment of reflection she said, "Is all of this necessary?"

"Regrettably it is and, with your permission, I'd like to leave it at that."

As their drinks arrived, Mike surveyed the area as if looking for someone. "Veronica, did you bring a crew with you?"

"I have camera and sound guys out in the van, but they won't come in until I call them."

"Why?"

"It's an unwritten policy that camera and sound crews don't mix and mingle. That's *my* job."

He thought about that for a moment. "You know, without worker bees there would be no honey and no need for a queen. Call them and have them join us."

Veronica sensed just a trace of authority in Mike's voice, but not enough to be interpreted as a directive. She made the call.

At precisely the time the interview was scheduled to start, J.B. came out on the veranda and spoke into a bank of microphones, looking directly into numerous TV cameras. "Ladies and gentlemen, it is my privilege to introduce the next governor of Oklahoma, Mike O'Reilly."

Mike told Veronica to not go away; he would be back in a few minutes. He then approached the podium, set his glass of tea down, and took a moment to look at each person before speaking. Noticeably, he dispensed with the typical upfront small talk and quips.

"We will grow to know one another well before this campaign is over. I already know your names, but that's not what I'm talking about. You will know me as a man of integrity and honor, and I will hopefully know you as honest, objective, professional journalists and reporters.

"I know there are age-old protocols in the news business; some of them I know through my experiences with the media in the conduct of O'Reilly Corporation business.

"Starting today, however, I want us to form our own set of rules that will apply to every aspect of this campaign, as well as my term as governor, should that be the will of the people. You may write or report objectively anything I say—or any member of my staff says—so long as it is verbatim. That is to say, it is my desire that you not take things out of context, embellish or otherwise change the original intent of any statement for personal or political gain. In my view, that is a reasonable request. You expect me, and rightly so, to be honest and forthright. I expect nothing less of you.

"Secondly, be assured, before I make any statement, claim or promise, it will have been thought out in great detail. Unique in the political arena, I do not use written speeches and therefore my staff will be unable to give you advance copies.

"That, by the way, scares the hell out of them, but they will adjust and learn to live with it, just as you will. However, you are more than welcome to call my campaign headquarters, stop by if you like, and someone will tell you what the topics of any given talk will be.

"The reason I don't use speeches is straightforward. How can one understand and be committed to an issue if he has to use a cheat sheet to remind him what to say? You must have conviction, and if that's the case, the subject will be known in infinite detail, thus negating the need of the written word.

"J.B. Hawkins, the distinguished gentleman standing over there, is, among other things, managing this campaign. J.B., how many speechwriters do we have in our employ?"

"We have no speechwriters, sir."

"How many researchers and analysts are on the payroll?"

"Counting myself, sir, we have seventeen researchers and twelve analysts."

The newly announced candidate looked over at J.B. with a smile. "*Damn*, am I paying for all that?" A few chuckles came from the assembled body.

"Indeed you are, sir, but given your propensity for not using the written word, we need to be sure you have the best, most factual information available."

Mike returned his gaze to the media. "That's how we do business here. For the record, I'm running for governor of Oklahoma. This is my platform: The way we handle crime, education and welfare is not acceptable. The good people of

Oklahoma deserve better, and I know how to fix it. I'll give you some specifics at our next media briefing. "

"When is that, J.B.?"

"It is scheduled for next Thursday at 1400, sir, Chamber of Commerce in Oklahoma City."

Mike smiled at his trusted friend. "For the civilians in attendance, which I assume is everyone, that is two o'clock sharp."

"That's it! Anyone have any questions or comments?"

One of the columnists from the Tulsa World raised his hand. "Mr. O'Reilly, we know the family name and have some exposure to you, but there is a lot of background detail that we don't have. Do you plan on preparing a dossier of some type to provide general information?"

"Good question, Ralph. We have prepared a packet for each of you. We hope all of you have time to join us for lunch. The information packets will be handed to you by security personnel at the front gate as you leave.

"By the way, we will be having a number of these informal press meetings as we go along. Everyone is invited to attend and I mean *everyone*! Hell, one of the camera or sound guys might choose to vote for me; who knows. Thanks for coming folks, and now please join us for some of the best BBQ in the state."

As he took a sip of his iced tea, Veronica approached him. "Well, that was certainly different, Mr. O'Reilly. I'm not sure media reps have ever been given a set of rules before."

Mike looked down at her—she stood barely five-two, her petite frame perfectly proportioned. "It works better if everyone understands the ground rules. It levels the playing field, as it were. Let's grab a bite to eat. I'm famished."

Veronica sort of wrinkled her nose and shrugged her shoulders saying, "It's so messy! It gets all over the place."

"Well, Miss Veronica, it's my intent to marry you, so I suggest you start acquiring a taste for it...*today*!" He put his arm around her and moved her in the direction he wanted her to go.

"I don't even know you!" she said, laughing, as she allowed herself to be gently guided toward the serving line.

"That's why I'm giving you an info packet. Read through it and see what you think."

"You're impossible! You don't know me either and maybe I don't want to get married. Have you thought of that?"

"No! Until you pass the BBQ test and become a viable candidate for marriage, I will simply relish the opportunity to spend a little time with you. That's a good start." Mike pulled her a little closer, thinking...'this is the woman for me, whether she likes it or not.'

17

Newbrockton, Alabama

Small southern towns have a lot in common. They are chockfull of friendly, God-fearing people. Seemingly more churches than there are people and everybody knows everybody else's business. Quaint! Consequently outsiders stand out like the proverbial sore thumb. Everybody not born within a stone's throw of town or lived there for a hundred years is an outsider.

The two operatives had been briefed on this phenomenon and decided to pull into a rest area outside the college town of Troy, Alabama, about thirty-five miles north of their destination, until after midnight.

They knew there was always a risk of discovery by either an insomniac farmer; a hapless cop making an infrequent pass through town; a wayward husband returning from a late night tryst with his neighbor's wife; or something really freakish, like hitting a deer on Main Street.

Everything considered, they felt the predawn hours of morning would give them the best opportunity to get in, conduct their business, and leave before anyone knew they were there.

Their target this morning lived off the main highway about a quarter mile down a dirt driveway. The lights on the large SUV they were driving flicked off just before the vehicle turned onto the dirt drive. Both men donned night vision goggles before slowly proceeding.

About halfway between the main road and the house, the driver stopped the vehicle by gently applying the emergency brake to eliminate illumination. The passenger had already removed the bulb from the interior light to keep the vehicle dark when the doors were opened. They left nothing to chance.

The ARC operatives sat for a moment in total darkness listening for any sound that might suggest they had been discovered. With the exception of a whippoorwill and the faint barking of a dog in the distance, it was quiet.

The ex-Navy Seals wore black clothing and pullover face masks. Before exiting the vehicle, they chambered hollow-point cartridges into their 22LR Rugers and ratcheted the silencers in place. Each had razor-sharp Randall fighting knives strapped to their legs. For this assignment, they were traveling light.

Their target was a Grand Wizard of the KKK—even friendly southern towns have the occasional embarrassing bad apple—but not for long!

This would be one sheet-wearing son-of-a-bitch that would never again see the light of day. Old man Briley was a slow learner and didn't quite understand that there was no statute of limitations insofar as Sean was concerned. He had been given fair warning many years ago that he would be held personally responsible should any harm come to Ezekiel or his family.

Sean received word and later confirmed that the KKK was again raising its ugly head by burning crosses at rallies on the Alabama-Florida border and had run a young couple of African ethnicity off the road as they returned home after evening church services. Fortunately neither was seriously hurt. The young man, however, was Ezekiel's eldest son and the grand poobah, or whatever he was called, was Briley.

The horrific sight that greeted the small town the following morning made national news. Mr. Briley's torso had been impaled on a sharpened shovel handle that had been wedged into the cattle grate at the entrance to his property.

Pinned to the body for all to see was a warning to the KKK to change their ways or meet the same fate. The note listed every known member in the local area. The list of names would rock this small town to its core and prove most damaging to local troublemakers and pillars of the community alike. More importantly, a photo of the list was carried on national television and published in newspapers across the country.

Old man Briley's head, cleaned of all flesh, was later found in the nearby Pea River. Crayfish, turtles, and other river-dwelling scavengers had benefited from his inability to follow simple instructions.

18

Oklahoma City Chamber of Commerce, Thursday, 2:00 PM

As Mike entered the large auditorium-like room just hours after the American Relief Committee (ARC) strike team had successfully completed its mission and crossed the Alabama state line into Florida, he noticed it was standing room only. 'The word is obviously out that I'm either a freak of nature or, best case, different from other gubernatorial candidates, and you wouldn't want to miss the opportunity to see this guy fall on his sword. If nothing else, it would be entertaining.'

He wasted no time moving to the podium. He didn't like time-consuming formal introductions or biographies that droned on ad infinitum by self-serving politicians. His advance team cleared the way for him to move directly into his own introduction and the issues at hand. Not only was this process efficient; it also negated any perception the candidate was sponsored by special interest groups.

Mike took a drink of water as he surveyed the large audience prior to speaking. "Ladies and gentlemen, I want to thank you for taking time from your busy schedules to be here today. Given the recent media attention, I'm sure you're all aware that I want to be your next governor.

"I will discuss three topics that I believe Oklahomans need to focus energy and resources on: education, crime and welfare reform. I have strong feelings about these topics and have a detailed plan on how to fix the problems associated with them.

"I'll tell you upfront that to fix the problems will require citizen involvement and pressure on the legislature to provide good laws and leadership. Changes will be needed in both areas. If elected officials choose to maintain the ineffective and inefficient status quo, the citizens of this great state need to demand with a *single voice* that they do their jobs…or replace them.

"I don't see running for governor as a play for power and prestige. Rather, I see it as a movement by Oklahomans to fix a system that is simply not functioning in the best interests of the people.

"Once I have shared my ideas, the floor will be open for discussion, and I'll stay here until every question is answered." Mike reached under the podium for his water glass and took a long drink. He then turned to a member of his campaign staff and asked him to check on how long the conference hall was available to them.

The president of the Chamber of Commerce overheard the question. "Mr. O'Reilly, you may have the room as long as you like. No other activities are scheduled today."

Mike thanked the gentleman and turned back to the overcrowded hall.

J.B. slipped him a note. He looked briefly at the message and then smiled. "I just this moment found out three members of Governor Dodd's senior staff are with us today. Gentlemen, I admire your initiative and want you to know you are always welcome. In the future, if you will contact a member of my staff beforehand, we will ensure you have seating on the front row.

"J.B., these gentlemen need to be provided information packets, because I don't remember seeing them at the BBQ. By the way, you missed one hell of a spread. While I'm thinking of it, background packets have been prepared for all attendees, and you may pick them up as you exit the briefing.

"What's needed for a society to succeed and prosper? Some would say a strong economy with jobs aplenty, and they would be right. Others say education and a safe environment wherein people can raise families out of harm's way. They too would be right. Still other more liberal souls might suggest the underprivileged and downtrodden must be provided for and, of course, most of us would agree that needs to be done as well." Mike paused for a moment to let those thoughts sink in.

"Strong economies are technology driven, which implies the need for a good education. All work is honorable, but really good, high-paying jobs are generally reserved for the educated. Why, then, if education is so important, are parents so willing to send their children off to be schooled by under-qualified teachers or teachers that may be qualified but have lost their zeal to teach because of frustrations derived from a tolerant school system?

"In my former life, I had the privilege of serving with the 75th Ranger Regiment. For those that do not know, airborne troopers are required to routinely jump out of perfectly good airplanes on parachutes packed by total strangers. So how can you be certain the guy who packed *your* chute did the very best job possible? Simple; chute riggers are selected at random to strap on a parachute he or she packed and jump with the rest of the regiment. I call that the ultimate test of one's chosen profession. You can bet your sweet bippy he does the very best job possible…every time.

"My question to Oklahomans: How well do you know the teachers involved daily with educating your children? Can you trust them to properly pack your children's parachutes—their young, impressionable minds?

"I have no speechwriters on my staff. I have opted instead to employ specialists in various fields as researchers. Guess what they have found? There is no systematic procedure in place to periodically test the proficiency of our teachers.

"Why is that? Certainly the well-qualified educators would not object; such a process would quickly weed out the under-qualified. This in turn would breathe fresh air into the good teachers who daily witness substandard performance on the part of some of their contemporaries. Sounds like this would be a good place to start the revamping process.

"If you want to ensure you have the best qualified educators teaching your children, you have to pay them an acceptable wage. What is that wage? I don't know at the moment, but I have a team working that issue, as we speak.

"I guarantee you it is one hell of a lot more than they now receive. If we are going to hold our teachers to the highest standards, they damn well deserve a good wage. Why should they have to use their own money to buy school supplies needed to support their class curriculum? That's crazy! I say let's change it.

"The long pole in the educational tent, however, is the family unit. If parents are not involved and aware of their children's strengths and weaknesses, the probability of them succeeding in the classroom is greatly reduced. Parents *must* get involved.

"Internationally we are losing ground rapidly, backsliding into an abyss of ignorance and apathy. Once we were among the leaders of the academic world. We have now been surpassed by some third world countries producing students better prepared to meet the technological challenges of the future. If we are to maintain technological advantage in the future, we need to work together to fix this problem right now!"

Mike paused to get a visual from J.B. on the audience's acceptance of a hard line they were not accustomed to hearing from politicians. An imperceptible nod told the story, and he stayed the course.

"One of the greatest challenges is to be a single mom. If you are a single parent—particularly a mom—who is busting her hump just to put food on the table and some sort of shelter over her children's heads, it is a hard sell to convince her to go to a PTA meeting or the school play after she gets home late from her second job. She needs help! We have provisions in our educational plan to see that she gets it.

"Freeloaders, breeding like rabbits, so they can continue to gorge themselves at the government welfare trough, fall into an entirely different category. I'll address them later.

"Part of that plan is aggressive pursuit and prosecution of deadbeat dads or single guys who think impregnating unwed women is a badge of honor. They have no responsibility for their actions. The message is clear. Support your offspring or go to jail, doing hard labor until you change your mind."

The audience erupted in cheers and clapping to the extent that Mike had to wait a few moments before he could continue.

"One of the longer-term challenges we must address soon is how to get uneducated, welfare-oriented, unemployed adults to care about their children's education. Many of these households are second and third generation welfare recipients who know no other way of life and are not smart enough to see a need for their children to be educated. Most of these kids see only underachievers and, worst case, deadbeat, abusive parents, so they are not exactly candidates for the fast track.

"We need to start working people out of that mode or it will simply continue generation to generation and that is not acceptable. It drains the resources of state and federal agencies and our society as a whole.

"Everyone deserves an opportunity to improve their lot in life, but few deserve to simply have it provided for them as an inalienable right. We have a solid plan, and I will talk about it more when we get to welfare reform.

"However, one aspect of it is a moving scale of incentives based on daily school attendance by children of welfare and low-income families and participation in mentor and tutoring programs.

"Ladies and gentlemen, there are kids out there who have no idea what a father figure is. We need to give them one so they at least have some idea of what the norm is. I believe we will find that such actions will have a positive impact on young minds and perhaps be seen as a good thing by the older folks, as well."

As he waited for the applause to subside, he motioned for one of his young staffers. "Would you please get me a bottle of pop or something?"

"Get you what, sir?"

Mike looked at him, shaking his head and whispered, "I'll bet you're a bloody Yankee, aren't you?"

"Boston, sir," replied the somewhat confused but bright staffer.

"I thought I recognized that accent. In that case, a soda would do nicely."

The young man went in search of refreshment, returning in a moment with an ice cold soda. He handed it to Mike, obviously embarrassed and turned to walk away.

Mike touched his shoulder and said, "Hey, Yank, it's the little things that make the difference and I really appreciate your effort. Thanks a bundle." The difference in his stride and attitude was obvious as he realized he was part of a team and not catering to the whims of a single all-important man seeking high office.

"As we talk about the three topics that constitute the major theme of my campaign—education, crime and welfare reform— you will become aware of how inextricably they are interrelated.

"Crime, for example: why do we have so much of it, particularly drug-related? The answer is not as complex as you might think. The assholes that commit the crimes know our over-burdened and often dysfunctional criminal justice system—made up of slick lawyers; soft or inept judges; and an unmanageable docket—will have them back on the street before the arresting officer gets halfway through his report. That *won't* happen on my watch! I can promise you that."

J.B. cringed as he quickly approached the podium in a crouch to avoid obvious notice by the audience. He whispered something to Mike and then returned to his chair in the same manner.

"My surrogate conscience has recommended we strike the word *assholes,* so if you would please when you print this piece just draw a line through it. That way my campaign director is appeased to some degree. You get to print exactly what I said, and I get to feel warm and fuzzy knowing I have perfectly described the superfluous mass of protoplasm that is a bane to society. How's that, J.B.?"

"Oh, much better, sir. Thank you."

The audience seemed to enjoy the lighthearted banter, responding with smiles and nods. It was refreshingly obvious that this man was truly a different kind of candidate, a dynamic force to be reckoned with if one was at all interested in running for governor in the State of Oklahoma.

Mike knew he had won over this audience, at least, and felt comfortable his ideas were being well received. "In my view, criminal law, as administered by the courts this day and age, does little to help law enforcement officers in the conduct of their duties and may actually place them at risk.

"A good example is the Miranda Act. If not followed to the letter of the law, hardened criminals caught in the act can walk free. That's nuts! No question, there have been improprieties in the past with regard to civil rights violations by law enforcement officers. That was the genesis of the act.

"We have, however, moved well beyond the caveman mentality that prompted this legislation. Guidelines are certainly needed and in fact the Miranda Act, in many ways, is a good piece of work. But under no set of circumstances should a piece of legislation release dangerous criminals onto the streets to kill, rob and rape again.

"I have a team of legal beagles evaluating the Miranda Act and preparing a dossier outlining recommended changes. It is my intent to personally deliver these recommendations to Steve Humphrey, attorney general of the United States. We were classmates in college and I know the man well. I'm quite sure, in fact positive, he will wordsmith this document until he passes out or falls over dead.

"If you would permit me to reminisce for a moment, Steve and I were roommates at Harvard and though we have been friends all these years, he still believes I'm a Neanderthal scribbling with the end of a burnt stick or at best capable of drawing unintelligible pictures with a number ten crayon.

"When one arrives at Harvard as an army ranger, fresh from a recent combat assignment, it takes the locals a while to adjust to his mannerisms, colloquialisms and speech impediments.

"Oh, forgive me! You probably didn't know everyone born outside the city limits of Boston is considered English language challenged. As far as I could tell back then, certainly insofar as the honorable Steve Humphrey was concerned, they viewed Okie-speak as an emerging means of communication, not yet fully evolved."

Those in attendance seemed to enjoy the candidate's down-to-earth humor and quiet intelligence.

"The good news is Steve is a smart guy. I think he will see the wisdom in our recommendations and initiate those actions necessary to amend the act so hardened criminals will no longer escape prosecution due to administrative oversight. Hopefully, this will be accomplished during our lifetime.

"In the interim, the state legislature needs to get proactive and make the necessary changes to Oklahoma's statutes so they enhance our law enforcement initiatives. Secondly, we must ensure every police officer whose duties require him to be on the street and in harm's way be properly equipped to meet the challenges he may face.

"I am reminded of Sean Connery's comment to Elliot Ness in the movie, 'The Untouchables.' He asked Mr. Ness if he really wanted to get Al Capone. 'If one of his guys pulls a knife, you pull a gun. If they put one of your guys in the hospital, you put one of theirs in the morgue. That's how you get Al Capone! Are ya prepared to do that?'

"That same question could be asked here. Are we prepared to do what is necessary to retake the streets and create a safe environment for our families and future generations of Oklahomans? I think we are and, further, I think the time is now.

"Arming a police officer with a six-shooter to face off against a lowlife carrying a MAC-10 automatic pistol won't stand the test of logic. Very few, if any, law enforcement agencies train their personnel to make head shots when deadly force is required. The standard two-shot burst to the chest is probably still the norm. If that is the case, then those two shots need to be from a heavy-caliber weapon, a .40 or .45 caliber multi-shot semi-automatic.

"If the situation is critical enough for an officer to un-holster his or her sidearm and engage an armed suspect, then we want to ensure that egg-sucking dog goes down for the count. I know of cases where doped-up felons have been shot several times with a standard-issue sidearm and still live long enough to kill the officer and, in some cases, innocent bystanders.

"Cops know what it takes to put a man down and consequently countless officers across the country wind up purchasing their own weapons, usually a heavy-caliber, multi-shot semi-automatic. That's not good policy, folks. It won't happen on my watch.

"Therefore all law enforcement agencies will be given adequate funding to properly equip and train their people with the latest in lethal and non-lethal weaponry. They must also have the best lightweight self-protection gear available on the market. I will see that they get it whether I'm elected as your next governor or not. That's a promise!"

Knowing the average person finds discussions about armed conflict, weapons and shooting people an uncomfortable topic, Mike took a moment to let the audience mentally regroup before proceeding,

"Folks, complacency and disassociation are insidious. We seldom know we are victims of it. How many in attendance here feel safe? Let me see a show of hands." The majority raised their hands without giving a thought to being baited for follow-up questions.

"How many here find it uncomfortable or distasteful to openly discuss lethal force or the use of weapons in general?" Again, though fewer hands were raised, they represented the majority.

"How many of you have ever gone on a 'ride along' with a police officer to gain an understanding of what they face daily? I see only about eight or so hands out there, so what does that tell us? It may suggest—and this is not a criticism, just the way it is—we have fallen victim to complacency and disassociation.

"We want our police officers to go about their business, facing the filthy, lawless dregs of our society on their own while we remain securely tucked away in suburbia. Oh, and by the way, *don't* bother us, we'll read all about it in the newspaper.

"If you want to conduct a quick self-evaluation with regard to disassociation, ask yourselves these questions: How often do you actually look an officer in the eye and say hello when you see them in a restaurant or on the street? How often do you nod or wave at an officer when your vehicles pass? And lastly do you get nervous and a little antsy when you see a patrol car in your rearview mirror? *Why* is that?

"If it were a friend or an associate we saw in the restaurant, passing us on the street or driving behind us, we would smile and wave, wouldn't we? Now ask yourself, which friend or associate of mine would put his or her life on the line in an effort to make my world safer?

"The operative words here are *friend* or *associate.* Most of us don't necessarily see cops as friends or even associates because we don't know them, and the only interface we have has generally been unpleasant and often cost us money. Superimpose the fact they're in uniform, which we have been conditioned to see as an authority figure, and they're armed.

"That brings us full circle back to the questions I posed to you a few moments ago. Our comfort level is challenged by these good public servants. I recommend we all make a concerted effort to have a greater respect for cops and give them the support they so desperately need.

"They go to work and do their job every day without you, but think how much better they could do it if we were all proactive in our efforts to keep our streets safe.

"Now for those in law enforcement, there is a flip side as well. Police departments have a responsibility to the public they protect and serve, to ensure their officers are well trained, physically fit and honest.

"I'm not suggesting every officer be able to run a four-minute mile. I am suggesting, however, they be physically fit, present a neat appearance and be able to hold their own against most adversaries. Anything less is unacceptable.

"With regard to the officers who have chosen to be slovenly, apathetic, bullying or, worse, dirty cops, my advice to them is to follow the gubernatorial race closely and if it appears I might win, pack your bags and get out of the state.

"You may not be my first order of business as governor, because each city or municipality has a mayor and elected officials who are supposed to be managing these kinds of things. Be assured, however, I will have a contingent of well-qualified gentlemen looking into municipal law enforcement and leadership.

"If your city has gang problems, I want those gangs to know that my *gang*, made up of committed and physically fit police officers, is bigger and tougher than *their* gang and we are, from this moment on, dedicated to reclaiming our streets, all streets."

A standing ovation came at the close of Mike's proclamation, and he was unable to continue for several minutes.

"I'm dead-nuts serious. If you're dealing drugs, committing felonies, not paying court-ordered child support or any number of other sorry-ass criminal acts, you better get your act together or get the hell out of Dodge. I have a plan and the resources to track you down and exact a fair measure of justice from your worthless carcass."

Mike stepped back for a moment and cleared his throat. "I guess you'd better put a diagonal line through *ass* also or J.B. will be low-crawling over here to chastise me again."

He looked over and smiled as he took a quick sip of soda. He then surveyed the audience, noticing many journalists on their cell phones which made him a little uneasy. He must have just said something that got their attention and God only knew what would be on the evening news.

He had entered the campaign knowing that running for political office was tantamount to walking through a minefield and decided early on he would articulate the issues as clearly and succinctly as possible and let the chips fall where they may.

Mike had no intention of changing his mannerisms or the way he spoke simply because he was running for governor. He would either win on the merits of his credibility and campaign issues or he would remain in the private sector and use his own resources to ensure the promises made concerning law enforcement came to fruition.

When he said earlier "not on my watch," he did not necessarily mean as governor of Oklahoma. Mike was dedicated to the long overdue task of getting these issues on the right track, whether he held political office or not.

"One of the key points I want to make here today is that law enforcement, like teaching, is grossly underpaid. Without these two professions we would run a very high risk of being both dumb and dead! As governor, one of the first tasks I will lay on the legislature is to appropriate funds to fix this problem."

Before Mike could get into his last topic—welfare reform—he noticed a man moving down the aisle toward the podium and intuitively sensed there was a rat in the sandbox. He glanced over at J.B. and inconspicuously motioned with his eyes and slight movement of his head in the direction of the man.

J.B. had already seen the man and casually nodded as he moved in that direction while speaking into a lapel mike. Almost immediately, seven highly trained bodyguards materialized out of nowhere to form a shield around their charge. Mike took this opportunity to diffuse the situation before some unsuspecting soul bit off more than he could chew and created an embarrassing, as well as a disruptive situation.

"Before we get into the welfare fiasco, I would like to introduce members of my staff. Names are not important and for security reasons we prefer you not know them by name. The seven gentlemen you see before you are all highly trained ex-military special operations personnel. The two on the left are battle-tested Green Berets who speak something like six languages between them.

"They also finished first and second in the International Military Marksmanship Competition held annually in Sydney, Australia. For those of you not familiar with this competition, which is probably all of you, each country having a uniformed military service may send their best marksmen to compete in rifle and pistol competitions.

"Each of these gentlemen, in fact all seven of them, can place fourteen rounds in a target at fifty feet and cover them with a coffee cup. That's a pretty darned good shot group for a sidearm!

"The big ugly guy here is an ex-Navy Seal. Other than being an excellent shot and a third degree black belt, he has no particular talent. He doesn't play well with others, so we keep him out of sight as much as possible."

There was a low rumble of laughter throughout the audience as they focused their attention on the seven men with renewed respect and a better understanding of just why they were on the payroll.

"He wants to turn around and stare me down so bad he can taste it, but he can't. His job is to stare *you* down. He's really a sweetheart when you get to know him, although he has a tendency to kill and eat anything that gets too close."

As Mike continued the introduction of the remaining security personnel, the man making his way down the aisle slid into a vacant seat about the time J.B. reached him. A few moments later, after a brief discussion, both men left the auditorium quietly, and for the most part, unnoticed.

As it turned out, the man was armed with an eight-inch butcher knife. J.B. turned him over to police officers stationed in the foyer and as he was about to re-enter the auditorium he was reminded of an over-used southern quip: 'Just like a dumb ass redneck to bring a knife to a gun fight.'

One of the police officers called to him as he was about to open the auditorium door. "Sir, you can tell your boss we fully support what he's saying and welcome the changes. He's got our vote." J.B. thanked the officers and returned to his seat.

Mike continued, "The last topic this afternoon is welfare reform. If ever there was a subject to raise the ire of mortal man and create discontent and controversy within the ranks of our citizenry, this is it.

"First and foremost, we need a plan that gets to the root causes of the controversy while restoring the dignity of welfare recipients. I have such a plan and will give you the highlights here today.

"You may recall earlier I mentioned the inextricable interrelationship of education, crime and welfare reform. This is where we pull it all together.

"If you look at the welfare rolls and dig into the empirical data, you will find the majority of recipients—notwithstanding illegal immigrants and other ineligibles which we will discuss another time—are Americans of African or Hispanic ethnicity, but primarily African.

"I didn't choose my words here for the sake of political correctness. One of the major underlying problems in this country is that we continually make distinctions between black and white. It's been going on for over 200 years and if we are to ever get over this huge cultural bump in the social progress of our country, it has to stop!

"Think about it for a moment. The blending of ethnicities from every corner of the world embodies the term *American*, yet we continually and harmfully make the distinction of *African American*. Why is that? The answer lies in the history of our great nation. It has been 'us' and 'them' from day one.

"Early immigrants, our ancestors, were predominantly impoverished and oppressed Caucasians from the British Isles and Europe—*us*. Later, unscrupulous slave traders introduced cheap labor by way of kidnapped Africans—*them*. Most and I suspect all at that time were uneducated natives from various coastal tribes in Africa. These hapless souls arrived in chains and were put on auction blocks in the same manner farmers bought and sold their mules, horses and oxen. Consequently they were viewed as little more than livestock.

"These folks had no rights or entitlements and were fed out of necessity, not compassion, to keep them strong so more work could be exacted. Furthermore, a strong well-fed field hand brought more money on the auction block.

"Overlay that traumatic experience generation upon generation of Caucasians and Africans, cradle to grave, having that 'superior-subservient' mentality reinforced on a daily basis. The stigma associated with such a tragic beginning may never vacate the subconscious of some Americans, but perhaps we can work our way through it and in time change how we view demographics and cultural differences. I submit the present approach is not the way.

"I won't portend to give you an American history lesson, but I can tell you from personal experience that as recently as the '50s, in rural Alabama, and I'm sure other parts of the country as well, folks of African descent were still denied proper education and for all intents and purposes were indentured servants laboring as sharecroppers or field hands for white landowners.

"Account ledgers and grocery bills, which many workers could not read, were manipulated in an effort to keep workers indentured forever. I bear witness to it.

"If you pass on to your children, through words or actions, the insecurities and animosity that must surely be associated with this tale of woe, and they see nothing but underachievers who have chosen to sponge off of the welfare system instead of seeking honorable employment, what kind of message does that send to impressionable young minds?

"What is their incentive to achieve anything? Many of these kids have nothing that even vaguely resembles a positive role model. They need our help in breaking this mold. It's not an easy task, and we don't have all the answers. But we definitely have some of the answers, and we need to stop side-stepping sensitive, hard-to-solve issues and get on with the task.

"There are able-bodied welfare recipients who see no need for their offspring to be more educated than themselves. This is the ingredient of social disaster. That, ladies and gentlemen, is where we are today."

Mike stopped long enough to take a drink and to let his comments sink into the psyche of all present. "When you live in a culture where impregnating unwed young women is viewed as a badge of honor; a way for the young woman to collect a larger welfare check; children who have no idea who their father is and have no father figure to teach them right from wrong, how do you think that will turn out? Let me help you out a little. It won't turn out worth a damn!

"Without proper parental guidance and involvement, the children—unless they are very strong willed and have a reasonably high intellect—will fail in school because the single mom, or in some cases a wayward dad, won't or can't help them with basic reading, writing and math skills. In other words, they're on their own. If on their own and no one at home places any importance on education, why learn? Many minority children don't.

"They drop out of school for numerous reasons: they get behind in their studies and there is not enough money in the school budgets to provide tutors; and they come from families either on welfare or with incomes well below the poverty level. Consequently they may not be dressed as well as their more affluent contemporaries and, like any child, they are self-conscious about it.

"Many see crime, primarily drug-dealing and robbery, as an easy way to wealth and self-esteem. That, ladies and gentlemen, is a sad testimonial and we cannot allow it to continue. It may take years to reverse this trend, but it has to be done. We need to start finding ways to resolve this problem now.

"To compound an already desperate situation, many agencies, institutions and organizations have adopted the attitude that this untenable mess will go away or somehow be mystically fixed by the government. It *won't* be! It must be fixed by you and me.

"That's what our discussion here today is all about: a plan to fix the problems. For the plan to be successful, community leaders of African ethnicity must dedicate themselves to a long, costly and tireless effort to reverse the present trend of underachievement.

"Within our respective communities and churches, many stalwart ladies and gentlemen have risen above the drawbacks I have just mentioned and have become successful in their chosen fields. Unfortunately those still on the lower end of the spectrum can't seem to jump quite high enough to reach the bar that leads them out of the quagmire of poverty and ignorance.

"We must provide the stepping-stones to elevate them to that bar. I know how to do it. One of the plan's major themes is to provide the necessary tools to enable community leaders, educators, businessmen and clergy, as well as mothers and fathers, to set a good example for our youth. That is no small task, given where we're starting. Critics may say I'm broad-brushing the entire black community. That is simply not so.

"The problems identified here, aside from being a victim of crimes, have nothing to do with honest, hard-working citizens of which there are many. I am talking about the subset of the community as outlined earlier, the crux of the problem.

"If there is anyone here today who thinks everything is peachy dandy and nothing extraordinary needs to be done, pass around that fine grade of rope you're smoking so we can all enjoy your utopian world.

"We need a collective wake-up call. The clock is ticking, and we have children and undereducated parents slipping deeper and deeper into the abyss of poverty and ignorance every passing day. We cannot allow this to happen; we must start reversing that trend...*right now*!"

Almost on queue, a young intern approached the podium and handed the candidate a cold soda which he polished off in one long drink.

"I believe we can all agree there are significant cultural differences within our respective communities. That is both good and bad. Good from the standpoint that keeping the quality aspects of one's culture alive is commendable and important. Bad in that even referring to 'respective communities' takes us full circle to the psychological barrier that is at the core of our racial problems: *us* and *them*. I despise that.

"I'm not sure how we can ever get completely over this mammoth hump. For now, however, my focus is on making sure that we have policies and procedures in place that will lead to a better education for minority youth, as well as adult education programs for those that want to better themselves.

"I don't mean to imply that nothing is being done. The government is doing some of this. Unfortunately it is being done in an enabling way, as opposed to providing the tools necessary to help the people involved to help themselves. We need a cohesive plan to do more and work smarter. This initiative will not be accomplished at the exclusion of non-minority citizens. This is an important point.

"Remember empirical data indicate higher drop-out rates among youngsters of African descent. Further, while they represent about 13 percent of Americans, inmates of African ethnicity constitute 60-plus percent of our prison population incarcerated for drug-related crimes.

"What does that tell us? If you look at the data and profiles of individual prisoners, they magnify the inextricable interrelationship between the lack of education; an inefficient, demeaning welfare program; and crime. If, under present policy, the government could fix the problem, you must then ask why it isn't fixed.

"One must remember that the movers and shakers in government at every level are career politicians elected by constituents just like you and me, who expect them to be proactive and to perpetuate those things that are in the best interests of the people.

"What is the probability, J.B., of a career politician vying for re-election of addressing these difficult and racially aligned issues, knowing that representatives from the media and every agency that would be impacted would be in attendance?"

J.B. said nothing as he held up his hand forming a zero with his thumb and forefinger.

"That's my read, also. In my view, most politicians are self-serving egotists, far more interested in self-perpetuation than addressing hard issues that may put them in a negative light. When enough of our citizens realize this, we can start electing hard-charging patriots that really give a damn, not only about the welfare of our people, but also about the welfare of our country.

"Until then, we will continue wallowing in the fat of fiscal irresponsibility and ineptitude, accomplishing very little. Ladies and gentlemen, that's not going to happen on my watch.

"I heard an interesting description of a politician the other day, and it seems to hold true more often then not: A politician is like a banana. They start off green and have a relatively short period of good before they spoil, turn rotten and have to be thrown out.'

19

While Mike was wrestling with the issue of unchecked crime at the town hall meeting, his father, under the guise of the ARC, was involved in a more direct and effective approach to crime fighting…one that could not be shared with his son.

Fourteen hundred miles to the southwest in the border town of San Luis, Arizona, an army aviator flying an OV-1 Mohawk, a twin-engine turbo-prop with Side Looking Aerial Radar (SLAR) on a border surveillance mission had just reported a building explosion to Yuma Air Traffic Control.

"Roger, control, it looks like it *was* a metal building of some type. I'm going to make a low pass. Stand by." A few moments later, "Control, this is Army 6549. I can see four bodies or what is left of them, and the building is burning. It is totally destroyed."

"Roger, 49. Yuma fire and rescue has been notified."

"By the looks of things down there, I don't think there's a need to hurry. What the… Control, be advised at least three sub-surface explosions just went off, two south of the border and one about 400 yards south of the building."

The four ARC operatives in the green Suburban driving north on US-95 saw the twin-engine aircraft as it screamed in low over San Luis. Their work, however, was done. It would take several more days before local authorities, the DEA and U.S. Border Patrol personnel understood the full scope of what had happened.

In the interim, eight more bodies in the tunnel leading to the storage building would be dead from high explosives or suffocation. Either way, dead is dead!

An estimated four tons of cocaine were obliterated by the blasts and another drug-smuggling tunnel and storage facility destroyed. The men in the green Suburban knew this was just a small skirmish—a victory nonetheless—in a major war to keep drugs out of the United States.

They also knew there were at least twelve bad guys spread across or under the desert that they would no longer have to contend with. That would put a dent in the psyche of other smugglers and perhaps give cause for them to rethink their career choice; not likely, but perhaps.

20

After the break, Mike picked up where he left off. "It seems to me, if we truly understand the problems facing us, we should be able to fix the majority of them. Take crime, for instance. Habitual criminals know, if caught, they will be placed in an air-conditioned cell with a television; access to a telephone; three squares a day; and physical fitness equipment to make them stronger, more dangerous criminals when they get out. What's the deterrent? That's ten times better than they have it on the street in most cases. That's pure nonsense!

"My plan calls for something a bit different and one hell of a lot more cost effective, freeing up large sums of money for education and welfare reform programs. It costs somewhere in the neighborhood of $40,000 a year to keep an inmate confined under the present system of luxury. It is no wonder they have multiple offenses; and lenient judges continue to release these morons time and time again, due to overcrowding, ineptitude and administrative error.

"Let me give you an example of just how inept our criminal justice system really is. Judges, as often as not, set bail for hardened felons without knowing anything about their previous records. They say they're too busy and don't have time to check!

"I say they're inept, irresponsible and should be fired! The criminals, who were so haphazardly released, re-offend the moment they hit the street.

"We're not talking about stealing candy from the local grocery, folks. These douche bags are out there *again* molesting our children, robbing, raping, killing and committing all manner of heinous crimes.

"Over the past ten years in Oklahoma alone, 5,000 of these dangerous thugs have simply disappeared after posting ludicrously low bail bonds. It is estimated they will commit tens of thousands of crimes before they are recaptured. One thousand of these criminals are known to have committed capital crimes.

"It is unconscionable that judges, who make such poor decisions, not only remain on the bench, but also do so with total impunity. I believe they should be held accountable for their actions.

"I assure you, if there was a possibility their black-robed little butts could wind up in prison for cases of flagrant neglect, you can bet your firstborn they would find time to check criminal records before allowing dirt bags to skate out of the grasp of law enforcement.

"Interestingly the only people on Earth that like the 'revolving door' syndrome are bail bondsmen and defense lawyers. That's how they make their living.

"The O'Reilly plan is different on several levels. First and foremost, not many violators and no previously convicted felons would have the opportunity to post bail. It makes no sense to release a criminal when you have him in your hot little hands. It's one less bad guy our police officers have to contend with. Keep their sorry asses locked up! That's so obvious to me; I can't believe it's not the standard.

"Perhaps the most troublesome aspect of the plan to those of liberal persuasion is that most prisoners would be housed in tents surrounded by concertina and razor wire.

"A general purpose (GP) tent, used by the armed forces, is rectangular and houses about thirty people. It would be equipped with army-style cots, air mattresses and mosquito nets, as needed.

"If it gets hot, and Oklahoma does get hot, the sides can be rolled up to capture whatever breeze passes through. If there's no breeze, that's too damn bad...don't come back, assuming you ever get out.

"Adjacent to the compound will be a garden plot also surrounded by razor wire, where inmates will raise vegetables for their own consumption during the growing seasons. Port-a-Potties will be provided by local services contracted by the Department of Corrections.

"Inmates will be used as day laborers for many local and state government agencies. A nominal surcharge will be collected from these agencies for every hour of inmate work. This revenue will be used to offset the cost of operations.

"Prisoners will be fed three meals daily, consisting of Meals Ready to Eat, better known as MREs. These are highly nutritional rations used by the military. Inmates incarcerated during Christmas and Thanksgiving will receive hot turkey dinners.

Mike took a moment to take a drink and to get a sense of how the audience was reacting. Some were huddled, talking animatedly; others stared back at him in disbelief; but the majority were nodding in approval, smiling or firing up their cell phones to give early warning for blistering hot headlines. So far, so good!

After getting a positive nod from his campaign manager, Mike continued. "Each facility will have a full-time nurse or practitioner and a doctor on call to handle situations referred by the medical staff. There will be no weightlifting or physical fitness equipment, no television, no radios or personal belongings, other than perhaps a picture of loved ones. Music may be piped in via loudspeakers at the discretion of the camp commander.

"A nondenominational chaplain will be available for Sunday services, the only day that inmates will not be required to work. Prisoners will wash clothes, get haircuts, take showers, write letters and conduct other personal maintenance on this day.

"Personal hygiene inspections will be conducted military-style each morning prior to work detail. Failure to pass the inspection will result in a day of hard labor to be administered the following Sunday, meaning there will be no day of rest that week.

"Punishment for infractions will consist of breaking great big rocks into tiny little ones. These rocks will be used primarily on the shoulders of unimproved roads leading to incarceration sites.

"The plan goes into great detail on these issues and has been reviewed by several law firms and seems to pass the litmus test with regard to harsh and unreasonable treatment of inmates. If the living conditions and provisions for subsistence are good enough for our patriotic young soldiers, then they're plenty good enough for wayward meatheads who break our laws and prey on our citizens.

"The plan will be refined as we move forward, but I'm sure you get the idea. Prisoners will have few rights and even less free time. The plan has provisions for working your way out of jail through good behavior and hard work. Only the very stupid—I'm talking dumb as a stump stupid—will be repeat offenders in the State of Oklahoma.

"I've addressed general population inmates. Incarceration and treatment of hardcore cases is outlined in the packets you will receive on your way out. They don't fare any better but are handled a little differently. As we move forward, you will hear more about the dysfunctional criminal justice system and treatment of those incarcerated. Believe me, there is much to say and even more to be done if we are to salvage this over-burdened institution from the quagmire of ineptitude and indifference.

"Remember this, if nothing else: The criminal justice system is supposed to protect you from hardened criminals; it doesn't! It enables them through early release due to overcrowding; unwarranted paroles; or inept or soft judges approving bail for hardened felons, so they can *again* commit heinous crimes. Not on my watch, they won't!"

21

It was fitting that Mike's father would be discussing the criminal justice system at precisely the same time. Though their ideas on just how to fix the problem were at opposite ends of the judicial spectrum, they were both patriots and had the best interest of law-abiding Americans at heart.

As the Gulfstream IV sliced through the cold air at 500 miles per hour, its beautiful white paint and bright green shamrock glistened in the afternoon sun. Inside the eloquent craft, the CEO of the O'Reilly Corporation slipped into a pair of soft lambskin slippers while cradling a STU-3 encrypted telephone to his ear.

"So we agree that our present strategy is working and favorably impacting the institution which is near and dear to my heart? Good."

Ron Snyder was 2,500 miles away and 30,000 feet below Sean as they discussed the impact the ARC was having on what they believed was a criminal justice system wallowing in its own dysfunctional fat.

Said another way, the justice system was totally screwed up and unable to heal itself. It needed help. The ARC had been covertly providing unsolicited assistance for more than a decade in an effort to eliminate the flow of drugs into the country and to neutralize drug dealers and vicious criminals hell-bent on victimizing innocent citizens.

"We've crunched the numbers," Ron said, "and to move to the next level as planned, we need additional technicians with unique skill sets…perhaps as many as a 130."

Both men knew the success and longevity of their covert initiative to make the streets safer and rid the country of countless bad guys—something the government was unable to do—depended on absolute secrecy. Therefore, even when discussing business on an encrypted secure phone system, the true nature of their business was cloaked in the rhetoric of corporate America.

"Ron, they're already in the pipeline. It's a matter of a few more tests, some administrative details, and completion of background checks on the last twelve or fifteen candidates. If all goes well, they should be on the payroll by this time next month and fully operational in about six weeks."

"It sounds like you're on top of it, sir. Is there anything that needs to be done from my end?" asked Ron.

"Just continue to monitor our friends in Washington for any mood swings or information that would be beneficial to our expansion plans. I'll see you next week and, as I recall, it's your turn to buy."

"I'm sure it is. Do you even carry any cash? I'd be surprised if you had twenty bucks hard cash on you right now. It seems like it's *my* turn to buy every time you come to Chicago. Surely you don't pay for jet fuel out of your pocket, though that would not at all surprise me."

"No, the guys upfront have their own credit cards for fuel, thank you. I just don't have a need for a lot of cash," Sean said.

"I've seen you eat, Tiny; you *do* have a need for a lot of cash. I'm going to sign off now and see if I can float a loan somewhere to cover your dinner. Stay in touch."

It was not unusual for conversations between these two old friends to end in nonsensical bantering, even when the nature of the conversation was deadly serious.

Sean held the phone until he heard the distinct tone that let him know the encryption device was off. He then placed the handset back on the receiver base and, out of curiosity, reached into the pocket of his Armani slacks and pulled out his money clip. What he saw brought an involuntary smile to his face. 'The little, one-legged shit is right, seven bucks! Now that's downright pitiful.'

22

As his father's encrypted conversation concerning covert operations ended, Mike was gearing up to discuss perhaps the most controversial subject in the political kickball arena.

"If you would permit me, I want to quickly give you a snapshot of what I believe is one of the most abused and mismanaged government programs ever conceived: the welfare system. As poorly run and corrupt as it is, I have a plan to fix this insatiable blight that continues to devour the coffers of state and federal governments.

"Those who believe this program, as presently administered and policed, is in the best interest of the United States are either uninformed, hopeless liberals or drunk as a skunk. In my view, it is a national disgrace.

"Don't get me wrong; there is some good derived by truly needy citizens, but far more often than not, it is laden with abuse, corruption, unimaginable amounts of money and other entitlements delved out to ineligible recipients.

"I won't take time here today to outline documented program shortcomings because they are a matter of public record and available through your respective research centers or archives.

"I will, however, give you a feel for *our* plan to overhaul the system, insofar as the State of Oklahoma is concerned, and inform you that the plan when finalized will be submitted to the United States Congress, along with projected cost savings or, in some cases, cost avoidances.

"It is my intent to make this happen whether or not I am your governor. However, it seems to me if I *were* the governor that would be a more suitable position from which to launch these and other initiatives yet to be addressed. The punch line for those napping or daydreaming: I need your support.

"I'll hit the highlights of the proposed Welfare Reform Plan and then open the floor for questions."

Mike stepped from behind the podium as he polished off the last of a lukewarm soda and held his glass up in the direction of a young campaign worker, who quickly brought him another cold drink. He held it out in front of him as if he were savoring the moment, "This is the elixir of the gods!

"It's funny how the strangest things find their way to the forefront of memory at the most curious times. I was just thinking that in my former life as an infantry lieutenant on assignment deep in the hot, steaming jungles of an unnamed country, how I would have willingly paid a hundred dollars for a bottle of pop, had there been one available. Now, here I am with this young, bright future leader replenishing my glass as fast as I can drink it at no cost. It is at no cost, right, J.B.?"

The subtlety of Mike's humor was not lost on the audience. "Interestingly I have not used the term 'pop' since I attended law school in the Northeast and the fine citizens up there looked at me like I had two heads when I tried to order one. He quipped in an exaggerated New York accent, 'Yuz musta come from south of tirty-tird and tird stweet...'" Mike was unable to finish his comments.

The audience, for the most part diehard southerners, dissolved into laughter, since poking fun at their Yankee brethren was tantamount to a national pastime.

After the crowd quieted down a bit, Mike continued, "I learned quickly that colloquialisms play a significant role in defining the boundaries of North and South. In fact, we Oklahomans are a bit confused on the *pop* vs. *soda* issue ourselves. Most of us migrating from the Deep South or Texas refer to soft drinks as pop. Those of us who ventured down from Kansas and Missouri, both considered Northern states at one time, and those returning from California after the Dust Bowl days, seem to lean toward the soda side of things.

"All said and done, I guess you might say we're an amalgamated people living in what used to be known as 'no man's land.' This small piece of nonsensical trivia is provided free of charge and no way endorses soft drink manufacturers."

Mike took a moment to set his glass down, collect his thoughts and transition back to a more serious subject.

"I believe the place to start welfare program reform is in the name. The word *welfare* is in and of itself demeaning. It strikes me a more suitable name might be something like Government Assistance & Recovery Program or perhaps Humanitarian Assistance Program. Assistance and recovery suggests a temporary state, something out of one's control. Perhaps from loss of a job or for medical reasons, and those involved need temporary assistance moving toward normalization of their lives.

"The United States provides billions of dollars annually to support international humanitarian initiatives. The majority of these funds—at least the part that can be accounted for—provide shelter, clothing, subsistence and medical care for indigent people around the world. This is a good thing as long as it is done in an efficient, controlled manner, which is not always the case. Accountability and supervision have never been our government's strong suits.

"I'm focused on devising meaningful ways to help the needy in Oklahoma to recover and get back on track toward better lives. It has always struck me that we should take care of our own first, so we are better positioned to help others.

"We lose credibility when we start throwing vast amounts of money and resources to help people around the world, when the *world* constantly observes through the media that we have serious humanitarian problems right here at home. Let's first get our house in order.

"Let me say upfront, I'm all for helping those truly in need and unable to help themselves for whatever reason. I would never do anything to make their lives worse.

"However, I don't want one thin dime of my tax dollars used to support healthy individuals who happen to be shiftless, lazy, scheming opportunists. Those who routinely take advantage of the welfare system whenever and however they can. I feel pretty confident each of you feels the same way."

The audience showed how much they were in agreement with the candidate's views by giving him a standing ovation—continuous applause for the better part of a minute—during which he looked over at J.B., who nodded approval.

"You know, during the late '20s and carrying into the mid-'30s, this country had major economic and humanitarian problems. They started well before the October 1929 stock market crash, though that is the infamous date associated with the Great Depression. Millions of Americans were out of work, money and hope.

"People lost their homes to foreclosure, literally putting hundreds of thousands on the street. Soup kitchens kept destitute people from starving to death, and once proud financiers, businessmen, dishwashers and janitors stood in line for hours just to get something to eat.

"As humiliating as that must have been, moms and dads were willing to do it so their children would have a little food that day. Closer to home and to ensure all Americans had the opportunity to suffer equally, the weather gods conjured up a major drought lasting for years that settled over the grain, agricultural and cattle-producing states.

"One of the hardest hit was right here: Oklahoma. The Dust Bowl years served as the genesis for the cliché, Okies. Though it is not likely any of us plan to head west in a jalopy with a mattress tied to the top, we are Okies nonetheless and proud of it."

Many in the audience smiled and nodded their heads in approval, having either experienced tough times or heard similar accounts from parents or grandparents.

"What does this have to do with anything? Actually, quite a bit when you think about it. We are still saddled with major humanitarian issues. Nothing approaching the Great Depression, thank God, but moms and dads still suffer a degree of humiliation to see their children are clothed and fed. It would be naïve to think anyone would enjoy presenting food stamps at a checkout counter.

"We can learn from the past. We don't have to continually reinvent the wheel, generation after generation. President Franklin Delano Roosevelt confronted the problem of unemployment, bank closures and despair head on with a program called the New Deal.

"It was far from perfect, and they made a lot of it up as they went along. Many aspects of it were pushed through by perseverance, bluster and the personality of the man. It was never intended to provide a paycheck for deadbeats or to pick up the tab for the subsistence of illegitimate children born to lazy, promiscuous women. It was envisioned as a tool to jump-start the U.S. economy; to get Americans working again; and to restore hope and pride in one's self. It worked!

"It was designed to quickly put millions of unemployed Americans back to work on projects such as the Tennessee Valley Authority, the WPA and other programs that gave people hope.

"The plan I am proposing is multi-faceted and strikes right at the heart of the problem: removing those that are ineligible to receive welfare benefits, as well as able-bodied recipients. If there are mitigating circumstances, they will be addressed on a case-by-case basis. The number of people who fall into this category, and the amount of money that will remain in the state coffers by removing them, is staggering."

"The flip side of removing healthy adults from the program is creating employment opportunities for them that benefit both the individual and the state, with a focus on work that improves state infrastructure.

"The day of healthy welfare recipients saying they can't find work will quickly disappear. Once enacted, people will either take the initiative to find jobs of their choosing or be assigned work under Oklahoma's 'New Deal.'

"All work is honorable and being involved in things that benefit Oklahoma, and therefore Oklahomans are bound to instill a sense of pride in those that participate. This sense of pride, over time, will permeate whole neighborhoods, be uplifting and make life better for everyone.

"Let me back up a moment to make a point clear. The cost savings or cost avoidance of this action will not be a dollar-for-dollar exchange. There is some amount of sunk and continuing cost in establishing employment opportunity programs. However, paychecks from these new jobs will flow back into our economy, stimulating new job opportunities and an increased tax base that is necessary to feed the beast that keeps everything moving forward.

"The important point here is that people who have seen welfare as a way of life are now gainfully employed, pay taxes, have more self-esteem and are making significant contributions to society. That, folks, is a classic win–win scenario.

"In parallel with this initiative, we focus on blatant abuse of the food stamp program, imposing stiff penalties to include jail time or facility closure for retailers that continue to accept food stamps for anything other than basic subsistence. No more booze, girly magazines, drugs and countless things they are traded for today. No more!

"Older recipients not yet eligible for Social Security and unable to work will remain on the rolls until a determination can be made with regard to why they *can't* work. Obviously a medical problem constitutes a good reason. You will find more on this issue in the information packet.

"This is the connection as I see it. Education and hope are the keys to reducing minority focus on crime as a way out of poverty. Education provides opportunity. Opportunity instills hope and a more positive slant on the game of life.

"The proposed plans, properly executed, will help all of our citizens help themselves. The byproduct: far fewer drug-related crimes perpetrated against fellow Oklahomans. This is the right thing to do, ladies and gentlemen, and I'm prepared to do it."

Mike looked over at his campaign manager and smiled. "Have I said enough?"

J.B. repositioned himself on the hard stage chair. "It sure feels like you have, sir."

Mike chuckled at his friend's dry humor as he turned back toward the audience that was also smiling.

"Up to this point, I've done all of the talking. I think it's only fair you have an opportunity to take a shot or two."

The first hand to go up belonged to Veronica Witherspoon, KVOO TV news anchor. "Mr. O'Reilly, your discussion today has been uplifting, but it seems there are a few major obstructions that need to be removed or perhaps a better word might be overcome, before these plans could be implemented. What are your thoughts on this?"

As the petite news anchor finished her question and started to sit down, she cocked her head slightly and pursed her lips as if she were blowing a kiss.

As Mike stepped from behind the podium and moved forward to the edge of the stage, he smiled down at her showing perfect white teeth, the capstone of his gregarious personality.

"Oh, there are a number of hurdles that we have to clear, no question about that. But my first challenge will be how to get you to address me as Mr. O'Reilly after we're married next month."

Many in the audience did not know they were engaged and turned to look at Veronica who was by this time blushing and more than a little embarrassed at all the attention.

The only response she could spontaneously muster was, "Fat chance, Buster!" Everyone in the auditorium laughed, and all of the media representatives in attendance realized they had just been handed a great scoop and several more good headlines.

Mike grinned. "It's good to come to an understanding early. I think we can now put this issue to bed." He realized the instant he used the word *bed* that he had made a mistake and tried to no avail to quickly recover. "Scratch that last sentence." He felt pretty confident that, given the fevered pitch of note taking and snickers throughout the auditorium, he would be seeing those poorly chosen words again real soon!

"I'm assuming, Ms. Witherspoon, you're referring to the state legislature and attempted intervention by the ACLU and other agencies that feel their authority challenged.

"With regard to the legislature, Oklahomans placed them in office to accomplish good works, to do those things that are in the best interest of the state and the people. What I have proposed is in concert with their duties and responsibilities. Further, I know most of the fine men and women making up the Oklahoma Legislature and some of them played a significant role in the formulation of my proposed plans. A few details remain to be hammered out, but by and large, we're all in concert and ready to hit the ground running, given the opportunity.

"Aside from the ACLU being the ACLU, I see nothing in the proposed plans they could challenge with any degree of success. Having said that, I would submit that they will try to put a self-serving spin on about any issue presented.

"I am not now, nor have I ever been, an advocate of the ACLU. In my view, it is a socialist-dominated organization, far more interested in stirring up discontent and social unrest in the United States than in protecting the civil rights of Americans. I believe they have done far more harm than good to America and her citizens. They have had a modicum of success in eliminating or changing America's traditions. That in itself should be viewed as an un-American activity.

"I fail to see how children reciting the Pledge of Allegiance in a classroom; a nativity scene being displayed in front of a church; or publicly displaying the Ten Commandments violates the rights of our citizens.

"Most of the ACLU's leverage within communities is the threat of expensive ongoing lawsuits that they know the community or individuals within the community can ill afford, and so their challenge goes unanswered and they get their way. I will have no part of that.

"As governor, I will challenge any and all ACLU-initiated actions I feel are not in the best interest of the people or the State of Oklahoma. If they challenge something that truly is a violation of civil rights, I would applaud the initiative and work with the state attorney general to correct the injustice. But they'd better be damn sure there's meat on *that* bone before they pursue it."

Mike pointed to a reporter sitting on the front row. "Ron Blanchard, sir, Fox News Network. One could not help notice your proposed initiatives have national as well as state implications. Was that your intent?"

Mike thought for a moment and then responded, "There are specific points mentioned today that really can be addressed only by Congress or the U.S. Attorney General's office.

"For example, revamping of the Miranda Act; I can put forward recommendations for change, but I can't revise federal enactments. Congress has to do that, though the Supreme Court seems to think not even Congress has the authority to change Miranda.

"Unless there has been a significant change in the way we do things in this country and I missed it, only Congress can make laws. Judges, even those on the Supreme Court, are there to ensure the laws of the land are not violated and are properly interpreted. They don't *make* laws!

"In any event, there is much we can do at the state level to enhance law enforcement initiatives. We can ensure our officers are well trained and properly equipped to do their job. We can enforce stricter sentencing guidelines for criminals and rid ourselves of inept judges; things of that nature. Next question, please."

A little skinny weasel of a man in a wrinkled, cheap sport coat stood up in the middle of the pack. "Brewster Ames, Tulsa World. Mr. O'Reilly, I have two questions…"

Mike held up his hand, palm extended toward the man, and said, "Mr. Brewster, I have only one answer, so let's spread the questions throughout the audience. I will come back to whatever your second question is later."

The little grease ball seemed a bit rattled but continued, "Earlier you mentioned that you wanted to raise the standard for Oklahoma teachers. Are you saying that our teachers are not qualified?"

Mike took a deep breath and slowly exhaled. "How would you know if they are qualified or not if there is no procedure in place to measure proficiency in their chosen field? A college degree is not a testimonial to one's intellect. We would like for it to be, but it isn't. By and large, we have very good teachers but we also have some that would make a doorknob look like Einstein in comparison.

"We need to rid the system of the under qualified. I'm speaking of teachers who are unable to effectively perform the duties they were hired to do. Why should our highly qualified, professional teachers be subjected on a daily basis to under-achieving peers as they muddle through the day teaching our children nothing? Can you imagine how frustrating that would be?

"The only people that would fight the issue of measuring teacher skills, aside from the teachers' union, would be the under qualified who are trying to ride the wave to retirement so they can collect a good pension for a job poorly done. That makes no sense.

"The O'Reilly Corporation is heavily involved in the petroleum industry, and we have a gaggle of engineers on the payroll. Let me assure you, they are not hired solely on the basis of academic credentials. We measure their knowledge through a series of tests. We can then identify where their talents can best be utilized within the organization or refuse them employment before we spend a lot of money on them. Petroleum engineers don't come cheap, and you want to ensure you have hired the very best.

"Why should we accept anything but the very best educators for our children? Do you get my point? Using the engineer as an example, he didn't come out of the womb as an engineer; he had to be taught. Next question, please."

Mike politely answered questions for the next thirty minutes and then said, "Ladies and gentlemen, I want to thank you for being here today. I would appreciate your support in making those things discussed here today a reality."

Before he could disconnect his lapel mike, a final question came from an unidentified reporter in the back of the auditorium. "You've said nothing about Governor Dodd or whether it is your intent to schedule a televised debate with him. What are your plans in this regard and what do you think of the governor?"

Mike smiled. "I think he's a lousy golfer!" The audience, already standing in preparation to leave, laughed as they collected their things. "Sam is a fine and honest man and I like him a lot, but I think he has neither a big enough stick nor the name recognition needed to see the initiatives outlined here today through to fruition.

"He is nonetheless a dedicated, honest public servant and if I am elected governor, I will seek his counsel on a number of issues. Insofar as a televised debate is concerned, that is not likely to happen. In the military, there is an unspoken code among leaders: 'Criticize and chastise in private, praise in public.'

"Oklahomans are aware of how things are now. If I were not critical of how we are presently handling education, welfare and crime, I would not be gearing up to change them. I don't see how an open debate would be helpful to the governor, me or the people of Oklahoma.

"If our citizens are going to the polls to cast their ballots solely on the basis of honesty and integrity of the candidate, they could do no better than Samuel Dodd. While those traits are absolutely essential, we are at a critical juncture and must look beyond those qualities if we are to have any chance of fixing the problems outlined here today.

"I encourage all Oklahomans to consider the candidates objectively and then cast their respective ballots for the individual they feel is likely to be most successful in bringing about positive change in all state- related issues, but primarily education, welfare reform and crime reduction."

He hesitated for a moment and then added, "General George Patton once said, "Nothing is impossible provided you use audacity."

23

Two years later

Mike and Veronica had been married less than two years and had a beautiful baby girl they named Cheyenne. True to his word, the governor initiated plans to drastically improve the plight of educators and law enforcement. This day he was en route to visit the newest of thirty-two incarceration compounds that had been established since the state legislature voted in the necessary amendments governing the care and treatment of prisoners.

The governor had just returned from Washington, D.C. where he and a battery of lawyers, including his mentor Ron Snyder, had successfully defended Oklahoma's welfare reform initiatives and had briefed prominent U.S. legislators and the U.S. Attorney General on various changes that could be made at the national level.

Prior to returning home, Mike, Ron and good friend Steve Humphrey, the U.S. attorney general, had dinner at Hogates along the Potomac River. Of all the exclusive eateries in the D.C. area, Mike preferred the relaxed atmosphere of this restaurant, and certainly their famous cinnamon buns were not out of the question.

The discussion on this occasion was the remarkable progress that Oklahoma had made over the last couple of years in crime reduction.

Mike looked up as their server was clearing the last remaining plates. "Would anyone like another brandy while we have Sherie here?" There were no takers. "Young lady, if you could bring us coffee, a check and three cinnamon rolls to go, we'll get out of your hair."

After the server left, Steve leaned back in his chair, crossed his legs and said, "You have done well, my friend. I guess my initial assessment of you when we first met at Harvard was wrong."

"Oh, I don't know. I still write with a crayon now and again.

"I owe a great debt to my father and this fine gentlemen sitting here," Mike said, nodding at Ron. "If not for their guidance and tutelage, one can only guess how things may have turned out. As it is, I'm in a position to really affect change, hopefully for the better, and that is exactly what I plan to do."

Steve looked across the table. "I will help in whatever way I can, Mike; just keep in mind that D.C. is a different kind of animal and if there was ever an environment where you needed to protect your flanks, this is it. This town has a way of jumping up and biting you in the butt when you least expect it, so be careful."

Ron nodded in agreement. "That's good advice, Mike."

The coffee arrived and Steve savored a few sips of the hot brew. "I'm very interested in your sentencing criteria. It seems that your judges are imposing shorter sentences but getting much better results insofar as repeat offenders and lowering the overall crime rate is concerned. Tell me a little more about it."

"Stevie, me boy, I invite you to come pay us a visit. Seeing the process first hand is worth the trip. In the interim, let me say we have pretty well established that the length of the sentence is not as important as how you spend the time while incarcerated.

"You are intimately familiar with how our penal system operates at the national level. Taxpayers wind up paying big bucks to keep a dirt bag locked up, and the old school believes longer sentences are better. I don't believe that.

"I maintain, much as the Turks believe, that prison should be so tough that those in confinement will do about anything to avoid going back, even if it means going straight.

"The way we now operate in Oklahoma, our judiciary, with a lot of coaxing, prodding and a smidgen of intimidation from the O'Reilly Corporation but primarily the influence brought to bear by Ron's law firm, now sees the wisdom of shorter sentences coupled with ball-busting prison time.

"The stats speak for themselves, Steve. Once released, the majority of my knuckleheads want no part of a return trip. They may or may not be towing the line, but they are certainly not re-offending in Oklahoma. Since Texas is a ball-busting state as well, you might want to check crime rates in Kansas and Arkansas. See if there has been a migration of sorts.

"Steve, if we had tough policies and a functional criminal justice system at the national level, hardened criminals would have no place to run. Think how that would affect the nation."

The attorney general nodded. "I am thinking about it, along with the hysterical screams of the ACLU, the groaning of the American Bar Association and defense lawyers across the country that depend on the revolving door syndrome to perpetuate their livelihood, which, by the way, is considerably more than just a small cottage industry. If that pond dried up, where would all the bloodsuckers and their enablers go?"

Mike and Ron both knew he made a valid point but wanted to seize the moment to drive home their tough stance on crime philosophy in an effort to gain his support for other legislation that was or soon would be in the pipeline.

"We run a no-frills operation," Mike said. "Work hard and you get three squares a day. Keep your nose clean and you earn credits for early release. Screw up and your shit's in the street."

Steve smiled. "I see you have held onto your eloquent colloquialisms that endeared you so to our beloved Harvard professors."

"You bet your sweet ass I have!"

Ron smiled, leaning forward and shaking his head as if to indicate his protégé was a hopeless case.

Mike grinned. "The system is a work in progress. We started with a solid plan but have found better ways of doing things along the way. You must be flexible and willing to change things quickly.

"For example, we started out using military issue MREs."

"And just what might they be, sir?" the attorney general asked.

"Oh, yes, I remember now, you were raised in the fluffy world of the privileged. MREs are the high-protein packaged rations used by our armed forces. Add water, zip lock, place them in your crotch or some other heat source, and presto…a hot meal."

"No kidding?" Steve said.

"What we have found, however, even when purchased in large quantities, they are pretty expensive. So we have changed the menu. For breakfast, we now serve two small packages of dry cereal, a small carton of milk, a single-serving pack of orange juice and a couple slices of bread. We save about a buck eighty on each serving and give the inmate what he needs nutritionally. Lunch consists of two sandwiches, a package of juice and a piece of fruit, all in a paper sack."

"We have contracted with minority-owned businesses to prepare, package and deliver the lunches to the incarceration sites throughout the state before the inmates leave for work detail. I might add the employees providing this service are part of the new welfare reform, back to work program. It really works, my friend, and you guys at the national level need to take a serious look at something similar. The politicos in Washington need to start thinking outside the box for a change.

"Look at innovative ways to incorporate some of these policies, and to hell with the ACLU and the legions of bloodsuckers, as you so aptly called them. Ron's firm eats these pitiful little piss ants alive. He has done a masterful job of keeping them off my back. I'm sure he would love to work with you in smacking them around if they get in the way of progress."

Steve again smiled at Mike's way with words. "We are looking into it and hopefully we can make some changes during this administration."

Mike nodded approval. "In any event, we still provide an MRE for the evening meal along with inmate-grown vegetables that are in season. Daily cost per inmate is about six bucks, and since the work program levies a surcharge to state agencies using inmate labor, the State Department of Corrections pockets about twenty-two dollars a day per inmate to help defray overhead.

"Everyone benefits. The inmate earns his keep; state agencies can operate at a fraction of the cost it would take to have full-time employees pick up trash along state roadways; and the corrections guys can maintain facilities and staff. What say you, my friend?"

Steve smiled. "As I said earlier, you have done well."

He stood to leave, prompting five burly gentlemen at two nearby tables to also rise. "I'm impressed. I will schedule a trip out there to take a look. Have your staff prepare briefings for a target audience of senior staffers and congressmen. I will bring a few with me; I just haven't decided on the right set of eyes yet. I'll give it some thought and get back to you.

"In the meantime, pick up the check. Attorney generals are on a fixed income and not authorized to entertain guests who have more money than the U.S. Treasury. My sources tell me you both fit comfortably into that category. Besides, you owe me big time for tutoring you through international law.

"Ronald, nice seeing you again, and the rumors you may have heard about our main man here using a number ten crayon are true. He actually showed up for a lecture with a crayon—green, as I recall—and a napkin with a coffee stain on it. True story!"

Ron glanced over at Mike. "And I hired this guy?"

Steve then added, "What really ticked me off was he aced the exam."

Mike laughed as he thought back to the events of that day. "What you say is true, my friend, but taken totally out of context. I was running late, grabbed a cup of coffee that was so damned hot I had to wrap it in a napkin, and the only thing I could find to write with was a crayon I spotted in the gutter when I parked. The point you neglected to mention, however, is that I had been to the library and had just read three or four papers on the lecturer's subject. It was a slam dunk!"

"I share your frustrations, sir," Ron told Steve. "When he was with my firm I found it amazing he could read a legal brief once and remember not only the salient points, but recall them verbatim. It is a gift. Much to my chagrin, however, he still has a lot of his dad's traits. Have you had the pleasure of meeting the hulk, Steve?"

"I have. I thought at first we were experiencing an eclipse. He stood in the doorway of our dorm room and totally blocked out the hall light. Without question, Sean is the largest, most intimidating man I've ever met. He is a scary guy; his hands look like scarred hams. Once you get past the initial impression, however, he is also one of the nicest gentlemen I've ever met."

Ron smiled at Steve's accurate assessment of his longtime friend. "Don't ever go to dinner with him and get stuck with the tab; it is far more frightening than his gaze."

"Okay, gentlemen, you've had enough fun at the expense of the O'Reillys. Any more and I'll have me boys here do a tap dance on your slick little heads."

Mike always enjoyed a dig or two directed at Ron's bald head and Steve's rapidly receding hairline. After all, *they* started it.

A grin came over Mike's face as he picked up his sack of cinnamon buns. Gazing at the large aquarium in the foyer of the restaurant he mused, 'I wonder what the people of this great nation would think if they knew issues that could change our society were hammered out over dinner and cinnamon buns.'

24

The governor's black Lincoln pulled up to the newly established incarceration site west of Mustang, Oklahoma just as the inmate force was returning from work detail. Directly behind the Lincoln was a black Suburban carrying five more heavily armed security personnel. They worked directly for Mike and had nothing to do with Oklahoma, other than ensuring no harm came to its very capable governor.

As the men exited the two vehicles, they were met by the director, Department of Corrections. Mike shook the man's hand as they walked toward the manufactured structure that served as the facility's administration office and dispensary. Inside the air-conditioned building, they received the standard briefing before exiting for a first-hand look at the incarceration site.

As they walked around the perimeter of the concertina wire, Mike turned to his security detail, "I'll bet all this wire and tents bring back memories of your former lives, don't they?"

They all smiled, except for the ex-Navy Seal, who *never* smiled. "Yes, sir, they certainly do." One of the men commented on the peculiar smell of the weather-proofing materials used on the tents, "That's a smell not soon forgotten. It does bring back a few memories."

"You think about it; it really wasn't a bad life. I kind of miss it on occasion."

"And just what *occasion* might that be, sir?" asked the burly ex-Navy Seal.

"On those occasions when I have completely lost my mind," he replied.

They all chuckled, each conjuring up private thoughts of the life all had experienced in the not too distant past.

"Since we're here, let's go in and have dinner with these guys." The governor looked at his escort, "Do you think you could scrounge up some MREs for us?"

The director looked more than a little nervous, "Governor, I don't think that's a good idea at all. Some of these guys are really bad hombres."

Mike thought about it for a moment. "I'm willing to gamble that *my* hombres will make *these* hombres look like Boy Scouts in comparison."

The director, still concerned, made a final plea for reconsideration without success before he headed back in the direction of the administration building to direct his staff to provide additional meals and to get his guards in riot gear, just in case.

The head of Mike's security detail had accompanied the director and along the way had asked him to point out the inmates he was most concerned about and why.

The director pointed out two or three that he thought might be problems. "I've got my guys in full riot gear just in case things go south."

"That's fine, sir, but keep them out of sight. We don't want to stir the pot unnecessarily."

By now, the inmates were eating their evening meal. A moment later, most of them looked up when they heard the chains on the gate rattle. What they saw made them stare with that 'deer in the headlights' look. Entering the compound was the governor and his entourage, carrying the same meals they were eating or about to eat.

"You gents mind if we use your hot water to heat these things up?"

Hearing no objection—not that it would make a bit of difference to him if they did object—one of the bodyguards dumped the MREs in the pot while the others strategically positioned themselves around their charge, paying particular attention to the inmates identified as the most likely to cause trouble.

"Since I'm the guy that initiated the idea of incarceration sites, I thought I'd come out and see first hand how things are going and share a meal with you."

A number of inmates looked at each other with disgusted expressions and several got up and moved to the other end of the tent, but the majority seemed to welcome a break in the monotony of confinement.

As the governor sat down, he loosened his tie and rolled up his shirt sleeves as one of his men tossed him an MRE saying, "Watch it, sir; it's hot as hell."

"You're supposed to tell me that before you throw it, numb nuts."

The prisoners seemed to get a kick out of the exchange and visibly loosened up.

"Even the inmates have plastic spoons, guys. Do you think you could muster some sort of eating utensil for me?" One of his men handed him a plastic spoon rolled up in a napkin as he was speaking.

Mike looked at the inmates in mock disgust. "It doesn't matter who you are, gentlemen. You can't get good help these days."

As all the men in the compound ate, there was an open exchange of information, giving Mike the kind of feedback needed to measure the effectiveness of the program and to make changes, if needed.

"Speaking of good help, part of this program is to ensure each of you has an opportunity for gainful employment when you have served your time here.

"For those of you that have long rap sheets and have made rotating through the prison system a way of life, *those* days are over. You may have noticed your sentence this time was shorter than at any time in the past."

Several heads nodded and one of the younger inmates said, "Boss, this is a first class shit hole and I can't wait to get the hell outta here."

"Precisely! Incarceration centers are not here to rehabilitate you. They're here to punish those that have made bad choices and…"

One of the inmates, who had moved to the far end of the tent, interrupted him as he charged down the center of the large tent directly at the governor. Mike calmly fixed his gaze on the angry man, as other inmates scattered to get out of the way.

"This is a prime example," Mike said in a calm, steady voice "of what my security guys would call...a really dumb-ass decision."

Before the brawny prisoner realized what was happening, the ex-Navy Seal closest to the governor stepped to one side, spun and hit the attacker dead in the face with a maneuver known in the martial arts as 'spinning back fist.'

The force of the blow, coupled with the man's forward momentum, lifted the angry inmate off his feet, causing him to land squarely on his back...motionless. Unlike the fatal use of the knife-like side of the hand to the larynx, this expertly placed blow to the nose with a closed fist was meant to incapacitate and render an assailant unconscious. It did!

As one of the ex-Special Forces troopers knelt to check the status of the motionless inmate, Mike stood up. "I'll bet this fellow is the tent bully, right?"

A voice from somewhere in the rear of the tent said, "Not no more, he ain't! We can cut his nuts out from this point on, if he's got any left."

"If a plastic spoon is all you have to work with," Mike said as he walked over to discard his trash, "that could turn out to be one hell of a painful castration."

"As I was saying before this gentleman interrupted me, incarceration centers are not here to rehabilitate you. They are here to punish those that have made bad choices and to impress upon you the importance of changing your ways in order to avoid a repeat performance.

"So, young man, your strong desire to be elsewhere suggests the plan is working. I'm pretty confident you won't be back anytime soon."

"You got that right, boss!"

"As I mentioned earlier, part of the governor's crime reduction plan is to provide job opportunities to inmates ready for release. You all have made mistakes in the past and as far as I'm concerned, that's a done deal. I don't think you should be labeled for life as a deadbeat ex-con, unless of course you deserve it.

"I know each of you can turn this thing around and become productive, law-abiding citizens if you choose to. I'll help you by providing job opportunities but you have to suck it up, stay clean and stay out of trouble.

"To me, that's a far better choice than coming back here for more rest and recuperation. Don't you think? Now, I know you can do it, so pull your head out of your butt and do it! No one likes to be cut off from family and friends, and I'm sure you're no exception."

The center director and nurse had entered the compound by then, and the nurse was busy administering smelling salts to the downed inmate. She looked up. "Sir, he has a broken nose for sure and may have a fractured jaw."

The ex-Special Forces trooper who had initially evaluated the unconscious inmate addressed the young nurse. "Miss, his nose is not just broken, it's splattered with bone and cartilage fragments in his sinuses and probably very close to the right eye socket. I'm going to guess, by the blood in his right eye, that he has a displaced retina. He has at least three fractures to the upper jaw and one to the lower. There is considerable damage to teeth and gums, and he probably has a concussion from hitting his head on the packed dirt. Other than that, he's good as new."

The nurse, without looking up again, said, "Let's let the doctor be the judge of what *is* or *is not* broken, OK?"

"It's OK with me, Miss, but you need to keep him awake if possible, put his neck in a stabilization brace and get him prepped for surgery before all the bone fragments floating around in his head migrate into his brain."

Mike felt compelled to enter the discussion at that point. "Young lady, this gentleman is trained to perform emergency surgery in the field and has seen more death and mangled bodies than you will ever see in your lifetime. I highly recommend you listen to him and prep this fellow for medical evacuation right now."

The director touched the nurse's shoulder. "Darby, make the call."

She immediately keyed her portable phone and placed emergency calls to the resident doctor and the nearest fire station requesting immediate air ambulance service.

The fire chief knew that any calls from the incarceration center requesting evacuation by air would require a UH-1 Huey helicopter. Policy required two guards to accompany the inmate on the flight.

The director looked menacingly at the other inmates. "You boys just can't get it right, can you?"

Mike inconspicuously grabbed the man's arm and gently but firmly guided him out of earshot of the others in the compound saying not too gently, "Sir, two things you need to understand before I leave here today. One, a lot of inmates at this facility are of African persuasion, and while the term *boy* is common slang and of no consequence to you and me, it has a very demeaning connotation to them. If you are to provide effective leadership at this facility, you need to rid that word from your vocabulary.

"Secondly, your remark to the inmates was inappropriate. They did absolutely nothing wrong. Excluding poor judgment on the part of the injured man, we engaged in conversation that I found not only interesting, but also helpful in my quest to make the system work better.

"So here is what I want you to do. Let's go back and mingle for a few minutes and then I will leave. You will call the inmates together and tell them you meant nothing derogatory by your comment and will make every effort to refrain from using such language in the future. That will start the fence-mending and gain you respect and credibility and will probably make your job a lot easier.

"You can tell them our conversation here was all about my explaining they had done nothing wrong. Apologize for pre-judging them and thank them for their good conduct and cooperation. OK?"

The director thanked the governor for his comments and assured him he would take care of it the right way this time. They shook hands and returned to the group. Moments later Mike and his staff exited the compound.

25

O'Reilly Estate Airfield

The hangar complex on the estate was impressive by any standard. The long runway was fully lighted and had the latest in all weather instrumentation. There were six medium-sized hangars just west of the runway that housed two Lear jets and four shiny Citations when they were not in use by senior corporate executives. Next to the smaller hangars, and closest to the flight operations building, was a hangar large enough to accommodate a Boeing 707.

In front of the hangar being prepped for an afternoon flight was the queen of the O'Reilly aviation fleet, a beautiful, white G-4 with an Irish green shamrock glistening on its large vertical stabilizer.

Sean loved this airplane. It was a far cry from the beat-up old truck he had driven into Ozark, Alabama so many years ago to discover that his longtime friend Ron, with a few strokes of a pen, had made him a wealthy man.

He had used these resources wisely, building an empire around land, cattle, oil, banking and manufacturing industries. Ever present, however, were the nagging and painful thoughts of the injustice associated with the death of his oldest son Donovan who, for all practical purposes, had been beaten to death by an Alabama high school principal years ago.

There was some peace of mind in knowing he had exacted a full measure of O'Reilly justice, but nothing could bring back his son.

Some thought that entering the sanctity of a man's home and breaking his stinking neck was murder. Sean didn't see it that way at all, particularly since the legal system had no intention of bringing the guilty person to justice.

Though he didn't know exactly where or in what context, he knew the Bible mentioned "an eye for an eye," and that was good enough for him. Quite frankly, he really didn't give a damn in what context it was used.

Sean was a warrior and had a warrior's mentality. If the criminal justice system in the country he had fought two wars for and loved more than life itself could not deal with the explosive trend of criminal activity, he had no choice but to lend a hand…the O'Reilly way.

Years ago, and without his son's knowledge, he had formulated intricate covert plans; recruited operatives with unique skill sets; and initiated an aggressive campaign to help rid the country of those that would perpetrate heinous crimes against innocent citizens.

Sean believed in deeds, not words. To his way of thinking, he was willing to risk everything for the well-being and safety of his country and fellow Americans.

Buried deep in the subconscious of his military mind he found solace in the adage, "It is better that one man be sacrificed, if necessary, for the well-being of the unit.' In this case the unit was the United States of America.

The airfield was located about eight miles south, southeast of the mansion on the flattest piece of terrain on the estate. It was completely surrounded by a high chain-link fence that could be electrified with the flip of a switch. When it was initially erected, the plan was to keep it juiced up all of the time but nature didn't cooperate.

Security personnel were continuously called out to investigate probes to the perimeter only to discover fried jackrabbits, baked coyotes and other common variety crispy critters indigenous to the area. That led to the installation of security cameras and motion sensors, monitored twenty-four hours a day.

Set apart from the airfield complex were the communication and instrumentation towers one would automatically associate with an airfield. However, mingled amongst these towers were state-of-the-art satellite communications with secure downlinks for STU-3 scramblers that enabled a secure encrypted telephone link anywhere in the world.

One thing that was obvious and had been a concern of Sean's since it was pointed out early in the planning stages by his communications and information technology chief was the presence of high-powered electric lines terminating at the airfield. They were capable of carrying far more electricity than would be needed to power the base facilities and might raise suspicions if a believable cover were not found.

His solution: a flight simulation facility at the airfield, as a front, and the purchase of four three-axis flight simulators that he knew required enormous amounts of electrical power to operate. Only one of the simulators was powered up and actually used by his aviation staff to maintain instrument proficiency.

Most of the time, however, the simulators remained idle and provided a perfect cover for the power needed to operate the servers, computers and ancillary electronic equipment hidden in the underground complex at the far end of the runway. It was from this facility that all encrypted directives to ARC field operatives throughout the United States originated.

The complex had taken almost three years to complete under the guise of constructing an underground safe room, emergency living quarters and a bowling alley for the O'Reilly family and staff in the event of a man-made or natural catastrophe. In fact, the complex housed an indoor shooting range; living quarters for operatives flown in for special training; a gymnasium; a stocked galley; and the most sophisticated operations center money could buy.

The fully staffed Ops Center looked very similar to the one at the Special Operations Command (SOCOM) located in Tampa, Florida as well it should, since many of the special operations personnel on the payroll had served there at one time or another.

Large, computer-controlled color monitors lined the walls providing an endless stream of pertinent operational details concerning selected target profiles; relief maps; escape routes; location of safe houses; resource management information; and myriad data needed to ensure operational success.

A number of work stations were dedicated to monitoring FBI field offices, Federal Marshal Service, DEA activities and various law enforcement agencies in a given area of operation. Over a period of several years—and the selective recruiting of individuals from various federal agencies—state and federal law enforcement communication systems had been compromised to the extent Ops Center personnel could monitor most activities that could have a negative impact on covert operations planned by ARC.

Sean had taken literary license with the acronym ARC, because of resemblance in sound to its Biblical connotation. Noah's ark had protected the righteous in order to give the world a new beginning once the Lord had destroyed all of the wicked via the Great Flood.

The goal of ARC was just that: ridding the United States of wicked, dangerous undesirables. That meant anyone not acting in the best interests of the country and her citizenry. Dangerous criminals and their enablers were the primary targets. However, the sphere of influence was greater than that and included individuals or organizations bent on changing American values or the principles established by our Founding Fathers; they too were at risk.

Sean's goal, over time, was to put forth a message that permeated the very fiber of our society. The Bill of Rights gives citizens the right to believe and say whatever they choose. If, however, their words are treasonous or place our soldiers in harm's way, as the media so often does, *beware!*

If you are a criminal engaged in drug-related crimes, which is roughly 90 percent of all crimes committed, or perpetrating heinous crimes and acts of violence upon citizens of the United States, *beware!*

If you are a corrupt judge or shyster lawyer who, in any way, enables convicted felons to go free of punishment, *beware!*

Sean knew in his heart only immediate and direct action could provide a countermeasure to a weak and dysfunctional criminal justice system that was incapable of protecting the people by ridding society of those that would readily do them harm, given the opportunity.

He didn't give a damn about the particulars of how the system got screwed up. Ineffectual, outdated laws; weak judges; overcrowded dockets; plea bargaining heinous crimes; outrageous leniency with regard to bail bonds; inappropriate probation; administrative blunders that mistakenly released hardened felons back on the street; Sean simply didn't give a damn. The system was broken and he was dedicated to getting it back on track. If overcrowded dockets and jails were part of the problem, he sure as hell had a solution to fix that.

Since all of the O'Reilly Corporation enterprises, aside from Alaskan oil consortiums, were privately held, there were no shareholders to answer to. Consequently, access to essentially unlimited discretionary funds made the employment of highly qualified personnel with unique skill sets transparent and indistinguishable from, let's say, petroleum engineers, pipe fitters, software specialists, and so on.

To the world at large, ARC was a humanitarian organization dedicated to helping the downtrodden and impoverished and, on occasion, disaster relief around the world. In fact, that *was* its charter and all public documents established an excellent track record of humanitarian aid, both domestic and foreign.

Embedded in this organization, however, and operating covertly well below the radar of federal agencies, law enforcement and the criminal justice system was a cadre of skilled special operations operatives who were and had been for a number of years systematically eliminating the root cause of drug-related crime across the country. Man!

The justice department unwittingly aided ARC. Due to inter-agency squabbles, jurisdictional protectionism and petty differences in operational protocol, the feds simply couldn't muster enough synergy to get anything done. By and large, their people were dedicated but impeded by misguided directives from weak, self-promoting management and inept bureaucratic process. Sean knew at least for the foreseeable future this worked to his advantage.

ARC consisted of an operations center, regions with geographic orientation and a network of operational pods, working independent of one another within the region. Operatives in a given pod had no idea the organization extended beyond their activities, notwithstanding the regional director who provided target dossiers and special equipment as required. Even then, they figured he was an expendable messenger, certainly not an experienced, highly trained ex-senior military officer.

The defining characteristic of the organization was its ubiquity. Though omnipresent, each region operated separately and apart from the other. In fact, regional personnel were not even aware that the span of control consisted of more than their region. There were no group meetings or training off-sites. No senior management forums or company picnics. Nothing!

Sean and Ron were painfully aware that ARC would fold like a house of cards if the continuum of this organizational strategy were ever compromised. And unfortunately there was no safety net. It was the classic 'sacrifice a few for the benefit of many' scenario. As combat-hardened patriots, they dutifully accepted the risks associated with this all-important cabal.

ARC personnel had no idea where their operations center was located. For all practical purposes, it was a mystical place in cyberspace. On the occasion they were brought in for special training or re-certification of unique skills, they were flown in blindfolded. Since most operatives had received training, at one time or another in their military careers with regard to mentally recording time and directional changes while blindfolded, they were seated facing the rear of the aircraft and a surreptitious route was always flown.

Due to ever-changing business requirements, it was not at all unusual for O'Reilly corporate pilots to request in-flight changes to their original IFR flight plans. It was a perfect cover for clandestine operations.

Insofar as families were concerned, they knew their husbands were gainfully employed doing whatever it was they did best, other than military skill sets, somewhere within one of the many subsidiaries of the O'Reilly Corporation.

They were referred to as 'troubleshooters' by fellow employees, who had no idea how accurate the term was. This gave the operatives a reason to move freely around the country on short notice, as opposed to a nine-to-five desk job.

Operatives were paid well and had plenty of quality time for families, keeping their minds clear and focused for the *humanitarian* work they were hired to perform.

One man with courage makes a majority.
Andrew Jackson

26

Orange County, Florida

Martin McClary, ARC director, eastern region, had just received authorization from the Ops Center to proceed with established humanitarian protocol, an innocuous phrase for 'waste the slimy bastard.'

The unsuspecting target had been arrested at least sixteen times for numerous offenses, including child molestation, drug possession with intent to distribute and aggravated assault on a police officer. He served only four years for these transgressions and had just recently been paroled.

The criminal justice system was obviously overwhelmed. Perhaps broken is a better word and in need of immediate assistance. ARC aimed to please! Based on demonstrated performance over the past decade, they were more than capable of doing what the government and law enforcement was unable to do…efficiently rid society of all manner of bad guys.

According to Ops Center intercepts, the FBI had been called in to apprehend this perfidious reprobate as the prime suspect in the recent abduction, rape and murder of a thirteen-year-old girl. By monitoring FBI field office communications, ARC operatives determined they were just an hour or so ahead of the feds.

McClary, known to insiders as Marty the Merc, a nickname earned early in his career as a CIA asset specializing in explosive devices with mercury switches, relayed the message to the two-man strike team that had been shadowing this sleaze ball since his promotion to the immediate hit list. They repositioned their car from its surveillance spot in the rear of the parking lot to a space next to the target's old van...and waited.

The operative sitting in the passenger seat opened the glove box, removed the eight-inch silencer and secured it to the Ruger MK-III with a quick right-hand twist.

A light evening rain had started falling outside the rundown building that housed one of the lower class topless bars in the area. Of the six lights in the parking lot, only two were working, casting an eerie glow over the area. Atop the building was a huge neon sign proclaiming: We Bare All.

The unsuspecting man exiting the bar, where he had been holed up for the past couple of hours, was not aware his miserable, perverted, one-man crime spree was rapidly coming to an end with every step closer to his van. The to-go box containing whatever maggot-ridden food they served in there was held over his head in a futile attempt to block the rain as he fumbled for his keys. He walked with his shoulders hunched up and head down, as if that would somehow keep him dry. In a few more moments, that would no longer be a concern.

As he stood upright to get into his car, the tinted glass window quietly lowered behind him. The man didn't hear the expertly placed hollow-point bullet that penetrated the base of his skull, instantly ending his worthless life. His heart would try desperately to continue beating, before it realized it was an exercise in futility.

The shooter then opened the car door just enough to see the crumpled body and fired two more rounds into the dead man's temple. Gone was one more multiple offender that would not languish on death row for twenty years, costing taxpayers untold sums of money, while his shyster lawyer filed appeal after appeal, further cluttering the courts.

A quick, cost-effective solution to the criminal justice system's overburdening problems and, though not fully understood at this point by federal agencies, similar events were happening across the nation.

Across the country, ARC operatives had been carrying out professionally orchestrated hits for over a decade; to the degree that law enforcement nationwide was starting to notice a downward trend in all manner of criminal activity, but especially in drug-related crimes.

Sean O'Reilly's ARC was having a positive and profound effect on prison overcrowding and overburdened courtroom dockets across the country. The resultant eradication of dangerous criminals was front page news, and investigative journalists everywhere were scurrying to get an exclusive with the crime fighters responsible...if they could only find them.

Predictably, a number of police chiefs, county sheriffs, and particularly the New York City Police Commissioner—since a large number of criminals had been removed from the streets of New York—stepped forward to let the nation see what real heroes looked like.

That's fine! ARC operatives were not at all interested in publicity. They felt priming the pump, so to speak, might give these public servants an incentive to catch a few bad guys themselves.

The problem wasn't really law enforcement. Rather, an antiquated, dysfunctional criminal justice system, laden with ill-conceived laws that favored criminals, instead of dedicated police officers. That's dumb as dirt and had to change.

Interestingly ARC operations personnel monitoring law enforcement communications across the country had not heard even a whisper in back-channel messages that would suggest anyone was dedicating bodies or resources in an effort to identify those making their respective departments look like all-stars, while saving them lots of money, something they had precious little of.

People were starting to feel good about their communities again, as increasing numbers of hardened criminals committing all manner of heinous crimes were removed from the streets. Citizens were becoming more proactive, providing local police officers with valuable intelligence concerning illegal activities. Citizen involvement helped law enforcement build stronger cases, ultimately making the streets even safer.

Law enforcement across the country, though not complaining, knew they were getting unsolicited help from unknown Good Samaritans.

27

Oklahoma State Capital – Special meeting of the legislature

Governor Mike O'Reilly had just received a standing ovation by state legislators for the progress made in revamping the education system and in restructuring the State Department of Corrections.

He had often commented that getting anything done in government was tantamount to pulling teeth—stress-ridden and painful. This was no exception. As legislators began taking their seats, he nodded in appreciation.

"Ladies and gentlemen, none of our accomplishments would have been possible without the legislature's willingness to come together as a bipartisan body to draft the necessary amendments. And, in a couple of cases, write new law concerning the housing, treatment, and sentencing criteria of convicted criminals.

"Your actions over the last couple of years will stand as a testament to the nation of what can be accomplished if you have courage of conviction, persevere and view every naysayer's 'It can't be done' as one step closer to 'We did it'!

"My staff and I applaud you for a job well done." He then stepped from behind the podium and led the lieutenant governor, state attorney general and other senior members of his staff in applauding the assembly.

"All of the stats indicate our initial assessment was correct. Shorter, harsher jail sentences not only cut down on crime, as the underworld grapevine spreads the word that Oklahoma is not a good place to be in jail, but also decrease the number of repeat offenders. That tells me we must be doing something right.

"I don't have current numbers but Bob—Robert Langstrum was the chief financial officer for the State of Oklahoma—has indicated we have saved a ton of money by closing antiquated brick and mortar incarceration facilities and moving the majority of prisoners into tent cities.

"Some of that money has already been used to purchase new equipment…radar, video cameras, communications, new squad cars, more K-9 units, and the crown jewel to our crime-fighting initiative, over 200 more officers throughout the state and an additional 300 coming out of the academies over the next 18 months. That, folks, is measurable progress, and I've got to tell you, I'm very proud of this legislative body."

The assembly again stood and applauded their dynamic, forward-thinking governor, knowing none of this would have been possible without his energy, initiative and superb leadership.

Mike raised his outstretched arms in an effort to quiet the legislators. It did little good, so he resolved to let them have their moment. In the meantime he uncapped a bottle of water and took a drink.

He was an enigma among men. No question, he was different and only his closest friends knew anything at all about him, other than approved releases for media use.

Although extremely wealthy, he preferred simple things. Sitting next to his bottle of water was an unused crystal glass. When not dressed for business, he preferred old faded blue jeans, cowboy boots and a long-sleeved western-cut shirt.

These little idiosyncrasies drove his wife Veronica nuts, to say nothing about his public relations staff and senior members of his cabinet. When challenged about it, his standard reply was, "Among other things, I'm a rancher, first and foremost, and if you are one, you ought to look the part."

Moments later he was able to continue. "Bob also indicated the state has received several purchase offers on a few of the structures. We are now in the process of architectural evaluation to see if any of the prison facilities could be modified to accommodate state subsidized housing or perhaps quarters for our work release programs etcetera.

"My message to *you*…the plan is working and as we seek new and better ways of doing things, I'm confident our present model will become even more efficient. We have received no less than ten inquiries from various states and a couple from the federal government. Perhaps they will take notice and follow suit. Perhaps!

"Hell, I've even received inquiries from the ACLU. And you know how much I value *their* opinions." Polite laughter rumbled through the assembly. They were painfully aware of the governor's disdain for the far left, ultra-liberal organization he personally felt was borderline socialist and bent on destroying American values, traditions and culture.

"We all owe certain gratitude to the understanding and willingness of our judiciary in supporting Oklahoma's new no-bail amendment and for imposing swift, harsh punishment for crimes committed. That is precisely what the Sixth Amendment of our Constitution prescribes.

"Unfortunately most Americans, at least those that are paying attention, have grown accustomed to long, drawn-out legal proceedings, crafted by slick lawyers and endorsed by weak, liberal-thinking judges, concerned more about image than about taking a no-nonsense stand on crime and punishment. That is slowly changing. We have clearly demonstrated that positive changes can be made by those willing to go the extra mile and persevere.

"I simply refuse to quietly stand by while dangerous elements of our society break our laws, prey upon our citizens and run amuck, unchecked. I won't have it!

"I understand, just as you do, that 'bonding out' is a constitutional right. But I also understand the heinous crimes we experience in America today were seldom witnessed in the day of our forefathers. When they did occur, justice was instantaneous, by gun or rope, negating the need for bond. It is only logical that the bond process be administered judiciously and to the exclusion of dangerous felons.

"I was in China last month soliciting export opportunities for our state's agricultural products. Quite by accident, a mutual friend introduced me to China's philosophy concerning crime and punishment. Though I do not fully endorse their approach, it does have some interesting aspects. They believe in a speedy trial, immediate sentencing, and no appeal process.

"Folks, when I say speedy, I mean the whole process takes one day. My brethren in the ACLU would have a bloody field day with this bunch. Of course they too would be executed the next day and I would *surely* miss them!" This brought muffled chuckles from the assembly.

"Their anti-crime campaign is called 'Strike Hard.' In the four days I was in Beijing, they tried and subsequently executed 927 criminals for myriad crimes, but primarily murder, assaults and drug dealing…an expected manifestation of new-found capitalism.

"That is approximately one third of the number of inmates incarcerated in the U.S. prison system who have been on death row for ten years or more awaiting execution. Consider for a moment that it costs us somewhere around $40,000 a year to keep these guys, and a few gals, locked up. Does that make any sense? I submit to you that it does not!

"I also will go on record as saying I believe every inmate is entitled to one appeal and one only. Not numerous appeals, each of which must navigate through some eight judicial steps, taking years along its course of review.

"The present process is time-consuming; clogs an already overburdened and dysfunctional judiciary; costs the government a fortune; does not meet the litmus test of the United States Bill of Rights; and, in my view, is ludicrous.

"We need to start focusing on ways to change that process. I have a team looking at that whole mess right now, because I don't believe anyone understands it, including those filing and reviewing the appeals.

"I'm a lawyer and I sure as hell don't understand it. I don't know how we got ourselves wrapped around the proverbial axle so tight, but it is time to change the system and start doing things that make sense.

"In my mind, convicted felons are entitled to only their basic needs: subsistence, shelter and medical care when needed. All other rights are forfeited the moment the prison gate smacks them dead in the butt."

Mike knew he wasn't the only one holding high public office who felt this way; though he may well be the only one secure enough to state it for the record.

28

What the governor *didn't* know: covert operations were still ongoing across the country. Part of that ongoing process, and one of the main reasons Oklahoma was experiencing such a high degree of cooperation from the judiciary, was the pruning of ineffective, inept, and in some cases, corrupt judges.

Case in point was a district judge in Ponca City, Oklahoma who had been using heroin for years, undetected, until an ARC strike team inadvertently discovered her nasty little habit while monitoring the activities of a major drug dealer in the area.

Her secret started unraveling late one evening as four men in camouflage, equipped with night vision devices and armed with silenced Steyr AUG carbines, emerged from the trees above a log chalet overlooking Lake Oologah in northeastern Oklahoma.

ARC operatives preferred quarter-moon nights because they provided adequate ambient light for their night vision devices and the cover of darkness to the naked eye. Once the team left their concealed positions, only hand and arm signals were used to orchestrate the strike.

As the team approached the cabin from the rear and were about to deploy into pre-assigned positions for simultaneous entry, they saw headlights of an approaching vehicle through the scattered trees.

Moments later, a Jeep Cherokee pulled to a stop in the gravel parking area on the east side of the chalet. A well-dressed, middle-aged woman emerged from the driver's side door. She was greeted by a man standing on the porch just out of view of the assault team.

Had they been able to see who the man was, they would have readily recognized their target and the takedown outside the cabin would have been easy and far less dangerous.

The woman's arrival changed things. Who was she? Why was she here at this late hour? And what was her relationship to a high level drug dealer? These were questions the team would have to find out before they proceeded with their original mission.

The Jeep was a good place to start. It didn't appear the woman had locked the vehicle when she exited. The team leader motioned for the number two man in the strike team to check it out. He had to be careful. The Jeep was parked at the outer limits of the porch light but still visible if someone were to look out a window. A few minutes later he returned and motioned the team to withdraw to a safe distance.

Once back inside the tree line, he whispered, "Guys, you won't believe what we have here. Remember the intelligence reports suggesting this guy was being tipped off by someone every time the locals obtained warrants to search his home? You may also recall that the last time the district attorney prosecuted this low-life, a district judge dismissed all charges. Remember that? Well, that judge happens to be inside right now."

The four men just looked at each other in disbelief as the team leader collected his thoughts. "She has to be hooked. No woman, least a judge, would be wandering around out here in the middle of nowhere meeting with a known drug dealer.

"It does, however, explain the tip-offs and her motive for protecting her source. What address was on the vehicle registration?"

"Ponca City. I can't recall the street."

"This is too good to pass up, and I don't think we have time to check with Ops. I'll make the judgment call to go in. Any objections?"

The team members nodded approval, as they all prepared to retrace their steps back to the cabin.

Before leaving the cover of the trees, the team leader said, "Change of plan. Same assignments, but I want both targets secured…not wasted. Understood?" Each man in turn nodded affirmative.

"This could prove to be a fortuitous mission. I want you [tapping the number two man in the chest] to disable the judge's ride. Don't even breathe on the douche-bag's Bentley. It has more security alarms than Fort Knox.

"Before we move out, replace the power packs on your night vision devices. We don't need anymore glitches on this run." A moment later he whispered, "Okay, guys, let's do it!"

As the team moved into position, two team members made their way up the exterior stairs leading to the second floor loft and bedrooms, while the team leader approached the porch. He was joined moments later by the number two man who indicated the Jeep Cherokee had been disabled. Since they had not heard boards squeaking earlier when the man went out to greet his guest, they felt pretty confident they could make a stealthy approach, at least as far as the front door.

The plan called for entry from the second floor while the two team members positioned in front provided over-watch in case the target attempted to escape or go for hidden weapons.

From their position on the porch the two operatives made a methodical visual search of the interior. Only the man and woman were inside. Unlike the movies, where the high-rolling drug kingpin is surrounded by fifty armed bodyguards, most mid- and high-level dealers are so paranoid they don't even trust themselves, certainly not cocaine-sniffing bodyguards.

The woman was sitting on a sofa with her legs curled up under her, her head laid back and her blouse removed. The man was sitting sideways on the sofa and had just removed the syringe from the woman's exposed right arm. A piece of rubber surgical tubing was still wrapped tightly around the woman's arm to stem the flow of blood, making the task of hitting a vein easier.

The coffee table was laden with drug paraphernalia, along with two glasses half filled with bourbon and ice. These items did not bother the over-watch team. The 1911A1 .45 caliber semi-automatic pistol resting on the arm of the sofa did!

They noticed that to reach the weapon, the man would have to either lunge for it over the top of the woman or physically get up to get to it. That might give the entry team just enough time to secure the target. If not, the over-watch team was not squeamish about putting a bullet or two in his brain. After all, that *is* what they were sent here to do.

From his location by the front door, the team leader could see the entry team was now inside and one operative had positioned himself by the rail of the loft. The other was making his way down the stairs into the main room, where the drug-dealing puss socket had just injected another dose of slow poison into the woman's welcoming body.

Depending on the actions taken by the man, that injection could well be his last act on Earth. As the drug dealer reached for his glass of bourbon, he admired his handiwork and smiled as he thought of the fun he would now have with his hapless subject.

Unfortunately things don't always work out the way one would like, especially for drug dealing shit-heads unlucky enough to find themselves in the crosshairs of an ARC raid.

As he sat back on the sofa, drink in hand, he was startled by the cold barrel of the carbine that had been painfully jammed against the back of his head.

"Don't move a muscle, asshole, or there won't be enough left of you to send home. Slowly, *very* slowly, raise your arms and interlock your fingers."

The drug dealer started raising his arms as he looked over at the handgun just out of arm's reach.

As if on queue, he heard the cold, emotionless voice behind him say, "Go for it, you stupid son-of-a-bitch. I think you can make it!"

Those few words had a sobering effect on the man who, deep down, knew he would be dead long before he reached the weapon.

As the man slouched on the sofa, with his hands on his head, the operative roughly slapped the drink aside, secured his hands with plastic restraints and shoved him forward so hard his head hit the corner of the coffee table before he tumbled headlong to the floor.

"Ugh, you bastard! Why'd you do that?"

The operative, now standing over the man, snarled, "I guess drug-dealing sleaze balls just piss me off."

As the team member made his way to unlock the front door, the man on the floor struggled to his knees and started crawling toward his weapon.

By then, the second member of the takedown team was already downstairs and slammed the butt of his weapon into the man's neck so hard he temporarily lost consciousness.

As the hapless drug dealer regained his senses, he heard a deep voice, "Damn, Buster, you're a slow learner. Might I suggest you cooperate? Unfortunately for you, the team leader on this little foray is a no-nonsense kinda guy.

"Gentle and loving are not words I've ever heard when people describe him. He won't lightly tap you with the butt of a rifle as I did, if you fail to answer questions. He'll be far more apt to cut your nuts out or blow your friggin' kneecap into the next county. My advice to you is to give him what he wants."

Two team members set about the task of replacing the judge's blouse and walking her around the room in an effort to bring her back to the real world, though she was not likely to be a happy camper when she fully understood what her future held.

The team leader motioned the man to the sofa and as he slumped into a sitting position, his eyes met those of the team leader for the first time. His gaze was met by a set of emotionless, cold eyes that had long since lost any sparkle of compassion or happiness that might have once been there.

Four combat tours to Vietnam, two of them back-to-back with Fifth Special Forces SOG detachments, had taken its toll on this ex-Green Beret.

The horrific nature of his chosen profession had cost him his wife, his two children, and any semblance of love he might have once had for his fellowman. This was a dangerous man, a perfect fit for the kind of missions assigned by ARC.

After staring the man down for a few moments, the team leader stated coldly, "I was sent here to kill you!"

He then walked into the kitchen for a drink of water. As he held the glass in his gloved hand, his eye caught a glimpse of his favorite snack sitting on the counter—Oreo cookies. He poured out the water, opened the refrigerator and replaced the water with cold milk.

As the team leader intentionally delayed his interrogation, while enjoying a quick treat, the drug dealer was on the verge of pissing his pants. It is not uncommon for people to lose control of all bodily functions when they are frightened to death.

After a few minutes the ex-Green Beret returned. Standing directly in front of the man, he raised his right leg and rested his foot on the coffee table while leaning forward with his right elbow resting on his bent knee. This comfortable position took his body weight off an ankle screwed up a lifetime ago during a night parachute jump into Cambodia.

In his left hand, he held a razor-sharp Randal fighting knife with a specially designed eight-inch blade, its sheath securely strapped to his lower left leg. "It's crunch time, asshole. I can carve you into little pieces while you watch or you can answer every question truthfully. Your choice! This isn't my first rodeo, so I know truth from fiction.

"If I cut a slab of meat off your arm, you can assume I didn't like the answer. This is a deadly serious session, dick head, and unless you want to wind up filleted on the coffee table, I encourage you to not test my will.

"I want your black book. Where is it?"

The man was shaking so hard he could hardly speak but managed to mumble its hiding place in the loft.

The team leader nodded to one of the operatives who proceeded up the stairs to recover the book that hopefully listed all clients, lower level pushers, and perhaps even the name of Mr. Big...not likely, but perhaps.

"We'll just wait a moment before we continue...to see how accurate your answer is."

"There's nothing up here, boss."

Hearing these bone-chilling words, the drug dealer exploded with rage, "Don't give me that shit, you stupid prick! It's there, right where I said it was. Look again! The center shoe box under the rubber insoles."

The man in the loft chuckled, saying, "Oh, yeah, I looked in the wrong box. Sorry about that."

The drug dealer collapsed on the sofa, his face white, large beads of sweat forming on his forehead. For the first time in his miserable life, he was terrified!

The operative handed the book to the team leader who sheathed his knife and started paging through what appeared to be a treasure trove of names; telephone numbers; addresses of clients, distributors, lawyers and a judge or two, including his house guest.

"You're off to a good start. The next question is tougher, and I don't want to hear how you'll be killed if you tell me. I'm here now, dip shit, and I will surely kill you if you don't, understand?"

The man nodded his head and weakly said, "Yeah."

"Who do you work for and what is the name of Mr. Big?"

"What's this Mr. Big crap?" He had unfortunately just made his first painful mistake.

As the team leader reached for his knife, the subject was in the process of retracting his wise-ass comment when the blade sliced through the muscle of his forearm literally filleting a two-inch chunk of flesh and muscle.

The drug kingpin screamed and writhed in pain as he looked at the gaping wound, bleeding profusely all over his trousers. The blood drained from his face as he entered the first stage of shock, having just witnessed a significant piece of flesh carved from his body and unceremoniously thrown on the table.

"You're not too bright, are you? I told you not to test my will. Get this creep a cold rag and a shot of bourbon…we'll try again in a minute."

"Boss, you want me to stop the bleeding?"

The team leader looked over at the operative, who also served as team medic, and with a smirk said, "I personally don't give a shit, but if you feel strongly about it, go ahead."

As the strike team member moved forward to stop the bleeding, the drug dealer passed out.

"This guy doesn't have much staying power. It's not like I cut his damn arm off. Bring him back so we can get on with it. I want to be well down the road before daylight. How's the judge doing?"

One of the operatives supporting her as they walked around the room said, "She's coming around. A few more minutes and some smelling salts, and she should be good to go. He must've given her a pretty stout dose of that crap to put her in the twilight zone like this."

"Do I need to repeat the questions?" The subject, who had been revived and was holding a cold rag to his neck, weakly shook his head indicating he understood the question. "Good. Let's have it."

The man looked up at the team leader and weakly surrendered the name of the person who supplied him with large quantities of cocaine for distribution in Oklahoma and surrounding states. He also gave up the location of distribution sites; warehouses; money laundering facilities, and carriers. He didn't know the name of the Mexican at the top…only that the drugs were transported by truck from South Texas.

"Now I need to know where you keep the money that goes to your supplier and when it gets picked up?"

The drug dealer reluctantly gave up the information, knowing it was tantamount to a death sentence. It was academic. His sentence had been determined weeks before the ARC strike team showed up on his doorstep.

The storm cellar was located about a hundred feet west of the main entrance between the house and the boat dock. The door, which lay flat to the ground, was covered with pine straw in a haphazard effort to conceal it from prying eyes. Once the two operatives had checked it for booby-traps and tripwires, they pulled the door open and with flashlights, descended the cobweb-ridden stairs into the musty cellar below.

At first glance, all they saw was a crate of apples and some emergency staples on one of the shelves. As they stood in the center of the ten-by-twelve-foot room munching apples, while their eyes adjusted to the darkness, they noticed one of the shelf racks had recently been pulled forward, leaving marks on the dusty floor.

They tossed aside their apple cores and took a closer look. Sure enough, when the shelving was pulled forward, there was an access door. Cautiously, and with weapons drawn, one of the team members slid the secret panel open just wide enough to search the interior of the hiding space with the beam of his flashlight.

"Mack, you aren't going to believe this."

The second team member stuck his head around the corner to see what his partner was talking about. Stacked inside was more money than either had seen in their lifetime, and they had been involved in some pretty big busts over the last decade or so.

Inside the enclosure were apple crates filled with cellophane-wrapped packets of United States currency of every denomination. There were three duffel bags, as well as several large industrial-grade plastic bags, full of money. It must have just been delivered for counting, packaging and subsequent shipment to either a banking institution offshore or a cartel south of the border. It was clearly destined to go somewhere, and if the strike team's luck held, they could walk away with an opportunity to inflict significant damage to this operation.

"You'd best get the boss. This is no mid-level dealer we have here. This asshole is at the top of the food chain or damn close to it. After you notify the boss, bring the Hummer down so we can load this stuff."

The ARC team leader climbed the cellar steps just as their vehicle pulled up. "Load it up, guys, while I go back in and have a little chat with Junior. This stash will go a long way toward helping those in need.

"That's what I like about tapping these dirt bags…it gives us a chance to clean up the streets; get rid of dope and play Robin Hood…stealing from the illegally rich and giving to the poor.

"Get us ready to roll while I wrap up inside with the judge. Oh, while I'm thinking about it, be sure and bring that electronic money counter with you. Those things are expensive as hell and that one is top of the line, OK?"

As the team leader made his way back to the cabin, he stopped long enough to pop a stick of gum into his mouth and admire the natural beauty of the setting. In the semi-darkness he could see an outline of the waves lapping against the boat dock below and a few lights in the distance across the lake. There was the fresh smell of pine trees in the air, and the wind had picked up just enough to rustle the leaves of nearby scrub oaks.

It was hard to believe such a serene place could have been used to hide the terrible consequences and misery associated with the sale and use of the drugs that the confiscated money represented. How many lives had it ruined? How many deaths had it caused?

The strike team leader was agitated as he thought, 'It ends here, tonight. Right now!'

When the ex-Green Beret was satisfied he had gleaned all useful information from the high-rolling drug dealer, he turned his attention to the judge. "You're in a lot of trouble, Miss, and I'm not just referring to your addiction to drugs."

The judge looked at the team leader with an unsteady, dazed look. "Who are you and what are you doing here?"

"We represent the good, law-abiding citizens of the United States. And we were sent here to rid the country of predators like this," he said, as he motioned toward the sofa where the target of this mission was sitting.

The judge had a smirk on her face as she asked hostilely, "Do you have any idea who I am and how much pain and suffering I can cause you with just one phone call?"

"Lady, I know exactly *who* you are and how you have failed to judiciously carry out the responsibilities of your office. Further, what makes you think you're going to get a phone call?"

Hearing this took the wind out of the woman's sail. "Can't you just let me go? Please. You can arrest him," pointing to her drug source, "and I'll see he's punished to the full letter of the law when he comes before the bench."

"Like you have in the past? Dismissals, tip-offs, altered arrest records and soft punishments. I *don't* think so. You see, Judge, you and others like you are a big part of the problem.

"Cops bust their ass to do their part, expecting the courts to put these guys away so they can't hurt anyone else. You have failed miserably over a long period of time, and it has to stop.

"You will serve as an example of what will happen to other inept, corrupt, or soft judges, if they don't act responsibly. In other words, lady, we're shutting you down. You are no longer a judge."

Hearing this, her manner changed as she postured to counter the team leader's intimidation. "You can't scare me, and I know you aren't going to kill anyone, so why don't you just back off, arrest me or get the hell out of here?"

Without even turning around, the team leader said, "Put him down!" In an instant there was the muffled sound of gases escaping into the eight-inch silencer as the bullet exited the barrel and found refuge deep in the drug dealer's brain. He was dead instantly.

"Now, what to do with you," the man said coldly, his gaze never leaving hers. "I'm sure you now realize we are quite capable of killing, if it's in the best interest of the country. Your choices are simple, die here and now from a drug overdose or retire from the bench tomorrow morning and check yourself into a rehab center. Which will it be?"

The woman, shaking uncontrollably, whimpered, "I will resign and do as you say if you will just let me go now. OK?"

The team leader gave her a chilling stare before saying, "Good choice! We have your name and address from your vehicle registration. If we even suspect you renege on your end of the deal or say anything about what happened here tonight, we *will* come for you when you least expect it. Understood?"

The judge nodded and started to leave.

"Hold on, lady. Give us thirty minutes before you leave. Go in the bathroom and shut the door."

The shaking, broken woman quickly picked up her purse and sobbed as she staggered down the hallway.

Before exiting the cabin, the team did a thorough search to ensure the area was sanitized and, as a safety precaution, cut the phone line. They then silently faded into the night...ghost warriors!

29

Back at the special meeting of the legislature, Mike continued, "It's now time to focus on full implementation of our welfare reform initiative. The passing of Oklahoma's New Deal law speaks volumes about the legislature's sincere desire to help our people help themselves. It is a historically significant law that serves as the cornerstone of the program.

"Why do we need it? Simply stated, the United States has been wallowing in its own fat far too long when it comes to welfare.

"Inefficiencies are inherent in its design, and the country has long since grown beyond the capabilities of the program. If that were not true, why would the issue of reform always be a topic of great concern leading up to election years, only to subside once the Congress and other politicians have been safely seated for another term?"

"It seems to always be the topic of discussion, but other than an occasional Band-Aid for public appeasement and political pacification, the hard decisions necessary for meaningful reform are *never* made. The subject of welfare reform is too damn dangerous for most career politicians to tackle.

"My advice to the weak-willed, nearsighted representatives of the people: 'You had better do something pretty damn quick or the system will be bankrupt!'

"It was never designed to be a cash cow for the federal government, yet it has been tapped over the years for all manner of reasons and purposes. It was the intent of the government to pay the system back. Of course it was…and if *you* believe that, you're probably sniffing glue.

"When money is taken from savings or loaned to a relative, how often does it get paid back? Not very often. The government is no exception.

"If we ran the O'Reilly Corporation or any business for that matter in the carefree, fiscally irresponsible manner in which the federal government conducts its business, we would either be bankrupt or in prison. Said another way, folks…it is tantamount to giving the coyote a key to the henhouse!

"By passing this bill to correct those pieces of the program we have some control over, Oklahoma has set the standard for positive reform not only for Oklahomans, but for the nation.

"Implementation of the Back to Work program is progressing nicely. Fewer able-bodied men and women remain on the welfare rolls; the state infrastructure is noticeably better because of the hard work of those souls who heretofore were welfare recipients.

"Incorporation of inmates eligible for the Work Release program has had a positive impact not only in the self-esteem of the individual participants, but on lowering overall crime rates in the state, particularly by repeat offenders.

"That is what state government is all about…helping fellow Oklahomans to help themselves. If it works here, it can work nationwide. The only difference is the size of the political wheel that has to be turned.

"Implementation of anything new and innovative is difficult, but I have yet to be confronted with an issue or circumstance that is not manageable if well thought out and properly executed. Welfare reform is no exception."

There was polite applause and the customary murmurings associated with a large body of people, as the governor took a moment to survey those in attendance.

Old habits die hard, and Mike had learned years ago as an army ranger to expect the unexpected and to never let his guard down.

Though it was highly unlikely anything would, or even could, happen in the assembly hall, there had already been several attempts over the last couple of years to harm the governor and, on one occasion, an attempt to kidnap his daughter Cheyenne.

The plots were foiled by alert security personnel and good intelligence before they could be executed. In one, highly controversial instance, the would-be assassin received multiple fractures and irreversible brain damage after being run down by one of the SUVs in the governor's entourage as they exited the airport.

It was late at night and there were no witnesses, other than security force personnel. Purportedly, the would-be assassin materialized out of nowhere brandishing a handgun as he ran into the middle of the street and was unavoidably struck by one of the vehicles.

Had a thorough investigation been conducted, the evidence would have shown the man tried to jump out of the way, dropping his weapon in the process and was run down by the second vehicle before he reached the curb. He was now in a vegetative state in a hospice facility.

The group of Special Operations personnel—the governor's security team—had been handpicked by Mike's father. Their guidance very specific: Any action by a perpetrator to harm any member of the O'Reilly family will be met with deadly force. No exceptions and no questions asked. This was a perfect mandate for the psyche of the specialists that comprised the security detail.

Mike quickly regained focus and continued his unrehearsed speech to the esteemed body before him. "You know the problem of having a modicum of financial success is that those involved have short memories and seem to forget there is a whole bunch of folks out there who are barely getting by paycheck to paycheck. God help them if they get sick and can't work. That's just not right!

"I was talking to my dad the other day during one of those rare occasions when our schedules allow us to spend a little free time together. We were on Lake Hudson fishing in an old wooden boat he has had since I was a kid.

"It leaks like a sieve, so he carries an old coffee can to bail water when it threatens to sink. Getting the motor started is like shooting craps… you win some and you lose some."

The assembly hall was quiet in anticipation of another one of the governor's profound, real life stories that he had become well known for and often used to make a point.

"It was during one of the bailing periods that I said, 'Pops, what the hell we doing in this raggedy ass old boat? Don't you think you deserve something a bit more seaworthy?'

"He just shook his head and said, 'Nope, this is who we are.'

"For those of you who don't know my father, he's big enough to block out the sun, with hands as big and rough as a rain barrel. He has earned his stripes in two wars and believes talking is overrated. 'Deeds, not words' is one of the many life's lessons I learned from him at an early age. Six simple words, 'Nope, this is who we are'…spoke volumes to me.

"You see, O'Reilly men, including me, have lived the Spartan life of an infantry soldier, dating back to the 1600s. Our ancestry is one of poor Irish farmers.

"When I was a wee lad, my dad was poor as Job's turkey, and I won't even attempt to tell you what that means. It's something he always said to describe our station in life. I mean *dirt* poor Alabama farmers.

"Only through the grace of God, the generosity of a dear friend, and hard work was he able to make the quantum leap from poor to affluent."

Mike let that thought sink in for a brief moment and then continued. "Like a thunderbolt, my father's meaning hit me. He keeps that old boat and motor to stay firmly anchored in the real world.

"That's what I'm asking of you here today. We need to be bright enough to see the need for change, but poor enough to see what changes are in the best interest of those in need. They are counting on each and every member here today to make the right decisions and that is a tremendous responsibility.

"It is wrong and demeaning for our senior citizens to have to choose between food and life-sustaining medicines.

"It is wrong for a mother to pay half of what she earns to a daycare center so she can go bust her butt for low wages in an effort to keep her family afloat.

"I propose we formulate a plan that would bring these two groups together in a mutual effort to help one another. For example, why not let honorable senior citizens, who may be lonely and in need of income augmentation, staff state-run or sponsored daycare centers to provide quality care to children of working mothers? A floating fee, based on ability to pay, could be charged to help defray operational costs.

"In concert with that, we have already put in place an aggressive program to get deadbeat dads to pay child support. This dovetails nicely into the overall welfare reform plan. I am asking you to now go back to your respective districts, have some heartfelt, grassroots discussions with needy constituents, and let's see what we come up with.

"If you need assistance from me or my staff, give us a call. I see this as a high priority issue, and we can make it happen in the same manner we were able to greatly increase the salaries of educators and law enforcement personnel...a good plan, perseverance and a lot of hard work."

30

As governor, Mike had accomplished many good works and received national acclaim for a number of innovative initiatives. Most notable was his tireless efforts to shore up the ailing criminal justice system.

As his term as governor was drawing to a close, there seemed to be an ever-increasing swell and rattling of influential sabers in support of a presidential bid.

Mike had discussed this with both his father and his mentor, Ron Snyder. Since a run at the presidency had been their design from the beginning, they enthusiastically supported the idea. Truth be known, they were the power brokers behind the groundswell of influential supporters.

Even his wife Veronica encouraged him to at least think about it. She had played an active role and taken the lead on a number of state-initiated humanitarian projects and enjoyed myriad philanthropic endeavors that the O'Reilly family supported.

She had long since given up her career as a television news anchor and dedicated herself to family and full support of her husband. The idea of being First Lady had a nice ring to it, particularly to a small town girl from Oklahoma.

Veronica was born and raised in the small enclave of oil workers in Red Fork, Oklahoma but she was Ivy League educated, beautiful and smart. A perfect fit for Mike and whatever political aspirations he may have.

So when Mike informed her he was going to test the waters, she was very supportive, but also a little apprehensive. After all, she had already endured a number of attempts to harm her husband and one attempt to kidnap her only child Cheyenne. She knew of the dangers, seldom spoken, but ever present, in the lives of high profile personalities, and Mike was as high as they got.

As their limo drove through the gates of Southern Hills Country Club in Tulsa, she immediately noticed the presence of an inordinate number of security personnel strategically placed on the grounds and in front of the majestic clubhouse.

Mike saw the concern on her face and made light of the precautions. "Another prank call, babe, nothing to be alarmed about." Unknown to the O'Reillys, there was plenty to be worried about, and the threat was one hell of a lot closer than they could ever imagine.

Men who have experienced combat possess intuition, an early warning system alerting them to an unspecified danger. That's what Mike was feeling as he surveyed the surrounding area before leaving the safety of the vehicle.

His mind momentarily flashed back to the Congo, recalling what his friend Jeff Stone had said to him. "Always listen to the inner voice and trust your instincts."

Before his driver left the armored limo to open the passenger door, a ritual conducted hundreds of uneventful times in the past, Mike stopped him. "Phil, let's sit here for a moment. I need to touch base with J.B."

J.B. was presently head of Mike's security detail. A moment later Phil Burlingame, his personal bodyguard and driver, tapped his ear and pointed at the polished mahogany console housing the bar and the communications system.

Mike reached forward and removed the handset. "J.B."

"Yeah boss, I have the same feeling. Stand fast while we do another sweep. Damn! I hate this feeling. That *is* why you called…right?"

"It is indeed, sir. Take a look at the gaggle by the door. I have no real reason to suspect them, but it would not give us much reaction time if something came up as we walked by."

"Roger that. I'll take care of it and get back to you when we think it's safe."

The problem was not the people pushing ever closer to position themselves for one of Mike's customary handshakes and a good look at his beautiful wife.

As J.B. and members of the security detail completed another sweep of the clubhouse, finding nothing out of place, he returned to the foyer and was about to place a call to the limo, but still had an uneasy feeling in his gut. Something just didn't feel quite right. He keyed his lapel mike.

"Bob, do you still have the pictures we took of the facility yesterday?"

Bob LaGrone was one of the few guys on the O'Reilly security detail that did not have a Spec Ops background. He had been hired away from the FBI's counter-intelligence branch, where he had built an outstanding reputation for his uncanny ability to identify minute detail, often overlooked in surveillance and aerial photographs.

As Bob LaGrone received the call, he thought... 'how many times must I tell these knuckle draggers that pictures are painted; photographs are taken with cameras?' In reality, he was way too smart to have actually shared this disparaging tidbit with his more brawny teammates. So he treated himself to a slight smirk, shrugged and keyed his lapel mike. "J.B., I have the *photographs*. I'm in the kitchen area. Where are you?"

"I'm in the foyer."

"I'm on my way."

As Bob entered the foyer and handed the photos to J.B., he said, "Somebody must really like silk flowers. There were only four arrangements in here yesterday."

Bob's observation registered in the deep recesses of his boss's mind a few seconds later. He jerked his head up to gaze at the six decorative pedestals and the lavish flower arrangements sitting atop each one. The head of security quickly shuffled photo after photo until he found the foyer shot. Sure as hell, there were only four pedestals in the photo.

Standard protocol states that once a security sweep is completed, nothing can be taken out or brought in. He had made that crystal clear to both club management and the Tulsa chief of police.

J.B. immediately keyed his lapel mike as he started a visual inspection of the two arrangements he thought had been added to the foyer décor. "Boss, we may have something. Don't get out of the lim…" As he took a closer look, he added, "Oh shit, stand by."

He had quite a bit of experience with explosive devices, but he had an expert on his team and called for him as he continued to evaluate the situation.

It seemed like an eternity, but only a few moments had passed when J.B. again keyed his mike. "This is what we have, Mike, and how I think we should handle it. We have two C-4 packages on either side of the foyer. They are rigged for electrical detonation, which means we have a set of eyes, line of sight, to the entryway.

"We'll be alright as long as you don't enter the building, but as a precaution, we need to move the people away from the foyer without causing alarm. I recommend we…wait one."

J.B. had alerted the sniper team on the roof of the clubhouse of the situation and they were up on the tactical frequency. "J.B. here, what do you have?"

The voice on the other end said, "We have two possible threats. One is a golf course maintenance worker leaning on a rake about 300 yards out. He is looking in the direction of the clubhouse, but given the magnitude of the visit, that seems pretty normal.

"Second threat is a suit, sitting on the railing of a little bridge, about 400 yards out. He has binoculars and seems very interested in the activities over here."

"That's our guy! Send a four-man package out the delivery entrance of the club. Cross whatever main road that is out there and get in position to either capture or tap this guy on my command. We will keep the tactical channel open. Tell the team leader to contact me when he is in position. You keep him fixed and let me and the team know if there is movement."

"Yes, sir."

J.B. switched channels and called Mike. "Boss, we have two possible threats, neither appears to be armed and both are over 300 yards out. I recommend you and Veronica exit the limo now. I will tell the people at the entryway that you will avail yourself to a brief meet-and-greet opportunity by the trees, opposite the driveway to the club. That will clear the area, should there be a mishap during the removal of the explosives.

"That will give us time to disarm and low profile these devices out through the pro shop and away from the building. Give me two minutes to get a security perimeter set up for you. This is a diversion. When it's safe, I'll call you to enter the club. One of these turkeys is going to key an electrical transmitter, and when he does, we'll nail him, one way or the other. Sound OK to you?"

Mike grinned. "Sounds good; let's do it. There is one small detail that concerns me, however. I don't believe the Democrats use *their* candidate as a decoy. I've always been under the impression you guys were supposed to take the hits."

J.B. laughed. "I have a wife and three kids in college. You surely don't want *me* to volunteer, do you?"

Both devices were reasonably sophisticated C-4 wrapped in cellophane to help mask the smell from bomb-sniffing dogs, should there be any, and rather intricate electronics to the detonator. The bomb maker evidently was not anticipating the devices would be found, because there was no false circuitry or clever secondary fusing.

Once the bombs had been secured, the pro shop loaned the detail a golf cart to take the devices out to the maintenance buildings for safe keeping until the Feds showed up.

The two-man security detail was told to stay with the explosives to negate any future attempt by a slick defense lawyer claiming continuous and positive control was not maintained at all times. Consequently, someone could have replaced his client's inert package, a poor attempt at a harmless joke, with real bombs. The simple-minded, immoral bastards care nothing about justice; it's all about money.

J.B. alerted the sniper and capture teams that their charge would be entering the clubhouse momentarily and to prepare for a takedown.

The perpetrator on the bridge was so preoccupied with trying to send an electronic signal to the explosive devices he didn't hear the team approach from his blind side. One member of the team put his face next to the man's ear and, as loud as he could, yelled, "Bang!"

The man was so surprised he wet himself and fell headfirst over the bridge railing into the dry creek bed eight feet below. It was over!

31

Over the next few months, Mike made numerous swings across the nation speaking from the heart about the kinds of changes needed to revitalize and perpetuate this great nation, keeping it strong and prosperous for future generations.

Fortunately not all stops were as eventful as his visit to Southern Hills Country Club. He had many concerns, but unlike other presidential candidates who provided endless pontification, he also had well-defined plans.

In concert with Mike's campaigning, his father Sean and mentor Ron Snyder used their resources and influential connections to ensure their candidate of choice was always in the right place at the right time to achieve maximum exposure.

The campaign was not the only place resources were being dedicated. Unknown to the promising candidate, ARC was ramping up its covert operations.

Sean had made a number of key personnel changes. Expanding any operation or business, regardless of the end product, requires realignment and the placement of key personnel, possessing the right skill sets.

J.B. and Dave, as examples, were an inseparable team, experienced in the planning and execution of complex covert operations. Together, they had orchestrated the humanitarian initiative in the Congo.

They were reassigned as director and assistant director of the ARC Operations Center, located underground at the far end of the O'Reilly estate's airfield complex.

Patriots, by and large, do not necessarily do what they do for financial gain. If money was the driving force, the armed forces of the United States would be nonexistent.

Their families have a different perspective and are far more supportive if they have discretionary funds to spend at the mall, beauty shop, or a car for junior.

So when Dad comes home with the announcement he has just been promoted, given a nice title, and oh, by the way, a six-digit salary, he experiences family enthusiasm tantamount to a sixteenth century hanging in the town square…jubilation!

Selection of ARC personnel was based primarily on character, demonstrated performance, honor, courage, loyalty and an unwavering desire to make the country a safer place for all Americans.

A candidate could be rejected based solely on Sean's intuition, when all other data suggested the candidate was sound. It had to be that way.

One weakness on the part of an operative, one slip up, one moment when attention to detail is not quite as keen as it should be and the entire ARC operation could be jeopardized. The organization's charter made it a prime candidate for compromise and implosion should a weak link occur.

As one would expect in the conduct of covert operations, information flows on a need-to-know basis, involving as few people as possible. In the case of ARC, field personnel were aware only of their specific assignment.

Operatives didn't need to know how big the organization was; where it was; or what it was. It takes a strong, self-sufficient personality to operate in this mode day in and day out, and that was the strength of the operation.

There were exceptions. Personnel selected to staff the operations center were personally interviewed by Sean; that would test the resolve of the most hardened applicant. Their duty station, once selected, was on the O'Reilly estate.

They were grilled relentlessly; administered lie detector tests; and underwent, as did field operatives, psychological profiles and in-depth background checks by the FBI.

These background checks were not the typical quick look…asking past neighbors if they had ever witnessed you spitting on the sidewalk. They wanted to know if you had blood in your urine at age ten; if you paid the ten-cent library late fee in high school; and if you had a history of amorous relationships with farm animals.

The FBI knows their business and they do it well. Of course they were not aware of the subject's intended purpose in life, thinking only he had been selected for sensitive positions within the O'Reilly Corporation's complex organization of companies and subsidiaries.

Sean had recently made other significant personnel acquisitions, much to the liking of his son. He had located and recruited one of Mike's closest friends, Jeff Stone.

Jeff had resigned from the CIA after seven years as a covert operator in Southeast Asia and had been training hired guns—mercenaries—for a private company headquartered in Ottawa, Canada. He was the embodiment of the quintessential killing machine…scary to look at and equally scary to be around unless you were counted among his few friends.

His sinister-looking scar was wide and ugly…clearly not the work of a skilled surgeon. Whoever had done the stitching—and it may have been Jeff himself—must have used a big nail and bailing wire. A daily reminder of just how tenuous life really is.

Jeff was recruited to replace J.B. as head of Mike's personal security detail. He would also serve as a special staff advisor, giving him reason to always be in close proximity to his charge. That really pleased Mike. It also pleased his father but for different reasons.

Mike and Jeff had formed very close bonds while fighting in the Congo many years before. Jeff had taught the young infantry lieutenant a lot about surviving in a hostile environment. Now he would be responsible for keeping Mike and his family out of harm's way in a totally different kind of hostile environment.

It was on this occasion that Mike and family were returning to the O'Reilly estate. Veronica had heard her husband talk about Jeff and the exploits experienced in their former lives, but had never met the man.

Sean thought it would be the perfect occasion to get his family home for a few days. What he really wanted, since he saw Mike all the time in the conduct of campaigning for the nation's highest office, was to see his beautiful granddaughter Cheyenne, whom he dearly loved.

As the G-4 turned on final approach this crisp, quiet morning, Veronica looked over at her husband and said, "What are you looking at down there?"

"Nothing particular," Mike said, as he continued to look out of the window.

The landing was uneventful and as the aircraft taxied to a stop in front of base operations they could see Sean, J.B. and Jeff making their way out of the warmth of the operations building and walking toward the aircraft.

By the time they reached the plane, the door was open and Veronica, her eager little daughter in tow, was making her way down the stairs. She turned loose of Cheyenne's hand and the child made a beeline for her grandfather, gleefully screaming, "Papa, Papa" at the top of her lungs. Mike exited the cabin in time to see Sean engulf his little sweetheart in his massive arms.

Since the arrival of their only child, Mike had always been curious how such a mammoth man could be so gentle. He recalled his own childhood, how he had been raised by this same man without the help of his mother who had been killed in an airplane accident when he was just a young boy.

How his father had picked him up by the belt buckle and swung him with ease over the boat dock at Lake Thollaco on their last day in Alabama before starting out on what his father had called, a 'new adventure.' In retrospect, Mike thought that was an understatement.

As Sean gently lowered his granddaughter to the ground, Cheyenne got her first look at the menacing figure standing beside her grandfather. The child's immediate reaction was to quickly put her Papa's massive frame between them, wrapping both of her little arms around his leg and hiding her face.

Only after her dad came over to hug the man did Cheyenne venture a quick peak from the safety of her grandfather's leg. It was just that…a quick peak. She then went back into hiding.

Mike called his daughter over to introduce her to his best friend. No dice. Cheyenne had no intentions of leaving the safety of her Papa's huge frame.

Sean picked his granddaughter up, letting her know that Jeff was not only a friend, but also would be spending a lot of time with Mommy and Daddy and she might as well get to know him right now.

The O'Reillys had always faced challenges, large and small, head on. It was their way, and this was no different. To Cheyenne, however, who was not fully acclimated to the O'Reilly way, it was a major problem. So she hid her face and blindly extended her arm out to shake this scary man's hand.

Jeff gently took the child's hand in his and said, "I'm happy to finally meet you, sweetheart. I've heard a lot about you. Your dad and I have been good friends for a long time and I'll bet by the end of the day, you and I will be friends, also."

With the honesty reserved for the very young, Cheyenne looked up saying in her soft little voice, "I'll bet we're not!"

Everyone laughed and Jeff patted the little girl's back saying, "She's definitely an O'Reilly...hardheaded and direct! Thank *God* she got her mother's good looks."

J.B. had left shortly after meeting the plane and the other three men had spent the evening rehashing old times over a bottle of Jack Daniels and discussing the nature of Jeff's new job. Sean had a meeting the following day in Chicago with Ron, so he bowed out shortly before midnight, leaving Mike and Jeff alone. The two friends talked a while longer, bringing one another current on what each had been doing since they had last been together.

A short while later, fatigue and the lack of anything else to say, along with the empty bottle of whiskey sitting on the coffee table, brought the evening to a close. "Well, Jeff, I've got to get some sleep. It's been a long day."

"It's good to be back with you, bud. I hope I can be of service to you."

"I'm sure you'll do just fine and I'm looking forward to it. It's good to have you on board."

"By the way, the guest suite you're staying in is that way," Mike said, waving his arm in the direction of one of the wide hallways leading off of the family room.

"Thanks, bud, your dad got me squared away before you arrived. This place is incredible," Jeff said as he gulped down the last of his drink and set the glass on the table. "How many rooms does this little shanty have, anyway?"

"I have no idea, partner, I never counted them. But it feels pretty big, doesn't it? It's too big for me. On the rare occasion I'm home, I usually stay down by the lake."

Both men started to shake hands but Mike pulled Jeff toward him and gave him a bear hug saying, "God, it's good to see you, my friend. I had forgotten how warm and cuddly you really are." Jeff pulled away and told him to go screw himself.

As Jeff turned to leave, Mike asked as an afterthought, "Do you ride?"

Jeff turned and with a wry smile said, "All depends what it is that needs riding."

"You're a *bad* pig, my friend. I was referring to horses. I thought we might give it a go in the morning if you're up to it."

"I rode one once up in Canada, hunting mountain goat. Damn fool thing broke its leg…only thing I shot that day was my horse."

Mike shook his head and smiled as Jeff walked away. "Maybe you'll have better luck tomorrow."

Though the O'Reilly estate was fully staffed, Mike always picked up after himself when he was at home. 'Old habits die hard,' his dad always said. As he carried the tray of empty glasses and bottles into the large ornate kitchen, he couldn't help but think how far removed they were from the small Alabama dirt farm of his youth.

He wondered if it was still there and if the old black man was still alive. Hell, he could even remember his name…Ezekiel! All of a sudden Mike had a vivid recollection of the day he and his dad first pulled into the old man's yard. He could see the heavyset woman sweeping the dirt yard with a broom made of small branches; the rundown shack with no windows; and the dirty little kids running out to take a look at his dad's new red pickup. But most of all, he remembered the headless chickens flopping around after the old man had wrung their necks with a flip of the wrist. How did he do that?

A flood of good memories rushed in as he remembered the old man's colloquialism: 'I surely do, Mr. Sean, I surely do.' He must have used that phrase a hundred times that day…the day his dad shared his good fortune with a stranger. In retrospect, he had given

Ezekiel and his family a new lease on life by giving him the 200-acre homestead. No question about it, the big guy was a compassionate man…sometimes!

All of a sudden Mike didn't feel tired anymore. He had too much on his mind. He poured a healthy portion of brandy from a crystal decanter sitting on one of the marble islands in the kitchen. With glass in hand, he checked on Cheyenne and Veronica. They were sound asleep.

He opened the glass doors leading to the veranda and walked into the cool, early morning air. He had been on the go for almost twenty hours and though it was almost two in the morning, he was wide awake.

Mike loved to sit on the large rock wall that encased the veranda and courtyard area. It was at least thirty feet above the meticulously landscaped grounds and provided a commanding view of the estate.

The moon was dimmed by early morning scud that blanketed the large lake and river basin in the distance. It created an eerie glow every time the light from the airfield's rotating beacon flashed around. This had to be the most beautiful, most peaceful place on Earth, he thought.

Mike was having doubts about his bid for the presidency. His view of politics, more specifically politicians, was not good. He perceived most of them to be self-promoting egotists who really didn't give a damn one way or the other about the people.

That was the prime motivator that led him into politics in the first place. He knew he could make a difference. As governor, he had indeed made a big difference, and if he could just find a way to navigate through all the political bullshit in Washington without killing someone, he'd do fine.

He knew there was a high price to pay. For every ounce of energy dedicated to public service was an ounce his family didn't get. His dilemma: Am I willing to make that sacrifice?

At moments like these, alone with his thoughts, Mike often fantasized—more for entertainment then anything else—about how he would have managed major crises in the country's history, and how his perceived actions might have changed history.

One incident that always seemed to work its way to the forefront of his consciousness was the hostage situation in Iran. He always felt that if the president had called the Ayatollah and the Iranian ambassador to the United States and said...'I have dispatched a 747 en route to Tehran's International Airport. I want all U.S. citizens held captive escorted to and placed safely on this aircraft for immediate return to the United States.

'Six hours after the planned departure of the 747, if you have failed to comply, I will direct the Atlantic fleet which, as you know, has been camped on your doorstep for the past several months to initiate offensive strikes that will ultimately wipe your worthless, raggedy asses off the face of the Earth.

'For future reference—given your country has a future—any attack on one of our citizens will be viewed as an attack on the United States, and we will respond swiftly and with extreme prejudice. In other words, we will find, fix and kill those responsible, even if it violates sovereign territory.

'That's a good piece of information to have. Pass it along to your radical friends and take heed or life as you know it will cease to exist. While I'm on the subject, you can take diplomacy and shove it right up your ass, at least for the remaining few hours you still have one!'

He smiled as he took another sip of brandy. The hypothetical scenario seemed to have a life of its own with a nuance here and there changed to make the story better each time it surfaced. He liked this one.

Mike sat outside for a long time relishing the privacy, as he watched little winged critters flutter around the horse stable lights in a futile attempt to avoid the diving bats that had an even keener interest in the insect world.

Through the light fog forming on the lake below, he could barely make out the derrick lights of a distant drilling site. He knew from personal experience, having worked his summer vacations on rigs like this one, the roughneck crews manning the rig would work round the clock until black crude surged upward through thousands of feet of piping or the site was declared a *dry hole* and they moved on to the next crap shoot.

Geological advancements had greatly reduced oil deposit speculation, but it was still a gamble. The rig he saw in the distance was too far away to determine whether or not it was an O'Reilly well site. During the day, each O'Reilly rig was easily recognizable by the large white flag waving atop the mast and sporting a green shamrock.

Some time around three-thirty Mike quietly made his way back into the house. He never liked being asked questions he didn't have answers to, so before retiring, he made his way into his father's study looking for blueprints of the house. After spending a reasonable time searching, to no avail, he left the study and spent the next ten minutes or so counting rooms.

32

Mike required only three or four hours of sleep nightly, which is fortunate because that is about what he got. He showered, slipped on an old pair of jeans, a long-sleeved western shirt and scuffed-up cowboy boots, and made his way to the kitchen for coffee.

Jeff was already up, working his way through a big plate of bacon, eggs, biscuits, gravy and a side of grits. He looked up as Mike walked into the kitchen. "About time you surfaced. I was starting to worry I might have to throw a saddle on something myself, and quite frankly it's not real clear to me if the horse is the one with or without horns!"

Mike patted him on the shoulder, as he pulled out a chair at the table. "It wouldn't take long for you to figure that one out," Mike said as he sat down.

Rosa Mendoza, a jovial, plump sweetheart of a lady, had been in the employ of the O'Reillys for as long as Mike could remember. He treated her like a surrogate mom, so when she brought him his first cup of coffee he put his arms around her waist and gave her a big hug. She kissed him lightly on the cheek and asked, "So, Senor Mike, biscuits and gravy?" She knew it was his favorite breakfast.

"Yes, Rosa, please."

Mike then looked over at his friend, "Twenty-eight!"

Jeff met his gaze with a perplexed look. "What?"

"The house has twenty-eight rooms, counting the laundry room."

Jeff sighed, as if a great burden had been lifted from his shoulders, "You can't imagine how that weighed on my mind all night. It must have taken me all of two minutes to fall asleep. I didn't really give a shi...darn, I was just curious."

"Well, you asked, so now you know."

"Are you telling me you scurried around the house last night like some kind of cheese-eating rodent, so you could tell me how many rooms the house had?"

"Yes, I did! No question goes unanswered in my world."

Jeff looked back at his plate of food. "*Your* world, sir, will take a little getting used to."

"You have about two days to master it before we hit the road again."

They finished their breakfast, thanked Rosa for a great meal, and Mike gave her a loving peck on top of her head before the two men made their way to the stables.

Rosa's son Miguel, a twenty-four-year-old ranch hand, had been placed in charge of the stables because of his uncanny way with horses. By the time the men arrived, he had already saddled Mike's horse. Flame, a spirited seventeen-hand gelding, dwarfed the smaller mare that had been saddled for the gringo with the sinister look.

Mike thanked Miguel for taking such good care of the livestock and watched as the young man's eyes lit up, as they always did when he was praised for good work. He then instructed Jeff in the way to properly mount a faithful steed before climbing aboard Flame.

Miguel told Jeff that he had selected the little mare for her gentleness and in the event something did happen, like stepping in a gopher hole or shying away from a rattlesnake, it wasn't very far to the ground.

His choice of words didn't seem to comfort the gringo from New York who asked, "Don't you have a Jeep or something we could ride instead?"

Mike and the young stable hand laughed, assuring Jeff he would be fine since the little mare was the same horse Miguel always saddled for Cheyenne. "Climb aboard, cowboy, and Miguel will adjust the stirrups for you. It makes for a more comfortable, controlled ride."

Their first stop was the lake. Flame always wanted a drink before hitting the trail. The little mare emulated Flame's every move and was, to Jeff's relief, quite gentle and easy to ride.

As they left the lake and headed toward the Kiamichi river basin, Jeff asked, "Do we have a destination or do horses just go where they want?"

Mike just shook his head and informed his friend that horses generally went where their riders directed them to go.

"I saw something peculiar as we were landing yesterday so I thought we'd ride over and take a look. It's only about six or seven miles; should be an easy ride. We'll be back for lunch."

"You've got to be shitting me!" Jeff said, "My butt's already sore, and I can still see the barn."

Mike kicked Flame into a comfortable gallop leaving Jeff behind. The little mare followed suit and the tough guy, hired to protect the O'Reilly family, held on for dear life.

It was obvious from the outset that Jeff was not an equestrian, and riding was not particularly high on his 'want list'...probably just below a colonoscopy. He was funny to watch though and Mike was enjoying the moment.

The ride over to the perimeter fence surrounding the airfield was uneventful, though several stops had to be made to let Jeff walk around and massage his tender Yankee butt.

"Not many horses in the Bronx, I gather?" Mike mused.

"Bite me, Mr. O'Reilly! We have a horse or two. I just prefer taxis, like most civilized people."

"*You're* civilized?...You've spent so much time in the jungle, rumor has it *whole* families of spider monkeys can be traced directly to your DNA."

Jeff looked up at Mike, who had remained mounted and while rubbing his tender backside said, "Cute! God forbid, I should trip as I'm diving in front of a speeding bullet to save your Okie ass."

"Don't worry, my friend, I'm bulletproof. My ranger tab will protect me."

Jeff continued massaging his sore tailbone as he prepared to mount again.

Mike pulled left on the reins and positioned Flame alongside the little mare. He reached down and released the slip knot holding a bed roll and rain slick on the back of the mare's saddle. He unrolled the bed roll and folded it into a square, making a multi-layered cushion for Jeff's saddle. "Try this. It should help some."

Jeff swung his right leg over the little mare's back and sat down on the new cushion arrangement. "Oooh! That feels *so* good. Why didn't we do this earlier?"

"I don't generally carry a 'sore butt' gauge, and you didn't say anything. I figured a big tough guy like you could handle it."

They walked the horses along the perimeter fence until they reached the furthest point from the operations building and Mike looked over at Jeff. "I want you to look around and tell me if you see anything peculiar or out of place out here."

Jeff, without hesitation, said, "I saw something long before we reached the airfield that looked a little strange."

"Like what?" Mike asked.

"Like those massive high tension power lines that terminate in the middle of nowhere. That's strange to me.

"And look over at that cluster of towers. The microwave tower sporting a variety of antennas mixed in with the others seems to me like overkill, even for a large corporation.

"And the taller one of the bunch, I can't be sure without a closer look, but it resembles those used for the old STU-3 scramblers. There are newer, more advanced encryption devices out there now, but the STU-3 gets the job done and is still used. If that's what it is, it's a little more than *strange*."

The observations caught Mike by surprise since that was not at all what had caught his eye on yesterday's final approach. "Interesting observation; I guess I've been in and out of here so much I haven't paid any attention to them and wouldn't know what I was looking at had I paid attention. Anything else, catch your eye?"

"That's about it, buddy," Jeff said as he continued to scan the airfield, dividing it into manageable sections and evaluating each section separately. "What were you looking for?"

"Yesterday, as we turned on final approach, I noticed steam coming out of the ground just off the end of the runway over there," Mike said pointing in the direction he thought was the general area he had seen the phenomenon.

"You landed around six-thirty or seven in the morning, right?"

"I think so. I've taken off and landed so many times lately, they all seem to run together."

Jeff continued, "Well, it's about twelve now and using one of your quaint southern quips, 'hot as a three-dollar pistol.' Not likely you would see steam this time of day. The ambient air would have to be considerably cooler than the air being released."

"It was probably nothing. As tired as I was, hallucination is not out of the question."

Jeff looked at Mike with skepticism, "You know as well as I do; it is totally out of the question. You may recall, sir, we didn't sleep for seventy-two hours on our Congo excursion, and you were pretty friggin' lucid then. I know damn well you've never been that tired since, and certainly not yesterday."

By the time they had made their way to base operations, following the fence line, Jeff had pretty much had all the horse riding he ever hoped to have in this lifetime. "If riding these damn things is in the job description, I quit!"

Mike laughed as they dismounted and entered base operations. The roar of a Learjet taking off momentarily filled the room. As the jet reached rotation speed and lifted off, Mike instructed the gentleman at the counter to call the stables and have Miguel come get the horses and trailer them back.

He and Jeff entered the pilot's lounge and took a couple of sodas out of the fridge. Lounging on one of the recliners was a corporate pilot who sat up the moment he saw Mike. "Hi, Ken. Relax, man." That was what all of the pilots on the O'Reilly payroll liked about Mike; he blended in and they saw him as one of the guys, as opposed to a presidential candidate and heir to one of the largest fortunes in the country.

"Ken, are you checked out on the SK-76?" Mike asked, nodding his head in the direction of the flight line and the glistening helicopter parked in front of base operations.

"Yes, sir. You need a lift?"

"That would be a real treat. And I suspect this bow-legged *cowpoke* here would probably kiss you on the lips for a ride back to the house."

"That won't be necessary," Ken said, as he got up to preflight the aircraft. Mike introduced him to Jeff and they shook hands briefly before Ken left.

Mike flopped down in one of the lounge chairs. "Have you ever flown in the Sikorsky SK-76, Jeff?"

"I've got tons of time in military aircraft, but not the SK-76. Is it different?"

"This thing is a marvel. It has a retractable landing gear and is sleek as a newborn baby's butt...and comfortable, too. It is really a sweet aircraft, queen of the fleet as far as I'm concerned; though Dad would have you believe the G-4 holds that honor. The way he talks about her, you'd think they were married!"

"Now that I think about it, they're about the same size." Mike smiled. "Hell, maybe that's where all the little Citations came from."

Jeff just stared at his friend as though he'd lost his mind. "Maybe hallucinations aren't out of the question after all."

After a few minutes they heard the distinctive whine of the turbine and the thump of rotor blades as the SK-76 sprung to life. The two men walked out into a bright, cloudless sky and made their way to the aircraft.

As the pilot pulled collective pitch and brought the aircraft to a hover, checking the instruments to ensure all systems were functioning properly, Mike looked out the window and saw the horses straining against their tied reins in an effort to somehow avoid the rotor wash created by the massive blades slicing through the air.

As Ken moved the cyclic forward, the aircraft nosed over and began moving toward transitional lift at which time it seemed to rocket down the runway, making a lazy turn back to the east.

The flight was short and before the two men could really get settled into the flight, it was over. The beautiful chopper made an effortless approach to the helipad located in the mansion's courtyard.

Sean and his little shadow, Cheyenne, were there to meet them. The big man gently shielded his granddaughter's eyes with a huge hand as the aircraft touched down, dropped off the passengers and just as quickly rose and headed back in the direction of the airfield.

The three men, with Cheyenne in tow, headed for the house and relief from the midday sun.

Rosa had lunch ready for the family and as Mike excused himself to go wash up, Veronica gave him a kiss and handed him a stack of messages as they both walked toward their suite. He scanned them quickly, selecting those requiring immediate response, made a few calls and then they made their way back to the dining room to join the others.

As they sat down, Mike immediately saw his favorite meal had been prepared...fried chicken, mashed potatoes and gravy, biscuits, sliced tomatoes and iced tea. Rosa came around the table and Mike gave her a hug and kissed her cheek. "Thank you, sweetheart, you know how to win me over."

After lunch, the men entered Sean's study to talk about the challenges that lay before them. The study was masculine—clearly a man's sanctuary—with heavy leather furnishings, bookshelves and a large ornate desk. A number of original western sculptures by Charles Marion Russell, notably *The Bucking Bronco*, and numerous paintings by Frederic Remington, including his most famous works...*Cavalry Charge on the Southern Plains*; *A Dash for the Timber*; and *The Scout: Friends or Enemies*.

"This is a beautiful place, Mr. O'Reilly," Jeff said. "I would find it hard to leave...once I sold all the damn *horses*, that is!"

Sean smiled saying, "Call me Sean, Jeff. It sounds like you and horseflesh aren't all that compatible."

Jeff shifted his weight to gain relief from a chafed area on his lower torso. "Oh, I have no problem with the flesh part. I've eaten horse before... and liked it. It's riding them that I find painful!"

"Pops, I'm not sure this little sissy, *girly man* is up to the task. Maybe we should send him packing," Mike said as he winked at his father.

"Keep it up, sir! I don't forget much. Refresh my memory...Am I supposed to jump in front of the speeding bullet or duck?"

Sean leaned forward and rested his massive arms on the ornate desk. "Regardless of what this little shit says, we're glad you're here, Jeff. I think you will find it to your liking, though the hours leave a bit to be desired. As we discussed during our initial meeting at Niagara Falls, you will head Mike's security team and be responsible for the safety of the O'Reilly family. No small task. In the event he has not already told you, there have been several attempts on his life and a failed kidnapping involving my granddaughter.

"As harsh as it may seem, Jeff," Sean said, as he looked at the man with a penetrating gaze, "if anyone dies, I want it to be you and your detail, not my family.

"You will be compensated in ways you have not yet dreamt of. In other words, for your service and expertise, it is my intent to make you a wealthy man during your tenure here. My demands are straightforward: Be a man of honor, loyalty and courage... anything less is unacceptable."

Mike interjected, "He's got a real way with words, Jeff. It just makes you feel warm and fuzzy all over, doesn't it? I've seen grown men salivating at the very thought of being his little buddy."

Sean looked over at his son. "Don't make me hurt you, you little shit. President or not, I can still stomp a mud hole in your gut and don't ever forget it."

"Yes, Daddy!"

Jeff smiled and shook his head. "Are you sure you want him protected?"

Sean grinned. "Sad as it seems, he's all I got!"

"While I'm thinking of it, Pops, what's with all the power lines and antennas at the airfield?"

Sean seemed taken aback by the question and looked at his son for a moment while he carefully chose his words. "Don't tell me this is the first time you've seen them?"

"Well, let's just say it's the first time I paid any attention to them."

Jeff looked on with interest as Sean explained, "The heavy duty power lines are needed to power the flight simulators at the airfield. They really suck up the juice. The other towers are for microwave communications around the country and mixed in there somewhere is a proprietary tower used solely for corporate communications when security is paramount."

To the elder O'Reilly's relief, J.B. Hawkins was shown into the study. Sean didn't want to reveal the real purpose for the cluster of state-of-the-art communications towers, though he knew he may have to one day. "I've asked J.B. to join us to help Jeff transition into his new assignment. J.B., there is coffee in the server and cold beer at the bar."

The three men were sequestered in the study for the better part of four hours going over every facet of the security assignment.

J.B. provided Jeff with a dossier of after-action reports concerning all of the attempts made to harm Mike and his family.

The file included incidents at the incarceration center, the Oklahoma City Civic Center, the attempt to intercept Mike's motorcade at the airport and most recently, the attempted assassination at Southern Hills in Tulsa. Each report, eight reports total, contained location and date of the incident, a summary paragraph of salient points and in bold type the actions taken to neutralize the threat.

Jeff briefly thumbed through the papers, with the intent of reading them in greater detail later in the day. One thing stood out and immediately caught his eye. The 'actions taken' on an inordinate number of the reports contained a phrase he was very familiar with…Terminated with Extreme Prejudice.

Jeff closed the dossier, laid it on the arm of the chair and looked over at J.B., as he took a long pull on a warm beer that had been brought in a couple of hours before.

J.B. read the look on the ex-CIA operative's face. "Business as usual, Jeff!"

Sean alleviated all doubts concerning standard operating procedures by saying, "That's the way we do it here, Jeff. Any problems?"

Jeff shifted in his seat a little. "No problem here. I share Mike's view on resolving danger close situations… 'Kill um all and let God sort um out!'

"I assume, by the looks of these reports, the men assigned to the security detail are highly qualified professionals?"

Mike answered, "The team was hand picked by Jeff. The crème de la crème of *our* world…army rangers, Green Berets, Navy SEALS, jar heads and a few feds from the FBI, secret service and state department to add an air of sophistication to an otherwise rather vulgar group. They all know their stuff."

"When do I get to meet these guys?" Jeff asked.

"I'm hosting a presidential campaign planning meeting here tomorrow afternoon," Sean said. "The whole team will be on hand. That will be a good opportunity to put your signature on how things will be done in the future. I think the last of the detail flies in about 1900 hours this evening.

"We can have Rosa and crew whip up some BBQ and beer for an informal icebreaker out on the veranda. How does that sound, Mike?"

"Any occasion to have BBQ is a great idea; it will give Jeff a chance to huddle with the team and get acquainted. Managing any group of highly qualified men is tantamount to juggling Jell-O, even under the best of situations. So, the quicker you can make your presence felt, the better."

"I suggest that I make the introduction," said Mike, "give a brief *hoorah* pitch endorsing this fine figure of a man and highlighting his illustrious career, our longstanding relationship, and why he was chosen to head the security detail. I think that's the best way to handle the transition." Though he made it sound like a suggestion open for debate, it was not. It would happen just as he laid it out, with no variation.

After the meeting, Mike, Jeff and J.B. left Sean in the study as they worked their way toward the kitchen to tell Rosa how many people would be at the BBQ and to talk her out of a glass of iced tea or perhaps another cold beer or two.

Hearing about a BBQ for the first time and having roughly four hours to prepare for it, Rosa was not a happy camper. After a brief tirade with her hands on her hips, in her native Spanish, she said, "Senor Mike, this makes me look bad. The meat must be prepared slowly with herbs, special marinades and smoked slowly for hours. I cannot do this in such a short time."

Mike smiled and gave Rosa a big hug. "You're right, as usual sweetheart. What do you suggest?"

"I can make a wonderful Mexican fiesta with chili, tacos, burritos, refried beans and rice. Would that be OK?"

Mike smiled at his surrogate Mom. "That would be just fine, Rosa. Be sure there's lots of cold beer, and if you would give us one now, we'll get out of your kitchen and let you get started."

Rosa opened one of the large Sub-Zero refrigerators which contained an assortment of beverages, including five or six brands of beer. She handed Mike a Corona, his beer of choice, and then asked the other two men what they would like to have. She gave each the brand they asked for and as they were leaving the kitchen, Mike winked at J.B. "You know we have some time to kill. We could mount up and take a quick ride if ya'll feel like it."

Recognizing the barb was directed at him, Jeff replied in an exaggerated Bronx accent, "Don't make me tell uze guys what uze can do with da horse! Don't make me do it."

Mike and J.B. laughed at their friend's response which was the one they anticipated. They slapped him on the back and, much to Jeff's relief, settled for a casual walk to the lake.

The rest of the time at the O'Reilly estate was occupied with campaign strategies, associated security requirements, small talk, relaxation and a great Mexican fiesta.

Early the next morning, the fleet of glistening white corporate jets displaying the bright green shamrock punched through the early morning scud to begin winging their way toward pre-assigned destinations across the country in preparation for the serious business at hand: Mike O'Reilly's bid for the highest and most important office in the land—president of the United States.

33

Everglades City, Florida

Mike never gave a thought as he walked toward the lake with his two friends what order of business might have caused J.B. to be late for the meeting in his father's study.

He had to first issue two deadly serious communiqués. Interestingly, the messages were transmitted via STU-3 scramblers from the very tower Jeff had pointed out to Mike, and from the underground compound whose vented air Mike had seen, or thought he had seen, on final approach to the airfield.

The sleek, black Mosquito boat, powered by three of the most powerful outboard motors available, sat low in the water as it slowly transitioned from the open sea into the twisting channels created by the Everglades mangrove thickets.

A sentry, standing on the bow of the boat, could barely be seen in the early morning fog rising from the water. The pilot of the craft was painfully aware of just how tricky navigating the ever-changing shallows of the mangrove swamps could be. A month earlier on a similar run he had fallen prey to the tide and run aground. Fortunately they were close to the edge of the mangroves and were able to camouflage the hapless craft, going undetected by DEA and coast guard aircraft, until the tides changed.

The low guttural sound of the engines carried across the water, but could only be heard for a short distance due to the buffering created by the thick outcroppings.

Up ahead, a smaller boat and two locals awaited the sinister cash crop...two tons of cocaine, already packaged and ready for distribution throughout the eastern states.

The sentry on the bow of the boat used hand signals to guide the large craft toward the faint glow of the pin light ahead. As they approached their destination, the ever-present paranoia of drug smugglers kicked in.

The men aboard both boats were armed to the teeth with automatic weapons—TEC-10's, M16's and one AK-47—and tension was high, as it always was during the transfer of drugs and vast amounts of cash, though this ritual was performed many times during the course of a year and often by the same players.

Federal and state law enforcement agencies routinely provided media releases concerning drug seizures and how they had crippled a particular cartel. They dutifully submitted their reports up the chain of command as directed, with estimates of the amount of illegal drugs entering the country.

These reports brought a whole new meaning to the term 'literary license.' For the most part, the reports served the same purpose as old Sears catalogs before the advent of indoor plumbing: It made good ass wipe and that was about it! The field agents knew this better than anyone. Nonetheless, the further up the line the reports navigated through the bloated bureaucracy, the more embellished they became.

Truth be known, the government didn't have the foggiest idea of what was getting through the anti-drug net sieve. And their solution to the problem was to throw billions of dollars down the proverbial rat hole, trying to plug up the shortcomings, within the parameters of the law, of course.

Sean's position, under the auspices of ARC, unencumbered by parameters of law, most of which favored the criminal, was different...*liquidate* the drug-dealing bastards and you never have to worry about them again.

Every peddler tapped is one less you have to deal with. Simple solution! From his point of view, it sends a clear message to other worthless scumbags looking for a quick score that maybe the fast cash wasn't worth the life-threatening risks.

No question, since the inception of ARC over a decade ago, involvement in the drug trade was definitely life-threatening. The events about to unfold would magnify that message.

As the Mosquito boat got within fifteen or twenty feet of the smaller craft, the guy on the throttles heard several light thumps from beneath the heavily laden boat as he slipped the motors in reverse to help slow the closure rate. Given the deep draft and shallow waters, thumps were to be expected.

The sentry on the bow was so preoccupied with throwing a rope to the smaller craft he didn't see the occasional bubble coming from the dark waters under the boat.

Following an exchange of preplanned passwords, everyone, with the exception of the sentry on the bow, laid their weapons aside and started the arduous task of off-loading and stacking the packaged cocaine onto the smaller boat.

The transaction complete, the Mosquito slowly rumbled out toward open seas while the smaller craft, with two uninvited guests in tow beneath the hull, slowly made its way toward the wooded shoreline just below the boat ramp at Everglades City.

The intelligence provided the ARC strike team by the larger of the two men in the small craft was very specific about where the rendezvous would take place; where the small craft was to make landfall once the cocaine was onboard; and even which house the packages would be delivered to.

The heavy-set drug smuggler didn't arbitrarily come forward as a Good Samaritan. The promise of safe passage, help in relocation and a large sum of money had a lot to do with his level of cooperation. The term 'safe passage' simply meant he wouldn't find himself cut up and used as bait in someone's crab trap.

Over the past three or four days, the strike force had filtered into Everglades City in pairs, posing as fishermen out for a few days of Snook fishing. In actuality, they were not *posing* as fishermen, they *were* fishermen who did all the right things…trips to the store for more beer, bait, etc. and supper at the restaurant closest to the little motel they were staying in.

Two of the operatives entered the village in an RV that must have cost half a mil. From an operational standpoint, they were careful not to fraternize with anyone other than their fishing buddy.

The latter was not difficult. ARC was organized in such a way that respective spheres of influence assigned to one of the three ARC regions were organized into two-man teams. Unless there was a mission requiring more than one strike team, such as the one they were preparing to initiate, they really didn't have the opportunity to know one another.

Teams were stacked as needed to tailor a strike package for a specific mission. Because of the large sum of cocaine allegedly involved in this operation and the number of bad guys they might encounter, there were five teams in Everglades City on this predawn morning.

Before Morning Nautical Twilight (BMNT) is a nice time of day. It is still dark but ever so slight traces of light are preparing to start their daily trek westward. Most mornings, it is a peaceful time in this sleepy little Everglades fishing village.

Unfortunately, this was not to be one of them. The two men from the boat completed the arduous task of off-loading the packaged drugs into an older van with faded blue paint and touches of rust around the headlights and double cargo doors.

The uninvited ex-Navy SEALS, using suction cups designed to provide divers with a handhold on submerged objects, while performing myriad underwater tasks, were now out of the water, flippers and tanks removed.

They advanced unnoticed in black wetsuits and waited for the large man to slam the cargo doors of the van to twist-lock silencers onto their drawn Sig Saur semi-automatic pistols.

As the smaller man climbed into the passenger seat, a 9mm projectile entered the open window and quietly dispatched the unsuspecting soul and his brains to a happier place, though they would not be traveling together!

The large man was cuffed, using plastic restraints, and escorted a short distance to the luxurious RV, where he was blindfolded, gagged and hogtied in such a way that any movement would essentially choke him to death.

The two teams assigned to over-watch duty covered the single-story house front and rear. The six-man entry team, equipped with night vision goggles, gained entrance through unlocked windows on either side of the house and systematically eliminated four targets in less than a minute.

They spent another ten minutes looking for large stashes of cash. They found nothing and silently slipped back into the predawn darkness. All of the weapons and scuba gear were checked in at the RV using an equipment inventory list to ensure nothing was left behind.

With the exception of one team of 'fishermen' left behind to keep an eye on the van, the remaining teams made their way up the two-lane road leading to Alligator Alley and obscurity.

The Florida Highway Patrol or local sheriff's office would be notified by the locals sooner or later and descend on the small village to claim personal victory for the takedown and drug cache. Of course a convincing media release to explain all of the dead bodies would have to be fabricated.

Unfortunately the fat guy hogtied in the RV must have *moved*! His lifeless body was unceremoniously dumped into one of the canals just outside Everglades City. Alligators and turtles have to eat, too!

The ARC mission was cruel but necessary. Government laws and rules of engagement, severely handicapping law enforcement initiatives, were slow, cumbersome and ineffective. If that were not the case, Sean rationalized there would be no need for a covert organization whose only charter was to make the streets of the United States a safer place. Perhaps one day that would be the case. Until then, ARC would continue to selectively eliminate the dregs of society…the worst of the worst!

Before leaving Everglades City, the last remaining strike team witnessed the distant unexplained glow in the western skies over the Gulf of Mexico. One can only assume it had something to do with the C-4 satchel charges affixed to the underside of the fast, sleek Mosquito boat.

34

Centralia, Washington

Centralia, originally settled in the 1800s as Centerville at the junction of the Chehalis and Skookumchuck Rivers, is a quaint community of about 14,000 snuggled in a setting of beautiful green mountains and clear water.

To a passerby, it has the appearance of a place time has forgotten. Old dilapidated buildings, some of them long since deserted, and neglected railroad tracks serve as a reminder of a once busy hub for the logging industry that disappeared decades ago, along with the local sawmill.

Small cafés, antique stores and an assortment of small businesses associated with a town this size line the main street.

It's the kind of town that makes one feel good, a nice place to live. That was the impression at least of the two men who had spent the last few days in a budget hotel along I-5 just south of Olympia.

This mission was different. The targets were two elusive cop killers right off the FBI's 'Ten Most Wanted' list: a man and a woman, released from an east coast jail after posting a ludicrously low bond for several aggravated assault charges. They killed a police officer the day after they were released by a judge who had not taken time to review their extensive and violent rap sheets.

The strike team knew this was not an isolated case. Across the country, due to overcrowded dockets, inept or soft judges, and mistakes, thousands of felons—many of them repeat offenders—

were being bonded out of jail without even appearing before a judge...to continue a life of violent crime against unsuspecting citizens.

The strike team knew, as many informed citizens knew, that the criminal justice system was broken for countless reasons, all academic. If it doesn't work; if it places our citizens at risk; if it releases tens of thousands of hardened criminals back on the streets to rape, rob and, in this case, kill a police officer, then it has to be fixed. The ARC charter was to do just that: Fix the problem!

Two of the problems were holed up in a small motel that had seen better days about a block from a park bordering the Skoocumchuck River. A gravel road made a big loop about half a mile long through the park, providing two entrances into the area. Huge tree stumps lined the road suggesting that at one time, it must have been a majestic sight. It was less than that now.

The last several days of surveillance recorded only three vehicles entering the park, two of those were after dark and parked in a remote area...probably not picnickers!

The only other traffic involved the two cop killers who seemed to have established a daily ritual of taking evening walks to the river. They would not forget this one, at least for the short time they were blessed with memory.

Observing the fugitives approaching the fast-moving river shallows, the strike team noticed every detail. Clearly they were not intimate, at least not in public. Both smoked. The woman, short and heavyset, wore a flannel jacket opened in the front and was holding what appeared to be a bottle of beer.

The man wore a dark parka of some type, probably to better conceal a weapon. They casually walked the gravel road, turning off at a small opening in the foliage next to the river.

The woman sat on a downed log that had been lodged between two trees during a previous flood. The Skoocumchuck had a tendency to do that on occasion and seemed to have more water flowing this evening than it had over the last few days of observation.

The man appeared to be about six feet tall, 150 pounds, and he entertained himself by trying unsuccessfully to skip flat rocks across the river.

A slight drizzle had started to fall, which was not uncommon for this part of the Pacific Northwest, and an evening chill was setting in.

It became noticeably darker and the white caps created by rushing water over rocks in the riverbed appeared phosphorescent. After a few minutes the man tired of rock throwing and sat down next to his companion.

The faint sound of voices could be heard above the roar of the river, but the operatives could not discern what the conversation was about from their position fifty feet away.

Sometimes, even the best of plans can turn to shit right before your eyes, and there isn't much can be done about it. The dense cloud cover that had rolled in producing drizzle had obscured what little light there was, rendering night vision devices all but useless.

One of the operatives wore glasses so he had to constantly wipe the mist off them, lest his vision be distorted. They both knew that in covert operations, movement of any kind could be the kiss of death.

To complicate things further, the two fugitives were wearing dark clothing and sitting on a log with dark foliage as a backdrop. Suddenly there was zero ambient light and no light poles anywhere within the park.

The first indication the strike team had that the subjects were no longer in the kill zone was the sound of a discarded bottle hitting the gravel road as the couple made their way back toward civilization.

Both men swore under their breath, as they came off an adrenaline rush, knowing they had been only moments away from neutralizing two of America's most wanted. There was no way to work their way in front of the two cop killers before they reached the relative safety of the motel. The mission was scrubbed for the night. However, unfinished business was not part of the ARC psyche.

The bloated bodies of a man and woman were found down river several days later, forced under a pile of rubble created by the swollen river. Both had two grayish holes in their chest and one in the temple.

Fingerprint analysis from law enforcement's Automated Fingerprint Identification System (AFIS) would later positively identify the two, thus removing two dangerous fugitives from the FBI's Ten Most Wanted list, ending one manhunt...and initiating another.

Who was out there systematically eliminating the worst of the worst and with military precision? *Why*? *What* was their motivation? *Where* did they get their intelligence and *who* could fund such a major undertaking?

Federal agencies and state law enforcement didn't have an answer, and only one of them had the resources to find out...the FBI.

35

Philadelphia Civic Center weeks later

Mike had spent most of his time, since visiting the O'Reilly estate weeks earlier, stumping across the country delivering a powerful but simple message. "If you love this country, it's time to become proactive and *demand* that the government start acting in the best interests of the people. The Republic is in trouble and hurdling ever closer to the edge of an abyss from which there is no return. It happened to the Roman Empire, and it is happening to us at this very moment."

His message was candid, articulate and cut right to the bone. "United we can make the changes necessary to keep this great nation strong. If we continue on the present course, the country runs the risk of economic and political implosion." There was no better place, in his mind, to drive this point home than here...the cradle of the Republic.

"Ladies and gentlemen, look around you. There are great Americans everywhere. There may be people in this very room that are descendants of our Founding Fathers. Remember them? They spoke eloquently of things like: in God we trust; life, liberty and the pursuit of happiness; aiding and comforting enemies of these United States is an act of treason; and all manner of things needed in the design of a cohesive democratic government process.

"Freedom, after all, is not a new concept. *We* have it in writing!" As he waved his outstretched arm from one side of the packed meeting house to the other, Mike said "Collectively, *we* are the problem.

"Fortunately we are also the solution. Right now, the tail is wagging the dog. Because of apathy, inaction or inattention to detail, we have fallen asleep at the wheel.

"Under what other circumstances would we allow an organization like the ACLU, under threat of a lawsuit, to manipulate a law-abiding nation to agree to nonsensical laws that force their extremism and liberal will on the people?

"What other explanation is there for allowing an atheist...an *atheist*, mind you...to bring so much pressure to bear that prayer and the 'Pledge of Allegiance' is removed from our schools?

"What the hell could we have been thinking when we allowed the judiciary to introduce the concept of plea bargaining in lieu of being judged by a jury of your peers as outlined by our Founding Fathers?

"The job of the prosecutor and the judge in our judicial system is to ensure that the defendant gets a fair and impartial trial and that the law of the land is upheld. Is that what we have today? I think not!

"The degeneration of the criminal justice system has eroded to the point that most prosecutors are interested only in self-promotion. Wins! Tick marks in the win column of the ledger that will ultimately propel them into the political arena and higher office. And if they can win via a plea bargain, that's a win without effort. It's also nonsense!

"To use the media as a means of foreplay, so to speak, to publicly put an individual on trial by releasing information that is tailored or less than full disclosure in an effort to ultimately sway public opinion, reeks to high heaven and needs to be nipped in the bud right now...*today*!

"Keep in mind, the jury of one's peers is selected from those the prosecutor is trying to sway via the media. In other words, folks...there's a rat in the sandbox, and if we allow it to continue unabated, shame on us!"

In unison the audience stood and applauded this dynamic, forward-thinking candidate who, by almost any measure one could think of, was the darkest of dark horse candidates.

"Believe me when I tell you, folks; I don't give a rat's ass about endorsements from special interest groups. If, within their esteemed body, individuals do not have the moral courage to step forward and be counted in such a way that it is in the best interests of the country and her citizens, then I sure as hell don't want them on my team…votes be damned!

"This is my pledge: If elected president, I will do everything in my power to see that public servants elected to the United States Congress dedicate their efforts to enacting good laws that are in the best interests of the people. I will ensure proposed legislation presented to me for signature is not laden with self-serving pork barrel amendments. If they are, I'll veto the proposed legislation, send it back and tell them to clean it up.

"These gentlemen are used to getting their way. I say enough is enough. It's time for them to become the moral voice of the people. Quite frankly, based on their demonstrated performance to date, I'd fire the whole damn bunch and start over."

The shouting, whistling and raucous behavior from an overwhelmingly supportive audience was far more characteristic of a baseball game than a serious political rally. Mike was pleased, but taken aback by the demonstrative nature of those in attendance.

When the hall had settled down, he was able to continue. "I plan on doing many things with your help, and if I do nothing but that, it will be a giant step forward for the citizens of the United States. The amount of taxpayer dollars dedicated to self-serving congressional initiatives is mind-boggling, hundreds of millions of dollars every year. If we committed those resources to research, we would have cures for about everything that ails mankind or be damn close to it.

"I will put the full weight of the presidency behind three initiatives. I will lead the way for national prison reform, outlining harsh sentences for our wayward brethren, similar to those that are presently in place in my home state of Oklahoma and in Maricopa County, Arizona. They work there and they can work equally well for the nation.

"Tents, razor wire and hard work, serve as strong deterrents to those that would commit heinous crimes. It all but eliminates the revolving door syndrome. I assure you, inmates in Oklahoma and

Maricopa County will do everything in their power to avoid a second trip through the system...even honest work.

"Secondly, but of equal importance, is the revamping of the country's welfare system, again tailored after the successful programs we have implemented in Oklahoma. I see no need to reinvent the wheel. The programs I will recommend for the nation are time tested and have proven successful in reducing welfare rolls; putting able-bodied people back to work and providing a boost to the economy. That sounds pretty good to me, but then I'm a simple farm boy."

Not everyone in attendance knew a lot about Mike, but they knew for sure he was anything but a simple farm boy. He was dynamic, articulate and obviously a candidate whose thinking was outside the proverbial box...a futurist.

"Let me give you something to think about. It's not presently in the welfare reform package we passed when I was governor, but I have given it a lot of thought, and I think it is worthy of analysis and consideration.

"In our respective places of employment, many of us are subjected to random urine or drug tests as a condition of employment. We pay taxes and the government spends that money as they see fit. Part of it goes to welfare checks.

"If the hard-working citizens who constitute the tax base are subjected to drug testing, shouldn't those receiving welfare and unemployment checks also be tested as a condition of receiving the government's money? I'm inclined to think they should. It's logical."

"Education is the third and perhaps the most critical piece of the O'Reilly plan. It is unconscionable to think that the youth of America place lower academically than some third world countries. We have students graduating high school and college who find it a major challenge to read and write the English language. Let me rephrase that...the *American* language. Hell, I have trouble reading and writing the *English* language."

Light laughter came from the hundreds of people who had crowded into the assembly hall to listen to Mike in his bid for the presidency.

"We must ensure that our educators at every level are the cream of the crop, and we must be willing to pay them good wages to not only keep them in the classroom, but also to provide economic incentive to young people who may be considering education as a chosen profession. Education is the future, my friends, and we best not lose sight of that.

"We live in a highly technical world and to stay abreast of the phenomenal growth of technological innovation, our young people must be properly educated in order to meet the challenges of the future."

Mike took a moment to scan the audience to get a read on whether or not his messages were being favorably received. He didn't see anything alarming, so he continued.

"I'm an advocate of simplicity. In that vein, what you see is what you get, insofar as my campaign is concerned. I have had a reasonably high national profile over the last decade or so and I'm sure if there's a blemish it has already been pointed out. If you have criticisms, be my guest. That's one of our inalienable rights.

"My staff is even critical. They think I should be more eloquent, more *presidential*, as it were. I think they're nuts! I'm a rancher from Oklahoma and the only cowboy I know who even came close to being eloquent, in a quaint sort of way, was Will Rogers." The audience chuckled and a few even clapped.

"I have good credentials. I am an alumnus of the long gray line and will be forever grateful to West Point for the leadership lessons learned there. I graduated cum laude from the Harvard School of Law and predictably, they were taken aback by southern colloquialisms but, bless their little hearts, they soon learned dialect is a poor barometer for measuring one's intelligence.

"I have served in our armed forces as an infantry officer. I was a partner in one of the most prestigious law firms in the country before running for governor of Oklahoma. And intimately involved in the management and leadership of one of our countries most successful and prolific private corporations.

"Undoubtedly everything I just said plays a role, but most important in the scheme of things is that I come from good Irish stock and believe in honor, courage and loyalty.

"O'Reilly men have always been infantry soldiers, dating back to the 1600s and duty with the Queen's own 18th Royal Grenadiers. My great grandfather fought in the Civil War with the Kentucky Long Rifles. My grandfather fought in World War I as an infantryman with the Big Red One. My father Sean, God love him, is a distinguished infantry soldier, having fought in both World War II and Korea. He was awarded the Congressional Medal of Honor for his selfless actions and heroism while serving with the 101st Airborne Division at Bastogne.

"These kinds of things don't just happen. They are matters of heritage, patriotism and a firm belief in duty.

"Together, my father and I have dedicated ourselves to helping others through humanitarian relief efforts and employment of tens of thousands of hard-working Americans across this great nation, including our frost-bitten brethren in Alaska.

"This country has afforded us the opportunity to work hard and be successful. My goal is to see that every American, young and old, has that same opportunity.

"There will be no free rides or slackers on my watch. Coining one of my father's favorite sayings, "You can lead, follow or get the hell out of the way...but do something!

"I couldn't carry a tune in a wash tub, but there is one part of the theme song for the mountain man movie 'Jeremiah Johnson' that I think sums up my view on about everything...'the day that you tarry is the day that you lose.' I'd be happy to sing that for you but I'm afraid it would cause a mass exodus, and the folks most likely to vote for me would be trampled to death. I can't take the risk."

The audience had a genuine connection with this candidate and most in attendance gave him a standing ovation as he concluded his remarks and opened the floor to questions.

Mike pointed to a gentleman in the front row. "Mr. O'Reilly, during the conduct of your campaign have you had occasion to meet with special interest groups and, if so, what promises did you make to them?"

Smiling, Mike stepped from behind the podium and walked as far forward as possible without falling into someone's lap. "I have met with all manner of special interest groups...longshoreman, American Medical Association, American Bar Association, Autoworkers of America, Greenpeace, respective state governors, convention of city mayors and many, many more. The only organizations I have not, and will not, meet with are those I consider subversive and a danger to our American way of life.

Ranking at the very top are the KKK, the Aryan Brotherhood and my all time favorite, the ACLU.

"The second part of your question, concerning promises made. I made *no* promises beyond the pledge that I gave here today and further that I respectfully would decline all contributions.

"Let me make my position concerning campaign contributions clear. I will *not* accept contributions. End of statement!

"The costs associated with my presidential campaign will be borne by me and none other. Further, should I become president of the United States, every nickel I am entitled to will be diverted back into the government coffers. That's a promise!"

Mike pointed to a lady in the extreme rear of the assembly hall. "Sir, it is common knowledge that you have your own hand-picked security detail. Is it your intent to dismiss the Secret Service agents assigned to the presidential protection detail, should you become president, and how do you envision the transition into the Oval Office?"

"The short answer to your question…I have no intention of dismissing the Secret Service. It is mandated by law. I will also tell you my guys will remain in my employ; be paid by me; and will continue doing what they do best…protecting me and my family. We will work together to see that the relationship within the security details are as transparent and seamless as possible.

"I already have plans in place that will give me and those I have chosen, or will choose, an opportunity to hit the ground running. But you have to realize, this is a new experience for me and one would be naïve to think the transition into the highest office in the land would be made without a bump or two. Did that answer your question?" The lady nodded and took her seat.

A voice from somewhere said, "Mr. O'Reilly, your Democratic challenger and previous presidential hopefuls have gone on record stating they would provide full disclosure of their finances and, if necessary, divest themselves of all areas where a conflict of interest may arise. What is your position?"

Mike scanned the audience, "You're a voice from nowhere, sir. Where the hell are you? I like to see the person I'm talking to." Midway back and to the left a man stood and raised his hand.

"Thank you, sir," Mike said. "There are certain things required by law to disclose. To the degree I understand that law, I will comply. As long as the disclosure does not jeopardize in any way the O'Reilly Corporation; proprietary information; or somehow disclose corporate intent regarding future business ventures or acquisitions.

"Secondly, under no condition I can think of would I be willing to divest my interest in anything. We are speaking of my family's livelihood and that would not be a reasonable request.

"The O'Reilly Corporation, as you surely know, is up to here," Mike said indicating a level just above his chin, "in oil, cattle, agriculture, manufacturing, real estate and a host of other subsidiaries doing all manner of things. How do I divest from that? If I were president, would I be involved in any of these things? Absolutely! Would there be conflict of interest? Most likely there would be.

"The more important issue is the integrity and intent of the man you elect as your next president, and I can tell you unequivocally, under no condition would I intentionally influence an action or law for self gain. The litmus test for my entire adult life, not just my political career, has been the simple question: Is what I'm about to do in the best interest of the people? If it will not pass muster, then I don't do it. It's that simple."

He pointed to a lady three rows back from the stage. "Let's say you *are* elected, what influence will your wife have on your decisions and in what areas might she become involved?"

Mike flashed the woman an exceptionally warm smile before saying, "Wow! I wish she were here to answer this one. If it is a decision concerning me or my family, she certainly has a lot of influence. The word that comes to mind is *absolute*!

"On the other hand, if it is a decision impacting the nation, it is not likely she will know anymore than you can glean daily from the media. Rarely has business been a topic of discussion in our household. I see no reason why the color or size of the house would change that policy.

"With regard to interests and things she may choose to pursue, she is very much interested in issues impacting education, the arts, and all manner of humanitarian initiatives. Veronica has an innate love of her fellow man and doesn't want anyone to suffer hardship. You can just about count on her deep involvement in these areas and, as I have done in the past, I will seek her counsel on some of these issues. She is an incredibly bright lady."

Mike looked out over the audience and with a wry smile added, "I know what some of you are thinking so let me intercede. Even bright people have weak moments, and it was during one of these moments that I proposed to her." Half of the audience chuckled and the other half had that 'deer in the headlight' stare, having no clue to what he had just alluded to.

A gentleman halfway back in the seating area raised his hand. "Mr. O'Reilly, your prison reform initiatives are harsh, to say the least. I know you and the Oklahoma State Legislature have taken some pretty heavy hits over the years from liberals, the ACLU, and I don't doubt others. At the national level, one can only imagine the pressure to soften your stance on crime will be overwhelming. How do you plan on dealing with that, sir, and would you be amenable to softening your position or perhaps even offering a whole new tact?"

Mike thought about the question for a moment before answering. "Well, sir, here's the deal. The policies and procedures governing incarceration in Oklahoma work. They evolved over time into a system that has not only lowered the incidents of crime, but also reduced what is referred to as the revolving door syndrome, the continuous re-incarceration of repeat offenders.

"What exactly, would you have me change, sir? It is clear my plan works and, short of being shown proof positive that there is a better, more effective way, I would not be inclined to soften my stance. No, sir, I would not be a willing participant to that. Let me say here and now that any legislation presented for signature alluding to a soft stance on crime would be vetoed if I were president.

"That is one of our problems today. Every bleeding heart liberal out there is so wrapped up in political correctness and protecting the rights of criminals, they totally forget about the victims. That's nonsense!

"I'm an advocate for citizens' rights and, as far as I'm concerned, prisoners have limited rights…food, if they work for it; shelter, if they don't destroy it; adequate medical care, as needed; and an opportunity to work hard in an effort to reduce their sentences. That's it!"

The majority of the people in the assembly hall applauded, and a number of them gave him a standing ovation, but not the gentleman who asked the question. He looked sullen as he stood in preparation for asking a follow-up question.

"Mr. O'Reilly, are you saying convicted felons should not be given a second chance?"

"Did you hear me say that, sir?" Mike said, as he fixed the man with a cold stare.

"No, but I…"

Mike interrupted the man. "If you care enough to ask a question, then it is incumbent upon you to at least listen to the answer.

"Excluding capital crimes, for which there is no second chance in my plan, all other convicted felons are entitled to right the ship, so to speak, after they serve their full sentence, minus time off for hard work. There is a subtlety here you need to pay attention to. I didn't say time off for *good behavior*, and I didn't say anything about *parole*. In my plan, if you commit a crime, be prepared to serve the full sentence. All of it!"

Mike drank some water while the audience settled in and then continued. "It is important for everyone to know why I'm so hard-over on soft, inept judges, parole and bail.

"In my view, each represents a leg of what I call the 'triangle of regret.' We've all heard it a thousand times, after the fact: 'I regret not reviewing his rap sheet before granting bail. I regret signing his parole papers. I regret he killed or raped again after being released.' I regret, I regret, I regret!

"And the beat goes on. If we keep the egg-sucking dogs locked up or execute them at the earliest possible date, you won't have to regret a damn thing. Let him *regret* he committed the crime!

"It is very hard for most law-abiding citizens to understand that there is an element of our society that is pathologically evil and takes immense pleasure in being the purveyors of death and destruction. These people must be identified and permanently removed from society.

"Since this is a common theme in my talks about prison reform and crime in general, some of you may have already heard this, but it is important enough to say time and again. The criminal justice system is a *train wreck*! Judges are either lazy or overworked to the point they don't take time to check the records of criminals coming before them to bond out. In many cases, the criminals don't even have to appear.

"Thousands of hardened criminals, with rap sheets as long as your arm, are released daily to continue preying on law-abiding citizens. They commit tens of thousands of crimes before they can be re-apprehended and locked up…again!

"By any standard, that's *dumb as dirt*! It is an irrational, nonsensical practice that must stop. Once you have the squirrel in your grasp, why would you want to turn him loose again?

"I may not be the smartest bird in the nest, but I'm sure as hell smarter than that. That won't happen on my watch, and if you think that's too hard of a position, I encourage you to cast your vote elsewhere.

"Voters must choose between two camps: the liberal status quo or dramatic change in the way our government, our representatives, and our criminal justice system functions.

"If we continue on the present track, the United States runs serious risk of imploding. Our future will be managed by foreign entities; our Congress, through ineptitude and fiscal irresponsibility, will bankrupt the country; and our streets will be so overrun with crime and corruption, the good citizens of these United States will be unable to walk the streets. Collectively we must draw a line in the sand and say *enough is enough*!"

Mike must have struck a nerve. The meeting hall erupted in applause and raucous shouts of approval. He sensed perhaps the citizenry was starting to see the light. After a few moments the majority of those in attendance settled back in their seats, and he was able to continue.

"There are those who would have you believe there is nothing we can do to reverse this mess we have made for ourselves. What kind of testimonial is that? United there's a hell of a lot we can do.

"Write, call or send the Pony Express to your elected representatives and tell them to knock off the nonsense and refocus on passing good laws without self-serving pork barrel attachments and start making decisions that are in the best interest of the people and the country. That's what you elected them to do and demand that they do it. If they don't, put their rosy red butt out on the street.

"Ladies and gentlemen, I am reminded almost daily by my staff that I don't sound presidential. Decades of people with a focus on sounding *presidential* are what got us into this mess in the first place. Frankly, I don't give a damn how I sound.

"I know how to fix the problems and I have the moral courage to do it. I have a plan to successfully lead our country back toward fiscal responsibility; to ensure our streets are safe and our children are well educated; and to make sure government represents us as *we the people* want to be represented, fair, just and with high moral standards."

36

The good people of Philadelphia and elsewhere around the country were not the only ones who felt it was time to act. Unexplained incidents resulting in the seizure and subsequent destruction of countless tons of illicit drugs; the death of those selling and distributing the deadly substance; and professional hits on high profile criminals, many on the FBI's 'Ten Most Wanted' list, could not continue unchecked.

The recent discovery of two cop killers found in a river in Washington and the efficient elimination of a large drug-smuggling operation in Everglades City, Florida made this a federal case. It was the catalyst that forced the fed's hand. The FBI had to do something...*but what*?

Many in the FBI and the DEA were willing to leave well enough alone on the premise that 'you don't fix it if it isn't broken!' What they were really wrestling with was *where* to start.

There were no obvious starting points or good leads pointing to who might be behind these 'good deeds.' Secondly, how do you motivate an investigative team to track down a person or persons unknown who were systematically ridding society of the worst of the worst?

They were doing what the federal government, due to antiquated, ineffective laws, judicial procedures, and bureaucratic nonsense, seemed unable to do. One agent assigned to the newly formed detail asked the rhetorical question, 'Tell me again why we want to catch these guys?'

The daunting task would initially be given to the FBI's Criminal Investigation Division, since the majority of the unexplained, unsolved assassinations that had taken place across the country over the last decade or so were drug-related, crossed state lines and resulted in the death of both foreign and U.S. citizens.

Lou Hanson, FBI deputy director, soon realized a small, clandestine investigative team approach was tantamount to placing a Band-Aid over a sucking chest wound.

He decided getting to the root cause of these mysterious and unexplained incidents would require the combined efforts of a task force made up of his agency, the DEA and other federal and state law enforcement agencies as required. His first call was to Steve Humphrey, United States attorney general.

Within two weeks, Lou had organized Task Force Checkmate and was within a few moments of hosting the kickoff meeting in one of the Bureau's conference rooms used primarily by the deputy director's planning office.

In attendance from the Bureau were hand-picked agents from the Criminal Investigation Division; Office of Law Enforcement Coordination; Information Technology Operations Division, as well as Joel Armstrong, the chief information officer responsible for all aspects of the FBI's information technology.

Overkill was the natural inclination of the deputy director anyway, but in this case, he felt a strong presence by the Bureau was warranted to send a clear message to other members of the task force with regard to just how serious this mission really was.

The deputy administrator, Drug Enforcement Administration, was there with agents from the DEA divisions responsible for special operations and intelligence.

Also in attendance were legal beagles from the general counsels of both agencies and a representative from the U.S. attorney general's office.

Present for the kickoff meeting, but not part of Task Force Checkmate, were a number of state law enforcement representatives who had been called in to provide overview briefings of incidents that had occurred in their respective states that met the arbitrary criteria assigned by the Bureau.

To say the least, it was an interesting mix. The large conference room was well appointed for a government facility, with a large eight-by-ten-foot screen and retractable projector imbedded in the heavy wooden conference table.

Because of the importance of the meeting, a court recorder, in addition to the normal recording devices, was on hand to ensure every word was captured. Not a bad idea, given the relationship that normally prevailed between rival government agencies.

Cloistered next to the large stainless steel coffee urn was a bevy of pin-striped suits with highly shined black wing-tipped shoes. Most of the talking heads atop these suits had that 'holier than thou' expression associated with FBI agents. It's the same one New Yorkers give a Texas cowboy as he stares up in disbelief at skyscrapers...*that look*!

In the corner furthest from the door were the more relaxed and less formal DEA agents who were laughing, probably at an off-color joke from one of their own.

The state law enforcement cadre was easily recognizable, decked out in the colorful uniforms of their respective agencies. Most of them appeared to be somewhat uncomfortable sequestered in the Washington, D.C. offices of the FBI. Who wouldn't be?

The lawyers were chatting as lawyers do; observing this menagerie of cultures was the matronly, gray-aired recorder sitting quietly, hands folded in her lap.

At precisely 9:00AM, Lou Hanson with the deputy administrator, DEA, following close behind, entered the conference room and proceeded directly to the podium.

Lou was a no-nonsense kind of guy and got right to the point after introducing the deputy administrator. "Gentlemen, this assignment will *make* you or *break* you, myself included. Excluding our friends in uniform, you're all now part of Task Force Checkmate and will be under my operational control.

"All investigations and additional duties you had prior to walking in here this morning will be placed on backburners or transferred to other agents. Our sole purpose in life will be to find the genesis of unexplained incidents, some of which, you are about to be briefed on.

"The FBI, DEA and attorney general of the United States believe there are enough similarities in these cases to suggest that an efficient, well-trained group of individuals are responsible. By no means do we believe the list to be complete. I'm sure there are a number of unreported incidents that have taken place in rural areas, international waters, or even foreign countries that have not yet bubbled to the surface."

The deputy director, though slight of build, was blessed with a confident, deep voice that somehow held one's attention. If that were not enough, his reputation as a *hatchet man* was.

Practically everyone in the Bureau was aware that he had relieved two agents who dozed off during one of his briefings. It didn't seem to matter that the agents in question had not slept in almost twenty-four hours and had just dragged their rumpled butts off of a red eye from LAX.

There were no second chances in Lou Hanson's world, so it was wise to pay attention and to focus all of one's efforts on whatever task he assigned.

Lou looked over at the lawyers. "You gentlemen can pull together all of the intra and interagency agreements over the next couple of days, but I wanted you in here to hear the scope of work and to get a feel for the magnitude of the task.

"We need a wide berth on this one, and when the time comes, we will need to act quickly. I don't want to be sitting around yanking my crank while you guys ponder whose jurisdiction it is or who should issue the warrants. You understand what I'm saying?" They nodded in unison.

"Let me tell you what we know for sure. Without exception, every hit has the earmarks of assassination…neat, clean, and I'm going to guess, quiet. Each incident has been well planned and executed.

"So, gents, we are either dealing with a *superman* who leaps tall buildings and scoots around the country at the speed of light or we are dealing with a well-funded, organized group of highly trained professionals. I opt for the latter.

"Our analysts reviewed what little data we have and came up with a hypothesis to at least give us a point of departure on this thing. Hopefully, as we work our way through it, each piece of information will give us a clearer picture of what we are facing.

"I've asked Vince DiMarco from the lab to give us an overview. Vince."

Lou took a seat at the head of the table as the gangly, self-conscious analyst made his way to the podium. Vince was about 6'6" and weighed maybe 150 pounds. His first task was to wrestle with the podium-mounted microphone in an effort to raise it a couple of feet.

As is the case with most analysts, public speaking was not his strong suit. He spoke in a very low monotone and as he started to lay out the basis of the hypothesis, a loud, crude voice from the rear of the room shouted, "Speak the f--- up!"

Lou Hanson quickly rose from his chair and with his face already starting to flush said, "One more unsolicited interruption, sir, and you're out of here."

The discourteous culprit, a large, tough-looking DEA agent in a well-worn sport coat replied, "I don't give a shit."

Lou fixed him with a cold stare. "I'm afraid you may have misunderstood me, sir. When I said 'out of here,' I meant you would no longer be employed by the DEA or any other government agency as long as you live. Do you now understand?"

The agent paled noticeably, as he tried to disappear in his seat before saying, in a somewhat subdued voice, "Yes, sir."

"Good! Please continue, Vince, and move a little closer to the mike so everyone can hear you, OK?"

Vince was visibly shaken but continued as ordered. "The absence of clues at the crime scenes suggests a disciplined, well-planned assault. In reviewing the various cases that will be presented here today, I had the sense that each was devoid of emotion. In other words, gentlemen, no bravado or passion one might normally associate with the killing of a drug dealer, had he been shot by a rival or perhaps a drug deal gone bad. There was none of that.

"Further, projectile analysis of the 22 LR and 9mm rounds recovered suggests a professional hit. Both are subsonic and easily silenced. Two well-placed rounds to either the head or chest, with a good luck tap to the temple, suggests the shooters knew what they were doing.

"The location of the incidents tells us quite a bit as well. Dark, secluded, and at a time when few, if any, witnesses would be around.

"These gentlemen," Vince said, pointing at the chairs against the far wall where the uniformed officers were seated, "will get into the various incidents, but my group thought a couple of them were interesting in terms of information gleaned.

"One took place a while back in Orlando. The subject clearly didn't know what hit him. He was tapped as he was getting into his van in the parking lot of a strip club.

"Interestingly, agents from the Bureau's Orlando field office were en route to apprehend the victim about the same time. Perhaps it was a coincidence, perhaps not. If it was not, then a rather alarming scenario emerges…compromised communications within the agency."

The thought was chilling and reflected in the concerned faces of the agents now assigned to Task Force Checkmate.

"In a more recent case, two cop killers that every law enforcement agency in the country had been looking for and unable to find were found in a Washington river…two shots to the chest and one to the temple. Sound familiar? As an analyst, I have to ask…*who* could do that?

"With all of the resources available to federal and state law enforcement, we were unable to find and subsequently bring these two to justice. Yet this organization not only found them hiding in some obscure, out-of-the-way place, they terminated them…a different form of justice, I guess. At least *they* must think so.

"The *who* and *why* pieces of this puzzle are not clear at this time. One thing, however, is certain. If we find all or a portion of the incidents on the list are connected, then we are dealing with a level of organization and sophistication never before encountered by the federal government. Our hypothesis is based on such a scenario.

"The bright spot, at least for the moment, is we can eliminate organized crime, and that will save us time. All of the crime scenes are devoid of an organized crime signature. Furthermore, hate groups, militia and outside entities such as cartels can be eliminated. None of them are smart enough or have the wherewithal to accomplish this, even if they wanted to. That's about it, gentlemen. It's not much but we have to start somewhere."

Vince looked down and nodded at Lou as he turned to leave. He was so unaccustomed to public speaking, it never entered his mind that someone might have a question.

Lou stood facing the task force. "Are there any questions you wish to ask Vince before he leaves?"

One of the DEA agents raised his hand and Lou nodded at him. "Sir, do we know if the 9mm rounds were factory loads or were they self-loaded?"

Vince returned to the podium and leaned into it as if to answer the question, and then make a run for it. "With one exception, there were no exit wounds in any of the cases involving 9mm projectiles. That may suggest self-loads, but not necessarily; all projectiles recovered have been hollow point."

As he turned to leave, Vince stopped and returned to the podium. "This may be important to you as we start filling in the blanks. There was an incident in Everglades City involving, I believe, six subjects. One was shot in a van which had a large quantity of cocaine still in the cargo compartment. If it had been a drug deal gone bad, certainly the drugs would not have been left there.

"Furthermore, in a house about a quarter of a mile or less from the van, four heavily armed men were found dead. Each had the signature wounds of a professional hit.

"Let's assume for a moment that this operation was conducted in the dead of night. Someone may be able to observe the loading of the van and subsequently take out the subject found in the front passenger's seat. But it raises a flag to guys like me. Who was driving? Only brains were in the driver's seat.

"It also raises the question of how the shooters knew where the house was or how many people would be in it. How could they so easily have gained entry into a house full of traditionally paranoid drug conspirators? I believe, in this case, they were helped.

"Gaining entry into a strange, dark house would certainly be made easier if the good guys, or *bad guys*, depending on how you look at it, were using night vision devices. I say that because there was no sign of a struggle or any indication the victims had attempted to reach their weapons.

"If our assessment is anywhere close to right, then it doesn't take much imagination to also tie the reported explosion of a suspected drug runner's boat to this case.

"That opens a whole new can of worms. Who planted the explosives and where did they do it? Certainly not while it was docked at the marina; the boat that blew up was too large, with a draft too deep to navigate the shallows, even at high tide. And, we have reviewed the tidal charts which indicate low tide conditions, given our estimated timelines are correct.

"Finally, initial interviews of locals by the Florida Highway Patrol didn't turn up anything unusual. The DEA reports, however, were a bit more thorough. Evidently there had been several small fishing parties come into the small enclave prior to the incident.

"No one really remembered when they arrived, but they did remember what they looked like and that may be a significant piece of information. All of them were physically fit. One witness described a couple of them as 'hard as nails' with short-cropped hair. He said they didn't strike him as all that sociable…loners!

"We ran a quick profile of the typical fisherman, just to give us an idea of the probability of that many *super fit* fisherman showing up at the same time in a place like Everglades City.

In contrast, most guys that like to fish also like football and beer. Statistically, they are twenty-five to fifty-five years of age, somewhat overweight and out of shape, noticeably different from the description given by the witnesses. Our suspects sound more like combat-ready soldiers."

Vince could see he had the attention of everyone in the room and kind of liked it. It beat the hell out of banging on a computer eight hours a day and staring at a cubicle wall. All of a sudden, he didn't want this briefing to end and became emboldened, even his voice became stronger and exuded a certain confidence.

"As an analyst, I only provide information. I'm not in the recommendation business. However, I've been doing this for over twenty years and I might suggest, in this case, you narrow the search by first identifying who has the wherewithal, outside the government, to orchestrate something like this and what their motive would be.

"Trying to react to specific incidents that meet the profile is going to require a lot of men and man hours. If what we have seen to date is an indication, not likely you will find much at the scene. It's something to think about as you gear up Task Force Checkmate."

After thanking Vince who was somewhat reluctant to leave the room, Lou turned to the group. "We may not have much to go on, but Vince has provided some meaningful information. What I would like to do now is to break into study groups to brainstorm this thing. Assignments have already been made, and you will find them in the folders in front of you.

"We will reconvene after lunch to discuss the findings of each group. Keep in mind, this is a non-attribution session and there is no right or wrong conclusions. We simply need to put some meat on this bone, and *quickly*."

37

Chicago, law offices of Greene Laverish Santine & Snyder

Ron and Sean had just finished lunch in the executive dining room and were settling into plush leather chairs in the chairman's large corner office. A few minutes later, an assistant served coffee and then promptly and quietly left the room, leaving the two men alone.

"How do you think the campaign is going for the little shit?"

Ron smiled, always amused at his friend's unique way with words. "He has a way about him most people seem to like. I would be far happier if he sounded more presidential, but that is not his way and you have to admit, he has captured the imagination of the media."

As an afterthought, he added, "Most of it is positive, at least. I think the thirty-second TV spots are good…upbeat, to the point and most importantly, a welcome relief from the negative ads we've been seeing so much of."

Sean nodded. "I think people like the idea that Mike is not accepting a nickel of their tax dollars. We're picking up the whole tab and if elected, the presidential stipend will be returned to the government. Not that it makes a difference, given the size of the national debt, but it sounds good and at the moment; that's what counts."

Ron stood, limped over to the floor-to-ceiling glass walls that covered two sides of his corner office and stared out at the Chicago skyline. "I received an interesting call this morning from the attorney general's office."

"I think I know the nature of the call. That was to be the next topic of discussion. What did he have to say?"

Ron turned and looked at his old friend, "It wasn't the attorney general. It was one of our guys in his office. It seems he has just been assigned the task of drafting a memorandum of agreement between his office, the FBI and the DEA. They have been working the last couple of weeks to form a task force to investigate a series of serious incidents, resulting in the seizure and destruction of large quantities of drugs and assassinations of really bad guys across the country."

"Yeah, I know, Task Force Checkmate. They're huddled in D.C. as we speak. We've got a Bureau guy assigned to the task force. I'll get a data dump later today or first thing tomorrow morning. I'll let you know something as soon as I find out."

Ron poured another cup of coffee and held the silver server up toward his friend. Sean nodded, and Ron poured him a cup as well.

As he sat back in his chair, Ron said, "We knew it would only be a matter of time before someone in the government did something. Quite frankly, I'm surprised it took them so long."

"Ron, these guys are so micro-managed they couldn't find an egg if they knew it was up the hen's ass.

"They have some bright guys, but the bureaucracy has them handcuffed. That's why we've been able to accomplish so much with absolute impunity for all these years, and *they* continue to come out of the chute backwards.

"To prove my point, I'll make a wager with you. I'll bet you ten big ones it'll take them at least two months to finalize the draft inter-agency memo…and that's the easy part."

Ron laughed and shook his head. "No way am I going to buy into that, Tiny. I know you're right! But is there anything we need to be doing that we're not presently focused on?"

"Ron, I can't think of a thing. We have quality people in the field, the org structure has been refined to a fine science and, as you know, we've made some recent personnel changes in the op center that has proven to be a godsend. J.B. and Dave have added a whole new dimension insofar as efficiency and effectiveness are concerned.

"As an example, they know people are far more apt to make dumb mistakes if they're mad. And there is nothing more maddening to a drug czar then to have his bounty confiscated or, worse, contaminated to the extent it no longer has street value."

"So from now on, drug caches will be saturated in diesel fuel, making it worthless. That also eliminates the opportunity for dirty cops or those on the fence from taking the drugs themselves. That's a pretty nifty idea.

"They have also refined the criteria used for allocating confiscated cash more equitably across the humanitarian spectrum. More money now goes to hands-on construction projects like Habitat for Humanity and support of church building projects, as long as they're in the best interest of those in need."

Ron redirected his gaze from the Chicago skyline and made eye contact with Scan. "Who would have ever thought that an old peanut farmer from Alabama and a one-legged Jew from New York could have made such a positive and dramatic impact on the reduction of drug-related crime...in fact, on the criminal justice system itself?

"We've come a long way, my friend, and I wouldn't have missed it for the world. If the feds busted through the door this very moment and cuffed us, I'd have absolutely no regrets. It had to be done; we were in a position to do it; and we did it!

"I've always wondered, though, if Mike had any idea as governor of Oklahoma of what the *real* driving force was behind the cooperation the judiciary gave him in cleaning up their ranks; revamping of the Department of Corrections; and getting the criminal justice system back on track."

Sean, without hesitation, said, "Nope, he had no idea. Had he known, I'm convinced he would've gladly dumped politics and joined us."

"He is a bright lad, always on the leading edge of the intellectual power curve, and one step ahead....in your case, light years ahead!"

Sean gave the smaller man's neck a light squeeze as he pulled him closer. "You just have to get a shot or two in, don't you? I'll bet you wouldn't be grinning like a shit-eatin' dog if I ripped that leg off and beat your skinny little ass to death with it, would you?"

After several hours of open discussion about Mike's ongoing campaign, ARC operations, and of course, the ritual showing of photos of Sean's granddaughter Cheyenne, the big man hugged his friend and left for O'Hare International where he would board the glistening G-4.

Next on the agenda: a flight to Anchorage to finalize agreements with the consortium involved in the production of natural gas from the North Slope and inspection of new pumping facilities at Valdez, Alaska.

38

J. Edgar Hoover Building, Washington, D.C. (1400 hours)

The deputy director, FBI, and deputy administrator, DEA, entered the conference room and, as if on queue, the room fell silent. Lou Hanson opened the afternoon session by instructing the uniformed representatives from state law enforcement agencies to brief Task Force Checkmate on unsolved incidents of interest in their respective areas.

"Gents, I want you to pay particular attention to what these gentlemen have to say. We will be relying heavily on outside law enforcement to help us piece this thing together. Sooner or later mistakes will be made and as likely as not, state and local police will be the ones who pick up on it.

"Let's start with you, sir," Lou said, pointing to one of the uniformed officers. "If each of you would preface your remarks by stating your name, state and title, it would be most helpful." He then sat down.

The first briefer made his way to the podium. "I'm Captain Demeitry, California CID. We have three incidents that meet the criteria outlined. In the first case, the subject had twenty-two arrests for domestic violence, aggravated assault, robbery and a raft of drug-related charges. He served a total of five years and was released due to overcrowding last year.

"A lenient judge placed this animal on house arrest. A week later he killed his parents and two nieces, ages ten and seven, but not before taking time to rape both of them repeatedly. The department responsible for overseeing house arrest candidates found the bodies and the ankle bracelet a week later after he failed to show for a court hearing.

"He had been on the run for the better part of a year when he was found outside the little town of Ely, Nevada along U.S. 93. He had been hogtied, much like the guy in the Everglades City report.

"The difference was he was missing his testicles and his penis had been severed and crammed down his throat. According to the coroner, they let him bleed out before tapping him twice in the chest and once in the temple. The crime scene was clean. No indication of who may have taken this guy out. I would be remiss if I didn't say we appreciated the help."

Officer Demeitry laid out his other two cases. They were similar in that the assassinations were professional; the victims had long rap sheets; they had escaped custody, and for whatever reason, law enforcement had been unsuccessful in apprehending them.

The next officer was a tall, physically fit gentleman from the Oklahoma Highway Patrol. "Colonel Sam Weatherby. We have one case we believe fits the profile you are looking for. It involves the death of a known, high level drug distributor found dead in his lake lodge by a housekeeper.

"It was obvious he had been tortured. I'm going to guess it had something to do with his connections to the drug world. When we arrived, there were slabs of fly-ridden, human flesh lying on the coffee table. It was a pretty bad scene, but that isn't what killed him. He was shot dead nuts between the eyes at close range with a 9mm.

"It appeared he had been entertaining a lady friend. We found drug paraphernalia on the floor, a bottle of bourbon and a glass with lipstick smudges on the rim.

"There was a storm cellar down toward the lake, but if anything had been there, it was taken before we arrived. This was a professional job, gentlemen, and I encourage all of us to proceed with caution. Whoever is behind these incidents if, in fact, there is a connection is well trained, disciplined and very dangerous."

Lou thanked the officer for his input as he left the room to catch a five o'clock flight out of Reagan National.

Next to speak was a tall, amiable officer who approached the podium with the confidence of an Old West gunfighter. Unlike most of the Type-A personalities in the room, there was not a trace of urgency in his gait.

In a pronounced southern drawl he said, "Since I'm the only hombre in town wearing cowboy boots and a Stetson, I'd be hard pressed to convince ya'll I'm one of New York's finest."

Members of the task force either chuckled or smiled at the affable peace officer's comments. Even the deputy director cracked one of his infrequent, thin-lipped smiles.

"Name is Rosco Boulliard. I'm a fifth generation Cajun, born so far back in the bayou it took the Texas Rangers a week to work their way in to recruit me. Even now, I'm not sure they all made it out! My kin still find a badge now and again, usually close to somebody's moonshine still."

Rosco was by far the most laid-back lawman this group had ever seen. One might say he was an unpretentious island in a sea of arrogance. Unpretentiousness is not a common trait within the federal law enforcement fraternal order.

"We had a cop go bad in a little West Texas town. He was doing school security work on the side and molested several little girls over a period of time. He was given a slap on the wrist and house arrest by an inept lady judge who knew him and didn't think he was a real threat to the community. Makes ya kinda wonder what ya have to do to be considered a 'real threat,' don't it?

"Well, boys, rest assured, there is a God...and *he* does work in strange ways. Sure as hell, this ole boy lured an eight-year-old to his house, raped and mutilated her body. That beats all I ever saw!

"I'd of killed the bastard myself if we could've found him. This happened a number of years ago, but the captain said it fit the profile and that I needed to come up here and let ya'll know about it. So here I am!

"Like that other fella said, he was found hogtied, his gonads to hell and gone, and his puny little pecker dangling out his mouth. He either took one to the head or one of our wily West Texas centipedes bored a hole clean through his temple.

"That's not all, though. You know that lady judge I was tellin' ya about? They found her at home, hangin' from a basement rafter. You care to venture what was found in the pocket of her sleepin' gown? Yep, you guessed it ...the ole boy's shriveled up testicles just a-layin' there.

"They also found a note, makin' it crystal clear that bad judges were no better than the douche bags they released and warned um all to do right by the people *or* else!

"Maybe that's why Texas justice is so tough today. If that's the case, suits me just fine."

As Rosco Boulliard turned to leave the podium, almost all of the agents clapped in appreciation of his informative but humorous break from a day of serious police work.

The gangly Texas Ranger touched the brim of his hat and nodded as he casually strolled to the back of the room.

A parade of six more state law enforcement representatives from New York, Michigan, Kansas, Ohio, Maine and New Hampshire briefed the agents on a series of cases with very similar characteristics. Professional hits; no clues; and almost all drug related.

In every case involving rape or molestation, the bodies were mutilated. And the victim appeared to have died a slow, painful death, culminating in finishing rounds to the chest or head.

After all of the state officers were released, the deputy director again approached the podium. "What have we got? No, wait a minute. Let's take a ten-minute break for coffee or whatever."

Once everyone was back in their seats, Lou continued. "Let's start over here and work our way around the table," he said pointing to the group on his immediate left.

The group's spokesman sat up. "Sir, there are over seventy incidents of interest in the portfolios provided earlier today, so at best, we have only scanned the content. A quick look, however, suggests there are some interesting similarities.

"For example, excluding the three or four that were hogtied and managed to choke to death, most were double-tapped to either the chest or head and then hammered once to the temple. As we continue to collect data, I believe we can catalog each case and, in short order, come up with a pretty good profile on the modus operandi.

"Then, we can get serious about finding who provides that sort of training. My best guess, at this point, is it will lead to some pretty interesting places…the agency, Quantico, Camp Peary and no doubt, the military.

"As you are all aware, most federal agencies still teach a two-burst shooting technique. I believe that started when it became apparent a single shot from the smaller caliber side arms most officers carried wasn't enough to put a man down. Even with the advent of large cal side arms, I don't think the practice has changed. If I'm not mistaken, most law enforcement agencies across the nation use that technique."

With a smile, the group leader added, "The exception might be our friends here from Texas and the DEA. They just keep *shooting* until they run out of bullets."

There was the expected backlash of inter-agency scoffing but most everyone in the room had a good laugh, particularly the DEA guys, since they felt it dovetailed nicely into their perceived 'wild west' image.

The group leader added, "Because it's a common practice amongst trained shooters, I'm not sure what we can glean from it, but it's worth a try."

"Do it and get the analysts involved," Lou said. He then pointed to the next cluster of men.

Their group leader was a senior DEA agent. "We picked up on at least ten or so judges and shyster lawyers getting caught up in this thing. That can't be a coincidence."

Lou asked, "What do you mean by *caught up?*"

"Well, sir, some flagrant miscarriages of justice, resulting in decisions to give hardened repeat offenders a slap on the wrist and releasing them, have taken place. Whether it was probation, early parole or bonding out, the results are the same…recommitting heinous crimes. The inept judges involved, and more than a few shyster defense lawyers, have met with all manner of sudden, unexpected deaths.

"Interestingly their demise coincided within a week or so of the perpetrator's death, and in some cases on the same day. We think there is intent to send a strong message to those involved in the criminal justice system: Do your job and do it right!

"If I were out there whacking bad guys, I'd be doing it to make things better and safer for everyone, wouldn't you?"

Lou thought about the agent's comment for a moment. "You may be onto something we can catalog and evaluate. It should be relatively easy to match up incidents involving players in the criminal justice system with specific members of the criminal element, particularly if both are terminated. Yes, sir, this could be very helpful later.

"Let's feed this into the lab. Better yet, take an action to review all of the incidents of interest we have to date; trace the bad guys back to judges and defense lawyers; and see if there are even more deaths linked to the judiciary then we are aware of.

"Gentlemen, this could be *huge*! If we discover there are quite a few of these coincidental events, we will definitely know we're dealing with a level of sophistication far removed from anything organized crime syndicates could manage.

"Further, what organized crime element would want to terminate judges that seem to favor the criminal? Crime bosses aren't the brightest stars in the galaxy, but they sure as hell are smart enough to know popping a judge would make it a federal case and they wouldn't want that.

"Do the legwork necessary to eliminate them, but I'm convinced this is not organized crime seeking retribution. This is something far more dangerous. I want this action moved to the top of the priority list of things to chase. OK?"

"Yes, sir."

The last group of agents produced a single point of interest that tied right in with the deputy director's line of thought. Whoever was behind these separate incidents was well organized, possessed intelligence-gathering capabilities at least equal to the federal government's, professional with unique skill sets, motivated and well funded.

Now all that remained was to *find* them. Without exception, every man assigned to Task Force Checkmate intuitively knew the task was daunting…assuming it could be done at all.

39

Presidential debate, Manchester, New Hampshire

Because of the importance of New Hampshire in the race for the presidency, candidates of both parties and the single independent that had entered the foray were working hard to bring their campaign positions into focus.

Mike was not saddled with the problem of focus. His message had been crystal clear from the start, forcing the other candidates to play catch up, and quickly!

He was not, and had never been, an advocate of political debates. He enjoyed the cerebral jostling but viewed them as a rehearsed dog and pony show serving no real purpose. He felt if people didn't understand a candidate's position by now, given all of the media coverage and advertising, then perhaps the country would be better off if they didn't vote. Nonetheless, it was a burden one had to bear if interested in higher political office; in this case, president of the United States.

His political advisors were going nuts ensuring the playing field was level...lighting, position of their candidate's podium in respect to the audience and myriad other small, and insignificant details they felt were important based on previous experience.

Even the other candidates were busy reviewing talking points, opposition platforms, national and world events they felt might be raised as an issue by the commentator.

Mike, on the other hand, was backstage with Jeff Stone enjoying a glass of freshly squeezed orange juice, much to the dismay of staff members. One staffer sarcastically commented, "All we need is to have a close up on national television of orange pulp dangling between those pearly whites."

Jeff looked at the preppy little man with disdain. "Is that all you mullets have to worry about? Get the hell out of here and leave us alone. I'll ensure he's pulp-free before the lights go on. Damn!"

After the flustered staffer left the lounge, he added, "Buddy, are you sure these Ivy League assholes know what the hell they're doing? They give me the creeps, scurrying around like rats on a sinking ship."

"Yeah, supposedly they're good at what they do," said Mike, "but they can get on your nerves if you let them. Interestingly, only yesterday one of them said you gave *them* the creeps."

Jeff shrugged off the comment and as an afterthought, smiled and asked, "*Which one?*"

A few moments later, someone stuck their head in and said, "Five minutes, gentlemen."

"Better go brush those pearly whites, Boss, before Tweety bird has a shit fit. Our guys are in place and, short of some diehard liberal setting himself on fire in protest to your prison reform policies, we're all set. As a precaution, I'll escort you to the stage when you're ready."

The next several minutes were occupied with brushing, flossing, gargling, and tie-straightening and lint removal, assuming any lint dared attach itself to his Armani suit.

Mike thought as he and Jeff headed for the stage entrance, 'How I hate this nonsense! Why can't I debate in jeans and a flannel shirt? What would that hurt? Am I really up to four years of this nonsense?'

As debates go, this one was par for the course, a few slash-and-burn runs by the candidates as they took negative shots at one another, pontificating infinitum about why the opposition programs simply wouldn't work or, at best, would bankrupt the country.

Mike O'Reilly was the exception. Not once did he speak poorly of the other candidates...other than to say, "It strikes me, gentlemen, that making another look *bad* simply to glorify yourself is a pretty lame approach to leadership. If you are of that ilk, who is to say you will not carry that philosophy into the Oval Office and continue to use it as you try to navigate through the quagmire of national and international affairs?

"I would like to share with you one of the key leadership tenets taught at West Point, and one that served me well as a military officer and in the conduct of my private and political life: 'Praise in public and criticize in private.'"

Because of his tough prison reform policies in Oklahoma, no debate would be complete without first having the various candidates address their views on the subject. Each candidate discussed this issue and, not surprisingly, the opposition filled the time with all of the right buzzwords for a liberal New Hampshire audience.

Prisoners have rights, too; educate them; show leniency; provide essential amenities, such as unending access to the court system to give platform to frivolous complaints; television; refrigerators; open access to telephones so they can continue a life of crime behind bars; weightlifting equipment to ensure they are bigger and stronger when released; etcetera, etcetera.'

In other words, make going to prison a real deterrent to crime by making conditions there better than they had it on the street. Now that's a real plan! And these brain-dead mullets want to hold the highest office in the land...*God help us*!

After listening to their meaningless, uninformed, gibberish, Mike was given an opportunity to speak. "I need only ten seconds. If you're really interested in a plan that works, look at the effective prison reform policies now used in Oklahoma."

"Mr. Commentator, with your permission, I would like to use the remainder of my time addressing the byproduct of leniency within the criminal justice system. It has a direct impact on all Americans and we all need to be aware of it."

The commentator grudgingly nodded his head and said, "Mr. O'Reilly, you have just under five minutes, sir."

"My remarks, ladies and gentlemen, are not designed to entertain you with superfluous buzzwords or to make you feel good. They are a matter of public record and with just a few minutes of your time, each of you can verify the validity of what I'm about to say by beaming up public records which are available for all to see. For those too busy or not wanting to take the time to seek out the truth, I'll give you a snapshot."

Mike didn't have adequate time to fully address the issue so he carefully chose his topics. "Regardless of what you conveniently choose to believe, our criminal justice system is dysfunctional. Daily, due to a full range of inefficiencies, the system flushes thousands of hardened criminals back into society to again commit tens of thousands of crimes against *you*," he said, pointing his index finger and waving his arm left to right across the audience, "the American people. That won't stand the test of logic, folks!

"We proved beyond a shadow of doubt in Oklahoma that the problem can be fixed quickly by taking three words out of the criminal justice equation...leniency, parole and bail!

"Lenient, slap-on-the-wrist sentences, and parole are the culprits that have created what is known as the revolving door syndrome. Criminals, inept judges and less then honorable defense lawyers have made a mockery of our judicial process. Collectively we can stop this nonsense.

"Why do you think repeat offender stats in Oklahoma dropped by 90 percent? I'll help you with that one. They don't want to spend another damn minute in a ball-busting system that makes them pay a full measure for crimes committed...*that's why*!

"My staff has compiled files reaching clear to the ceiling on case after case of felons and the crimes they committed after posting bail. The stats are horrifying, something one would expect in a lawless third world country. The analysis clearly indicates that *bail* is a green light for the commission of additional heinous crimes against society.

"If bail is the problem, then the solution is quick and easy: Eliminate bail for hardened repeat offenders.

"Because of antiquated, ineffective and, in some cases, ludicrous laws, our criminal justice system is overburdened to the point that judges don't have time or, worse case, don't care enough to look at a prisoner's rap sheet before deciding whether or not to bond him out. That's dumb as dirt, even for the most liberal amongst us.

"Can you even imagine how frustrating and disheartening it is to law enforcement officers who bust their butt daily, as well as risk their lives, to apprehend these knuckleheads, only to have some diehard liberal judge release them back into society?

"Why go to the trouble and expense of apprehension if you don't plan on keeping them locked up? I can tell you this with certainty. That *won't* happen on my watch. I will not be a party to ludicrous policy and procedure.

"The criminal justice system is in the toilet and in need of immediate overhaul and reform. We must demand change to ensure the safety of our citizens. If our judiciary and elected officials can't grasp that concept, replace them with those that can.

"We must stay the course until our judiciary and courts are again aligned with the provisions laid out in the Constitution by our Founding Fathers...a system that is swift and harsh, provides equal justice for all and does everything within its power to protect the law-abiding citizens of the United States."

Mike quickly calculated about how much time he had left and it wasn't much, so he quickly added a few stats for the New Hampshire citizenry and everyone watching across the nation.

"Most of us, as we muddle our way through life, give little thought to things like prison populations or what that whole inefficient mess might be costing us as taxpayers. Let me give you a couple of data points to think about. There are over two million prisoners locked up as we speak, and each one of them is costing us, on average, $40,000 a year to maintain. That, of course, doesn't take into account the millions more spent to process and, at some point, address thousands of frivolous, nonsensical claims submitted through the legal system by inmates with too much time on their hands.

"Let me give you just one example of this nonsense. There exists this very day an inmate who has submitted over 600 separate actions pending review by the courts, some of them handwritten on toilet paper. If that makes sense, I'll eat your bloody hat! If he has that much free time, put his little butt to work doing something that will benefit infrastructure, like mopping floors, washing dishes or making license plates.

"With regard to death row, you may recall that's where we supposedly send the worst of the worst to meet their maker...someday!

"Let me tell you a little about these blood-sucking leeches. There are about 32,000 hammerheads on death row across the country, and they stay there while our ludicrous legal review process runs its course processing appeal after appeal, as many as six or more, at every level imaginable, up to and including the Supreme Court.

"On average, a death row inmate spends eight years, ten months before we finally get our chance to *kill* them back."

Mike could sense the uneasiness within the audience and thought, 'I really don't give a shit. Even the most liberal of our brethren needs to wake up and smell the roses or, better yet, pull their head out of their ass!'

He continued his hard line, knowing it was not being well received by this ultra-liberal audience. "However, there are many, many cases where an inmate is there for fifteen years or longer. The longest stay, I believe, is twenty-four years. Now, these are high-dollar incarcerations. Forty thousand annually won't even start to cover the taxpayers' tab associated with these guys.

"Do the math! It costs more for the United States to keep hardened multiple offenders locked up than the value of the gross national product of many third world countries."

Mike paused briefly, distracted by one of the debaters feigning the need to clear his throat in order to indicate that Mike had run over his allotted time.

The commentator picked up on this. "Mr. O'Reilly, your time is up an…"

Mike politely but firmly cut him off. "Give me one moment, sir, to capstone my comments. This is one of the most important topics facing this nation, and the audience needs to hear my position on it."

The commentator nodded and said, "You have thirty seconds, sir."

"Thank you."

"Ladies and gentlemen, my position is clear. Everyone on death row is entitled to one and *only* one appeal…to provide the legal system every opportunity to ensure justice has been served. Subsequently, however, the death penalty imposed should be swiftly carried out. Folks, the Constitution of the United States calls for swift punishment; anything less is pure nonsense."

Mike nodded at the commentator. "Thank you, sir, for the extra time and I will use less than my allotted time on other topics during the debate."

He reached for the glass of water sitting on the podium as he surveyed the audience. What he saw wasn't reassuring and his political advisors, standing just out of sight, seemed distraught. Mike thought, 'Wimpy little freaks! They wouldn't know an honest conviction if it hit them dead in the ass.'

One of the staffers muttered, unfortunately within earshot of Mike's security chief, "Has this guy lost it? You can't come into the very heart of liberalism and deliver that kind of message. We're screwed."

Jeff, who was positioned to observe the vast seating area for security purposes, turned briefly to give both staffers a stare that froze the blood in their veins, "At least he has the balls to say what's on his mind. You gutless wonders scurry around in your high-dollar suits thinking you have all the answers. You don't know *shit*!

"Mike O'Reilly has more courage, honor and integrity than the whole damn bunch of you put together. Why he keeps your sorry asses on the payroll is beyond me."

As quickly as possible, the stunned staffers moved as far away from this obviously upset and very dangerous security chief as they could get without tumbling unto the stage.

For the next twenty minutes or so, the presidential debate in New Hampshire droned on with a predictable conclusion.

Senator Steven Lombardo, Democrat from Massachusetts, promised to take from the rich and give to the poor; revamp the senior healthcare plan to the extent that it was practically free, bordering on socialized medicine; increase the minimum wage to almost double its present level; and endless pontification about fixing everything broken.

Mike stood there thinking, 'Surely these liberal mullets are smart enough to see through this guy's smoke screen, aren't they? He mentioned nothing about what this grab bag of goodies would cost the taxpayers. Hell, he doesn't even have a plan!'

As he went through the courtesies of thanking the commentator and shaking hands before leaving, Mike knew with certainty that New Hampshirites—or whatever they called themselves—didn't share his views on anything debated here this evening.

As Jeff and his security team formed a cordon around Mike, he mused, 'You can't win them all, buddy...but a tie now and again would be nice.'

40

Kraft Plantation, Eufaula, Alabama (1100 hours)

Deer season in this part of the country is a major event, tantamount to the Second Coming, and anticipated by avid hunters biting at the bit to get back in the woods.

Schools close on opening day and production falls off, due to the number of sick days taken by workers with a sudden case of the flu, a rare strain of the virus that seems to infect only men on opening day of deer season. Strange, indeed!

The Kraft Plantation located twenty miles or so west of the Alabama–Georgia state line is particularly popular because it is one of the few places in the state where hunters are allowed to use rifles.

The plantation covers about 300 square miles of heavily forested area abutting a national wildlife reserve in one of the more mountainous and scenic parts of the state. It is an ideal setting for taking a trophy buck...and hundreds of hunters flock there annually in anticipation of doing just that.

Bambi, being one hell of a lot smarter and faster then most of the good ole boys that show up each year, retreats deep into the national wildlife reserve after the first shot of the season is fired.

Fortunately for the hunters, there are always a few deer failing to realize what time of the year it is. That's what keeps bringing these guys back year after year.

Three of these hunters, actually five, were staying at the Lakepoint Resort overlooking Lake Eufaula. In the predawn hours on this particular day, it was especially serene. The morning air was crisp with a layer of fog hugging the lake and surrounding mountains.

In fact, the fog had delayed the departure of the hunters because finding the specific hunting area identified the day before in the fog-shrouded mountains would be almost impossible.

The three men decided to have breakfast instead and give the fog a chance to lift. The smell of bacon, eggs and coffee wafted through the crisp early morning air outside the cabin as one of the men carried three rifle cases to the large Dodge Ram pickup parked in front of the cabin.

The two 'hunters' in the cabin approximately 200 feet to the east had no need to arise early. They too had scouted the area for ideal shooting positions and as planned would have a casual breakfast in the historic City of Eufaula, and then make their way into the mountainous terrain off U.S. Highway 431.

Roland Blankenship, a high-dollar shyster defense lawyer, and his two companions laughed and joked about the stupidity of the criminal justice system as they ate breakfast and drank coffee. Roland was a high profile lawyer who specialized in defending major drug dealers.

His tactics and courtroom manner skated on the ragged edge of acceptable legal standards and conduct. He had been reprimanded a number of times by exasperated judges, tired of his arrogance and courtroom bullying of witnesses.

Nonetheless he was very good at his chosen profession and more often then not found loopholes in the letter of the law or improprieties in law enforcement arrest procedures, allowing his clients to go free... though guilty as sin.

This hunting trip was a perk, above and beyond the $100,000 fee he had been paid, for getting his two clients acquitted on the charge of masterminding one of the largest illicit drug distribution organizations in the Southeast.

DEA agents and state law enforcement officers had made forty-three arrests, resulting in a number of convictions, as the result of an eighteen-month undercover investigation. But the two heavy hitters, now enjoying their early morning breakfast, escaped successful prosecution due to technicalities and the antics of the slick lawyer sitting across the table from them.

Unfortunately this is too often the case, and the real threats to society remain free to continue profiting from the addiction, misery and frequent deaths caused by their illicit products.

Sometime around 0630, a soft breeze came up from across the lake and dissipated the fog enough for the three men to see. They left the warmth of the cabin and stepped into the cool morning air.

In less than thirty minutes, they had found the site identified the day before as a promising crossing for deer en route to a stream at the base of a relatively steep slope, about 300 meters from their position.

The men were dressed in dark camouflage and armed with top-of-the-line equipment, two Weatherby bolt-action rifles (a 270 and a 30-06), and a Henry 44-40 lever action. All three rifles sported high-dollar Bausch & Lomb scopes of various magnifications.

As the three men settled into their firing positions about fifty yards apart, Roland Blankenship was still puffing on his cigar, the first clue that he was not an outdoorsman and new to hunting. In fact, the 44-40 he was cradling belonged to the client that was frantically sending hand signals in an effort to get him to extinguish his nasty smelling cigar. What a dumb ass!

The driver of the large Dodge Ram had pulled off the main logging road and driven about a hundred feet up a small splinter trail and military parked, facing back toward the road, probably from habit.

As the three men settled in and focused on the hunt, they had no way of knowing they were now the hunted.

The two-man ARC strike team had been handpicked for this assignment, as they often were when special shooting skills were needed. Both were military-trained, combat-tested snipers and had been working together as a team for a number of years.

As they turned the old, rusted-out Jeep Cherokee, which someone had unsuccessfully attempted to camouflage with a paint brush, off of U.S. 431, they couldn't help but laugh at the circumstances placing them in this unadulterated piece of junk.

They had spotted it the day before, parked down by a dock across the bridge from the cabin they had rented under assumed names and thought it would be perfect for their needs.

The Jeep belonged to a kid in his teens. As the two operatives approached him, he was sliding a ten-foot Jon boat into the gaping cavity at the rear of the vehicle, where normally doors would have been. They weren't there now. The two men looked at one another, biting their lips in an effort not to laugh, as they walked up to the young man.

"Hey, bud, you got a minute?"

The young man was startled and jumped a little as he quickly turned to see who had snuck up on him. "Yeah, I guess so."

"Did you do this paint job yourself or have it done?"

That broke the ice and the young man laughed. "What do ya'll think? Shit, fuzzy man, you can see the brush marks."

The two older men laughed. "How does it run?"

The teenager, still chuckling, replied, "Awesome, dude. Four-wheel drive even works. My girlfriend said she wouldn't be caught dead in it. No matter, she don't fish or hunt so screw her."

"Would you consider selling it?"

Without hesitation the young man said, "Can't do that, man. Haulin' my boat or a big buck on my Harley would really be a bitch."

The two operatives chuckled at the thought, as did the young man. "Yeah, I see your point. We came down to do a little hunting and after driving on some of the logging roads, decided our SUV might get torn up pretty bad out there. Would you consider renting it to us for a couple of days? Say, 200 bucks?"

"For 200 I'll tote ya'll up on my back. Hell, yeah, man, but I gotta tell ya, this piece of shit ain't registered. You ain't the law, are ya?"

"No, son, just businessmen from Atlanta, anxious to get away from the city for a while and do some hunting."

The young man then cautiously explained the license tag on the Jeep actually belonged on his brother's pickup. But his brother was away at school and his truck didn't run, so he didn't see any harm in using it.

One of the men peeled off $200 in small bills and handed them to the excited teenager.

"Here's the deal. Are you familiar with the little airport café up 431 toward Columbus?"

"Sure am, best damn sandwiches around these parts. It's just a hoot and a holler up the road."

"OK, then, when we're finished with this thing, probably tomorrow afternoon sometime, we'll leave it in the café parking lot. We may even try one of those sandwiches."

The young man, still looking at the handful of bills, said without looking up, "You're good to go, just let me yank my boat out." The kid then pulled the small Jon boat to the ground and left it where it fell.

The two men laughed and one of them said, "Are you just going to leave it laying here? Do you need some help carrying it somewhere? Like, maybe the *lake*?"

The young man looked up. "Who the hell would steal this thing?" He shrugged his shoulders and as an afterthought added, "Now that I think about it, that's how I got it. But other than me, who'd take it?"

The next day, as the old Jeep wound its way up the ridgeline on the opposite side of the valley from the big Dodge truck, both men surveyed the area with trained eyes, looking for any sign of hunters in close proximity.

It appeared they were alone on the ridge. It took them about twenty minutes of scouting to find a shooting position that afforded line of sight across the valley to the pickup parked some 500 meters away.

They then went back to the Jeep, which had been pulled well off the logging road and hidden behind a thicket. It was time to suit up. Ghillie suits, by design, are shaggy looking camouflage made of strips of material, usually burlap, that closely match the coloring and texture of the natural setting. Grasses and foliage are then added to create a perfect blend with the surrounding foliage.

They were first used in Scotland by hunting guides in the employ of land barons. These expert marksmen were called Ghillies by the aristocracy, and the name stuck.

The shooters carried their individual weapons in specially designed high impact, plastic cases. Pre-formed foam covered in felt protected each piece of the weapon system.

The operatives picked prone firing positions ten yards apart. One of the shooters extended the bipod legs of the McMillan .50 caliber sniper rifle, until the weapon was essentially bore-sighted on the Dodge Ram, while the second shooter used a laser to range the target.

He whispered the distance to the man positioned directly behind the large .50 caliber weapon system, "5-6-2 meters. No wind."

The primary shooter nodded as he loaded five rounds into the bolt-action rifle's magazine and chambered a round. All movements by both shooters were slow and deliberate. Like all ARC missions…nothing would be left to chance.

The second shooter was armed with a 7.62 Parker-Hale sniper rifle. Both men removed the protective lens caps off their Leupold 10x30 sniper scopes, just long enough to make adjustments, and then replaced the caps to safeguard against glare.

They blended into the natural surroundings so well that a hunter passing just a few feet away would not have been able to see them. Now, they waited, with the patience accrued through training and hundreds of similar missions.

A .50 caliber sniper rifle can reach out and literally blow a man apart at over a mile. The shooter positioned behind this one had personally scored kills at over 1,500 meters. This shot was about a third that distance; guaranteeing the concept of one shot, one kill!

As the morning hours passed, the shooters heard the report of a number of rifles from deep within the Kraft Plantation and observed several vehicles moving down the logging road back toward civilization.

One of them had a small six-point buck strapped to the luggage rack atop the vehicle. Between now and next hunting season, the story of how this expert woodsman took his monster 14-point, 600-pound trophy on the run at, let's say 400 yards, will have been told a hundred times in every beer joint in the county.

The day remained overcast, which was ideal. It was almost ten-thirty before the strike team saw their targets emerging from the wooded area just above where they had parked their truck. The Dodge Ram had been backed into a clearing, and the shooters had already determined they would take their shots once all three men were in the clearing, with little or no cover.

The operative armed with the 7.62 Parker-Hale would take out the smaller of the two drug kingpins first, and then engage the other.

The intent of this mission, in addition to ridding society of two more drug-dealing sleaze balls, was to send a clear message to greedy lawyers who chose to defend them and to irresponsible judges who released them back into society. They did so at great personal risk.

With this in mind, the sniper positioned behind the McMillan knew, given the unbelievable destructive power of the rifle, a chest shot would be required. It was critical to mission success that Roland Blankenship, attorney at law, be identifiable.

The McMillan's report, as it sent the heavy .50 caliber projectile down range, would sound like a cannon as it reverberated through the valley; it was impossible to silence.

The business end of the cartridge was capable of penetrating light armor. One can only imagine the trauma it caused to soft tissue and bone. Certainly Mr. Blankenship would not be able to attest to its power.

The strike team removed the end caps from their high-powered scopes and laid the crosshairs on their respective targets.

The smaller man had walked to the far side of the Dodge Ram, propped his rifle against the truck, and was in the process of unzipping his fly when the 7.62 projectile entered the back of his head.

The resultant thud and subsequent spray of blood and gore to the side of the truck or perhaps the sound of his lifeless body hitting the ground attracted the attention of the other two who looked in his direction and were saying something that couldn't be heard by the two shooters.

When they didn't get a response from their hunting buddy, the second drug dealer started walking toward the other side of the pickup. He didn't make it!

Roland Blankenship, attorney at law, was leaning back against the truck, having just taken a long drag on a freshly lit cigar, when he heard the unmistakable thud of the projectile entering and exiting his client's head, then smashing into the windshield of the pickup.

He was more confused and startled by the shattering of glass than by the guttural moan of his client's last utterance before entering the gates of hell. He watched the surreal scene as his client's lifeless body crumpled to the ground directly in front of the truck.

The lawyer had less than a nanosecond to be startled. The loud report of the .50 caliber rifle could be heard for miles, or so it seemed to the strike team. The velocity of the projectile, impacting dead center of his chest, sent him airborne almost the full length of the pickup, and then slamming him unceremoniously to the ground in a lifeless heap; his upper and lower torso, held together by ripped ligaments and shattered muscle tissue, was all but severed.

The shooter slowly exercised the bolt of the McMillan, collecting the brass casing in his right hand as he chambered another round. He carefully placed the expended casing in his pocket and placed the engine compartment of the truck in the crosshairs of his scope and slowly squeezed off another round.

Within a couple of minutes the sniper team had broken down their weapons, shed their Ghillie suits and were moving back down the logging trail, just as a number of other hunters had done earlier.

Shortly thereafter, the Jeep Cherokee was inconspicuously parked at the Airfield Café, as agreed, and the two 'hunters' were crossing the Chattahoochee River Bridge at Phoenix City into Columbus, Georgia…and obscurity.

41

Albuquerque, New Mexico

Mike O'Reilly had made so many stops and campaign speeches he wasn't sure where the hell he was. His staff had advised him to concentrate on the heavily populated states and to avoid less populated areas in the Mountain Time Zone.

That made no sense at all to him, and he started to believe Jeff may have been right about these guys; they had their head up their ass! There were plenty of hard-working Americans in *every* time zone and he was going to see as many of them as time would allow. After all, he was footing the bill for this Kabuki dance and he would go where he damn well pleased.

Hardheadedness was an O'Reilly family trait and Mike had been issued a double dose, as his father's genes rose above all others while he was still in his mother's womb.

Mike thought he could make a swing through the Mountain Time Zone and then maybe squeeze in a few days at home with Veronica and Cheyenne. He really hated to be away from them but Jeff felt the risks of having them accompany him were too great…too many crazies out there.

The center that had been reserved was packed full. Every seat was taken and people were standing along the walls on either side of the cavernous hall. This made his security detail nervous. Capacity crowds were difficult to observe, and standing room only just complicated an already difficult task.

Jeff had insisted on roving agents as well as a tighter than usual perimeter detail around Mike. Additionally, a couple of spotters with binoculars had been positioned in what appeared to be a projectionist booth overlooking the hall.

These high-visibility precautions didn't go unnoticed. Mike decided to take the opportunity to short circuit the inevitable question from some rookie reporter out to make a name for himself: 'Don't you trust the good people of New Mexico?'

Mike thought, 'It's not the *good* people I'm worried about. It's the armed squirrel that mistakenly thinks the O'Reilly Corporation and its petroleum interests are screwing up the habitat of the Chi Chi fly or some other obscure biting insect no one gives a shit about that bothers me.'

As the chairperson of the New Mexico Republican Party approached the podium, he announced, in what Mike embarrassingly thought to be an obsequious manner, "Ladies and gentlemen, it is my distinct honor to introduce Mike O'Reilly, the Republican candidate for president of the United States."

As those in attendance respectfully applauded, Mike made his way to the podium. "I'm happy to be with you this afternoon on my first stop of a swing that will culminate in Great Falls, Montana later in the week.

"So if I momentarily forget where I am, don't think too poorly of me. The last couple of months have been a blur. However, my grade school geography teacher would be very pleased with my ability to recite state capitals and historic detail about this great country of ours."

There was polite nodding and murmuring from the crowd. "Before I get into the message I want to share with you today, let me say a word or two about these rather large, good-looking fellows who have failed miserably in their attempt to blend in."

Mike waved an outstretched arm in the general direction of his security detail that was essentially everywhere. "Security is a very difficult thing to accomplish, particularly in an overcrowded, standing room only gathering. So when we find ourselves in this situation, my chief of security insists on high-visibility scenarios.

"One of his conditions of employment, I might add, is that I cannot override his decision. And I would not want to, anyway. He is very good at what he does and the gentlemen you see before you, and some you don't see, are all highly trained professionals.

"If you have yet to notice the eye in the sky," Mike said as he pointed in the direction of the glassed-in projectionist booth at the top of the hall, "his job is to watch you watching me. So if you are so inclined to suddenly reach in your pocket, be sure you pull out a handkerchief," he said smiling at the audience, "or there is a high probability your day will not end on a happy note."

As Mike took a drink of water and again smiled at the audience, he could sense they were warming toward him and appreciated his levity concerning a deadly serious topic.

"You know, I think back to when I was a kid and how different things were. When I was just eight or nine, I roamed all over the place *alone* and often swam by myself in the Pea River. That's spelled P-E-A, but given what I now know about it, the spelling is probably interchangeable. Aside from water moccasins that occasionally chased me out of the muddy water, there wasn't a soul around, and my parents never gave it a second thought.

"The greatest danger we faced was getting hit by a farm tractor and the probability of that was pretty low." Many in the audience smiled and nodded as their thoughts returned to simpler times.

"We may never see those days again, but we owe it to future generations to make their world as safe as humanly possible and that is exactly what I plan to do. If we can reduce drug-related crime by 85 percent in one state, and we have, we can do it in every state in the union

"Given 90 to 95 percent of all crimes in this country are drug related, in one way or another, just think how much safer law-abiding citizens would be. It may not be quite like it was when *we* were kids, but we can get pretty damn close to it."

The audience applauded and even a few whistles were heard. Mike had time to take a drink while the audience settled down.

"Ladies and gentlemen, in my estimation, there are just too doggone many things in this country that are not working right and are in need of revamping.

"For the most part, we have a self-serving Congress, far more interested in tenure, pork barrel projects and partisan politics than in the welfare of the nation and her citizenry. Our criminal justice system is absolutely in the toilet…totally ineffective. That is unacceptable and I'll have no part of it.

"Whether I become your next president or not, I plan on using all the resources available to me to change the way we do things in this country…*enough is enough!*"

"Every so often stories concerning organized militias make the headlines or at least page two. We have been conditioned to dismiss them as fanatics, rabble rousers, hate mongers and so forth. Perhaps the ones that make headlines are; I don't know.

"What I do know is that many of them are well-trained outdoorsman with military backgrounds and armed to the teeth. That, folks, is something we need to take notice of.

"Just a little over 200 years ago, militias took exception to the way things were going in this country. And you may recall from history books, they reacted rather violently. Revolution quickly followed. The circumstances we face today, in my view, are not dissimilar.

Our government is bloated! It is top heavy with pontificating, fiscally irresponsible wind-bags, with an insatiable appetite for your tax dollars. Their ineptitude and indifference to the real world needs and desires of the people places all Americans at risk.

"The attitude in Washington, certainly Congress and the executive branch, is that the supply of money is endless. It is not! I forewarn you here today that when taxation and government stupidity reaches an untenable level—and we are close to it now—Americans *will* rise up in strong protest and, if necessary, may exercise their constitutional right to bear arms, just as they did in our country's fledgling beginning.

"The social welfare system is on the verge of bankruptcy, in great part due to the number of illegal aliens feeding from the government trough.

"They are violating U.S. law, folks! Why on God's Earth would we then allow them to suck the benefits out of a program that is designed to help U.S. citizens in need?

"The answer, though painful, is really quite simple: Congress, as an institution, is totally inept. I assure you that if any one of us here today were king for a day, we wouldn't allow it; collectively we're all crazy as hell if we allow it to continue unabated.

"Don't tolerate mediocrity from those you have sent to Washington. Demand that they take the necessary action to get things back on track and be sure they understand they won't be around for another term if they don't. That's how you bring about meaningful change...and *change* we must!

"The quality of education in our country now lags behind some third world countries. I am appalled at how poorly many of our youth read and write the English language. Their knowledge of math, geography, history and the sciences is sadly lacking. The government, past and present, professed a circuitous fix that has led down the road to nowhere. To fix the problem you have to fix the quality of educators, both present and those that will enter the pipeline later on, and find ways to get families involved in the education of their children.

"You do this by recognizing the importance of the teaching profession and by providing financial incentives for their efforts. In other words, pay them a professional wage. There is no mystery about how to go about it, and I have a plan ready for implementation within the first week I am in office, should that day come."

He took a breather to get a feel for how this startling, rather candid message was being received. There was a look of real concern on the faces of most in attendance. It was not disbelief he saw. Most people had simply shoved these critical issues into the recesses of their mind, hoping they would be fixed or miraculously disappear.

Mike had a unique talent for getting to the heart of an issue and as those listening would attest, he was not blessed with subtlety or political correctness.

Jeff Stone received a curt warning from the projectionist booth that a late arrival had just entered the room and looked a bit peculiar. His mannerisms were overly nervous and he was overdressed for the weather in Albuquerque.

The man was wearing a light raincoat which made no sense at all. It hadn't rained here in weeks, and none was forecast for the foreseeable future. A closer look was in order and Jeff wasted no time as he spoke into his lapel mike. "Alfa Team to main entrance...man in light gray raincoat may be armed; move!"

Jeff ordered the loose cordon of security around Mike to tighten their positions, and immediately seven physically fit, heavily armed men migrated to predetermined security positions directly in front of the podium and at seating level. Two others materialized on either side of the stage and took positions in plain view of the audience.

Though these security measures are handled professionally, it is difficult to saturate a possible trouble spot without someone noticing something is amiss.

Such was the case in Albuquerque this day. Low murmurs emanated from the audience and heads began to swivel, and bodies turned one way or the other in an effort to discern what the unidentified disturbance was. One lady in attendance was heard to say, "Oh, God, what's happening?"

Security personnel had taken positions on either side of the suspect and two directly behind him. Jeff approached the man and quietly said, "Excuse me, sir, may we speak with you in the outer hallway?"

He was all too familiar with the darting, unfocused eyes that were staring back at him and the man was perspiring profusely, so Jeff knew he had a drug-ravaged nut on his hands.

The real question at this point...was he armed? Jeff called upstairs to see if the over-watch could see any better than he could; he doubted it, but it was worth a try.

Before he could get an answer, the man looked over his shoulder and, seeing the two beefy security men behind him, he freaked out. One of them zapped him with a taser, which momentarily stunned the man and dropped him to the floor.

As he fell, the raincoat opened revealing a sawed-off, single-barrel, twelve-gauge shotgun. Jeff jumped on top of the writhing figure and quickly broke the weapon down. A magnum shell ejected half an inch or so out of the chamber. Jeff grabbed the shell, wrested the shotgun from the man's weakened grip and held it up for one of the detail to secure.

He then rolled off the man and other security personnel whisked him outside as quickly and quietly as possible, turning him over to Albuquerque uniformed police officers, who none too gently threw him into the back seat of a patrol car and left.

The incident lasted only a moment or two, and Mike observed the whole event. He smiled at the audience. "Some people are a little slow on the uptake. Didn't I *just* get through telling everyone that if you reach into your pocket, it better be for a handkerchief? Didn't I just say that?"

There was a small amount of strained, nervous laughter from the audience but with a few moments of small talk, Mike had everyone settled down, at least enough for him to continue.

"A little pre-dinner entertainment is good for the digestive tract. I know most of you don't have this level of excitement in your daily lives, so look at it as a story to be told for the rest of your lives to whoever will listen.

"Let's move on. I feel strongly that anyone violating the law of the land should be punished accordingly. I make no distinction between rich or poor, illegal immigrant, United Nations or foreign embassy personnel. If you come to the United States, you must obey our laws; there should be no exceptions. I'll work hard to have those laws amended, if in fact change is in our best interest. To date, I'm inclined to believe *change* is warranted.

"I believe we need to again address the issue of universal jurisdiction, particularly as it may relate to the prosecution of drug dealers and capital crimes against our citizens.

"As most of you that have followed my crusade to draw attention to a dysfunctional criminal justice system know, I have real concerns about the value of what the legal profession refers to as the 'books of precedent.'

"What's that all about? I'm a lawyer...and I even think it's dumb as dirt. Why shouldn't each case stand on its own merit? Are we to believe that our esteemed judges are incapable of determining and subsequently administering a fair and just sentence commensurate with the crime to which an individual has been found guilty?

"Ladies and gentlemen, I'm inclined to believe we should shelve these books and let every case stand on its own merit. If there is an overwhelming argument that the books of precedent should, for some reason, be maintained as empirical data or for some other reason I'm not aware of, then so be it. They should *not* be used as a basis for establishing punishment in new cases.

"The last topic I want to share with you...taxes! One could build a pretty strong argument that the reason we have not had a serious revamping of tax laws in this country is the government has no idea of what to do with the legions of Internal Revenue Service employees no longer needed.

"I have a possible solution for that predicament. They *are* federal employees, right? Keep them on the payroll, retrain them and send the whole bunch down for border patrol...that should plug up *all* the holes that exist today."

The audience laughed and applauded Mike's unique solutions to what otherwise seemed to be insurmountable problems for the Congress. Many thought maybe, just maybe, this was the guy that could make sense out of it all and get things back on track.

"I have a team of green-shaded wizards looking into every aspect of a flat tax, perhaps 10 percent or whatever the research suggests. It would pertain to every nickel earned in this country, whether corporate or an individual's income. The exception to taxable income might be the very lowest of wage earners...below poverty level. They would not pay tax.

"No loop holes. No hiding places for the very wealthy or corporations, etcetera. It is simple, and our quick look suggests the federal coffers would swell to new levels, giving us an opportunity to quickly pay down the national debt.

"So why hasn't it been done if it's so *simple*? Two primary reasons as I see it. It is a radical change from the status quo, and our gutless wonders in Washington are afraid to tackle the issue. Additionally there are so many incestuous relationships with special interest groups, Congress may be afraid to air their dirty laundry. It may prove to be just that simple.

"Now before we get into questions and answers, let me just say we have many issues in this country that need to be thoroughly and intelligently addressed and fixed. It is not, as our legislators would have you believe, an impossible or overwhelming task. It *can* be done if we collectively apply our minds and will to it. So, *let's* do it!

"To the good folks of New Mexico and across this great nation, I submit we are no different than the patriots of a bygone era. They had problems not unlike those we face today. They united, realizing *they*, not their elected officials, were the government, and with a single strong voice took the actions necessary to return the government to the people.

"It is now up to us...*we the people*. Let history show we had the fortitude, foresight and will to do those things necessary to guarantee the welfare of future generations of Americans. Something Thomas Jefferson said comes to mind, 'It is incumbent on every generation to pay its own debts as it goes. A principle which if acted on would save one-half the wars of the world.'"

42

The deputy director, FBI, Lou Hanson, stormed into the conference room where Task Force Checkmate had assembled. "Gentlemen, we don't have much time, so let's get to work. It appears our friends have been working overtime this past month or so, and we might have the closest thing to a lead we've seen to date.

"I'm going to turn the meeting over to J.C. Holder, chief, Special Operations Division, DEA. He will be replacing the deputy director as the senior DEA member on the task force…J.C."

J.C. Holder was a no-nonsense senior agent with a low threshold for bureaucratic bullshit. A rough and tumble man who had forgotten how to smile at childbirth.

He had been the All Army middleweight boxing champion three years running while on active duty at Fort Lewis, Washington with the 10th Mountain Division. He was a little less than 6 feet tall, with a weathered ruddy complexion and, at age 44, weighed in at a muscular 210 pounds.

His nose had obviously been busted several times, and chances are good none of the breaks came inside the ropes. That's probably why he had the distinction of making corporal three times before receiving a general discharge from military service.

He successfully petitioned a Minnesota senator and eventually was given an honorable discharge. Subsequently he had been accepted by the DEA and had quickly navigated to the top spot in special operations.

As he positioned himself behind the podium, he looked at everyone in the room with the same disgust and suspicion you would expect if he were making an arrest of a dirt bag drug dealer.

"I'd rather be anywhere in the friggin' world than here. Let's knock off the interagency crap I've been hearin' about and wrap this thing up, so I can get the hell out of here and get back to work."

Lou had been forewarned by the DEA deputy administrator about J.C.'s mannerisms and less than eloquent use of his native tongue, but had also been told that if he wanted to solve this mystery, J.C. was definitely the right man for the job.

"Deputy Hanson, I can't tell ya how to run the show, but I can tell ya suits and shiny shoes ain't gonna cut it. If you wanta identify these bastards sometime during *your* lifetime, get rid of the ties and suit up for field work.

"By the way, other than violatin' a dumb ass law or two, it's not real clear to me why we're goin' after these assholes. Let's deputize the whole damn bunch of um and turn um loose to do what they do best: catch bad guys!

"I've spent the last week and a half readin' summary briefs and talkin' to analysts from both agencies. No question in my military mind that we're up against a well-organized, well-funded, and well-trained group of hard-hitting professionals.

"Let me feed that back to ya in reverse order. There are only a few places these guys coulda learned the special skills needed to do what they're doin'…the military, which is my guess, Langley, Quantico and maybe state.

"Secondly, it costs lots of money to operate on this scale nationwide. Who could fund this thing? Don't you have someone pullin' that list together?" J.C. asked, looking down at the deputy director.

Lou nodded. "We have identified a laundry list of wealthy people that could probably do it. However, I think the list is suspect. Most extremely wealthy people are more concerned with social status, image and philanthropy. Not likely they would have the stomach for this kind of thing and, of course, most of them would not be inclined to break the law."

"If I could have a copy of that list, maybe I can weed out some of um."

The deputy director pulled a copy of the list from his briefcase and handed it to the agent nearest him to carry up to the podium.

J.C. continued without looking at the list. "It seems to me, based on what I got out of the summary reports and the geeks behind closed doors, that we should be lookin' for someone with tons of cash, who knows damn well that the laws *we* have to operate under won't allow us to get the job done.

"Whoever it is, we know for sure they're willin' to spend whatever it takes to recruit the right kind of skills. Perhaps it's a patriot, a veteran or maybe just an angry asshole that's fed up with crime and drug dealers. It don't matter! They're out there poppin' bad guys and, as strange as it sounds, that's against the law.

"I recommend we have our wizards take a look at men on this list that might fall into one of those categories and then rank um highly probable, possible, and not likely. That might keep us from chasin' our tail any more than we have to."

J.C. walked down to the table and poured himself a glass of water from one of the metal water pitchers on the table. As he did so, the condensate that had formed on the outside of the cold pitcher, dripped over the notepad of one of the agents sitting at the table.

As he turned to walk back to the podium, he patted the agent's arm saying, "Sorry about that, chief. Fortunately, you don't have anything but doodles on it anyway, so no harm done."

Lou looked over at the agent with a cold stare, assuring the pad would be full of copious notes before the end of the meeting.

"Mr. Hanson, with your permission, I'd like to bring the task force up to speed on a recent DEA case," and without waiting for the deputy director to acknowledge his request, he continued. "For those of ya that wanta follow along, pull out case file 42328.

"For the better part of two years, my guys worked this case under cover. I won't waste time with details, you can read um yourself. When we pulled the hammer on these assholes, we arrested forty-three of um. Seven flipped and turned state's evidence, which really put some starch in the DA's case, resulting in solid convictions with lots of jail time for thirty-one of um.

"Three were popped by persons unknown while out on bail and the two heavy hitters…the *really* bad guys walked! Technicalities and a slick lawyer bit us in the ass yet again!

"Not to worry, there is a God. A few weeks ago, the exact date is in the file, these two slime balls lost their heads...*literally*. And we got a big break. It gets better. Their asshole lawyer took a heavy tap to the chest right along with um.

"It seems they went huntin' in sweet Alabam and became the *hunted*. What I'm about to tell ya is pretty well documented in the file. I have put an asterisk on those parts of the summary that represent speculation on my part, but I'd be willin' to bet a dime to a donut it's right on the money."

Lou had not read the latest summary reports, so all of this caught him by surprise. "Mr. Holder, other priorities have occupied most of my time lately, and I must say I have not read the most recent summaries concerning incidents we may want to investigate. Am I right to assume you believe this was a professional hit and, more specifically, by the group we are attempting to identify?"

J.C. looked at Lou with contempt. "The short answer...*absolutely!* Since you've not had *time* to read my report, sir, I'll give ya a quick overview. The two dealers were hit by 7.62 NATO rounds. Both head shots from about 600 meters.

"We were able to recover one of the rounds from the interior of the truck, which means it exploded the target's head, shattered the windshield and still had enough zip to lodge in the steel frame of the truck's cab. That suggests to me, it could've been a special load, similar to those used by military shooters...snipers or, if you prefer, assassins.

"The shyster...geez, let me tell ya about that poor bastard. A well-placed .50 Cal round all but disemboweled the scum sucker. It looks like the velocity of the projectile may have blown him fifteen feet or so from where the round impacted and essentially cut him in half. It happened so fast, he still had a cigar clenched in his teeth when the sheriff got to the scene. What a mess!"

Lou squirmed in his seat a little, probably from J.C.'s graphic description of the hits. Dealing with assassins, blood and guts was not his cup of tea. He was tough, but still a senior level bureaucrat, not a field agent.

"You mentioned we got a break," Lou said, as he changed positions in his chair in anticipation of hearing something that might move the task force closer to their objective.

"You bet. When my guys got wind of this thing, I went out to the site with a couple investigators. We did trajectory analysis of the four shots taken."

Lou perked up, "Four shots? I thought you mentioned only three."

"That's correct, and that's one of the breaks as I see it. The fourth projectile was a .50 caliber armor-piercing round. It had been fired into the engine compartment to ensure no one stole the truck before law enforcement showed up. I don't personally think that was the reason, but possibly.

"Keep in mind we're dealin' with professionals, and a shooter with a lick of sense—and these boys have plenty—would know a trained monkey could do the trajectory work to find out the firing position in a heartbeat. No, sir! These folks wanted to be sure we got the message."

"And what do you perceive that message to be, Mr. Holder?" Lou asked, as he leaned forward and placed his elbows on the table.

"There are several messages in my estimation. First and foremost, we have to ask ourselves, why not three head shots? Why the overkill with a .50 caliber weapon system? The shooter's position was only about 600 meters away...child's play for a military-trained shooter with any number of sniper rifles available, and in a caliber that could be almost totally silenced.

"I've qualified with the Barrett .50 caliber sniper rifle out to a range of a thousand meters, and it sounds like a thunderbolt when you squeeze off a round. The report of that round in the valley where this incident took place would've been heard by just about everyone on the mountain.

"I was trained as a sniper at Fort Benning, Georgia and, as you might imagine, drawing attention to yourself is *not* part of the curriculum. So, I asked myself, why use a high caliber, sophisticated weapon system, not readily available to the average gun enthusiast, and one that would most assuredly be heard?

"What message might that send to someone, let's say, a government law enforcement agency...like us? Someone really interested in identifying a covert group?"

J.C. scanned the room of very attentive faces, "Let me share my thoughts and we'll get a group consensus later. The messages I glean from this and other incidents we've looked at to date follow. One, the .50 cal chest shot ensures we know they have access to the most sophisticated weapons available and expertise in their use.

"Two, a chest shot would make identifying the body or what's left of it easy. Which suggests they want players in the criminal justice system to know they are responsible for their actions and, if justice is not served, there will be no distinction made between so-called good guys and bad guys. That's a damn good message," J.C. said as he paused for a moment. "We could damn sure use that in *our* business.

"We now must ask ourselves, how did they, this mystery group, know where these guys would be and when? Not just in this case, but all of them? Where do they get their intelligence? I think they have an unequaled and unencumbered intelligence network.

"In other words, they don't have to play by our stupid ass rules. They get information by breaking a low level druggie's legs, by tapping phones whenever and wherever they damn well please and without legal authorization. That makes their intel timely. Something they can act on immediately, instead of waiting days or even weeks like we have to.

"The real kicker, you ain't gonna like. I also think they get a hell of a lot of information from us. I feel pretty sure law enforcement communication networks, to include ours, have been compromised."

Lou stiffened. "That's absurd. We have more firewalls and security blocks then any system on Earth; it can't be done."

"You're right about the firewalls and security blocks, but don't for a minute think it *can't* be done, sir.

"Systems one hell of a lot more sophisticated than ours have been penetrated...the Pentagon a number of years ago comes to mind. Remember, in our budget-conscious world, system upgrades are usually the first thing the bean counters look at when they start sniffing around for a cash cow. It *can* happen and in my best judgment, it has happened."

"I just don't believe that to be the case," said Lou in somewhat of a huff.

J.C. stared at him for a moment and then said, "Who knows? But let's not take the possibility of it off the table just yet.

"If that observation twisted your shorts, the next one will be a real ball buster. I think it's conceivable this task force has been compromised as well."

The deputy director was becoming more and more agitated by the moment, and the veins in his neck were starting to show as his face became more flushed.

"Do you have proof of the compromise, sir, or is it speculation?"

"It is a logical assumption at this point, sir, and I have no proof or the culprit would be face down and cuffed by now.

"Of my own admission, Mr. Hanson, I'm one nasty, suspicious son-of-a-bitch, but as I'm sure you've been told, my intuitions are right far more often than they're wrong. When I say compromised, it doesn't necessarily mean it's someone on the task force.

"It may be clerical or administrative staff. Hell, it could just as easily be the nimble-fingered recorder over there in the corner. They're an excellent source of accurate information and reasonably easy to recruit, if you throw a chunk of money at um. We sure as hell don't pay um nothin'. And given the 'cover your ass, every man for himself' world our agencies have degenerated to, loyalty may not rank too high on their list of considerations. It's somethin' to think about."

Lou's shorts would have been more than just twisted had he realized how accurate J.C. Holder's assessment really was. Some of the federal government's law enforcement agencies' communications network had indeed been compromised.

More importantly, and closer to home, the federal agent Lou had dispatched like a school boy to take the list of wealthy candidates to the podium, was in fact, an undercover ARC operative.

J.C. looked around the room. "I have one final piece of speculation to share with the task force. I'm convinced they already know we're lookin' for um. That's the principal reason I'm goin' with the compromise hypothesis.

43

Space Needle Restaurant – Seattle, Washington

"Who is this guy, Frankie?" asked Jeremiah B. Hawkins, director, American Relief Committee, Operations Center. J.B. generally served as the buffer between Sean O'Reilly and patriots recruited by ARC.

For a number of reasons, Sean seldom got involved in one-on-one meetings with operatives. He was extremely busy directing the affairs of one of the largest privately owned corporations in America and, secondly, as one of the wealthiest men in the country, he was a high profile figure whose likeness regularly appeared in major newspapers and magazines. Then there was the issue of size; he didn't blend in very well.

Special Agent Frank (Frankie) Moreno, a twelve-year veteran of the criminal investigation division, had been recruited by the FBI the day he graduated from USC School of Law. He was smart and considered a rising star by his superiors at the Bureau.

What the Bureau did not know, he had also been recruited by ARC several years earlier and was presently serving as their eyes and ears on Task Force Checkmate.

A fortuitous temporary assignment for a mission-oriented special agent, frustrated by the shackles of bureaucratic policy and ineffective laws that had for years precluded government law enforcement from effectively achieving their charter…crime fighting!

He had not had a vacation in almost a year and a half and had finally talked his supervisor into convincing the deputy director that he needed to get away for a few days with his family to recharge his batteries. He chose the Pacific Northwest, a perfect cover for a clandestine meeting.

Frank Moreno smiled at the server as she removed what was left of an excellent salmon fillet. "May I have a cup of coffee?" he asked, smiling at the attractive young woman.

She looked over at J.B. who nodded that he too would like to have a cup. When she turned to walk away, as an afterthought, Frankie said, "Thanks, you're a doll."

He scooted his chair from under the table so he had room to cross his legs and get comfortable. Then he reached inside his suit coat and pulled out a folded eight-by-ten manila envelope and pushed it across the table.

"J.B, I don't know the man, but from what I saw at the meeting, he's not the kind of guy that's likely to back off. He has a better understanding in just a week than the task force has been able to muster in months. Some of his speculation is spot on.

"One look at this sucker and you know he's a real life tough guy. You could slap a green beret on him and he'd be a recruiting poster boy. I mean...he really looks the part."

J.B. had already started looking through the data Frank handed him and didn't say anything immediately. Moments later, as a smile crept into the corners of his mouth, he said, "You've got to be shitting me!"

"What?"

"I know this guy! He looks older in the photo, but that damn nose is unmistakable. Unless I'm terribly mistaken, Frankie, I interviewed Mr. Holder a number of years ago and was involved in reviewing his application for Special Forces. As I recall, he was rejected outright. He didn't have the temperament, self-control or psychological profile required to be SF.

"Though he didn't make the cut, I remember thinking he'd be a damn good man to have around when the serious shit started kicking up. No mistake about it, I know this guy.

"I clearly remember telling someone on the review board that his name and mannerisms conjured up an image of a rodeo cowboy: 'J.C. Holder, out of chute four, riding Whirlwind!'"

Both men were laughing when their coffee arrived and the server smiled. "What are we so happy about? If you gentlemen just won the lottery; propose and I'll say yes."

Frank looked up at her. "No, nothing like that sweetheart; just a couple of blokes having a good time. However, if I ever win the lottery, I'll be back to hold you to it."

After she had walked away, he said, "Whirlwind is a good descriptor of the impression he left with most of the task force. You can see by the information I gave you there that Mr. Holder knows his stuff and moved through the DEA ranks faster than shit through a goose.

"I listed the salient points of the meeting in the papers. What is not there is the sense of focus he had. I mean he cut right to the meat of the issue and did it in a hurry. There was no question in anyone's mind about who was really in charge.

"Mr. Holder overshadowed the deputy director, and that's not easy to do. This guy has his act together, J.B., and in a very short time, it would be my guess he will narrow the field of probable players."

J.B. sipped his coffee while pondering the content of the papers and Frank's observations. "This is good stuff, Frankie. It helps a lot. Let me ask you, do you have a feel with regard to Mr. Holder's loyalty to DEA? Said another way: Do you think he might be amenable to joining us? It sounds like he operates on the ragged edge and is mission oriented. He might be one hell of an asset if we could find a way to keep his energies harnessed."

Frank thought for a moment. "I don't know. But in the short time we were together in the conference room, I sensed he would be absolutely loyal right up to the moment he punched the director in the mouth and turned in his resignation.

"He is street savvy...that I know. And it strikes me that someone like that would consider alternative employment if he felt in his heart he could make a difference. He hates drug dealers with a passion. He was really upbeat as he described the eighteen-month investigation and the resultant convictions.

"But when he mentioned the two key players that got off on technicalities and a slick lawyer—and those were his words—his whole demeanor changed. You could sense he was seething with anger and disgust.

"You know, this might be important, J.B, he also said something to the effect that it was not clear to him why the task force was looking for a covert group that was accomplishing what the government had been unable to do. He posed this question, and I quote: 'Why not deputize the whole damn bunch of them and let them do what they do best?' Of course the deputy director cringed and glossed over the comment, but that might give you insight to how the man thinks."

"If we *were* to approach him, any feel for how we might go about it?" J.B. asked. "What type of person would he most likely relate to?"

Frank thought about it for a moment while he unwrapped an after-dinner mint and popped it into his mouth.

"Well, he's clearly a 'no guts, no glory' kind of guy. He's smart and tough mentally and physically. He loathes suits and ties and, I sense, the men who wear them. He's a field guy through and through and I'm sure if someone put him behind a desk for more than a few minutes, he'd cut their nuts out."

"You know...now that I think about it, he really reminds me of that guy you had with you the first time we met."

J.B. looked surprised, "I was alone the first time we met, Frankie. You may recall we were at the Viet Nam Memorial."

"I know exactly where we were. It struck me as quite a coincidence that the Neanderthal in the brown leather flight jacket...you know, the one with the scar running across his face where someone tried to cut his head off with a meat cleaver, stayed about the same distance from us no matter how far down we walked.

"Have you ever tried to find someone's name on that wall? Even with the guide, it takes some doing. But somehow, Scar Face was able to find and trace names at precisely the same height all along the wall. And by coincidence...I'm sure; his dead buddies were all about twenty feet from us, no matter where we were.

"Come on, J.B., I didn't just fall off the turnip truck! I don't know where you found him, but by the looks of his face and neck, he's had some pretty interesting up close and personal encounters.

"My guess...he's from *your* world! Or maybe an agency asset who probably knows his stuff in the woolly wilds of the jungle or other God-forsaken places, but doesn't have the foggiest idea how to conduct over-watch operations on Main Street, USA. You surely don't think I slept through Surveillance 101 and counter-espionage for the amateur sleuth?"

J.B. looked at Frank for a moment. Then a broad smile crossed his face. "Frankie, you're too slick for an old warrior. I had no idea you were on to us. You hid it well...maybe that's why you're on the team. You think this Holder fellow is cut from the same cloth?"

"I didn't say that. I never had a chance to talk to your *shadow*, but they have the same persona...the same bad ass look about them. I can't quite put my finger on it, but he's the guy that comes to mind."

"Well, see what you can find out about him. We don't want to act prematurely or do something really stupid that might jeopardize all of the success we've had to date."

As he talked, J.B. inconspicuously slipped a large sum of money into the same envelope that Frank had given him earlier. "Be smart with this, Frankie. Unless you can afford to run out and buy a new Mercedes on your government salary, don't go out and buy one now. I'm sure, based on what you've said, the deputy director is going to be looking at all kinds of scenarios; we don't want to give anyone a reason to be suspicious of you. OK?"

Frank nodded and slipped the envelope into his suit coat.

As the two men finished their coffee, J.B. looked at the tab and left a fifty-dollar bill on the table. "We've turned so many times [referring to the rotating restaurant atop the Space Needle] we'll be lucky to find our way out of here."

"This would *not* be a good place to come for happy hour," Frank said, as they walked slowly to the exposed elevators and queued for the 600-foot drop to the bottom.

J.B. looked down at the street below. "You know, I was a paratrooper for over twenty-five years and probably jumped out of perfectly good airplanes maybe 700 times, but if I stand on the edge of a place like this, it makes me a little queasy to look down.

"Same goes for rappelling. I always felt a bit squirrelly before I went over the edge. I was okay once I got started, but in the back of my mind I was always conscious of what the young troopers under my command would think if I chickened out. I think, in retrospect, the fear of failure is what drives us so hard to set the right example for those in our charge."

"I don't know how the hell you Special Forces guys do all the things they ask of you. I know I couldn't do it. Hell, Quantico was a cakewalk in comparison, and I thought that was pretty tough."

J.B. touched Frank's shoulder as they got on the elevator. "Quantico's tough enough. The Bureau's mission is simply different. Consequently the training is understandably tailored to the mission. In my view, the FBI is second to none at what they are trained to do, if only the bureaucrats would cut you loose to do it."

"Amen to that."

Once on the ground, the two men parted company as though they had never met. Two patriots, working in different circles, but with one cause—to do what the government of the United States had failed to do, protecting her citizens by eliminating selected targets, *the worst of the worst*, thus reducing the incident of drug-related crime and making the streets of America safer.

44

Governors Convention, Ritz-Carlton Hotel, Alexandria, VA

Regardless of the outcome, Mike had already decided this would be the last major campaign stop. TV spots, interviews and guest appearances would have to carry the day. He was tired of all the nonsense, the coddling, glad-handing and what seemed to be ubiquitous compromise.

He didn't like being in the nation's capital. There was a certain feeling about the place...a sleight-of-hand that reminded him of a cheap carnie's shell game.

He had long felt the city was awash in ignorance, indifference and ineptitude. Superficially it is a beautiful city with a lot of history and many things for visitors to see and do. However, just under the surface was layer upon layer of corruption, malfeasance and self-importance by elected officials at every level, including the United States Congress.

Mike wanted to go home, be with his family and breathe fresh air. Shake hands with friends and honest, hard-working folks that could be trusted to tell you the way things really were, not what they thought you wanted to hear or what they perceived would be advantageous in perpetuating their personal agenda.

As he prepared to leave his suite, his mind was in another place. Surrounded by five-star ambience, he knew what he really wanted, at that moment, was to smell fresh hay in the early morning dew; to breathe in the rich smell of saddle leather as he prepared Flame, his seventeen-hand gelding, for their morning ride to the river; to hear the familiar squeak of cowhide as he settled into the saddle and the snorting of his mount as the cool morning air flared nostrils; that's what he really wanted. This was not the place for Mike O'Reilly.

If there was a bright spot, he no longer had to contend with the bevy of political advisors that had surrounded him from the outset of the campaign. He had finally taken Jeff's advice and sent them packing.

In the process, Jeff became a special staff member with oversight responsibility for O'Reilly family security. Day-to-day security operations were given to Phil Burlingame, an ex-Navy SEAL and henceforth Mike's personal driver and bodyguard.

The O'Reilly team seemed to function more efficiently now that all of the silver-tongued strategists had left the camp. One thing that was comforting: Jeff wouldn't follow him around with hair spray or give a damn if he had foreign matter wedged between his teeth. Jeff had already made it crystal clear earlier in the week when he had said something to the effect: 'If you can't comb your own hair and brush your teeth, why on God's Earth would I want you to be president of the United States?' Mike smiled at the candidness of his longtime friend as he left his suite to be escorted to the Governors Conference by his new chief of security.

During the hour-and-a-half talk, Mike drove home the salient points of his presidential platform as well as the politically charged issue of immigration. During the question and answer session that followed, several governors had questions about meaningful immigration reform and wanted to hear the Republican candidate's views.

After setting his water glass down, Mike stepped from behind the podium and moved toward the room full of governors assembled before him. "Ladies and gentlemen, you are in unique positions to bring about meaningful change. I have had the great privilege of serving as governor of Oklahoma. I know first hand what can be accomplished. The issues of illegal aliens, border security, and immigration in general are no where near as difficult to resolve as the executive branch and our Congress would have us believe.

"The United States already has a good set of immigration laws. The problem is our weak-willed representatives don't have the courage or intestinal fortitude to enforce them. We have a border that leaks like a sieve. Seal it!

"Purportedly our country needs migrant workers. Those jobs should be filled with foreign workers only after we have exhausted all means to ensure gainful employment for Americans.

"In that vein, state and federal welfare reform is needed, just as we have done in Oklahoma, to get all able-bodied individuals stricken from welfare roles and placed in jobs. If migrant workers are needed in your states to harvest crops, offer those jobs to able-bodied welfare recipients and to work-release candidates. It works!

"It also dovetails nicely into crime prevention or reduction initiatives. Listen, all work is honorable and that is the approach you have to take to interest people that have grown accustomed to making a living off the welfare system and crime.

"One of you had a question earlier that I said I would address when we reached the question and answer session. The question was: 'Mexico does not seem to be cooperating with the United States in our ongoing efforts to stop illegal immigration. What pressure could we bring to bear to encourage the Mexican government to cooperate, and where would the issue of illegal immigration fall in your presidential agenda?

"Do I have that right, sir?"

The governor of Illinois stood. "That is correct, sir."

"Before I answer that question, let me share with you the *real* reason the government of Mexico is not cooperating as they should. The peso, as a currency, has little value, and inflation continues to erode what value it does have. The more U.S. dollars that are pumped into their economy, the better off they are.

"According to our government talking heads, there are over twenty million illegal aliens in the country. I have a specific number from the latest government report. But if I share it with you, one would have to ask if the government knows *exactly* how many there are, they must know *where* they are. And if they know where they are, why haven't they been arrested, imprisoned or deported?

"That would be a pretty good question to ask, wouldn't it? So when we take a break, why don't you get on your cell phones and ask it! Each of you has a hot line to the Oval Office, the attorney general, director of Homeland Security, Customs and Immigration. Make the calls!

"Should I become president, and you have not made the call, be assured I will be calling you. If ever in our country's history it was time for a full court press, it's now!

"Where will it be on my agenda? Hopefully the same place it will be on your agenda...close to the top. We must work this one together and with a single voice to the extent statehood in the Republic will allow.

"Let me give you some pretty shocking numbers. Just within the last eighteen months, more than $22 billion have been wired to Mexico by Mexicans working here in the United States. One would have to assume that many of those wiring American currency to Mexico are illegal aliens. That is 22 billion reasons the Mexican government is reluctant to help curb illegal immigration.

"Over the last decade, illegal aliens who should not even be candidates for benefits have cost the social welfare service over 397 billion dollars. That's welfare and medical support the Mexican government doesn't have to provide.

"Are you starting to get the feeling that their government officials are one hell of a lot smarter than those we have elected to represent us?"

"We have over half a million illegal aliens in the U.S. prison system. They are incarcerated for all manner of criminal activity. The cost of that incarceration to U.S. tax payers is close to one-and-a-half billion dollars annually.

"From a purely economic point of view, why would the Mexican government want to assist in stopping illegal immigration? Their economy is being bolstered by U.S. dollars; they are avoiding the expense of welfare and medical attention for their impoverished citizens; and they can literally dump their unwanted criminal element across the border by the truckload, getting rid of undesirables, and avoiding the high cost of incarceration.

"There is also the lucrative business of state-sanctioned, or at least tolerated, drug trafficking across our southern border. You should now have a pretty clear understanding of why the Mexican government turns a blind eye to the issue of immigration.

"It's one hell of a deal if you can find someone *stupid* enough to let you get away with it…and they have! That, folks, is the *real* reason we get only lip service from our neighbors to the south."

Mike observed a certain nervous shifting and fidgeting in the conference—particularly from governors representing Border States and states heavily involved in agriculture. He wondered if this was driven by concern or embarrassment for their inaction, not having aggressively voiced their displeasure in the performance of an impotent U.S. Congress. He didn't know, but he was certainly going to do all he could to get them moving in the right direction.

"The second part of the question concerning what pressure the United States could bring to bear on the Mexican government in an effort to enhance cooperation, it seems to me—and, by the way, this would apply to all countries involved in illicit drug trafficking—that an aggressive, multi-faceted program, incorporating trade embargos; withdrawal of U.S. funding where applicable; and the threat of cancellation of all NAFTA and other economic support agreements, would go a long way in getting an uncooperative governments attention, don't you think?

"There are very few things—none that come to mind—U.S.-based manufacturers are presently having produced in foreign countries that we cannot do in the United States, and do it better. We did it for over 150 years. We can and *should* do it again!

"Affordable labor is the issue here. We have shot ourselves in the proverbial foot, not with the creation of unions, but by allowing them to become mismanaged, cash-consuming albatrosses—in many cases, dead weight around the neck of our most crucial industries. As a businessman involved in a large U.S. corporation, with a number of subsidiaries, I can tell you unequivocally…that's not a good position to be in.

"Surely with our combined acumen for business, we can devise an incentive package to offset the delta cost…foreign versus made in the U.S.A. I'm sure you're all familiar with 'favored country' and 'preferred trading partner' agreements. There are numerous incentive-based agreements floating around, and we're taking it in the ear on most of them.

"If that were not true, how would one explain the trade deficit imbalance which, by the way, becomes increasingly worse with every passing day? Let's focus on incentives for American-owned enterprises and bring the products...and jobs back home.

"Our Congress is fiscally irresponsible, gentlemen, and unless we stand together—with a single voice—they will continue to drive this country into bankruptcy, or worse, sell us out to foreign entities. It not only can happen...it *is* happening as we speak."

"As an alternative approach to business as usual, I suggest we give some of these incentives to U.S. manufacturers of goods and services, thereby proliferating the economy with 'made in the U.S.A' products. We do that by offering them at affordable prices offset by cost incentives, keeping U.S. currency here at home and circulating and strengthening our own economy, as opposed to sending it offshore. We must find smarter ways of doing business, no question about it, but not at the expense or to the detriment of the United States...not on my watch!"

45

Several weeks later

Mike had removed his tie, had the cuffs of his tailor-made shirt turned up and was enjoying a cup of coffee in his twenty-first floor office suite of the newly constructed O'Reilly Corporation headquarters building on the outskirts of Oklahoma City.

Floor-to-ceiling windows afforded him a panoramic view of the city to the West and North. Since he traveled less now, having greatly reduced his campaigning initiatives, he was rested and spent almost every evening with his wife and young daughter at the O'Reilly estate.

Though the new building had a luxurious penthouse for use when a trip home was not practical, the jet-powered SK-76 Sikorsky helicopter could wing Mike from the helipad atop the O'Reilly building home in less time then most people spent in rush hour traffic. Besides, he really got a kick out of flying the thing, once the senior pilot got it airborne and pointed in the right direction.

The sun was losing its luster as it prepared to disappear beyond the horizon, its last rays of light reflecting off of an advancing front of cumulous clouds, creating a beautiful array of soft pink and orange highlights.

He drained his coffee cup as he pushed the intercom to the outer offices. "Mary Elaine, are you still here?"

Mike's personal assistant had been trying for years to convince her boss to just call her Mary, like everyone else, but he couldn't bring himself to do it, partly because of his southern heritage, but mostly because he really liked to tick her off.

"No, boss, I'm home in my recliner watching television, but if you'll leave a message...of course I'm *still* here. I'm *always* here! I have no life!"

"Yeah, yeah, I've heard it all before," Mike said, chuckling. "Would you please round up Jeff and tell him we can get started early if he's ready. And please brew up a fresh pot of coffee for us. We'll be here for a while, so I'll trade you a pot of coffee for the privilege of leaving at a normal hour."

"Deal!" and the intercom went silent.

Ten minutes later, Jeff entered Mike's office with a briefcase and what appeared to be a rolled up sheet of easel paper. "I just got off the horn with an agency contact and got the last piece of data I needed to lay this thing out for you...fortuitous, huh?"

Mike smiled. "Stay away from the big words, buddy. They're not for you."

Jeff glared at his friend, extending his arm toward him with a balled fist and a curled lip but opted not to extend his middle finger. "If nothing else, you're a funny guy. Please tell me that's fresh coffee," Jeff said nodding toward the silver server on Mike's desk.

"That it is," Mike said as he poured two mugs of hot coffee and shoved one toward him.

Jeff sat across from Mike and took a sip of coffee as he admired the beauty of the last glimpse of sunlight. "I'm not complaining, you understand, but most people are heading home about this time. *Not* us though, right, boss?"

"You've never had it so good, so quit bitching. You remind me of a little crybaby...right after it came out of a meat grinder. You do understand you're not pretty, right?"

Jeff smiled saying, "Oh, I don't know about that. I have a chick or two. Unfortunately I have no time to see them. By now, I'm sure they think I was killed in the last war. You see, I work for a cruel taskmaster who is insensitive to the needs of mortal man."

"I heard something very similar to that just before Mary Elaine left. What have you been able to piece together and does it make sense to you?" Mike asked, as he sat back resting his mug on the arm of his plush leather chair.

Jeff unrolled a large map on the desk, moving several items to one side as he did and placing a couple of extra coffee mugs on either side of the map to keep it flat.

"Before we get too wrapped up in the latest incidents, let me show you what I meant by spheres of influence." Jeff had used a protractor to draw interconnecting circles covering the entire map of the United States.

Mike leaned forward with his arms folded and elbows resting on the massive mahogany desk.

"Now I set this up the same way we ran GRU units in Nam, just to demonstrate how it might work here. I think we can agree there has to be some means of controlling the activities of individuals in an operation of this magnitude, and I think, based on the data collected, we *are* dealing with an organization.

"Now, bud," Jeff continued, "imagine, that whoever is calling the shots in each of these spheres has no idea there are others. His whole universe, his area of operation is within the geography assigned. That way, should he be captured or his identity compromised, he knows nothing beyond his world…his sphere…and cannot, even if he wanted to, give up the organization." Jeff looked up at Mike as he reached for his coffee mug, "That's how it's done, pal."

Mike leaned back, deep in thought as he ran mental extrapolations about how such a complex initiative might be organized, controlled and funded. Given the long tentacles of the IRS, he knew it was not easy to hide or move large sums of money without attracting attention. He believed, however, that he knew a way it could be done. 'We'll just stick this in the data bank for future recall.'

Jeff knew the distant look Mike got when he was thinking and had learned to never interrupt him when he was in that mode, so he sat back, drank his coffee and waited for him to re-enter planet Earth.

A few moments later, Mike again leaned forward to examine the map. "What are these little stars pasted all over the place?"

Jeff sat forward. "Remember the judge that expired in a plate of sauerkraut some time back? *You* remember… That's kind of what started this whole inquiry."

"I do remember, now that you mention it."

"Well, that star right there," Jeff said, tapping his finger on a silver star just to the North of Atlanta, "is the sorry ass judge. A second, more thorough, autopsy revealed high levels of potassium chloride. Obviously I'm not the only one that felt he wasn't fit to be a judge."

"How have you managed to identify all of the rest of what I must assume are unfortunate incidents? There are so damn many of them, Jeff. What's the significance of the different colored stars?"

"There's a shit pot full of them, boss, no question about that. If my guess is anywhere near right, this has to have been going on for a long time. In answer to your question, the silver stars represent suspicious or untimely deaths involving players in the criminal justice system…judges, lawyers and dirty cops. Red stars are hits on known drug dealers. You may notice there are many more red stars than anything else.

"The black stars are hits on bad guys other than drug dealers, and run the full gambit. As an example, this one up here," Jeff said placing his index finger on a black star just below Olympia, Washington, "represents two cop killers fished out of a river. Both had been double tapped in the chest and one to the temple.

"You asked how I came by the location and detail concerning the stars," Jeff said, as he opened his briefcase and removed a large expandable folder full of incident reports.

"A friend of a friend of mine has a cousin who's an analyst with the FBI…"

Mike chuckled, cutting his friend short. "Holy crap, Jeff…that sounds like a hot tip you'd get at a race track! How good is the data?"

"Very good," Jeff said, shoving the folder across the desk. "This guy is working directly, maybe not directly, but is involved in identifying cases resulting in the death of bad guys and unsolved by law enforcement. Evidently they have a specific criteria or profile they apply to determine if a particular case fits.

"From what I can gather, boss, the Bureau is in the process of doing exactly what we're doing…trying to figure out who's wasting all these useless bastards.

"All the data pertaining to each star is right there," Jeff said, nodding his head toward the bulging expandable folder. "As you read through it, you'll come across a case where a shyster lawyer is taken out by a .50 caliber sniper rifle.

"That's a unique piece of equipment, requiring special shooting skills. The only one having a need to reach out and tap someone at distances in excess of a mile is the military, and within the military most of those weapon systems belong to Special Forces.

"Neither the agency nor the Bureau has occasion to use such a weapon, at least not to my knowledge. It's been a while since I was in the agency, maybe a few of their assets are now trained on such a system; I don't know. I do know however, that most of those systems reside in the military."

Mike was rubbing his hand over a full day's whisker stubble while thinking about everything Jeff had said. "Who has the wherewithal to do this, and what would be their motivation? It must have taken years to reach the point your map suggests they have reached. Hell, there are hundreds of stars on that map."

Jeff interjected, "There are probably many more; these are simply the ones that met an arbitrary criteria established by the Bureau."

Mike had the unsettling feeling that he may *know* the driving force behind all of this, but he was certainly not ready to share these unfounded thoughts, not even with his closest friend…not yet, anyway.

Jeff was looking right at him when Mike looked over to get an answer to his question. Jeff repositioned himself a little self-consciously in his chair. "Let's assume for a moment that we are looking for a person with an endless supply of money, who is very concerned with the trend of unchecked lawlessness our country is tracking to. He would be a proven patriot with military experience, a man of unquestionable integrity who places honor and loyalty above all other traits. Who do we have? We have *you!*"

Mike sat back in his chair, dumbfounded by what his long time friend and confidant had just said. After looking at him for a few moments, he finally said, "You're a real piece of work. No wonder someone tried to cut your friggin' head off."

Jeff laughed and stretched both arms toward the ceiling while standing on his tiptoes to stretch his legs at the same time. As he sat back down, he said, "Think about it, Mike. It's a pretty rational conclusion actually.

"Your track record on and off the political playing field is laced with honorable, patriotic and humanitarian initiatives. The very platform you are using to seek the presidency screams your concerns for the country and fellow Americans.

"For all the same reasons, I'm here with you at 2100 hours instead of out seeking more pleasurable releases for my pent-up energies. What say you?"

Mike had just checked his watch, having no idea where the last three hours or so had gone. "I think you're *nuts*! But hell, I thought that the first day I met you in the Congo. Before we knock off for the night, Mr. Stone, let me assure you, it's definitely not me...though I'm sure we could get a hell of a lot more done and with less nonsense, if it were.

"Thanks for your due diligence, buddy. I really appreciate all you've done for me and the family. If you want to stay here tonight, you know you're always welcome."

Jeff shook his head, "No, thanks. I still have time to get lucky tonight."

Mike smiled and shook his friend's hand. "Whoever she is, I'm sure she'll bring a whole new meaning to *blind date*."

"You're a smart guy, boss, but as a comedian, you really *suck*!"

"Yeah, I know. By the way, Dad's flying in from Alaska tonight, and we have meetings scheduled until about noon tomorrow. Why don't you plan on sleeping in after that hot date you have and join us for lunch around 1300?

"If she looks anything like the last date of yours I had the pleasure of meeting, it'll take you that long to get the ugly washed off." Both men laughed, and Mike added, "I know, I *suck*!"

Jeff turned to leave saying, "Sasquatch—a title Jeff affectionately used to describe Mike's father—now there's another solid candidate, now that I think about it. You guys are peas in a pod, though he is a slightly larger, more imposing pod."

"Enough of this babble; I'll see you for lunch." Mike smiled, as he watched his friend leave the office. Birds of a feather not only flock together, they obviously think alike.

46

Chugach Mountain Range, Alaska

As Mike and Jeff were wrapping up their meeting, it was a little after 1800 hours in Alaska. Sean O'Reilly, family patriarch, recipient of the Congressional Medal of Honor and chairman of one of the largest privately owned corporations in America, intuitively knew they were in serious trouble.

Their single-engine aircraft was being hammered by snow and sleet and violently tossed around as its engine surged in response to sudden wind shifts. Two of his traveling companions regurgitated and the third, pale as a ghost, was on the verge of following suit.

Sean, two geologists and a senior vice president for operations from the O'Reilly Corporation's oil exploration subsidiary had earlier departed Fairbanks for Valdez to visit the company's new oil pumping facilities.

On this leg of the trip, they were flying in one of the most dependable aircraft used by Alaska's bush pilots...a 1950s vintage DeHavilland L-20. The Beaver, as it was commonly called, was powered by a single Pratt & Whitney radial engine. Some of these aircraft had been equipped with anti-icing systems, some not.

Alaskan weather is unpredictable, particularly in the fall and winter. It develops quickly and can catch even the most seasoned aviator by surprise. It is the root cause of over 500 bush pilot fatalities. Such was the case on this day.

At 16,523 feet, Mount Blackburn and the surrounding Chugach range were high enough to create their own weather with vicious downdrafts and wind shifts.

Unlike the lower forty-eight states, bush pilots in Alaska generally do not have the luxury of flying to alternate airfields or finding a small strip to set down on to wait out a storm.

There were *no* alternate airfields, and the terrain, rugged as any on Earth, left few options...reverse course, assuming the weather had not already closed that option, or try to navigate through the weather at your own peril.

In just a matter of minutes, the aircraft was totally engulfed by freezing rain and snow. The build-up of rime ice on the aircrafts control surfaces quickly overtook the capabilities of the anti-icing equipment, and they started losing altitude.

"Mayday, mayday, this is Butch Robinson, iced over and losing altitude, visibility zero, zero...Northwest of McCarthy, approximately five miles west of Blackburn."

He was transmitting in the blind, but the savvy pilot knew it really didn't matter. From this moment on, short of a miracle, it would be a recovery operation. There would be no survivors.

Butch Robinson was right! In the white-out conditions, the disoriented pilot, along with all souls onboard, slammed into a mountain twenty miles further southwest than his reported position. Alaskan weather claimed another hapless aircraft, and Butch Robinson joined the ranks of hundreds of bush pilots that had perished in the Alaskan wilds.

47

Mike was awakened somewhere around 0430 by a call from Stan Wickham, Valdez pumping station general manager. The O'Reilly Corporation held the lease on one of the largest oil pumping and storage facilities in Valdez. He answered the phone but in the fog of early morning sleep did not immediately understand the significance of the message.

Mike knew they had facilities in Valdez but was not personally responsible for that part of corporate operations and consequently did not know anyone named Stan Wickham. A total stranger had just informed him that his dad had not arrived in Valdez as planned and provided very little additional information.

Sean was notorious for last-minute change in plans, so alarm signals did not immediately go off in Mike's head. Perhaps he chose not to go to Valdez this trip or didn't finish his business meetings about future exploration as early as planned or any number of other reasons that might have delayed his arrival...including a decision to be the oldest person to ever run the Iditarod.

Had the younger O'Reilly been more familiar with the dangers associated with flying in Alaska and known that bush pilots made a habit of staying in contact with whoever was monitoring their flight, whether it be their base operations, local air traffic control, or the Coast Guard, he would have been more alarmed.

Mike was an early riser and by the time he got off the phone, he decided to shower, shave, have coffee and make a few calls of his own. When he came out of the shower, however, he could see the red message light glowing in the semi-darkness of the bedroom.

It was from Darin McVeigh, president of the O'Reilly Corporation. Because of the hour and the previous call from Alaska, a chill went up Mike's spine. He knew the news would not be good.

Even before he had finished a silent prayer and mentally prepared himself to return McVeigh's call, the phone rang again, startling him.

The news was far beyond *not good*...it was life altering. Darin McVeigh, tearful and barely able to speak, relayed the latest information from Alaska. The plane transporting his father had departed Fairbanks and about an hour into the flight encountered severe weather and had not been heard from since.

A faint mayday had been picked up by an amateur ham operator who called the coast guard station at Valdez. The operator didn't get the aircraft call sign and with the low power of the transmission and the static created by the weather heard only bits and pieces of the transmission: *"mayday... robins... ice... los... altitude... wes... McCarth..."*

The ham operator was queried at length by the coast guard in an effort to extract as much information as possible so search operations could begin at first light or whenever the weather broke sufficiently to get aircraft off the ground and into the reported area of the crash.

Mr. McVeigh also said that he had been told by Stan Wickham, who had lived in the area his entire life, the probability of survivors in that area was at best, doubtful.

The temperature was already thirty below and would dip even lower as the expected front rolled in. Almost three feet of new snow had fallen in the area where they believed the aircraft went down. To complicate things further, there was really only one road into McCarthy and it was closed for the winter.

Darin McVeigh was crying and barely audible, as he told Mike that it was not unusual for aircraft in the Chugach Range to simply disappear, never to be found. The probability of locating the aircraft was slim, and even then, it would not happen until the spring or summer thaw.

He told Mike how terribly sorry he was to have to make this call, but felt he should be the one to tell him about his dad, since they had been friends for over twenty-five years. Mike thanked him for the call and slowly hung up the telephone.

Through all of the shock and pain he was feeling at the moment, Mike's only thought was how he was going to break this tragic news to Cheyenne. She and her grandfather were like one. She adored him and had even tried to pick up the tough persona of her beloved Papa, trying to emulate his every move. He knew this would be the most difficult and painful moment of his life.

"My God, what have you done to me and my family?" Mike said aloud, as he slumped to the floor and wept uncontrollably. Hours past before he could pull himself together enough to splash cold water on his face and finally get dressed. He finished a double brandy as he stood, lost in thought, on the balcony of the penthouse overlooking the awakening city.

As Mike returned the telephone to its cradle, having just informed Ron Snyder of the tragic news, he knew the pain and suffering he had just placed upon his old friend and mentor, but it was something that had to be done if they were to move on through these difficult times.

He decided to wait until he got home to break the news to Veronica and Cheyenne. In the interim, he held an emergency meeting of senior executives to inform them that the corporation had tragically lost its beloved chairman and mentor to a number of the executives seated around the table. Mike directed the chief counsel to take the necessary steps for an orderly transfer of power. He thanked everyone for their concern and support during this most difficult time. He pushed his chair back and quickly left the conference room.

48

Arlington National Cemetery

The burial ceremony was attended by hundreds of dignitaries, military and civilian. Sean O'Reilly's bravery and military exploits were highlighted with the recognition and reverence one would expect for an old warrior that had been awarded the countries highest decoration for valor, the Congressional Medal of Honor.

Following a twenty-one gun salute by the crack soldiers assigned to the 3rd Infantry detachment, the unit responsible for guarding the Tomb of the Unknown Soldier, an Irish bagpiper atop a hill overlooking the burial site played taps as Mike, Ron Snyder, and almost everyone in attendance wept or did their best to choke back tears in an effort to keep their emotions in check.

The officer, with his deepest regrets, presented Mike the flag that had draped his father's empty coffin. Sean O'Reilly was, in spirit, laid to rest.

Those in attendance included the vice president of the United States, Mike's college roommate Stephen Humphrey, the attorney general of the United States, numerous members of Congress, and senior executives from some of the largest, most powerful corporations around the world. The governors of Oklahoma and Alaska were there, too.

As Mike and Veronica accepted condolences from these prominent dignitaries, he thought, 'Dad, these fine folks have come to honor you. You were a great man, and I will miss you so much.

I promise to continue your good works just as though you were here. That's my promise to you, Pops!'

As Veronica, Cheyenne, the O'Reilly estate staff and other guests made their way back to the limousines that would take them to BWI and the flight back home to Oklahoma, Ron put his arm around his surrogate son's waist. "Mike, I promised your dad many, many years ago that I would always be there for you should something happen to him. I plan on honoring that promise just as I have since you were a small boy.

"We have many things to talk about and some things I want to show you. Do you think we could use one of the corporate jets for a day or so? Maybe leave tomorrow or the next day, if you're up to it?"

Mike nodded. "I really need to get away to sort through where we go from here. I can think of no one I'd rather spend time with right now." He could feel his chest getting tight as tears welled up. "This is *really* hard, Ron. I feel like my heart is about to explode; it just hurts so much."

"I know it does, son. Your dad and I were close friends for as long as I can remember. I know it hurts, but I think the little trip I have planned will make it easier for both of us."

As they moved toward the waiting limos Ron said, "Your dad was truly a hero, a patriot of the first order and one hell of a fine American. I am so proud to have known him, but it's time to leave now." Mike nodded and let his mentor guide him down the path to the limousines.

As the procession of countless automobiles prepared to leave Arlington National Cemetery, they noticed members of the Ancient and Royal Order of Bagpipers, 100 strong, had quietly taken positions along the full length of the driveway leading out of the cemetery. They were in full regalia, each wearing the plaid kilts of their respective clans.

The beautiful sound of bagpipes could be heard up and down the Potomac, as the procession was piped out of Arlington to the tune of 'Irish Soldier Boy.'

Aboard the large G-4, Mike thought how much his father had loved this airplane. It was plush and had all the amenities of home and office. It was magnificent, no question about it.

Mike took a few minutes to console members of the estate staff that were having a particularly hard time coming to terms with the loss of the man who had treated them so well; who had given them jobs when others would not; who treated them with respect and never once forgot a birthday. Mike thought, 'With all the things going on in his busy corporate life, how could he possibly remember such things? But he did!'

He checked on Cheyenne, who was already asleep half-sitting and half-lying in the seat next to her mother with her little head against her mother's shoulder. He gave Veronica a reassuring kiss. "Everything will be fine, dear. This is a strong family," and looking around the cabin added, "and we are surrounded by people that really care about us. What more is there?"

Mike slumped in his seat and slipped into a restless sleep with the full weight of his loss on his clouded mind. Where do I start?

49

Several days later

As the Citation winged southeast at nearly 500 miles an hour, a rested Mike O'Reilly looked over at Ron Snyder, "Exactly where are we going, kind sir?"

"We're going back to where it all began, and I'll say no more."

"Okay, then tell me how long you think we'll be gone?"

"Not long."

Realizing conversation with his mentor at this point would be like talking to a tree stump, Mike walked to the rear of the aircraft to get a soft drink and to see how Jeff and Phil were doing.

"I'd feel better, boss," Phil volunteered, "if we had a more substantial security contingent with us, but I understand Mr. Snyder wants to low profile this trip."

"Yeah, that's what he told me, too," Mike said as he squatted in the aisle between the two men and took a swig of his drink. "Hopefully we can get in and out before the media get wind of our little foray and turn it into a circus. It has to be a surprise to them, because I sure as hell don't know where we're going or how long we'll be there.

"Wherever it is, I want you two to be invisible. It makes Ron nervous to have armed men around, and I sense we will be having some serious conversations once we land, OK?" Both men nodded as Mike hoisted himself up and walked back to his seat.

The Citation glistened in the bright sunlight as it banked to pick up the assigned radial from the Montgomery omni-directional beacon and headed due south toward its destination: Dothan, Alabama.

Forty-five minutes later, with armed protectors in the back seat, Mike and his mentor drove north on Highway 231 to the outskirts of Ozark. Ron turned around in his seat and said, "Now, boys, I'm going to be telling Mike some things he probably never heard from his dad, so what is said here, stays here. Agreed?"

Both men nodded and as they approached Ft. Rucker Blvd. Ron motioned Mike to turn right and drive downtown.

Ozark, Alabama is a typical small southern town with the courthouse the center of the town square and all manner of small businesses lining the opposite sides of the streets that make up the square.

"Pull in here, Mike, and we'll get out." Ron said.

"Why are we getting out? There's nothing here."

"Humor an old man. This place is loaded with nostalgia, and I want to share some of it with you before I'm gone. OK?"

Mike did as he was instructed and all four men exited the vehicle. As the two men who had been sitting in the front seat walked over to a nearby bench in front of the courthouse, the other two took up strategic over-watch positions.

Smiling, and with moist eyes, Ron pointed to the old bank on the corner. "I'll never forget the time your dad and I were sitting in the 231 Truck Stop Café and he told me he had never had a checking account. Can you imagine, a grown man who didn't know how to write a check?

"Then when he told me he kept what little money he had hid in a sock out in the barn, I thought I'd fall on the floor." Both men laughed, fondly remembering the man that had been such a big part of their lives.

"I had to lie to get him to accept the property in Oklahoma…and then, only when I mentioned it was to ensure *little Mikey*," the old man said as he patted Mike's leg, "would have everything he needed for a decent life. He could be hardheaded if he set his mind to it."

"Tell me about it; I grew up in his shadow, literally!"

Ron continued, as his mind drifted back to another time. "Back then, old man MacDonald managed the bank. He told me your dad just about fainted when he found out how much money had been transferred into his first-ever checking account. I can't remember what it was, but a considerable amount of money for the day."

Ron smiled affectionately. "Your dad asked him if all he had to do was fill out one of these slips, meaning a counter check, and if he could buy a new truck."

Mike interrupted. "Pops paid cash for that red pickup truck, Ron."

"Yeah, at the insistence of old man MacDonald, who thought it would be a nifty way to start off a new life for the two of you. Hell, most of the time you guys didn't have two nickels to rub together."

Mike nodded. "You're right about that. Even as a kid I remember the lean times. But you know, it really wasn't all that bad...at least, not for me."

"Your dad was offered personalized checks, something like 400 for a couple of bucks. He turned them down when he found out he had to pay for them. He said he'd use the free counter checks and save the money.

"Think about it. Here he is, sitting on something like a couple hundred thousand dollars and he foregoes personalized checks to save a couple of bucks." They both laughed at the thought, and Ron added, "You have to love the guy...I really miss him."

Tears formed in the corner of the old man's eyes as he shared these fond memories with his surrogate son. Mike reached over and squeezed his shoulder. "Pops thought the world of you, and he never forgot all that you did for us. I really didn't fully grasp the magnitude of your generosity until I came to work for you overseeing the O'Reilly trust accounts and some of the O'Reilly Corporation initiatives."

Ron continued as though he had not heard a word Mike had said. "Over there is where the drugstore used to be," pointing toward one of the shops on the square, "where you sat having a burger while this drama played itself out in the bank."

"How can you remember this stuff after all these years?"

"I remember almost everything about the times your dad and I had; they were really special to me," he said as he began to weep openly. Mike could feel his own chest tightening as he consoled the old man and gave him a hug.

After composing himself, Ron said, "Let's go grab a bite to eat. There is something else I want to show you." He stood and limped toward the car.

The two-man security detail closed ranks as they looked around to ensure the area was safe and free of interlopers. A short drive north on Highway 231, the Truck Stop Café that held such special memories for this old man loomed ahead.

It had a different name, but other than that, it appeared as it had so many years ago when Sean and Ron pulled into the parking lot in Ron's new Cadillac convertible.

The two men in the back seat got out first, checked the immediate area and then went inside to look around before Mike and Ron got out.

Once inside, Ron asked the cute young lady that greeted them if it would be possible to have the far back booth, the same one he had used to jumpstart Sean and Mike's life so many years ago.

Mike followed his dear friend as they made their way to the back booth, thinking, "God love him…he's really showing his age now, almost as though this nostalgic trip was sucking the life out of him."

Jeff and Phil sat in different locations, one at the counter next to the cash register, the other toward the rear, next to the swinging doors leading to the restrooms. Not much had changed at the Truck Stop Café.

Only the two men in the booth ordered, and once the server had left Ron asked, "Aren't your friends going to eat? It's on me."

Mike smiled, "It's the nature of their business, sir…focus and constant vigilance. We'll get some burgers and fries to go when we leave. Besides, do they look undernourished?" The combined weight of the security detail approached 500 pounds, most of it muscle.

"I see what you mean," Ron said. "They seem like nice enough fellows, not very talkative, but polite."

Mike looked across the booth. "'Nice fellows' is not the first thing that comes to mind when I think of Jeff and Phil, but I'll tell them what you said. It'll make their day."

"Your dad sat in that very seat," Ron said, motioning toward Mike's side of the booth. "And he ordered enough food to feed a reinforced rifle platoon. It was downright embarrassing!"

"He could definitely destroy a plate of vittles, couldn't he?"

"Jeez, I think he ordered six or maybe eight eggs, a pound of bacon, grits, coffee and later downed a couple of burgers, fries and pie. I'll never forget it; neither will the little girl who waited on us."

Ron momentarily fell silent as his mind again wondered back to another more pleasant time. He then reached down for his briefcase, placed it on the table and removed several folders.

"There are several things I want to share with you and the only thing I request is that you hear me out before making any decisions, OK?" Ron said with the penetrating stare of a seasoned lawyer.

"Sure, whatever you want."

"Give an old man a few minutes to enjoy the moment," Ron said as he took a drink of iced tea. "We have come a long way, Mikey. The last time I was here with your dad, we drove my car because he wasn't sure his old truck would make it, and even if it would have, it was running on fumes. I remember so clearly how small his universe was…back then.

"Your dad's greatest concern was how he was going to come up with the money to buy your school supplies for the upcoming year. I don't know what supplies you needed, but I bet fifteen or twenty dollars would have covered it.

"Now look at us. I'm sitting across from a graduate of West Point and Harvard School of Law; one of the wealthiest men in the country; an ex-governor; a presidential candidate; a humanitarian and most importantly, a loving father…*just* like your dad."

Mike smiled, touching the old man's arm. "It would not have happened, sir, if it were not for you."

"Oh, I know I provided the means to get things started, but it was your dad and you that grew the O'Reilly holdings to what they are today. I have to say I do derive a certain pleasure in knowing I played a small role in the O'Reilly legacy."

"I don't think *a small role* quite covers it, Ron!"

"Well, in any event, this is where it all started…right here," Ron said, jabbing the tabletop with his index finger, "and knowing your dad, he probably never said much about it. I thought it might help us both move on with our lives if we came here. You should know how it all started."

Mike smiled as he patted the older man's hand, "I'm really glad we came, Ron. Thanks for thinking of it."

"Our journey is not over, son. There is much left to be done, and you will have to carry the standard alone. My health is failing and I won't be around much longer. That's one of the things we need to discuss today." Ron said as he opened one of the folders.

"This is my Last Will & Testament, a Durable Power of Attorney, a Living Will, and an itemized list of assets including locations and account numbers. I want you to be the executor of my estate, as well as the sole beneficiary." He shoved the documents toward a stunned Mike and pointed to where he needed signatures.

"Holy crap, sir! Are you sure you want to do this?"

"Have you ever seen me when I wasn't *sure*?"

Mike knew that to be the case. Ron always knew what he was doing, and it was well thought out before he committed to it.

Mike quickly scanned the documents and signed. He had, with the stroke of a pen, essentially doubled the assets and wealth of the O'Reilly family.

Jeff and Phil served as witnesses to the transaction, and Ron pulled out a notary seal to make the transaction official...and final.

Mike carefully eyed his mentor. "You're not going to die on me, are you?"

"Yes, sir, I am...and soon!

"The next order of business," Ron said as he pulled out another folder, "is the matter of the law firm. All of the partners, including the Laverish boy who was killed in an automobile accident, have passed, leaving only me."

He slid the folder across the table toward Mike. "This document initiates the actions required to give you sole ownership and chairmanship of the firm. Please sign here," he said, pointing to the signature line. "You know the firm and its clients as well as or better than anyone there, and they like you, even though you've not been in the loop for a while.

"The associates that are there now don't have the vision required to sustain continued growth. You do! One of the senior partners can manage the day-to-day activities. You will not have to move to Chicago or New York, just oversee operations; chair board meetings; and provide strategic guidance for the firm. Sign it…please!"

"Yes, sir." Mike signed the document and with a wry smile said, "Finally, after all these years, I can tell you to *shove it* if I don't feel like attending one of your mandatory meetings. Is that right, Mr. Snyder?"

"I wouldn't recommend that, not while I'm still around. I can fire your little butt and will at the drop of a hat." Mike handed the signed documents back across the table.

Ron pulled out a deed and handed it to Mike for signature. "This is a gift from the Snyder estate to you, Veronica and my sweet little godchild, Cheyenne…The place you both love so much on Long Island."

The place Ron was referring to was the beautiful, old-money mansion sitting on ten manicured acres in one of the most exclusive communities on Long Island.

"You've got to be kidding, Ron. Isn't there anyone in your family you would rather give it to?"

"I have no family left, and even if I did, I would still want you and Veronica to have it. You both seemed to enjoy your stays there so much, which always made me happy, so now you can go whenever you like…my treat, Mikey!" he said, knowing how much Mike hated hearing his childhood name.

Little did Ron know that Mike had long since considered it a term of endearment and had just acted mad to entertain the two men who meant so much to him his entire life.

"Let's talk about something else for a moment. Your dad and I, as you know, were the prime movers in getting you into politics.

"You did a magnificent job as governor of Oklahoma and I have no doubt you would make a good president, but I have a special favor to ask of you, and I have a good reason for asking it. Pull out of the presidential race!"

Mike stared across the table at his long-time friend, mentor and now benefactor, as he took a drink of coffee and smiled. "I have no choice but to pull out, Ron, but I sense our reasons for my leaving the race may be different.

"In my case, I have O'Reilly Corporation responsibilities and now, because of your graciousness, a large, very successful law firm to oversee.

"Further, there is simply no way I can divest my interest in either to the extent the public and Congress may demand; should I win this election.

"You, on the other hand, unless I have misread the tea leaves, are about to tell me why it would be a conflict of interest of the greatest magnitude. Am I right?"

The old man should not have been surprised. He had first-hand knowledge of Mike's great intellect and perceptive talents. It was one of the reasons he had just placed full responsibility, in fact, ownership, of his law firm in his care.

"Yes, sir, you are right. How long have you known about our patriotic endeavor?" Ron asked, as he looked around to ensure no one was within earshot.

Mike thought for a moment and then waved to get Jeff's attention. As he started toward the booth, Ron raised both hands in surrender and said, "You're not going to have the old guy rubbed out, are you, Mikey?"

Mike chuckled. "You've been watching too many James Cagney re-runs." He gave Jeff a quick rundown of meetings he needed set up and to arrange a press conference as quickly as possible. He needed to announce his withdrawal from the presidential race.

Jeff reached out, pulled his friend toward him, gave him a hard hug and kissed the top of his head, saying, "There is a God!"

As Jeff moved away from the booth with a cell phone jammed in his ear, calmness Mike had not experienced in years settled over him as he again focused on the issue at hand.

"There are varying degrees of knowing, Ron. Jeff was first to really connect the dots on the trail of 'good deeds.' I, on the other hand, knew how the big guy felt about things and his approach to fixing injustices…given the criminal justice system couldn't do it. All of the key pieces seemed to fit.

"Since you two had been partners in crime, so to speak, your entire adult lives, I just assumed you would know about it, if not be personally involved.

"Years ago when Dad informed us he was the prime mover in the untimely death of that dumb ass principal, who caused my brother's death, he mentioned it was obvious there would be no justice for the O'Reilly family in Alabama…so he fixed the problem.

"I noticed you were not surprised and had figured it out years before. It was so matter-of-fact, Ron, I knew then Dad had the disposition and wherewithal to *take care of business* wherever the criminal justice system failed. He loved this country more than life itself and you may recall, he wasn't a big fan of pontification. He believed in deeds, not words.

"He had the resources to employ the right skill sets on a large scale, and he had a corporation to hide operatives under the veil of normal employment.

"I recalled a conversation Colonel Hawkins and I had after I was released from 97th General where I had been treated for wounds received in the Congo. He said Dad had asked him and Dave Best to leave the military and come to work for the O'Reilly Corporation in some capacity, punching cattle or something.

"Keep in mind these guys and others like them had been trained and conditioned for years to do one thing, and to do it well…track down and kill other human beings. Most cowboys I know don't have that skill set in their resume.

"I checked personnel records in our Human Resource Department and crosschecked for military backgrounds with a particular focus on Spec Ops to narrow the search. I then checked what departments they were assigned to and specifically what they were doing. The majority of them were employed as consultants, inspectors or troubleshooters in corporate-owned subsidiaries all over the country. Which means they pretty much had free rein to come and go as needed.

"They were all hired at relatively high labor grades. This would probably go unnoticed by outsiders but I know what we pay most of our various disciplines and these hand-picked specialists were making a hell of a lot more than the average salary, plus a pretty significant bonus."

Ron leaned back in the booth and waved for the young lady to bring fresh coffee. He then looked at Mike, "Do you think any less of us?"

Mike smiled, "Hell, no! I love you guys and always will. I just wish you had included me from the get-go instead of backing my bid for the presidency.

"You know damn well I would have punched some degenerate dignitaries' lights out if they said anything derogatory about the United States. Wouldn't that be *cute*? I would have spent way too much time strangling congressmen...all said and done, it would have been a bad fit. I have to tell you; I'm more relaxed right now than I've been in a long time. The deeper I got sucked into the political vortex, the more convinced I became that Washington is a cesspool, and a good housecleaning is needed.

"You know my feelings about the criminal justice system; it needs serious reform. I'm convinced I can bring about change faster as an influential private citizen and corporate voice than I could as president, particularly if we optimize the resources you and Dad have set in motion.

"We can become serious movers and shakers for honest, long needed change; a strong voice and rallying point for the people. We *owe* this to future generations of Americans. If, along the way, we become cannon fodder, then so be it. At least we will have given it our best shot."

Mike looked his old friend in the eye, "This is the way to go, Ron...and we can do a hell of a lot of good in a relatively short period of time. Self-serving zealots in Congress have the means to tie up needed reform legislation for years, and I want no part of it.

"That would drive me nuts, given I already see them as self-absorbed, inept politicians. I'd probably wind up being the only president in history to go over on the hill and *literally* stab the stupid bastards in the back!"

Ron laughed. "Damn, Mikey, relax! I can see the veins in your neck standing out."

"Yeah, that happens when I get fired up."

"When we get back to the estate," Ron said, "I'll see that you're read into the Operations Center. We named the organization American Relief Committee, ARC, as in Noah's..."

"*Ron,* I'm aware of the Biblical story of Noah's Ark. And a trained monkey could figure out the correlation...rid the world of bad guys and start anew! Right?"

"As usual, you're light years ahead of us...me," the old man said as he sat back in the booth.

The light finally came on in the recesses of Mike's subconscious and he smiled like a little kid who just found a shiny penny. "The Ops Center wouldn't be tucked away at the airfield by chance, would it?"

"You're too damn clever for your own good, Mikey, me boy. You were always smarter than your dad and I. Hell! An *anvil* would be smarter than your dad."

"Watch what you say you, little shit; I'll take that peg leg and beat your bony ass to death with it."

Ron let out an uncharacteristically loud laugh. "You're Sean O'Reilly incarnate. He said almost the exact same thing all those many years ago. Oh, how I miss him; no one will ever know how much I loved that man."

Mike mustered a slight smile–though he could feel a tightening in his chest–at the thought of his father, as he reached over and squeezed Ron's frail arm, "Me, too, sir!"

"When your dad and I used to brainstorm what we would do if ever compromised, he'd just shrug his shoulders and say, 'I'd rather be tried by twelve than carried by six!'"

"Let me share with you how I see this venture shaking out," Mike said as he set his coffee cup down. "I don't fully understand the ARC mission, beyond greasing bad guys and the occasional legal beagle, the likes of which I have plotted on a map and color-coded by type. So, I'll reserve comment until I'm fully read in. But for my nickel, there are several subsets of bad guys who need to be pursued, if we are not already doing it.

"I believe the family unit is central to a strong, safe and prosperous country. If this is true, and I believe it is, we need to focus on making it better. One way to do that is to aggressively pursue deadbeat dads who fail to pay child support once they fly the coop. Single moms need cash to maintain the household and provide stability for her children.

"On my watch, I envision chasing these egg-sucking dogs to the ends of the Earth and doing what is necessary to put the fear of God in their cold little hearts. The same would apply to men who feel beating their wife is an inalienable right. Hell, I might go out on a few of those missions myself."

Ron patiently let Mike vent, as he worked his way through the necessary steps to take the ARC mission to the next level. He was a born leader; a creative thinker; a righteous person and clearly the right man for the job.

"One other thing, if we're not already doing it: we need to take the fight to the enemy, even if it means violating international law and sovereign territory. *Screw the bastards*! If they're determined to poison our kids and disrupt our way of life with their illicit drugs, we'll go in after them to the extent they won't even feel safe in their own houses.

"When we get to that point—and *we* will—we'll have them by the nuts. Mr. Snyder, sir, it's time to declare all-out war on the whole drug-related spectrum...producers, smugglers and dealers."

All of a sudden he was struck with clarity of purpose and anxious to meet the challenges head on. To meet these new challenges, given the federal government's determination to foil their activities, ARC would have to be ever vigilant; create a more sophisticated recruiting process; and develop even better security measures.

Perpetuation of the present ongoing-mission would have to continue uninterrupted while transitioning the organization into other society-enhancing initiatives as defined by Mike O'Reilly and his team of patriots.

At Arlington National Cemetery, he had made a promise to his father...to continue his good works. At the time, he was not fully aware of all the 'good works' his father had done, but it made no difference; a promise had been made and it would be kept. 'So help me, God!'

As he stood in this small Alabama café to take his first step under a new mantle, Mike had to smile as he thought, 'A befitting choice of words, Mikey me boy, *so help me, God*...the last four words in the oath of office for presidents of the United States.

He sensed his father reaching out to share with him one last important lesson: What's supposed to be will be...this is your destiny!

> The strongest reason for the people to retain
> the right to keep and bear arms is,
> as a last resort, to protect themselves against
> tyranny in government.
> *Thomas Jefferson*

ABOUT THE AUTHOR

Mike Clowes is the author of *We the People* and *Blood Mountain* (2011 release). He is a decorated Infantry Officer with a background in Tactical Intelligence and Special Operations. He is a rated Army Aviator and has had worldwide postings in Europe, the Far East, Southeast Asia and temporary duty in the Republic of Congo. He is married with three daughters and lives in Apopka, Florida.

LaVergne, TN USA
01 October 2010
199272LV00003B/1/P